Forger's Revenge

Book III
The Chesapeake Tugboat Murders

By Leah Devlin

www.penmorepress.com

Forger's Revenge by Leah Devlin
Copyright © 2018 Leah Devlin

ISBN-13: 978-1-942756-74-4(Paperback)
ISBN -978-1-942756-75-1(e-book)

BISAC Subject Headings:
FIC008000 Fiction / General
FIC031010 Fiction/ Thrillers / Crime

Cover Illustration by Christine Horner

Address all correspondence to:

Penmore Press LLC
920 N Javelina Pl
Tucson AZ 85748

Forger's Revenge

DEDICATION

For Bruce, Kenna and Camie

There's the scarlet thread of murder running
through the colorless skein of life...

—Arthur Conan Doyle

"We may brave human laws, but we cannot resist natural
ones."

—Jules Verne

Chapter 1
The Upper Chesapeake

Early May

"SUBMIT. Exclamation point." Nina hit the SUBMIT command on the software program that logged her final grades into the grade entry system at Tolchester College. She closed her laptop and locked her office door. SUBMIT meant Hello Summertime. SUBMIT meant weeks without students and administrators. SUBMIT meant Hurricane cocktails with Alex and her grandmother Julia, while the Glen River flowed gently by. That was the plan for the evening. Nina hurried from the academic building, climbed into her car and headed into the village of River Glen. She crossed the bridge and turned down the river road. Around the bend were Alex's cottage and Julia's house-next-door. Their yards were cluttered with kitschy Americana. Pink flamingos, green gnomes, pyrate flags, a VW with a birch tree growing through it and a rusted Harley Davidson-turned-bird bath blurred the lines between surreality and reality. And more River Glen weirdness... under Julia's house was a veritable Fort Knox of pyrate treasure.

Who could imagine that when Nina had taken the job at Tolchester she would discover that the Giles Blood-hand legend was true. Yup. It was. The Scottish pyrate Giles Hale had in fact been a real person and was the distant grandfather of Julia Hale and Alex Allaway. Crazier still, a clandestine community of modern pyrates guarded the River Glen treasure. Its use was largely for the benefit of the locals —hip replacements, teenage orthodontia, student loan debt, Alzheimer's care and the like. An incalculable fortune in barrels and sea chests was hidden in Julia's basement, a fact Nina knew because she and Julia had been taken hostage in that very basement by the serial killer Ricarda Sarova three summers before and only days after her move to the Chesapeake. Any sane person would have left the village after such a traumatizing ordeal, but instead she'd found herself swearing a blood oath to Alex and Julia to keep the treasure's existence secret. The only outsider, besides herself, who knew of the treasure was Detective Jay Braden because it was he who had rescued Julia and her from bondage.

Yup. Thar be pyrates in River Glen.

And there was one of them—the Pyrate Queen no less. Julia was surveying her riparian kingdom from her porch while flicking ashes from a black cigarette holder over the railing. Alex was in her usual place, flinging crab traps around the deck of the *Vital Spark*, no doubt searching for her lost cell phone.

A delivery truck suddenly appeared in Nina's rearview mirror and followed her into Alex's driveway. Julia flew off the porch, yanked the clipboard from the driver's hand and scribbled her signature across the paper. "Hurry, man, hurry!" Hands fluttering, she shushed him to the rear of the truck.

Down the ramp rolled a stunning piece of machinery—a shiny Royal Enfield motorcycle and sidecar painted with the Union Jack. Julia rushed inside her house and returned with matching Union Jack motorcycle helmets. Alex wandered curiously down the dock.

"Any time now," Nina thought to herself. "The challenge cometh."

Alex and Julia were ridiculously competitive with one another. They existed on the planet for one sole reason—to outdo the other in everything. If they weren't trying to out tango each other or see who could endure more hot sauce on their eggs, it was the sword-fighting... whacking away at each other with épées across the porch and beach and down the dock until collapsing in exhaustion on the gunwales of the *Vital Spark.*

"Race you to the Point, love!" Julia said.

Motorcycle racing would be added to the endless list of granddaughter-grandmother competitions. Though not much of a gambler, Nina would put her money on Alex because she always rode some form of two-wheeled transportation. In their college days at the University of Maryland, it was a decrepit moped that she pushed back to their apartment on most days. She presently owned an old yet reliable baby blue Suzuki sport bike.

"I didn't know you could ride," Alex said to Julia.

"Every Brit knows how to ride," said Julia strapping on a helmet. "Horses and motorbikes. It's in our blood."

"How many cc's does it have?" Alex asked.

"Five hundred."

Eyes narrowed, Alex circled the glistening contender. The Enfield had 500 ccs, her Suzuki 250. Nina was by no means an expert on motorcycles, or anything mechanical for that matter, but Alex's bike was smaller, lighter and had less power, but it wouldn't be dragging the weight of a clunky sidecar. The odds were certainly in Alex's favor. Alex must have drawn the same conclusion.

"You're on, Old Bat! You're gonna eat my dust!" Alex sprinted toward her cottage.

"Don't we have cheek!" Julia scraped a starting line in the dirt with her heel, handed Nina the spare helmet and climbed onto the Enfield. "Get in, Nina."

"What? Me? No!"

"Yes, lass. I need ballast. Otherwise, at the speed I'll be going, I might flip."

"Flip?"

Julia impatiently waved her toward the sidecar. "You'll be ballast, the starter and judge, all rolled into one."

"But Julia…"

"Hush now. In!"

There was no point in arguing with her Highness; besides, Nina's mouth had gone dry. She climbed into the cockpit and grasped the hand grips.

"Seat belt, Nina, and strap that helmet tight. We don't want it to blow off at the light speed we'll be traveling."

"Blow off? Light speed?"

Alex strode out of the cottage, jingling her keys. She flung her leg over the blue Suzuki, turned the ignition and worked the throttle back and forth. Exhaust blasted from the tailpipe as she rode to the starting line.

"At Nina's Mark-Get-Set-Go!" Julia called.

"Who can speak?" Nina muttered.

"Ready, Loser?" Julia asked Alex.

"Ready, Dust Eater." Alex flipped down the face shield of her black helmet covered with skull-and-cross bone stickers.

"We'll see who's eating dust!" Julia laughed and rocked her throttle. "Start us, Nina!"

Nina pushed her hand into the smoky air. "On—on your mark, get set, GO!" Her hand flew back to the grip, and good thing too. Julia jerked the throttle, throwing her back in the seat. The Enfield bolted from the starting line.

Alex stalled her bike. "Shit!"

"Who's the Dust Eater now?" Julia shouted gleefully over her shoulder.

Bushes, trees and the river beyond Nina's face shield became streaks of greens and browns. The Point wasn't that far away, maybe a half a mile. If she survived this insane race, she would insist on walking back to Alex's cottage. If she survived. The motorcycle and sidecar bounced over ruts and potholes; she tightened her grip. Dead ahead was the glimmering Chesapeake where a mandarin sun hung low in the western sky.

"Let me see one more sunset. *Dios ayúdame*," she urgently prayed. "*Por favor*, one more sunset."

A pebble plunked against her face shield; next a fly splatted. Through green bug guts she spotted Alex squinting in fierce concentration, her chin over the blue gas tank. Julia glanced over her shoulder and kicked the Enfield into a higher gear, snapping Nina's head backwards. Alex grinned and blew by, spraying them with dust and fumes. They rolled to a stop at the parking lot by the Point where families were packing their cars after a day at the beach.

Alex circled back and pumped a triumphant fist in the air. "Dust eaters!"

"Brilliant race, lass," Julia shouted over the idling engine. "Did I mention that the winner buys the pizzas?"

"What?"

"If not, then it's haggis for dinner."

"She feeds me entrails, Nina," said Alex grimacing. "It's grandchild abuse."

Julia gazed up at a lone planet in the blue-orange sky. "It's a glorious evening. Let's take a ride up the coastal road, but no more racing. I don't need to get another speeding ticket from Jay. The wanker. We'll pick up pizzas on the way back."

"Uh, Julia," she said. "I wouldn't mind stretching my legs and walking back to the cottages."

"No, Nina dear. Impossible. You need to hold the pizzas." Julia turned to Alex. "Ready?"

"Ready."

The motorcycles cruised in tandem onto the coastal road, through the pine forest near Alex's place of employment at the River Glen Marine Station and between a valley of early corn. Alex flashed her turn-signal and headed down a dirt road through a fallow field. Star after star appeared overhead and a quiet exhilaration eased aside Nina's initial panic.

"Mama is rolling in her grave at me motorcycle racing with two modern-day pyrates," Nina thought as the sidecar jiggled over the bumps. Her life to this point had been an orderly sequence of goals. She had been the first in her family to obtain a college education, earn a PhD and get a tenure track job; but when was the last time a goal had been a fun, just-for-the-hell-of-it one? Learn to water-ski? Rock climb? Scuba dive? Sky dive? Ride a motorcycle? Why did her every goal have to have a practical, monetary outcome? Julia was nearly seventy years old. If the old Scot could drive a motorcycle, well then damn it, so could she.

She tapped on Julia's knee. Julia squeezed the brakes and they rolled to a stop. The Enfield with a sidecar would be perfect to learn on because it would be impossible to tip; nor would there be the distraction of cars on the remote road.

Julia flipped up her face shield. "Are you okay, lass?"

"Yes. Show me how to drive this."

Julia climbed off the Enfield and Nina took her place.

"Brakes, needless to say, are very important," Julia said, pointing out the right hand- and right foot brakes. "It's all about timing with your hands. This timing, Nina: Rock down on the right, release on the left. Rock right, release left. Rock right, release left. And both movements slow and simultaneously."

"Sounds easy enough."

Julia pointed to the gearshift by Nina's left foot. "Kick it up for higher speeds, down for lower ones. But do not move it until you've pulled in the clutch and then release it slowly. Every time you shift gears, pull that clutch in first or you'll stall the bike."

She nodded. The concept of clutches and stalling was familiar because she had learned to drive in her mother's pastry delivery van that had a stick shift.

Julia climbed into the cockpit of the sidecar. "Ready?"

"Ready." She rocked down with her right and released the clutch with her left. They went nowhere. "What just happened?"

"Nothing, Numpty. You're still in neutral. Pull in the clutch again, then kick the gearshift down into first gear and kick up for all other gears."

Nina kicked the shift down and the motorcycle jumped underneath her.

"Now rock right, release left," Julia said.

She repeated the movement and the bike and sidecar rolled forward.

"Nina dear, more throttle!"

They gained speed. At the end of the road a manor house was silhouetted against the grey-orange bay. The place had once been inhabited by the Civil War spies Josiah and Abigail Wedgewood-Smyth. She had visited the derelict estate once before when Alex's half-brother James Collins had taken her for a spin in his new convertible and showed her the infamous maple tree where Abigail had died. Presently a tall wire fence surrounded the property to prevent trespassers, squatters and children from falling through the rotten floorboards of the house.

"Drive around the circular driveway," Julia shouted to her. "Practice braking and up-shifting and down-shifting. This is the ideal place to learn."

Alex roared up beside them and skidded to a stop. "We're outta here! Let's go! Didn't you see it?"

"Stop, Nina, stop!" Julia said. "See what?"

"The light!" Alex pointed wildly at the manor house. "Let's scram!"

"What light?"

"I swear I saw a light in the house! Very faint but I'm sure."

Julia squinted. "You're seeing things. A padlock's on the front gate. No one can get in there."

"Someone's definitely in there! Maybe it's the ghost that ate the Larson twins!"

Nina's eyes darted from one black window to another. What if someone was watching them from behind the jagged glass? What if Alex *had* seen something? The place was definitely creepy. There was that cursed tree, then there were the Larson twins who were last seen a decade ago, riding bikes near the old estate. Then they vanished. The only trace of them was their pink bikes pulled from a nearby creek. The girls' disappearance prompted rumors of a man-eating ghost that haunted the estate.

"There are no such things as ghosts, love," said Julia unconvincingly.

Alex's head shook vehemently. "Or it's a Whitby who has an assault rifle pointed at us this very second!"

That got Julia's attention and she sat erect. She and Alex had good reason to fear—loathe—the Whitbys, the mortal enemies of the Allaways and Hales since the River Glen pyrate massacre in the 1690s. In more recent times Frank, Clyde and Desmond Whitby had murdered Alex's parents Colin and Carole when Alex was mere months old. Colin had been Julia's son. All evil and misfortune in River Glen, the United States... Planet Earth, the two women blamed on "a deranged Whitby."

"I spotted a motorcycle at the side of the house, hidden behind the hedge!" Alex panted. "We've gotta get the hell out of here! We're sitting ducks! Which deranged Whitby rides a sport bike?"

Giles Blood-hand Day, two months later

"Baffling, truly, baffling." Detective Jay Braden faced the town pier while his Ray Bans concealed his oblique gaze to the village green. Under the giant oak tree sat a singular woman sipping from a water bottle. She seemed to be the only sober person at the pyrate festival; the blood alcohol content of the other tourists probably averaged 0.05%. Among the drunkest was that rowdy group from Baltimore. Their purple pyrate hats with the Ravens logo were a dead giveaway. No doubt he and the trooper Denny would be passing coffee through the bars of a holding cell to one of them by the end of the afternoon.

The locals were also a handful at the annual festival. By the bandstand a tipsy Alex Allaway was dancing with his partner Assistant Detective Will Wilkins. An equally tipsy Professor Nina Vega was spinning around with the village lawyer James Collins. Alex and Nina's outrageous twirls and chorus-line kicks were probably fueled by the free samples at the rum tasting booths, or Luna's marijuana brownies. Possibly both. Like last year, the line out the door of Luna's Psychic Reading Shack stretched to the pier. The old woman was selling more than palm readings. Maybe next year he'd do something about the enforcement of Maryland's marijuana laws, but for now it was best to watch the festivities from his inconspicuous position on the River Glen bridge. Harlow's Pub and the Dockside Café were likewise packed with thirsty tourist-pyrates. So was the tiki bar at the Nauticus where gay waiters in grass skirts were hosting a limbo contest. Just another intoxicated day in paradise. It was his departed wife Laura who, of the countless villages on the Chesapeake, had insisted on relocating to this oddball place.

Jay's gaze returned to the woman under the tree. Another baffling fact: she was solitary. Who went to a pyrate festival alone? The event was packed with families, couples and bikers. Among the bikers were the Chrome Divas, a pleasant, law-abiding group of motorcycle enthusiasts who ate breakfast at the Dockside Café, only to rev their engines and explore the back roads of the Delmarva peninsula. On the mornings of the Divas' monthly breakfast meeting, he and his ex-girlfriend Julia had had a long wait for a table.

The solitary woman under the tree was also a biker. His first guess was that she was a member of the Chrome Divas, however when she rose to pull a water bottle from the metal saddlebag on her sport-touring motorcycle the Divas' club patch—a blue crab riding across the Maryland State flag— was absent from her leather vest. Her vest was devoid of patches or rockers that might indicate a club alliance. She was a lone wolf. At some point during the festivities she had ridden her motorcycle between the orange traffic cones, across the village green near the Moon Bounce and pony rides and parked it under the oak. That told him enough. The rules, the boundary of traffic cones, didn't apply to her. His next impulse was to strut up the hill, flash his badge and tell her to move her bike from the lawn, but he decided to be a dick about the traffic infraction another day. Besides, it was too hot to be walking up hills in the insufferable heat and humidity, and leaning on the railing of the bridge kept the weight off his bad hip.

The third baffling thing about the biker was that she too was watching the crowd. She wasn't in River Glen to get sloshed and laid like the throng of pyrates at the festival; she was here on business, surveilling the partygoers on the pier. Who in particular she was looking at? Was she a cop, private detective or bounty hunter? She was muscular and lean compared to the average middle-aged American woman. Was she military? What was so goddamn interesting to her? Twice she held up her cell phone and snapped pictures of the dancers on the pier. She turned toward the bridge and flashed him a lethal glare. What provoked that? Did he know her from somewhere?

"Nibblin' on sponge cake, watchin' the sun bake... all of those tourists covered in oil..." the band played. Any song but that one! The crowd by the bandstand went berserk. The planks of pier shuddered under their stomping feet.

He tensed. "No. Oh no."

The rowdies from Baltimore inched to the edge of pier and locked hands. Their knees bent in unison. They whooped and leapt outward, disappearing beyond the bollards. Splash! Pyrates and wenches rushed to the pier and cheered. He dashed off the bridge, but something compelled him to look up at the oak tree. The biker chick was motoring between the orange traffic cones. But another thing now occupied his thoughts. It was time to make the coffee.

Ella Winston pulled a bandana and pliers from her metal saddlebag and returned to the campfire. She knelt next to a circle of stones, wrapped the bandana around her hand and reached toward the orange embers. With the pliers, she pulled a can of baked beans from the coals and placed it on the ground to cool. The Virginians huddled around the fire at the next campsite burst in raucous laughter. They had been drinking—Yuengling's lager from her home state of Pennsylvania—when she pitched her pup tent earlier that day. They were also drinking at Harlow's Pub during the Giles Blood-hand festival, though no one was as drunk as the pyrates from Baltimore who jumped off the pier into the Glen River. Most trailers, third wheels and tents in the campground were flying skull-and-cross bones flags in celebration of the pyrate festival. It was essential to notice everything and everyone. Not a single detail could be missed. Never let down her guard. No one was going to mess with her again.

Earlier that night one of the Virginians had invited her for beers. "Ya sure ya don't wanna join us for brewskis, doll?"

"Yeah, I'm sure." And don't doll me.

No brewskis for her. Not even a cold Yuengling. Until this mess was settled, there was nothing to drink about, nothing to celebrate. Why did people assume that a woman traveling solo required companionship? Why couldn't she be alone without a lecher asking if she wanted company? No one ever interrupted a man sitting by himself in a diner, bus station or on a park bench. Why the assumption that a woman could not be content with her own thoughts? Maybe a tattoo across her forehead that read *Beware: infectious* would do the trick.

Ella moved her hands toward the fire. Ignore the Virginians and focus on the important stuff: the crackling fire and still forest. Blissful thing, solitude. What a contrast to her existence for the past eleven endless years at Cambridge Springs where she was surrounded by maniacs 24-7! The worse part of it was the lake effect snow from Lake Erie. Cambridge Springs, Pennsylvania might as well have been Cambridge Springs, Siberia. A car crunched along the gravel road and her mental cop alarm dinged. It was the park police making their rounds through the campground. She slumped into her hoodie.

What was that plain-clothed cop with the snowy hair and sunglasses looking at from the River Glen Bridge? She could spot cops from miles away. She had been sitting under the oak tree, minding her own goddamn business. Why was he watching her? That devious warden at Cambridge Springs had probably implanted a nanoparticle homing device in her, possibly while she slept, that pinged and alerted the local police to her presence. Her destiny forever after was to be stalked by the police.

If only she could escape this planet!

Deep space was absent of people. She gazed upward. The stars were just visible through a black web of branches. If NASA had a mission that required a solo astronaut be sent to Mars or Jupiter for decades, she would be first in line for the job. NASA hired persons with some intelligence so she wasn't entirely out of the running. According to the psychologist Dr. Brant who conducted psychological evaluations on the inmates, she had scored "significantly above the average on the IQ tests."

"Yeah great," she had told Brant at that news. "My cognitive abilities have been minimized to a data point on a graph, a number on your spreadsheet."

"You have too much mental energy, Ella," the psychologist said. "Too much time on your hands."

"Inescapable amounts of time," she said dismally.

"How about you participate in a vocational training program?"

Ella mock-shuddered.

"What's so scary about that?"

"Participation implies interacting with a group."

Brant shrugged and pulled a notebook from her brief case, on it the iconic image of *The Starry Night* by Vincent van Gogh. Ella nearly wept as she had not seen the image in years, nor any painting for that matter. At that moment she imagined herself diving headfirst into the painting... swimming amidst sky swirls of blue and silver and undulating bows of the green-brown cypress tree... circling the church steeple and yellow-white stars.

"Quantum Physics," she blurted to Brant. "NASA astronauts need to know Quantum Physics. Maybe that's one of the training programs?"

"Possibly," said Brant cluelessly.

Ella scheduled an appointment with the prison jobs counselor.

"There are a number to choose from," the perky counselor had told her.

"Quantum Physics?" she said hopefully.

"No. Cosmetology and Custodial Maintenance."

"Only two?"

"Hair always grows. There's always a need for Cosmetologists."

"And morticians," she said bleakly.

"Some job training is better than no job training. And hair always—"

"Fuck. Okay."

Her decision had been instantaneous. Custodial Maintenance meant pushing a mop or broom around *by herself*. It did not involve participation of any sort. The hairdresser job was out of the question as it required monotonous small talk while snipping split ends. Custodial Maintenance was a smart choice because it allowed her an element of creative expression. Across the cement floors she swooshed the mop in watery strokes, depicting the yellow petals in van Gogh's *Sunflowers* of 1889. With a broom she swept dust balls to create the warden's face in the cubist style, reminiscent of Picasso's *Portrait of Marie-Therese* painted in 1938.

"Winston, cut that shit out and mop in straight lines!" her supervisor had shouted. "Straight lines save time!"

"Time? All I have is Infinite Time."

Eight infinite years to be precise. Until her sentence got extended by three years because of her unsuccessful jailbreak in a recycling bin of sticky soda bottles. The minimal security prison was not really minimally secure; nor was she as intelligent as Dr. Brant surmised.

Since Time was a limitless commodity at Cambridge Springs, what was the issue with mopping *The Birth of Venus*, *Girl with a Pearl Earring*, *The Persistence of Memory* or *Dogs Playing Poker* in soapy bubbles on the cafeteria floor of a women's prison in the most frigid corner of the United States, except maybe Alaska? At least mopping gave her a chance to utilize the skills mastered while almost completing an MFA at the best art school in the country.

Until her Big Fuck-up.

Mere art degrees in Art and Art History were clearly not going to impress NASA. They were not Quantum Physics or Computer Engineering from MIT or Stanford, but she was teachable. She could adeptly run the scientific equipment for a one-manned spacecraft to Mars, she might convince NASA's evaluation committee. The Scientific Method had been mastered in introductory biology when an undergraduate at Swarthmore. Truly, she got it. While tuning up her motorcycle, she had become a decent mechanic, she might inform the NASA engineers.

Ella's view moved from the starry night above to her sole earthly delight, her BMW F 800 GS adventure sport bike. Firelight danced off its chrome in shades and shadows of umber and orange. One day the motorcycle would carry her across highways, mountains, deserts, steppes and savannas—

once she earned enough money for a trans-global motorcycle trek. Working an under-the-table job as a tour guide on a ghost walk provided just enough cash to cover food, rent at the campground and gas for short motorcycle trips. During a previous road trip to River Glen, she had noticed that black-haired woman on the *Vital Spark*, unloading bushels of crabs at the town pier.

Eureka! A crabber was a solitary profession.

Who would pester her out on the water? A small workboat and crab pots would be required. If she could drive and fix a motorcycle, then an outboard motor could certainly be managed. Another bonus of working on the water would be a golden tan. For eleven years on the arctic tundra of northwestern Pennsylvania, her skin tone had taken on a new hue in the color palette: anemic white. The prison nurse gave her Vitamin D supplements to compensate for the eleven-month-winters.

Ella spooned the last of the beans into her mouth, rose from the fire and walked across the road. She heaved the can and plastic spoon into a dumpster by the bathhouse. No garbage whatsoever was to be left at the campsite. The last thing she needed was a wild animal wandering into her tent. It would be impossible to get the stink of skunk out of her motorcycle leathers. She dropped next to the fire and swiped through the images in her cell phone. One in particular grabbed her attention. Her former graduate school advisor Professor Monroe Hadley had been at the Giles Blood-hand festival that afternoon. At his side, by the wine-tasting booths, was his wife Ventresca. In another lifetime Ella and her then-fiancé Ian Kent had sipped wine and eaten hors d'oeuvres in the garden of the Hadley's elegant brick home in Old City Philadelphia, just blocks from the art college and gallery. It was unlikely that Monroe had recognized her that afternoon, especially after so many years. She had dropped over twenty pounds at Cambridge Springs since the substances that the so-called cooks alleged was so-called food tasted worse than garbage, and her spiky blue hair of her art school days had long ago grown out to its natural color. Nor had she ridden a motorcycle then. No, she had not been recognized.

Monroe Hadley and Ian Kent—the pricks—had set her up and become very wealthy men. Everything came down to the paintings owned by the Civil War spies Josiah and Abigail Wedgewood-Smyth. Her sole mission was to find those paintings. Then exact revenge.

From his house on the bluff, James Collins peered through his telescope to the harbor below. Tomorrow morning sanitation crews would be sweeping plastic beer cups, wine glasses and trash from the pier and village green, but presently seagulls feasted on popcorn and hot dog rolls spilt during the day's festivities. As a member of the secret community of River Glen pyrates, James made it a point to look for anomalies—unusual, discordant breaks in the rhythm of the sleepy village. His greatest concern was the obsessive treasure hunter—usually a deranged Whitby—who combed the riverbanks for the missing treasure of Giles Hale and the pyrates of the *Raven*. But long ago the treasure had been found. In fact, it had never been lost. Since the 1690s it had been under the watchful eyes of the founding families of River Glen: the Allaways, Collinses, Hales, Smyths and Wilkinses. Due to the complexities and vagaries of modern life, all roles in the pyrate society had been duplicated. He and Grandma Julia acted as the senior advisors, he specifically as legal counsel. His half-sister Alex Allaway and her boyfriend Will Wilkins served as the treasurers while the Wilkins and Smyth cousins were the scouts and infantry.

But now an unsettling blip appeared on James' radar.

She was not a treasure hunter but a historian of art. Or so she claimed. She had appeared months ago seeking documents at the River Glen Historical Society. Now she was back in River Glen. For the Giles Blood-hand festival? Really? Or for another reason? He had spotted her sitting in the shade of the oak tree next to her sport bike. His attention was torn between the biker and his dancing partner, the lovely latina Nina Vega. Everything about Nina that afternoon was arousing... unspeakably so! Her wild dancing was fueled by Aunt Luna's delicious brownies... her smoldering eyes were accented by copious mascara... and that velvet-corseted wench gown ... arousing beyond words! Were he not a gentleman, he might have flung her over his shoulder right on the pier, carried her up the bluff, slipped off the gown and pleasured her all afternoon in all ways imaginable. Just when Nina's lips grazed his, and he had sworn she was going to kiss him—at long last!—she gasped that she needed to pee and ran off to the ladies' room in the historical society. His impulse was to dash after her and make love to her on any number of tables in the archive room when the biker woman teased from the corner of his eye.

Why was she back in River Glen?

Months ago, he had received a call from Judith Ann Smyth, the librarian at the historical society. "James, a woman's here inquiring about documents related to Josiah and Abigail," said Judith Ann who had assisted him with his research on the Civil Wars spies for his debut novel. "Come and see what she wants. I can't talk to her right now. It's story hour. I'm about to read *Curious George* to a bunch of preschoolers."

He had hurried across the village green. An adventure motorcycle laden with metal cases was parked in front of the red brick building and a woman in black leather chaps and a leather jacket awaited him at the help desk. She had introduced herself as Ella Winston, an art historian.

"I'm researching Civil War art, especially pertaining to the battle of Gettysburg," she had explained while zigzagging with him through the stacks. "Josiah and Abigail Wedgewood-Smyth had an extensive art collection. Among their favorite painters was an obscure painter named Adam Eaton. Have you heard of him?"

"Only vaguely." He needed to appear as not prying so he asked casually, "Which university do you work for?"

"I'm... an independent scholar."

Pause noted. He nodded nonchalantly. This meant one of two things. Either she was a substandard academic that no university would hire or she was independently wealthy and could do whatever she damn pleased.

"The Wedgewood-Smyth papers are here," he said pointing to a metal bookshelf in the back room.

"Who's been reading the files recently?"

"Um, me. How'd you know?"

"No dust in front of the Wedgewood-Smyth folders. All of the other shelves are dusty."

"Yes, you're right. I'm writing a novel about Josiah and Abigail."

"Interesting!"

That was the only hint of enthusiasm from her. Up to that point she was about as neutral in tone and behavior as neutral could be.

"It's a historical novel," he said nudging her to divulge more. "My first. Slow going."

She responded with silence. He felt his blood pressure rise. What if she wasn't really an art historian but a competing novelist also intrigued by the Wedgewood-Smyths? It had been his dream since boyhood to write the definitive novel about the daring couple. He had majored in English Literature (creative writing emphasis) and History at Colombia University for the sole purpose of writing a captivating story about the two spies.

"Its title?" she asked.

"What?"

"The title of your novel?"

"Er, the working title is *Subterfuge*."

She changed the subject. "If I find something useful about the Wedgewood-Smyths' art collection or Adam Eaton, do you mind if I photograph it with my phone? No flash so it won't damage the old paper."

"Of course. Sure."

He had hovered around the archive for much of the afternoon, appearing to be busy, while she sorted through box after box.

"I'm done," she finally said. "Thank you for your help."

He had locked the door to the archive and walked Ella out to her motorcycle. She tugged on her helmet and in afterthought flipped up the face shield. Her next words, though seemingly innocent, shook him to the core. He had been positive—absolutely sure—that he was the only person in the world who knew this fact about Josiah's activities.

"You know, Mr. Collins, *Subterfuge* could fall into the genre of steampunk. Not many people know that Josiah and his pal Adam Eaton were building futuristic weapons of war for the Union army."

James had suppressed an outright gasp. His thoughts sputtered. How to respond to that staggering remark? Best to go with honesty. "You and I are among the very few who know this. It's going to be a large part of my novel. So, if you wouldn't say—"

"Mum's the word." Ella Winston winked, slung her leg over the motorcycle, revved it up and disappeared in smoke and haze.

The thought of Julia gave Jay Braden a pounding headache. He shook the last extra strength aspirin from the bottle and swallowed it down with a gulp of gin and tonic. He tossed the empty vial into his chiminea with a satisfying "Damn her." He was a fifty-eight-year-old man. One would think that by this age, he would be a better judge of women.

One would think... one would think.

He downed the rest of his drink. *Thinking* implies that the brain is involved in at least part of the activity. *Thinking* implies that the neurons are firing in a coordinated manner somewhere in the confines of one's cranial cavity. But no. Long ago his countless infusions of G & Ts, that certainly equaled the volume of the Chesapeake Bay, had dissolved his gray matter. Nothing had changed. His heart and cock vetoed all cerebral functions—vetoed all rational thinking when it came to women. From the first second he laid eyes on Julia Hale he knew that she was trouble with a capital T and yet he still wanted nothing else than to hump her, hump her senseless. No one should be allowed to be that gorgeous. It was a cruel joke inflicted on the male species by a god with a twisted sense of humor.

Every miscue with Julia, except one, was entirely his fault. First was his abominable behavior during the Cliff Top Murder investigation three summers ago when he had found James Collins in her bedroom. He had erroneously thought that James was her young lover, but James turned out to be her grandson helping her reset the alarm system to a fathomless pyrate treasure in her basement. Like everyone has a pyrate fortune under their house.

Why hadn't Julia told him that James was her grandson? Who was not related to one another in this incestuous village? This explained the good-natured insanity that characterized all of the villagers. Up to that point he and Julia had been as cozy as two scotch-swilling, dog-walking peas in a pod.

His second miscue was to ask her to marry him. Her protracted silence after his proposal was infuriating.

"Jay, lad, I'm flattered," she eventually said. "Truly, I am. And I love you dearly. But I've been married twice. Now I just want to have fun."

He hadn't expected the same resounding response as Laura's when he had proposed in her dorm room during their senior year of college. Laura had thrown her arms around him, squealed an emphatic "yes!" and they spent the weekend in bed. True, they were twenty-one and knew basically nothing, but they had jumped into marriage with mutual zeal. He had wholeheartedly supported Laura's erratic career as an artist and she his career on the Baltimore Police Force.

Julia, on the other hand, had considered his offer for an endless ten seconds before answering in the negative. Then she rose off the sofa and said that she was going to the dog park. Did he and his dog Clark want to join her and her dog Miranda? And that was it.

He supposed that his attraction to Julia, besides her otherworldly good looks, phenomenal skills in bed and likewise excessive scotch consumption, was a Freudian longing for Laura. Julia was a former actress for the Royal Shakespeare Company and Laura a painter; he clearly had an infatuation with artistic women. It was probably because he had grown up in an arts-parched household. His father was a dour minister, his mother an equally humorless CPA and his older sister an uptight tax attorney and closeted lesbian. His mother's idea of a creative endeavor was dying Easter eggs. At every family gathering his father would pull him aside and ask him when Laura was "getting a real job."

The final straw in the break-up with Julia was the Burning Man Festival last summer. The palm reader Luna was in part to blame for that. It was Luna that got Julia hooked on the annual bacchanal and orgy in the Nevada desert. As in previous years, the two women headed west for Black Rock Desert in late August. They miraculously returned home in one piece, claiming to have had a splendid time. That was no different from previous years. Julia seemed genuinely glad to see him and their time-wasting routine of dog-walking and scotch-drinking resumed. About a month later it became excruciating to urinate. He had rushed to his primary care physician, worried about a reoccurrence of his prostate issues.

"It's just chlamydia," said the doctor in a voice dripping with innuendo. "Easily treatable with antibiotics. You should let your young lady know about this."

"Just chlamydia? You're kidding me!"

He didn't even get a STD when messing around with the Jacobs twins in high school and that pair was *seeing* just about everyone. That evening he had stormed over to his 'young lady's' house, whipped the vial of antibiotics from his pocket and pushed it toward her.

"For chlamydia. Thanks to you, I've been pissing scalding water."

"Oops."

That was it?

She sipped from a glass of scotch and blew smoke rings into living room ceiling, struggling to recall which in a long line of admirers it could have been. "Maybe it was that cowboy from Wyoming. He was a wild young thang." Her American impersonations—especially of hillbillies and southern belles—were always spot-on and hysterical but at the moment, not! "Luna's ayahuasca tea left us having profound revelations about our purpose in the cosmic plan. Later that night we all—"

He had stood, mouth agape. Cowboys... profound revelations... cosmic plans? How about *I'm really sorry, Jay*? But no. She had wandered over to the kitchen counter and asked if he wanted a salad with his crab quiche.

Weeks after their split he had been sitting with Denny at the intersection near the strip mall when Julia's mini-Cooper blazed through the red light. Denny floored it, the siren wailing. Jay had sat silently in the passenger's seat while Julia shot him accusatory glares and Denny wrote her a speeding ticket for many hundreds of dollars.

Across the river the windows of Julia's house were dark. She had returned to Aberdeen, Scotland, her excuse "to take care of Aunt Beatrice who was deathly ill." Before her departure she had dropped by to ask if he would take care of Miranda. Miranda and his Clark were pups of Alex's amorous dog Water Boy. This explained the good-natured insanity that characterized all of the dogs in the village. He had reached for Miranda's leash. "Yeah, sure." Julia pressed an all-too-familiar tobacco and scotch kiss on his lips, climbed into her car and drove off.

"Women. Damn women." He crunched a gin-flavored ice cube and pointed his binoculars down river. The pyrates and wenches had dispersed from piers. Another Giles Blood-hand Day was thankfully behind him for another year. Starting tomorrow—for seven blissful days—was a sorely needed vacation. He whistled Clark and Miranda inside, locked the glass slider behind them and headed for the kitchen. Just one more G & T while he watched the last innings of the Orioles game.

Damn Laura for dying and abandoning him.

Damn Julia for breaking his middle-aged heart.

Damn Luna who wasted the tourists with *Cannabis* brownies. Never had he and Denny made so many arrests for drunk and disorderlies at a Giles festival.

"Goddamn women." He was through with them. He had two excellent though ditzy dogs, a case of gin in his garage and a bag of limes. What else did a man need? He filled a beer mug two-thirds full with gin, one-third full with tonic and had just enough room for an ice cube or two.

His cell phone buzzed. It was a text from the young detective Lisa Paco. Before leaving headquarters that evening he had asked her to run a Pennsylvania license plate on a sport bike.

"Why?" she had asked him.

"Just curious."

Paco's text read: *Sick sick ride! A BMW F 800 GS. Belongs to a forty-year-old. Ella Winston.*

Ella. An uncommon name for these times. Ella Fitzgerald was one of his and Laura's favorite singers. They had a ton of the First Lady of Song's CDs in their music collection.

Jay read and re-read the next line of the text.

Just released from a Pa. prison. An art forger from Philly.

Chapter 2
A Body on a Beach

The impatient click of dog claws by the sliding glass door woke Jay mid-morning. He groaned his way off the sofa, flipped off the TV that had been on all night and slid open the door. Miranda and Clark dashed across the deck and lawn to the water's edge. Canada geese took flight across the water, honking indignantly at the intrusion.

The housekeeper Mrs. Pulacki, whom he had hired when Laura's mental health started to decline, had recently retired with her sister to a fifty-five-and-older community in Florida. Her hot breakfasts every morning and unpronounceable eastern European dishes every evening had spoiled him. Now he was on his own. Instant coffee and a bowl of cereal were within his range of culinary talents. The one plus to his abandonment by Laura, Julia and Mrs. Pulacki was that there was no one to nag him about a G & T— just a small one—to remove the cobwebs.

He lumbered to the powder room and peed. No burning urine that morning—thank you very much antibiotics—but no thanks to you, Julia Hale. He whistled the dogs back inside and poured food into bowls at opposite ends of the kitchen island since pushy Miranda tried to poach Clark's every meal. He filled a bowl of cereal for himself and ate standing, forming a human barrier between Miranda and Clark's food.

Now what? What to do on the first day of vacation?

His Boston Whaler floated at his dock. Yes, perfect. Walk the dogs to the Point and back. That would tire them out, especially since they would be cooped up on the boat while he fished at his favorite spot—that secluded marsh back by the Wedgewood-Smyth estate that no one knew about but him. There was no need to shave or shower since he wouldn't be seeing anyone that day and he would just get sweaty on the dog walk and fishing expedition. He climbed the stairs to his bedroom, changed into fresh clothes and brushed his teeth. He returned to the kitchen, poured a G & T into a leak-proof travel mug, leashed the dogs, stuffed poop bags in his shorts pocket and headed out the back door. Clark and Miranda pulled him across his neighbors' waterfront lawns until he reached the village.

Sanitation crews were emptying overflowing trashcans on the village green. A few bedraggled pyrates wandered around the piers. The parking lot by the Dockside Café was packed with motorcycles. It was a riding day for the Chrome Divas. Among the bikes were Alex's blue Suzuki and Julia's Royal Enfield and sidecar that she had given Nina to use in her absence. Alex and Nina had become biker divas.

He took a long sip from his travel mug. "Well, well."

There she was again. The Philly Forger had ridden her sport bike onto the sidewalk of the bridge which incidentally was illegal because the sidewalk was for pedestrian use only. Since he was off-duty, he decided not to be a dick about it. Last night he never had a chance to Google the name Ella Winston to see what he might find. The Orioles game got too interesting in the ninth inning and he was too drunk to maneuver a mouse or punch the right keys on his laptop.

Ella Winston was wearing sunglasses. Unfortunate that. One's eyes revealed all. No truer words were ever written, that the eyes were the mirror of the soul. His dogs also spotted her and tugged him forward. Great excuse to meet women... dogs. She bent and scratched Clark and Miranda behind the ears but ignored him completely. She resumed her lean against the railing. She appeared to be watching the Divas at the Dockside Café.

"Clark and Miranda... they're overly friendly," he said prodding her to speak.

She didn't.

Maybe another tack would work. "Are you riding with the girls today?"

"They're grown-ups. Women."

No infliction whatsoever. Julia's Scottish brogue was a rollercoaster of thrilling ups and downs and Laura's every word had seeped emotion. Ella Winston had evaded his question entirely.

"One of the great mysteries of the universe is why a woman can't be alone in public for two seconds without some predator accosting her," she said with a frown.

"Ouch. Predator seems excessive." He was information gathering, nothing more. True, the black leather vest and black boots had a definite allure, but he was a cop on a surveillance mission.

"You could have used the other sidewalk," she said. "This bridge has two sidewalks."

"My dogs always use this one." He grinned.

Her deadpan expression made him feel like the village idiot, but he was not giving up. He shifted slightly so that he might see behind her sunglasses. She shifted out of his line of vision. Miranda and Clark sniffed her which gave him the same idea. Interesting—the scent of gasoline, leather and smoke. She had been sleeping by a fire last night. Her hair tied back in a single braid reeked of it. The only campground near River Glen was Seagull Cove State Park.

The wind shifted and she turned toward him. A breakthrough. She was capable of emotion after all ... vexation. She had obviously caught a whiff of the gin in his travel mug or him sweating out alcohol from the night before.

"Drunk," she proclaimed with an expression of disgust.

"Verb or noun?"

"Definitely noun."

"Drunk. Verb. Later today. I'm on vacation."

He half-expected her to call him "Pathetic" or its synonym, but again she opted for silence. He was altogether uninteresting to her so she departed for her motorcycle.

Time to disarm her. "*Ms. Winston*, what brings you to River Glen?"

The question, the use of her name, didn't seem to shock her in the least.

She turned abruptly. "I'm a tourist, *Mr. Braden*, minding my own business."

His strategy backfired; it was he who was disarmed. The use of his name indicated that she had not passed out while drinking G & Ts but instead used last night to do her homework. She pulled on her helmet. The defiant flip of her face shield signaled the conversation over. She flung her leg over the seat of her BMW, pushed the starter and rode straight off the curb toward the parking lot of the Dockside Café.

'I'm a tourist, *Mr. Braden*, minding my own business.'

If you say so.

The best part of the Chrome Divas' motorcycle club, Alex realized, was its inclusivity. The Divas were women from all ethnicities and backgrounds—all united by a love of exploring the road on the back of a motorcycle. She was a marine biologist, Nina a sociology professor, the club president Linda Radowski an insurance agent, the ride planner Janice Klein was a potter and beekeeper and the treasurer Blanche Hyde was a dog groomer. Their varied walks of life made for offbeat, interesting discussions over breakfast and again at the restaurant where the ride terminated. She and Nina had joined the club shortly after Nina learned to ride the Enfield and passed Maryland's motorcycle safety course.

Alex had eaten too much at the Dockside Café which meant that breakfast would be jostling around in her belly along the back roads of the eastern shore. That day's ride was to Cape Henlopen State Park in Lewes, Delaware. A swim in the ocean, an all-you-can-eat buffet and ride back to River Glen before nightfall. Ride, eat, ride, eat. She and Nina had found the perfect club. She paid her bill at the cashier and headed out to the parking lot to stretch her legs before the ride.

Odd. An unfamiliar sport bike had parked-in her Suzuki. She had come to associate each Diva with her respective bike, but she had no clue who the BMW adventure bike belong to. The bike was a stunner. It was the type of rugged machine that tore across the desert in long-distance races. Maybe this bike had been in the Dakar Rally across South America or had wound through the Swiss Alps? Every bike and its owner had a story to tell. Some women drove low-slung Harleys. Others went for a classic Brit like a Triumph, whereas others preferred a sexy Italian like a Ducati, Aprilia or Benelli. One's motorcycle reflected salient features of its owner's personality. It was a bit like owners and their dogs.

Admittedly, she and her Labrador retriever Water Boy resembled each other in both looks and personality. They were both black haired, green-eyed water fanatics and flakes. Her Japanese bike was old and dinged-up, through no fault of hers. The previous owner Gary Smyth had left it in a back corner of the marina where it had collected dust and rust for eons before he traded it to her for a summer's worth of crabs. So what the bike was not beautiful. It had a better feature. It was unwaveringly reliable. It started up every time, even after sitting in the shed all winter.

Until the BMW was moved, she was going nowhere. The bike must belong to the stranger with the long braid who was talking to Linda Radowski. Linda opened a leather saddlebag on her Kawasaki Vulcan and gave the woman a pamphlet about the motorcycle club.

"The Divas are a local chapter of a national motorcycling organization for women," she heard Linda explain.

The BMW rider nodded. She was obviously a prospective member wanting to join the ride. Linda showed her the hand signals that were passed down the line of bikes as they rode and the foot signal that warned for a pothole or dangerous obstruction in the road.

Linda pointed at Alex. "Alex is Sweep today. She's bringing up the rear. Why don't you ride in the back with her? That's her, by your bike."

"Sounds great." The stranger left Linda and approached her. "Ella Winston."

Alex shook the extended hand. "Alex Allaway. I love your bike."

"Thanks." Ella smiled fondly at her blue Suzuki. "I learned to ride on a Suzuki dirt bike. Good memories, good times."

"Where was that?" She slipped on the high vis yellow vest that the Sweep wears to be visible to motorists.

"Gettysburg. There's where I'm living for the moment."

"Small world. Our annual motorcycle convention is there this week."

"I know," Ella said. "I've been hired to run ghost walks for the convention."

"Ghost walks scare the hell out of me. They have them here on Halloween to tell the story of Giles Blood-hand and Headless Charles Allaway."

"Allaway? A relative?"

"Yeah, one of my ancestors. Lucky me."

Nina approached and dumped water bottles and a bag of ice into a cooler in the sidecar. "Ballast."

"Nina, Ella's a rider from Gettysburg," she said in introduction. "She's running ghost walks for our bike convention."

"Sweet," Nina said. "I've never been on one. We're going."

"Not me," she replied. "Ella, nothing personal, but I'll take a pass on the ghost walk. I'm a big chicken. No, a huge chicken."

"We're so going, Alex," Nina said.

"You don't want to miss it," said Ella in a low, mysterious voice. "Gettysburg's the most haunted place in America. Ghastly ghouls are all over the battlefield."

Detective Will Wilkins flashed his police ID and the security guard waved his unmarked police car through the gates.

"The Radcliffe on the Chesapeake, Golf Club and Spa, Will," said Lisa Paco reading the gold letters on the stone archway. "I'm uberpsyched. Who da thunk it? It's not like I'm invited to black tie affairs here every Saturday night."

"The resort is too blue for the blood of a Wilkins," he said. Instead every family celebration was held in the tiki room at the Nauticus. The photographs on his mother's mantle, of baby showers, wedding receptions and golden anniversaries, had in the background a mural of naked island girls, outrigger canoes and flamingos.

"The Radcliffe," Lisa said breathlessly. "With an e. It's my dream come true that someone would get whacked here!"

Will secretly agreed. River Glen was long overdue for excitement. The last murder investigation was years before. The Cliff Top Murder case had been a doozy; Ricarda Sarova had murdered five people with spider venom and buried them in a mass grave at the cliff's edge.

Lisa pressed her forehead and nose against the passenger's side window. "I'm not missing an inch of this view. I mean is that even grass or artificial turf? It's so perfect. It doesn't look real. I Googled this joint. Two hundred K just to join and that doesn't even include the monthly membership fees. I bet the guacamole in the macho nachos at the poolside bar contains real avocados instead of that gross synthetic stuff that resembles pea vomit."

"Yuck, Lisa."

"But it does."

"Who found the body?"

"A golfer who hit his ball off the green."

"Does Jay know?"

"Captain Taylor told us to handle it, since Jay's on vacation," she said between excited smacks of gum. "Anyway, he's probably sleeping one off."

He nodded sadly. Their boss was in one of his funks. Depressed and moody like after the murder of Laura.

"How cool will it be to wander around this joint, Will? Let's prolong the investigation, interviewing everyone...

gardeners, cooks, masseuses, caddies, cabana boys, chamber maids, everyone... so we get to hang out here for a while."

"Yeah. Okay."

"Captain Taylor said to drive to the left, past the tennis club and meet Zera Lim back by the pro shop. But let's definitely go into the main building today. I wanna check out the fountain with the mermaids. I wonder if the manager would mind if I took a selfie in front of it. The crystal chandelier in the entry way is supposed to be sick." She pressed her cell phone into his face. "I downloaded it from the web. See?"

He glanced at the image of chandelier. "Sick."

"How much do you think it weighs?"

"Two tons?"

"Maybe even three. I'll wiki its weight later." She unrolled her window. "Whoa, the hotel looks like a white castle! #socool. This is just like the Majestic, that seaside resort that Miss Marple visits in *The Body in the Library*."

"I've never read a Miss Marple story."

"You're bullshitting me. What did you read when you were a teenager?"

"Biographies of football greats like Vince Lombardi, Sonny Jurgensen and Joe Montana. Why are all the books about quarterbacks and coaches but never tight ends? By far the most important position on the team is the tight end who has to block, run and catch passes."

"You're asking me, a football ignoramus? With any luck, our murderer has genius level intelligence and will leave us all sorts of misleading clues that means we'll be searching the Radcliffe for weeks on end."

"It's always the same. A jilted lover. A revenge killing."

"How can you say that? The Cliff Top Murder investigation was all about chemically-engineered super spiders. How cool was that!"

"Not. Just sick."

"Cool sick or ill sick?"

"Disturbed in the head sick."

"I smell chlorine. #bummer. The pool's behind that high wall. Now I'll never get a photo of Bon Jovi, Bill Belichick or Cher. All of them have stayed here, you know."

"I might have played for Bill Belchick," he lamented. "If I haven't blown out my knee twice in college, I might have been a Redskin, Raven or Patriot. I might have received passes from Tom Brady."

"A detective is much cooler than an NFL player, except the pay sucks."

He stopped the sedan near a fleet of golf carts and they climbed out.

"Dr. Lim is back with the body," said a uniformed police officer. "By the water."

A forensic scientist from Zera Lim's team handed them disposable white jumpsuits which they pulled over their clothes. Anxious golfers, whose game on the back nine had been interrupted, watched them walk toward the bay.

"Maybe the murderer's watching us at this very minute," Lisa whispered to him.

"Maybe."

"#kindacreepy."

"Way."

They crossed the smooth expanse of the sixteenth hole, veered around a sand trap, passed through a row of pine trees, then skidded down a sandy slope. Yellow crime scene tape cordoned off a section of the shoreline.

"Lisa, how could anyone hit his ball on to the beach?" he wondered. "He must have a terrible slice."

"It must be him." She pointed to a golfer in a yellow shirt and yellow and blue-checkered polyester pants, speaking with two officers and a well-groomed man in a tan suit. "Look at his comb-over."

"Shh, Lisa."

"It must take Super Glue to hold that flap in place!"

"Shh!"

Dr. Zera Lim, the medical examiner, approached them. "The golfer Chet Hathaway…"

"Comb-over Guy," whispered Lisa barely containing her laughter.

"… found the body this morning at 9:14 and called 911," Zera said unfazed. "The other man is the hotel manager Lionel Stevens."

"How was the victim killed?" he asked.

"One cut to the windpipe," Zera replied. "Last night around midnight. With a razor or similar instrument. Pardon the pun, but your work's cut out for you. The victim is wearing a toupee, fake sideburns, mustache and beard."

"Any weapon on the scene?"

"None, so far."

"Let's see!" Lisa said.

She darted across the beach to Zera's assistant who was kneeling next to the body. He pulled back the plastic cover. Flies dive-bombed the red opening in the victim's neck. Will shook imperceptibly. The red slice looked like a taut, mocking smile.

"A scarlet thread of murder," Lisa said. "Freaky."

"Way."

The victim was on his back in the sand. His dress shirt had been ripped open, casting the buttons outward like meteors from an exploding star. Will's eyes returned to the wound. There was no sawing or frantic hacking. Just one clean slice.

"Will?" said Lisa pointing to the man's frail chest.

"What's it say?"

"Freakin' crazy."

"What, Lisa?"

"Traitor."

He bent over the body. Lisa was right. The killer had quite legibly carved the word Traitor into the victim's chest. Weirder still, the killer had placed on the decease's head a gray kepi worn by the Confederate army during the Civil War.

"Do we know who he is?" he asked Zera.

"The hotel manager identified him as one of the guests. Professor Monroe Hadley from Philadelphia."

Ella Winston never intended to ride all the way to Cape Henlopen, Delaware with the Chrome Divas. She had been on a group motorcycle ride before, that time with the Cannonball Cruisers of Gettysburg. Like that ride, bikers peeled off at various places as the calls and demands of life dictated so none of the Divas would think twice if she peeled off early. Gas to the shore and back and a seafood buffet were not in her budget, but she had accomplished what she needed to. New terrain had been explored. After years of freezing her ass off in the arctic snow and winds that blasted Cambridge Springs from September to July, she was looking to relocate to a milder climate. Though a few Divas complained of the heat and humidity, the warm air felt wonderful to her. Maryland's eastern shore seemed just the place. Plus, she now knew some of the locals.

Linda Radowski was a bit officious but pleasant enough. Alex and Nina were outgoing and free-spirited. Better still, Alex was the crabber who owned the tugboat *Vital Spark*. Next time she ran into her in the village, she would rally the nerve to ask if she might be taught to crab. It was not her intent to compete or usurp Alex's crabbing business, she would explain, but just make enough money for gas, the campsite rental at Seagull Cove State Park and to feed herself crabs. During her eleven years at Cambridge Springs they had served crab cakes exactly never.

Chesapeake country, Ella was certain, was the place to lay low until she made enough money for her trans-global motorcycle trek. The gin-sodden cop Jay Braden might be a problem—he was the cagey Inspector Javert to her Jean Valjean. Another lifetime ago Ian Kent had taken her to see *Les Miserable* in Philly for her birthday, before she discovered that he was a duplicitous weasel. If she quietly went about her business in the village, Braden might discover that she was not painting replicas of the *The Kiss* or *Nighthawks* to fence on the black market but merely rebuilding her life—seeking redemption like Jean Valjean— after a series of catastrophic mistakes.

She glanced down at her gas gauge. Enough gas and time had been wasted. At the intersection of Route 313 and 404 near Denton she told Alex and Nina that she had to break off and go to work. They wished her safe travels and she circled back to River Glen. She did have work to do and she was an art historian; those were not outright lies, although she was not on the payroll of the Met, Louvre or MoMA. She was on the payroll of herself and her paycheck was zero. On the ride back to the village she enumerated the ways that she was nothing like Jean Valjean. He had been jailed for a selfless act—stealing bread for his sister's starving family. She had been jailed for painting forgeries, motivated by selfish reasons: to make tax-free money and expediently pay off student loan debt.

For the forgeries, she was guilty—indubitably guilty. That she had confessed to the public defender. By telling the truth, her sentence would be reduced or so she thought. Her naiveté was stupefying. Community service... she could be so lucky! But some way, somehow, a Civil War document stolen from the National Archives also got pinned on her.

"What document?" she had cried to the stone-faced jury. "I've never been to the National Archives in Washington DC!"

But there she was in pixels, her blue spiky hair ablaze on the footage from the security cameras as she entered and exited the archives on the day of the theft. The FBI agent had played the scene again and again for the packed courtroom.

"That's not me! Can't you see that I'm being framed?"

"Guilty on both counts," the foreman stated.

"Eight years" was punctuated by the jarring crack of the judge's gavel.

She was given an orange jumpsuit, put in handcuffs and was driven across Pennsylvania in an armored van with a burglar named Samantha Ramirez and a drug dealer named Keisha Long.

It was hubris to put herself in the same category as the heroic Jean Valjean who stole food for his sister's children. She had copied the Adam Eaton paintings for entirely self-serving purposes. The number of heroic bones in her body was zero. She was no Jean Valjean nor was Detective Braden the obsessive Inspector Javert.

Any man that loved dogs could not be all bad.

Braden was a lonely drunk; there were a million men like him all over the world. When she had read the website of the River Glen Police Department on her cell phone the night before, his face, name and rank glowed in the darkness of her tent. When she had Googled the name Jay Braden, River Glen PD, an article published in the *River Glen Gazette* from years before appeared on her phone. The accompanying photo had been taken at the funeral of his wife Laura. Braden had appeared exhausted and shell-shocked. Laura had been killed at a place called Mutter Island by one Clyde Whitby.

That tragedy was why she didn't tell him on the bridge to "Get lost, loser." If he wanted gin and tonics for breakfast on his vacation, then that was his business.

After passing horse farms and one-intersection towns consisting of a gas station, beer store and boat dealership, Ella was back in River Glen. She motored across the bridge once again, but Braden and his dogs were nowhere to be seen. She headed up the coastal road, traveling through a pine forest near the River Glen Marine Station and a valley of summer corn. At the Wedgewood-Smyth mansion she turned off the highway onto a dirt road. She looked warily around. There was no one in the fallow fields to either side of her. She followed the circular driveway around a huge maple tree and veered onto the grass. She tucked her bike behind the overgrown hedge where she had stashed it during a quick foray into the abandoned manor house months before.

It was early evening when the three motorcyclists appeared. Scaring the hell out of her! Her frantic thought was that Monroe Hadley and Ian Kent had heard of her release from prison and hired biker-hitmen to track her down. Her imagination went crazy—the assassins would chase her through the dark rooms and up and down the creaky staircases until they closed in on her from all directions. Her remains wouldn't be found for months, maybe years—if at all. She had flicked off her flashlight and peered around a tattered curtain snagged on a shard of glass. The motorcycles were an old sport bike and a retro bike with a sidecar. She had listened intently. Female voices, thank God. They were not killers-for-hire but three women, one learning to ride. Earlier that day in the parking lot of the Dockside Café, she had recognized the bikes and two of the women.

In the shadow of the hedge Ella unzipped her leather vest and pulled on an old T-shirt. It was going to be a day of dusty, dirty work. Bright sunlight would illuminate the rooms. There would be ample time to search the bedrooms, servants' quarters and outbuildings, maybe even the underground crypt. If she could just find the Adam Eaton paintings belonging to the Wedgewood-Smyths, then she could exonerate herself and finger Monroe and Ian. Where were those originals?

"Be still, very still," Lisa Paco told herself. If she held her cell phone pointing outward, the walk from the crime scene to the Radcliffe's opulent lobby could be filmed without the prissy hotel manager Lionel Stevens noticing. She and Will deliberately lingered behind Steven's precise footsteps.

"It's not like I'm going to post the footage on You Tube or Facebook or anything like that," she whispered to Will. "I just want to make a short indie film for Mom and Aunt Helen. They'll be ecstatic to see the inner sanctum of the rich and infamous. Flippin' bad luck is that my phone is only thirty-two percent charged. What if I run out of battery power? #pacosfirstworldproblem. How could I know that a rich dude would get knocked off at the Radcliffe this morning?"

"Score your film to tango music," Will whispered back. "Tango music has such a catchy rhythm."

"I never considered a soundtrack. I now have footage for the golf course- and tennis court scenes, but the characters lack diversity. All fat white guys."

Lisa's spirits lifted when they passed by the swimming pool. The codgers' thirty-something-bleached-blonde-trophy-wives were flirting with the lifeguards, cabana boys and each other. The pool scene—skimpy bikinis and Speedos on gym-honed bodies—would change the film's rating from G to PG-13. Aunt Helen could handle it.

"Will, if my cell phone dies? #ugh. Can I finish filming with your phone? Then Norman from IT can splice the footage together with iMovie or zoom.us. Our indie film could have an artsy Norman Mailerish title like *The Naked Bimbo and the Almost Dead Geezer*."

Will grinned. "Of course. You're welcome to use it."

"Awesome. Thanks, partner. #willscoolabouteverything. It sucks that we didn't see any celebrities in the pool. I was hoping for at least Liza Minnelli. Then we'd have a real movie star in our film."

"Look where we're heading, Lisa."

"OMG!"

Automatic glass doors parted in front of Lionel Stevens. She muted a gasp. The lobby was an indoor rainforest suffused with muted jazz and trickling water. There it was... the gargantuan fountain with ten fishtailed beauties squirting water from their mouths. The chandelier entwined with vines—live ones, not plastic—was equally mammoth.

"Whoa, Will! #copacetic."

"Way."

There was no time to gawk and less time to film. Lionel Stevens made sure of that. He briskly escorted them to a golden elevator. Monroe Hadley's room was on the fifth floor. A red and gold carpet led them to Room 505. The CSI team was already there. She cut across the room to the balcony. The view was of the pool and golf course and beyond a row of pine trees was the sun-speckled bay. She stuffed her cell phone in her pocket. Enough film-making. It was time to get to work. There was a killer to catch.

It took a few hours to search the room and bag up Hadley's belongings. No female items were found because, according to Stevens, the wife Ventresca had checked out yesterday morning. Hadley's shaving kit contained the usual for an old guy: a razor and shaving cream, toothbrush, toothpaste, Viagra, aspirin, Ambien, blood pressure medication and aftershave. Pairs of blue contact lens and lens solution. In the closet hung a dinner jacket and a cane with a gold handle. His suitcase contained silk scarves, sports shirts, dress shirts, underwear, socks, shorts and khaki pants.

But one item was out-of-the-ordinary.

In the professor's suitcase was a circular case containing two identical white-haired toupees, extra sets of artificial sideburns and goatees and the sticky fastening glue to adhere them to the skin. Odd. Very odd. It was the type of make-up that an actor, or a spy, might wear.

Jay cast his fishing line into the water. His line and bobber were the only things that made the water ripple. The remote inlet by the derelict Wedgewood-Smyth mansion was that still. One whole week to himself. By himself. Alone. Completely alone. What the hell was he going to do with himself for an entire week? Last summer he and Julia had taken a cruise to Bermuda and when Laura was healthy their vacations were spent in southern Europe where she had dragged him to art museums. He had never visited northern Europe, Iceland or Scandinavia, but he had dithered too long to book anything. Besides, he wasn't really sure where to go. Julia and Laura had always dictated the destination of his travels. As long as he was going to get laid and there was a bar or liquor store within walking distance of the hotel, he would go about anywhere he was told.

What about day trips to the shore? The Atlantic beaches were only an hour away, but he'd be too drunk to drive if the routine of breakfast G & Ts continued. Plus, he'd miss his dogs. He needed a destination where he could take Clark and Miranda. No doggie daycare for them. Miranda didn't play nice with other dogs because she was convinced that she was human.

That was it! The dogs would love camping.

He had inherited his father's camping gear: sleeping bags, a propane stove, pots and pans, all of it. The tent was large enough for a family so it would certainly accommodate him and the dogs. The camping stuff was buried somewhere in his wreck of a garage. Where to go? The barrier islands of Assateague or Chincoteague? Were dogs allowed on the islands with the wild ponies?

A sound broke the silence of the marsh—a motorcycle engine started in the distance. Maybe it was a teenager riding a dirt bike in the fallow field by the mansion. No, it was something bigger than a dirt bike. The engine did not have the cacophonous grumble of a Harley. It was the purr of a high-end European motorcycle. Laura had remarked on the pleasant murmur of café racers and sport bikes when at the sidewalk restaurants in Italy and France. He inched his binoculars over the fringe of marsh grass.

"What the hell?"

The forger's motorcycle was stashed behind a hedge at the manor house. She looked nervously about, whipped off her T-shirt, wiped her neck and armpits with it and stuffed it in a metal saddlebag. She pulled on a fresh shirt, then her leather vest, helmet and gloves. The glimpse of her black bra was way too quick. She slung her leg over the seat, clicked the bike into gear and disappeared up the dusty road.

Why was she poking around the Wedgewood-Smyth place?

"I'm a tourist, Mr. Braden, minding my own business," she had said on the bridge that morning. He was not so hungover to have forgotten that remark.

Tourist? What a crock of shit. He reeled in his line. There was work to do. He tugged. The nylon pulled and stretched. He tugged again. No movement. Nothing.

"Fuck, not again."

His hook was definitely stuck on something. He knew better than to cast his line toward that deep hole where some jerk had dumped their garbage. Was he stuck on a rusty bicycle, washing machine, ghost net or crab pot? Whatever it was, it wasn't the first time his hook had snagged on it. With a filleting knife from his tackle box, he cut the line. He reeled in the limp nylon, pulled up the anchor and ripped the cord on his outboard. He turned the boat in the direction of the village.

An ex-con was poking around River Glen. And he was going to find out why.

Dr. Zera Lim leaned over the stainless-steel examination table. Strange corpses had passed through the morgue but this one was amongst the strangest. The method of murder was easy to determine, unlike that in the Cliff Top Murder investigation where the peptides in the spider venom had degraded in the victims over decades in a mass grave. In this case, one swipe of a large blade had opened Monroe Hadley's trachea and carotid arteries. The slice was as narrow as narrow could be—a scarlet thread of murder. Exsanguination and oxygen deprivation were the causes of death. The killer was right-handed like ninety percent of the population. The murder weapon had not yet been located, either around the shoreline or in the waters at the crime scene. Nor were Hadley's cell phone and wallet found on his person or among the belongings in the hotel room.

After Hadley collapsed to the ground, the killer tore his shirt, flinging the buttons into the sand and then carved

Traitor into his chest. Who was that message intended for? The only person privy to that info was the golfer Chet Hathaway who found the body and the police. And why the Confederate kepi? Brand-new. It still had a price sticker on it from a gift shop in Gettysburg, Pennsylvania.

The strangest feature of Monroe Hadley was his disguise. Yesterday the village had been filled with tourists dressed as pyrates and wenches. Pyrate costumes were the norm in River Glen and worn year-round by shopkeepers, waiters and tour boat operators, but Hadley's costume had consisted of a white toupee, bushy sideburns, pointy goatee and blue contact lens. According to Lisa's rapid-fire stream-of-consciousness texts to Zera's cell phone, in every image of Hadley on the Internet, his driver's license photo and the website at his art college, he had the same shock of white hair and beard, brilliant blue eyes and a silk scarf tied cavalierly around his neck. He was the picture—stereotype of —the flamboyant art professor. Yet now on her examination table laid a brown-eyed bald sixty-year old with a singular word carved in his chest.

Zera gazed into the jowly face. "Who the hell are you?"

James Collins rarely had visitors to his house on the bluff and he liked it that way. He delighted in hosting an annual Christmas party and pig roast on the 4th of July, but otherwise he savored his private time to write. After a decade of stewing about it, he had overcome the inertia and taken that tremorous first step into the unwritten novel. For years he had mulled over the story of Josiah and Abigail Wedgewood-Smyth. Should it be a work of non-fiction or historical fiction? Historical fiction, he finally decided, allowed him the freedom to fill in the blanks with action and suspense. Josiah and Abigail were Civil War spies after all; their lives oozed thrills and intrigue.

He had stumbled upon the Wedgewood-Smyth papers when he was a high school volunteer tasked with cataloging the documents at the historical society. To say that Abigail was a graphic writer was an understatement. He had read her letters, glancing furtively around the archive and wiping sweat from his teenaged brow. Abigail was in part the reason that he was still a bachelor. He had had no serious relationships in his life, but it was not for want of trying. He had tried and tried often, but no one woman in real life captivated him like Abigail. No physical description of Abigail was ever found and it made no difference if she was drop-dead gorgeous or hideously ugly. She was raw sex, a tiger stalking the manor house, waiting for Josiah.

Then all changed. He had been working with Burt Sweeny, a new employee at the archive, when Nina Vega walked in. Laptop in hand, she had asked if he was aware of any local fisheries reports in the stacks. He knew Nina from afar; she was Alex's friend and a new professor at Tolchester College. Nina's left hand had been bandaged at the time. Burt later told him of the bizarre accident that chopped off her two fingers. Burt had been working as a security guard at Tolchester at the time; it was he who had driven her to the hospital.

It was too weird to be coincidence. It was fate. How impossible not to stare outright at Nina's hand! Abigail had had two fingers blown off by a Confederate bullet when escaping a cavalry unit near Cashtown, days before the battle of Gettysburg. On her left hand!

He was not particularly religious or superstitious, but Hindu ideas on reincarnation had given him pause. In that inexplicable moment, at the historical society's help desk, Abigail appeared before him in the form of Nina Vega. He was sure of it. Never was he so attuned, enlivened by a woman's presence. He led Nina to the shelves where the fisheries documents were kept and left her alone (with great difficulty) so that she could work. He later offered her a cup of tea, which she accepted, and they chatted about her scholarly research and his idea of writing a novel. She was pleasant and professional, but behind her glistening black eyes was a raging inferno of passion. She was Abigail carnal and incarnate!

James sighed. Enough Nina fantasizing. Back to work. He returned his attention to the novel on his laptop. There were two ways to go with the hay bale scene. Write it in Abigail's pornographic sensationalism that would place *Subterfuge* in the erotica genre? Or write in sensual metaphors, similar to D. H. Lawrence, that would appeal to a general readership? Better to err in favor of subtlety rather than write a *Fifty Shades of Abigail*. If made into a movie, he would suggest to *Subterfuge's* producers that Abigail be played by an actress with the sizzling sensuality of Sophia Loren and the dashing Josiah be portrayed by an actor with the roguish qualities of Clark Gable or Errol Flynn. Would Nina be interested in a picnic in a barn... with hay bales?

The doorbell rang. He opened the home security app on his cell phone. That was peculiar. It was Jay Braden, Grandma Julia's ex-boyfriend. Strange that he would drop by. Jay had come to the Christmas party and pig roast with Julia, Alex and Will, but it was not like him to drop by out-of-the-blue.

"Hello Jay. Let me buzz you in," he said to his phone that was connected to an intercom at the front door. "I'll be there in a second." He saved the draft on his laptop, grabbed his coffee mug and wandered from his writing room.

In the foyer a sweaty, sunburnt Jay stood checking out the nautical memorabilia hanging from the walls and rafters. His dogs were panting.

"A pleasant surprise." He gave Jay a hearty handshake. "A cold drink? Water for Clark and Miranda?"

"Sure, thanks."

"A cocktail, soda, beer?"

"Beer's perfect."

"Dark or light?"

"Light's fine. I'm watching my calories."

He skirted the kitchen island and opened the fridge. He flipped the top off a summer ale and handed it to Jay, then prepared a water bowl for the dogs.

"I'm here to ask you about the Wedgewood-Smyth house," Jay asked after a long swig of beer. "What's going to be done with it?"

"Is this part of a police investigation?" he asked somewhat uneasily.

"No. Just curious."

"Oh good." He relaxed. "We were hoping to have raised more money for our fundraising campaign, but alas, with the new tax reform, no one is donating to non-profits. At the last meeting of the Friends of the Wedgewood-Smyth House, the treasurer Kenneth Radowski reported that we're only at fifty percent of our goal. We have quite a way to go before a renovation is possible. Despite noble efforts, Kenneth has had little success acquiring state monies from Annapolis or local granting agencies. Our ultimate goal is to convert the mansion into a museum and education center on colonial history."

"I was fishing there today—"

"And you saw a woman," he said preemptively. "Ella Winston."

Jay's eyebrows jumped. "How'd you know?"

"Because I go there occasionally to check that it's not being vandalized by teenagers, squatters and the like. A few months ago Ms. Winston came to the historical society asking about the art collection of Josiah and Abigail. It obviously triggered my alarm since I'm writing a novel about them. At first I thought she might be a novelist who might scoop me. She was mainly asking about Adam Eaton so I did some checking on her. She's an ex-convict and artist of considerable talent. When I went up to the manor house, she, or someone, had dug a hole under the fence. After that I installed a hidden camera in the house that's linked to an app on my cell phone. She was wandering around today. She didn't damage or take anything so I just let her explore."

Jay's eyebrows rose again. "Very interesting. Who's Adam Eaton?"

"Not much is known about him. He was a so-called idiot savant. He was probably somewhere on the autism spectrum. He was an itinerant painter who was taken in by Josiah and Abigail. Abigail adored him and his artwork."

"What was Winston looking for, do you think?"

"I have no clue but paintings would be my guess. That's what got her sent to prison—copying Eaton's paintings."

"Do you know where she lives?"

"Not specifically. When she signed the guest register at the historical society, she put down a town and state."

"Do you remember from where?"

"Sure do. Gettysburg, Pennsylvania."

Chapter 3
Gettysburg

Ella kicked her legs out of the sleeping bag and unzipped the tent flaps to release the heat. She rolled onto her back. Morning light and shadows shifted across the canvas, transitory hues of Windsor emerald, viridian and cobalt chromite green. When did this whole mess with the paintings begin? Life had been perfect to that point... in fact, all fun and games. When? The trouble, she supposed, started in high school when she worked as a student volunteer at the Battlefield Historical Society. Her supervisor had been the historian Dr. Hazel Worth who ran the archive. Hazel's sister Phoebe was the book-keeper for the Society's nominal operating budget, but as far as Ella could tell Phoebe did little more than watch Brad Pitt movies on her laptop and bake cookies in the tiny back kitchen. Though the two sisters were probably in their mid-forties at the time, to a teenaged Ella they seemed as ancient as the outcroppings on the Round Tops.

The Battlefield Historical Society had always been managed by a Worth. Before Hazel and Phoebe, it had been run by their father and his father before that, all dating back to the Society's founding by Captain Tobias Worth. Tobias' sword-wielding statue on the sidewalk out front now provided a rest stop for weary pigeons. Hazel and Phoebe's fates were immutable; they were born into a family of staunch Pennsylvania Yankees whose sole mission was to carry forward the vision of the heroic Tobias.

Another history geek to frequent the historical society was Old Man Detrick who offered Ella a job guiding ghost tours through the Ephram Whitson House on Baltimore Street. Sure, why not? The part-time job was just the thing to pay for art supplies, Netflix and upcoming college expenses. Detrick had asked her her dress size and shortly after appeared with a black velvet gown and cape, plastic skull earrings and a black belt with dangly plastic skulls, all purchased at a Goth website. She had objected to wearing black stilettos since she would be doing so much walking up and down creaky stairs so he finally relented as long as her sneakers were black. With white make-up plastering her face, gloomy black shadows circling her eyes and underscoring her cheekbones and blood-red lipstick, she was the embodiment of nubile ghoulishness.

The tale of terror and ghostly happenings at the Ephram Whitson House that Detrick had her tell was absolute bullshit. The house had never been a Civil War hospital, nor had a single Union or Confederate soldier ever stepped into the dwelling. But Detrick, a notorious scoundrel, decided that he could pay off the mortgage by running ghost tours through it every Friday and Saturday night. She became a genius at improvisation. Her wide gesticulations, cocked eyebrow, pregnant pauses and throaty gasps at a squeaky door or fluttering candle entranced audiences and earned her giant tips.

The ghost tour that fateful Friday night was for fraternity brothers from the local college. It was clear from the start that the boys had been lingering around a keg before coming to the Ephram Whitson House. A paunchy, loud one had complimented her gown while his eyes roamed the swooping neckline. The ways of men were not unfamiliar to her because she had recently lost her virginity to Ralph MacKenzie, the tight end on the football team, amidst the rocks at Devil's Den. But that was another story. Detrick had assured her that he would keep a watchful eye on the burping, shoving frat brothers. One of them however seemed different, a black-haired boy who stood silently at the edge of the group.

She began the tale of the Union soldier Robert Harper from New Hampshire who had been injured at the Wheatfield on the second day of the battle and the Virginian Elijah Jones who lost a leg during Pickett's Charge on day three of the battle. None of the frat boys had been sober enough to ask how two soldiers from the two opposing armies were both left behind by their retreating infantry divisions and ended up in the same house; otherwise she would have been forced to concoct a ludicrous backstory. It wouldn't have been the first. By candlelight she led the brothers through the colonial house, grazing the hidden buttons with her hand that turned on sounds of wind, rustling leaves and agonized groans. She had pointed out the rooms where the grisly surgeries occurred, where Robert and Elijah convalesced, where during a violent fight over the beautiful nurse Grace Morgan, the tragic fire ignited—and where the three charred ghosts of Robert, Elijah and Grace had been spotted since July of 1863. Despite initial misgivings, all went fine on the ghost tour. The frat brothers had been enraptured by the lurid tale, gave her a generous tip and went on their way.

So renown was she at yacking about Civil War ghosts that she was offered a second job as a storyteller on the

Ghost Bus through the battlefield. To top it off, she was the featured attraction on a glossy tourist pamphlet for the Best Amusements of Gettysburg. She was Gettysburg's Princess of the Paranormal. Cha-ching. Money was rolling her way. The whole thing was a hoot.

And life was good at home. Her parents had divorced when she was five yet remained amicable enough to run a business together on Steinwehr Avenue. Her father owned a souvenir store that sold T-shirts, plastic bugles, Union and Confederate caps and flags while her mother ran the adjacent art gallery.

Like her mother, Ella could paint.

Their paintings flew off the gallery walls, especially during July 1 to 3 every year when the town was flooded with reenactors. The two of them could barely replace the paintings fast enough. And made to order paintings—no problem. If some Joshua Lawrence Chamberlain wanna-be wanted a customized painting of himself and the 20th Maine fixing bayonets to charge down Little Round Top, or a James Longstreet groupie wanted a painting of the General contemplating the impending slaughter of Pickett's Charge, then she was the one to paint it. She knew all about Gettysburg art, the sketches of Alf Waud, paintings by Peter Rothermel, the photographs of Alexander Gardner, Paul Phillippoteaux's Cyclorama... all of it.

She had been in the painting studio when someone triggered the bell in the front gallery. Her mother had been transfixed by her current work and said, "You get it, Ellie. I'm busy." Up by the cash register stood the black-haired student from the ghost walk. She turned on the sales pitch. "Can I help you? Are you looking for anything in particular? A specific battle? From the perspective of the Union or Confederate side?"

"I'm just looking." He smiled directly at her. His eyes were nowhere near the paintings on the wall.

She tightened. He was a college boy. She was a townie though she had been admitted to a college way better than his. He had a swarthy appeal, but flings between college students and townies rarely had good outcomes.

He strolled along the wall, examining the paintings. Then he spun. "Those look just like Adam Eaton paintings!"

"They're supposed to. He's one of my favorites."

"You painted these?"

"Yes. I love his primitive style. How do you know who he is? He's pretty obscure."

"My... ur, uncle, an art professor, is an expert on Eaton. He's got to see these!"

Two weeks later she was wined and dined at the Dobbins House by the business student Ian Kent and the esteemed Professor Monroe Hadley.

"Me and my big mouth," Jay muttered to himself as his SUV rattled along Route 30 West. He and the village lawyer James Collins were going camping. Together. The two of them. This meant no gin and tonics for breakfast. It's not that he didn't like James. He did. James was altogether likeable and he was invaluable in extracting life insurance money from the vise-grip of the greedy insurance company after Laura's death. It's just that James was a painful remainder of Julia.

The first fracture in his relationship with her occurred when he found James in Julia's bedroom. His neurotic, possessive mind immediately leapt to the wrong conclusion. Julia had never told him that James was her grandson or that the bulk of Giles Blood-hand's treasure was hidden under her house. Why not? Why couldn't Julia trust him? He was her boyfriend and a police officer, after all. But in Julia's eyes he was not a descendent of the pyrate families of River Glen. Plain and simple, he was an outsider with inferior blood lines. Always was, always will be.

At the moment James was shuffling through the music CDs in his glove compartment. James had set up a security system in Julia's bedroom closet; now he finds that James also installed a hidden camera in the Wedgewood-Smyth house. Jeez, where else? Innocuous James Collins, or was he?

"Goddamn stupid, goddamn big mouth," Jay muttered again. Yesterday at James' house he had casually let slip that was taking the dogs camping.

"Camping?" Boyish excitement had appeared on James' face.

Jay's heart sank. How could he possibly know that this idea would thrill James? James was rarely dressed in anything but an Armani suit. James camping... two incongruous words.

"Jay, I'd love to tag along. May I? I've never been camping. What do you think?"

"Um, ur..."

"We'll have a ball!"

"Uh..."

"What about Gettysburg? I could check out the Battlefield Historical Society while you hike with the dogs. Things are slow at the law office right now. I could use a break. I've never stayed in a tent. My father's idea of roughing it was a four-star hotel."

"Um, I just have a small tent, puny, microscopic." The next comment would surely induce James to whip out his cell phone and book a hotel room. "There's the dogs, the ticks, their farting."

"Oh, I love Clark and Miranda. Besides, I can borrow a tent from Alex. She and Will camp all the time."

Shit! If he hadn't been so buzzed by the G & Ts in his travel mug and the thermos on the boat, then the beers at James' house, he might have come up with a credible excuse. Instead, "Ur, sure."

"Wonderful!" James pulled celebratory beers from his fridge. "Another?"

"Yeah, okay."

"How about we go tomorrow? Does tomorrow work for you?"

"Tomorrow's fine." My god, what just happened!

"Do you want me to find a place now?" James slid in his stocking feet toward a laptop on the kitchen island while he took a swallow of beer, a giant swallow, two giant swallows. "Jay, this one's closest to the battlefield. The Blue and Gray Campground. How's that one sound?"

"Great."

"Let's see if a site's available. How long should we stay? A week?"

A week? God, no! "Three days," he had said firmly. This would leave the rest of the week to fish and drink.

"Three days are perfect." James had studied the online map of the campground. "What luck! Many sites are available. Probably because it's the middle of the week."

"Pick one near the bathhouse. My prostate—"

"Sure." James continued to tap on the keyboard. "Done. We're good to go."

That's how he got himself into his present mess of a road trip along Route 30 to Gettysburg with James Collins. "Plain stupid."

"What, Jay?"

"Nothing."

"Sounded like you said something about playing Cupid."

"I'm just an old man rambling to himself."

"I haven't listened to this for ages," said James sliding a CD into the player.

"What?" Please be anything but one of Laura's Broadway musicals. He knew every song from *A Chorus Line, Rent* and *The Man of La Mancha* by heart. *To dream the impossible dream* would be circling like a rabid dog through his head all week.

"The Grateful Dead. *Shakedown Street.* It reminds me of college. I had this stoner roommate who listened to all the old stuff."

He exhaled. So far, so good. The trip was not as unbearable as first imagined. James had pulled up to his house that morning on time and, in addition to Alex's tent and sleeping bag, loaded a case of beer into the SUV. The Dead and Molson Golden ales floating in a cooler of ice. The trip had promise.

"Hey, Jay, there's something I want to tell you. I have an ulterior motive for coming along with you. I do intend to do research on Josiah and Abigail at the historical society. Really, I do. But there's something else."

"Yeah?"

"There's a women's bike convention in Gettysburg this week."

He smiled. "Beautiful things... women in leather."

James smiled also. "Nina and Alex are going to be there. I texted Nina and she and I one night are going to dinner and —"

"You dog, you!" Jay laughed. "This is all about the seduction of Nina Vega."

That morning Will Wilkins couldn't shake his dark mood. Perhaps it was the police cruiser inching through traffic on I95 in Philadelphia. Inching was an overstatement. It was half-inching, at times quarter-inching. The honks and clanks of cars and trucks were intolerable. How could anyone endure the clutter and noise? It wasn't the grimy, claustrophobic city that caused his gloom, he realized. It was Zera Lim's recent remark.

"You and Lisa can handle this case on your own," she had said to him. "Jay's not always going to be around. He's going to retire in a few years."

"What? He never mentioned retirement!"

For years Jay had been his and Lisa's boss and mentor. There was still so much to learn. Unlike Lisa, he had not spent his entire youth preparing to be a detective. He was supposed to be a tight end in the NFL, leaping for passes in the end zone. Zera was Jay's same age and confidante and privy to his thoughts. Her statement was certainly accurate, but Jay could not retire. Not yet.

It was plain unnerving that he and Lisa were handling this murder investigation on their own without Jay's guidance. What if they missed a critical piece of evidence? Or botched a procedure or protocol that unraveled the case for the prosecution and Monroe Hadley's killer walked, then killed again? That would be on his conscience. Then what?

"Grow up," he told himself. "Stick to the game plan." He would do the legwork in the field while Lisa worked at headquarters with Norman from IT. They would bounce information back and forth by text. That's how they always operated. Now he fought the compulsion to call Jay and tell him about the murdered art professor. But Zera was right, as usual. If Jay was told, he would rush back to work and that would end a badly needed vacation.

If... when Jay retired, would he stay in River Glen? Move back to his home state of Vermont or return to Baltimore where he had started his career? Or would he go to Florida to fish with the snowbirds? What if he never heard from him again?

There was another source of Will's unease. Julia Hale had lived next door to the cottage that he shared with Alex and his daughter Carly which meant that Jay was always available for impromptu career advice. Now that the romance had fizzled and Julia returned to Scotland, Jay never came around anymore. The round-the-clock mentorship had slipped away.

"We're here, Will," said Denny from the driver's seat. "Ya don't mind if I pick up soft pretzels while you talk to Hadley's wife, do ya? I can't go home tonight if the misses knows that I've been to Philly and didn't bring her pretzels."

Will fumbled in his wallet for dollar bills. "Here. Get some for Alex and Carly too." He pointed. "Stop right there."

Professor Monroe Hadley's Old City brick and ivy home was easy to spot on the cobblestone side street because a black police sedan was already parked out front. Leaning against it were two Philly detectives. Blaze Haskell was a tall African-American woman and her partner Arnie Block, an acne-scarred, bowling ball-shaped man. Yesterday Haskell and Block had the terrible task of informing Ventresca Hadley that she was now a widow.

At Will's bang of the brass knocker Ventresca answered. Her face had the white pallor of terror. Her swollen eyes looked skittishly down the sidewalk as if she might be the next victim.

"A-any news?"

"Not yet, ma'am," he said stepping inside.

The colonial townhouse had been beautifully renovated and was full of paintings, sculptures, bookcases and lush plants. The open floorplan allowed him a view through French doors to a landscaped garden with a fire circle, chairs and loungers.

Ventresca sniffed. Shallow wrinkles around her eyes and mouth led him to guess that she was in her late forties, possibly early fifties. Strands of brown-gray hair had escaped its tortoise-shell clip. It had been a sleepless night.

"I can make you tea or coffee," she said vapidly.

"Please don't go to the trouble," he said flipping through his notepad. "I need you to tell me everything that happened on the day of Monroe's—"

Her moist eyelashes fluttered. "I guess I don't know where to—"

"Just take your time."

She sipped from a jittery tea cup. "Uh, Monroe and I visited the eastern shore numerous times over the years. We enjoyed browsing the antique shops and visiting vineyards. The spa at the Radcliffe is to die for." She paused at the blunder. "Oh my, what a faux pas. That doesn't sound right, does it?"

"It's okay, Ms. Hadley. Then what? On the day... then what?"

"We woke up and ate in the waterfront restaurant. I had a massage and facial scheduled in the morning while Monroe took a walk and read his newspaper by the pool. In the afternoon we went to the Giles pyrate festival for wine tasting and a late lunch, then I dropped him back at the Radcliffe. I returned to Philly. We had taken two cars because I had to work the next day. He is... was a professor so he was off in the summers."

"What's your job?"

"I'm an art therapist for the Philadelphia Hospital Consortium. That's how I met Monroe. At a gallery opening years ago." She blurted, "If only I had stayed with him!"

He waited for her to compose herself. "His toupee, fake mustache, beard—"

She blew her nose. "Monroe was self-consciousness about his hairlessness. He never had hair, could never grow a beard. The condition's called Alopecia universalis. It's an autoimmune disease that destroys the hair follicles."

He gestured for Haskell and Block to jump in with their questions, but they shook their heads. They had interviewed Ventresca yesterday. A wary Haskell eyed the widow while Block was preoccupied with a sports app in his cell phone.

"Your husband was British," he stated.

"Yes."

"He was educated where?"

"At the Royal Academy of Arts in London."

"What brought him to the United States?"

"He was an Americanophile. He loved everything about the United States. His scholarly work focused on the art of the American Civil War."

Will pulled himself from the sofa. "If you don't mind, I'd like to have a look around."

"Of course."

He wandered the first floor, from living room to dining room to kitchen, then climbed the stairs. Ventresca and the two Philly detectives followed him from room to room. Two home offices overlooked the narrow street while their bedroom and its balcony overlooked a private back garden surrounded by a high brick wall. He sifted through Monroe's walk-in closet. Tweed suits and caps, monogrammed dress shirts and countless pairs of two-tone oxford shoes. It was the wardrobe of an English country squire, reminiscent of Sean Connery's Henry Jones in the *Indiana Jones and the Last Crusade*. Alex and Carly were wild about Indiana Jones movies. Ventresca's closet was full of designer dresses, skirts and blouses, shoes and high-end accessories.

The respective offices contained the usual: desks, bookshelves and filing cabinets. Philly's homicide unit had already impounded Monroe and Ventresca's laptops and documents from their filing cabinets so those items were absent. On the surface there was nothing out of the ordinary. It was the immaculate home of an affluent, artsy couple.

"Ms. Hadley, can you think of anyone who might want to harm your husband?" he asked. "Any recent disputes, problems at work, friction with other artists, family, anyone?"

"Everyone loved Monroe!" she said emphatically. "He was the dearest man. His students, colleagues, everyone adored him." She pulled a tissue from her skirt pocket and wiped her chaffed nose.

"Someone didn't," said Haskell gruffly.

Will handed Ventresca his business card. "In case anything occurs to you, Ms. Hadley, you'll call me."

"Yes, yes."

They returned to the first floor. In the dining room Will paused in front of a painting of a Union cavalry unit galloping along a dusty road. "Who painted this?"

"It's a Jeremiah Barton," Ventresca replied. "It's called *Hungry Riders*."

He leaned closer. "I love looking at the brush work up close. Paintings always look so different up close compared to far away. They're different paintings at different distances."

"How observant of you!" she said. "Exactly!"

"Is it an original?" he asked undeterred by Haskell's impatient frown.

Ventresca swept her hand through the air. "These are all originals."

"Valuable?"

"Quite."

"Then they're insured and you have a good security system, I hope."

"Mr. Wilkins, my husband was in the art business. Of course, they're insured. We have the best security system on the market."

"That's good. And this one?" He pointed to the painting next to *Hungry Riders*. "It's very peculiar."

"And painted by a very peculiar man, a dunce actually, who happened to be a very good painter."

He craned his head forward. "What's in the water? The two grey things? Dolphins? Logs?"

"Whales. Art historians like Monroe believed that the painter's hallucinations and fantasies were depicted in his paintings. I'm highly doubtful that there were ever whales in the Glen River."

Will's eyes widened. "No kidding! The Glen River? That's where this was painted? River Glen's my hometown."

"Have you ever seen whales there?" she said with a hint of absurdity.

He grinned broadly. "Never. Only sea monsters like Chessie."

"Chessie?"

"The Chesapeake Bay sea monster."

"Get real," Haskell grumbled.

Ventresca seemed to appreciate his levity and smiled back at him. "This is just another of Eaton's preposterous paintings."

"Who?"

"Adam Eaton, the man who painted this."

"What's it called?"

"*Whales*."

"An original also?"

"Yes, of course."

Will pulled out his cell phone and stepped back toward Jeremiah Barton's *Hungry Riders*. "Do you mind if I take a picture of this one? My daughter loves horses."

"Jesus Christ," Haskell said scowling at her watch.

Ventresca glared at her. "Of course, Mr. Wilkins."

"These new phones... with all... so many features... are completely befuddling." Will pushed the camera button on his phone, fumbled, swiped through the images, turned and fumbled some more.

"What the fu—!" Haskell cried. "We don't have time for this!"

"I'm totally helpless with these complicated new phones." He smiled sheepishly. "Thank you for your time, Ms. Hadley. You'll call me if anything else occurs to you, okay?"

"Yes, detective. Please, please get the man responsible for Monroe's—!"

He shook her clammy hand, then he, Haskell and Block stepped onto the brick sidewalk.

"That bitch is so guilty," Haskell snapped. "I don't know how the hell she did it, but she's so guilty."

There was no time for speculative small talk with the Philly detectives. A snail's crawl down I95 South awaited him and Denny. "Please call me when IT is done going through the Hadley computers."

"Will do, pal," said Block staring at his cell phone. "Fuckin' Phillies. Useless bull-pen. They completely bit it in the ninth."

"What a hayseed!" he overheard Haskell say to Block as he ducked into Denny's cruiser. He could hardly keep from laughing. Rube, yokel, hick ... call him whatever! Jay would be so proud of his pupil. Ha! This country cop had no interest in *Hungry Riders*. None whatsoever. During his fumbling bumbling act, he had taken photos of *Whales*. *Whales* was the vital link between Philadelphia and River Glen. *Whales* was the reason that a Philly art professor had been killed on the shores of the Chesapeake.

But why?

Will was all too familiar with the curious painting by the artist Adam Eaton because he had seen that exact one every Friday night for the past three years when he and Alex inventoried the pyrate booty. And oh, by the way, *Whales* in Ventresca's dining room was bogus, a copy. Because *the original* was sitting amidst barrels of gold, silver and gem stones in Julia Hale's secret basement storeroom.

Dr. Zera Lim's hand paused over the plastic sheet. This was the worst part of her job—revealing a corpse for identification. She had witnessed every human emotion during her decades as a medical examiner, from the kin fainting straightaway onto the morgue floor, disconsolate sobbing into the decease's chest, to one wife spitting into the face of her abusive husband. "I hope he rots in hell."

Zera slid the sheet no farther than Monroe Hadley's chin. Ian Kent's eyes skittered over the gray moon-face, then his hand slapped his mouth as if to prevent himself from vomiting, a reaction she had witnessed countless times before.

"Yes. It's Monroe," Kent uttered. "But I've never seen him without—"

"Without what?" She knew the answer but wanted to hear it from him.

"His toupee, his beard. I knew that they were fake. I just never saw him without them."

"His relationship to you?"

"My business partner at the gallery."

"He lived in Philadelphia, correct?"

"Yes."

"And you're from?"

"Philadelphia also."

She covered Hadley's face. "Are you also an artist?"

"No, I'm in investment banking. I run the business side of our gallery."

"My examination's complete. We'll need the family to sign some papers."

Kent glanced reluctantly at the body under the sheet. "It's certain that he was—? His wife Ventresca told me that he was—"

"Yes. I can show you the injury, but we don't usually advise it."

"No, no!" He backed away. "I don't need to see it."

She pushed the stainless-steel shelf holding Hadley back into the wall fridge. "You'll need to stop by the River Glen PD barracks and speak with Detectives Wilkins and Paco. They need to ask you some questions."

"Sure, I'm happy to help."

She tugged off her disposable gloves, washed her hands at the sink and escorted him through a series of doors.

"Please stop at the front desk," she said. "My secretary will walk you through the paperwork."

"I'll take care of this for Ventresca. She's an absolute wreck."

She stopped at a water cooler in the hallway and filled a paper cup. "I'm so thirsty. I should have waited to run this evening, but I had so much energy this morning." She gulped down the water. "Would you like a cup? It's important to keep hydrated in this scorching heat."

"Thank you." Kent filled a cup, drank it and tossed it in a trashcan. "You know, this sounds inappropriate in light of the circumstances, but I'll be here through tomorrow at least, handling things for Ventresca. Are you interested in dinner tonight? I'm over at the Radcliffe."

In all her years as a forensic pathologist, never once had a visitor—suspect?—asked her to dinner. "Thanks, but I have plans."

"Can't you change them?"

"Nope. Can't."

"The chefs at the Radcliffe make a wonderful crab cake."

She shook her head.

"And a jazz ensemble's playing in the bar. Crab cakes, hot jazz, great conversation. You sure?

"I can't tonight."

He pulled a business card from his wallet. "In case your plans change."

She reached for the card. "In case."

"Ever hopeful," he called as he disappeared around the corner.

She pulled a pair of forceps from the pocket of her lab coat, bent over the trashcan by the water cooler and lifted out a paper cup. She hurried back to the lab. From the cup, her team would obtain fingerprints and extract DNA from the saliva of the slick operator named Ian Kent.

Ella pulled down the throttle of her BMW. That was the secret to good traction going into a bend, slight acceleration. The best sensation in the world was the smooth dip of a motorcycle in a curve. The road trip to River Glen hadn't been a total waste of time and money. There had been positive moments: decent bands playing at the Giles Bloodhand festival, the ride with the Chrome Divas and her discovery that the monthly rate for a campsite at Seagull Cove State Park was cheaper than at the Blue and Gray Battlefield Campground where she currently lived.

Would her trailer-mates Samantha and Keisha want to move with her? A more affordable cost of living, milder winters and the chance to catch their own food—crabs and fresh fish all summer long—were compelling reasons to relocate to River Glen. The trailer they shared was cramped, but that was no different from the lack of privacy and tight quarters at Cambridge Springs. The three of them could just as easily utilize their Custodial Maintenance skills cleaning houses and motels in River Glen as they could in Gettysburg. According to the manager at Seagull Cove, the campground was only busy twice a year—during the Giles Blood-hand festival and the October ghost walks in the pyrate graveyard. In contrast, the Blue and Gray Campground was packed year-round with horny, beer-belching reenactors: Robert E. Lees, George Armstrong Custers and Lewis Armisteads swaggering in their military finery into her campsite! As a deterrent to them, she had started to construct a tripwire around her campsite's perimeter until the campground owner discovered her plan. "No, absolutely no! An electric shock might harm the wildlife."

"Which wildlife? White-tailed deer or Pettigrew's Brigade?"

A move to River Glen was sounding better by the minute. If between crabbing and cleaning Chesapeake tourist hotels, she was still short of cash, she could always sign on to an October ghost tour. If she could pontificate about ghostly soldiers and nurses, how difficult could it be to blab about ghostly, headless pyrates?

Ella glanced in her rearview mirror again. That UHaul truck had been driving the same back roads as her since north of Baltimore. It was hard to tell for certain, but the driver appeared to be a woman. Perhaps it was an elderly biker with a bad back who was traveling cross-country to the women's bike convention in Gettysburg?

Focus on the road. Savor the ride. The best stretch, wooded and windy, approached. Exhilarated, she breathed in the moist forest air and leaned into another curve. Were the bike not laden with camping gear, her knee would be inches off the ground. The bike dipped left right left right on the snaking road.

Snakes had been a constant worry yesterday while climbing around the old Wedgewood-Smyth mansion. Fortunately, the only critters encountered were spiders, ants and a nest of barn swallows. She had explored the upstairs first where only sleigh beds and heavy bureaus remained. Which bedroom had been Josiah and Abigail's and which Adam Eaton's? Which was the room in which Eaton had set up his studio? She had circled the bedrooms, searching for paint droplets on the floorboards, but long ago they had been erased by gusts of dust and sand. The construction of the colonial house had occurred in a time before closets so it didn't take long to search the upstairs. At one point a sparrow swooped down the hallway, just missing her head. She had ducked and her flashlight clattered to the floor, but there were no other mishaps. If there had been Eaton paintings on the bedroom walls, they had long disappeared.

The ground floor of the manor house showed the most wear and tear. A beer party had occurred decades ago because rusty Schlitz cans were scattered around the-once-ballroom. Bird doo spackled the floor and dried leaves clung in the corners, but no Eatons were found on the walls downstairs either.

Ella's heart pounded upon entering the small bedroom off the kitchen that had once belonged to the cook. The trap door had been discovered during her quick trip through the house months before. At that time, dusk, there was no way she was going into the dark underground space. What was it anyway? A crypt, cellar, dungeon? But yesterday it was daytime and sunny. There were no excuses. The trap door was hidden under a rickety bed whose moldy straw mattress bowed between the slats.

She had flicked the flashlight on and off. Despite dropping it when ducking the sparrow, the light still worked. "It's just a basement where the family stored food for the winter. It's not a torture chamber where Josiah and Abigail imprisoned enemy spies. There will be no bones of Confederates, nor rats, bats or snakes. It was for storage. Really, only storage. Could it be Abigail's pleasure dungeon? She definitely had appetites." She tested the flashlight once again. "Go down there. Just do it. Find those paintings!"

She slid the bedframe aside; the scratch of wood echoed through the empty kitchen. She froze. There was no one in the house. She was alone. Alone, really. She listened and listened for a moment longer. Then she knelt on the dirt floor and worked her fingers into the crack of the trap door. She lifted, but the rusty hinges resisted. She inhaled and jerked up with all her weight and power. The hinges shrieked and she tumbled backward. The door slammed to the ground, poofing up dust. *Plunk plunk plunk.* Down each earthen step *plunked* her flashlight. It finally stopped in its own glow at the bottom of the black cellar.

A shadow arched over Ella like a crashing wave, ripping her mind from the cellar to—the road! Her eyes zipped toward her rearview mirror.

"What the!"

The UHaul was inches from her back tire! Her head swiveled over her shoulder. The truck's bumper shoved her bike forward. She toed the gearshift up, yanked down the throttle and swung the handlebars to the right. *Bumpabumpabumpa* her tires bounced over the gravel shoulder. The front wheel plunged into a gulley, tossing her over the gas tank. She thrust herself back on the seat and clamped her knees around the frame. The bike reared and flew up the embankment. Bushes and trees skidded by. Branches smacked at her helmet and shoulders. A thick tree lay dead ahead. She veered, but the burdened back-end of the motorcycle spun out. She was catapulted through the air, then thudded and rolled in leaves until a thistle bush entangled her. Cursing, she wrestled herself from her thorny captor, dashed past the smoking bike and down and up the gulley to the shoulder. The UHaul had long disappeared around the bend.

She shook her fist in the air. "Crazy bitch! Get off your cell phone!"

During undergraduate days at the University of Maryland, Alex had rented an apartment with Nina Vega. Theirs had been an excellent living arrangement. She had studied marine biology and Nina doubled majored in sociology and economics. Different classes and schedules meant that they rarely saw each other during the day, but each evening after studying they ate ramen noodles and howled at reruns of *Portlandia, SNL, It's Always Sunny in Philadelphia* and *South Park*. Now she and Nina were roommates once again but at the Four Score and Seven Hotel and Convention Center down the highway from the Gettysburg National Military Park. The parking lot where they had unloaded their motorcycles was full of two- and three-wheeled vehicles. The next few days would be packed with demonstrations, exhibitions and lectures on motorcycles and in the evening would be a terrifying ghost walk.

"Just like old times, Roomie," she said stepping into the hotel room. "Except that our old apartment looked down on dumpsters. We've moved up in the world. A view of a pool and tiki bar."

Nina dropped her backpack on a chair. "I could use a drink. I'm parched from that dusty drive. Which bed do you want?"

"Either's fine. You know me. I sleep like a dead person."

"Then I'll take the one near the bathroom since I have to pee so often."

Alex slipped off her mesh riding jacket, boots and jeans and flung them on a bed. "I can't get into that pool fast enough."

"Thank god for air-conditioning," said Nina standing in cool air blasting from a wall unit.

"Shit. Not again. Why can't they give it up?"

Nina joined her at the window. "What?"

"At the tiki bar. Linda Radowski and Blanche Hyde. Tempers are flaring again."

"If I was Linda, I wouldn't be in Blanche's face like that. Blanche might deck her."

"The way I see it, it's all Kenneth's fault."

"Who?"

"Linda's asshole husband. Remember? The guy who tried to put his hand down my dress at the Giles festival."

"That's Linda's husband?" Nina groaned. "I can't stand him. I see him all over the village. Once he asked if he could join me for breakfast at the café."

"You didn't—"

Nina recoiled. "That snake wouldn't take no for an answer and slithered into my booth anyway. He wouldn't leave so I packed up my laptop and left."

"Kenneth's the one who sent Blanche the friend request on Facebook. She should have known better than to accept. Ever since then, Linda thinks that he and Blanche are bonking each other."

"How could Blanche be that stupid?" Nina said. "He's plain horrible."

Alex rummaged through her bike gear for her bikini. "It would have been a perfect ride to Gettysburg except for those two bickering at the gas pumps. Now this. I'm avoiding them the whole time. I'm here to have fun, not get anywhere near a cat fight. Boat drinks, Nina. Let's obliterate the thought of Kenneth Radowski with boat drinks."

"Here, here, sister."

"I agree with Detective Haskell, Will," Lisa said. "I don't know how Ventresca did it, but she's so guilty. There's probably a giant insurance policy and she probably has a boy toy on the side. Ventresca. What kind of a name is that? It sounds like the name of a travel agency."

"It's not her," Will said from his desk. "She was really broken up. Besides, the CCTV cameras from the Radcliffe confirm her activities. Everything she said exactly matches the footage. Look."

Lisa leaned toward his computer, stretched gum from her mouth and twirled it around her finger. "If we look hard enough, we'll find a discrepancy."

"On the day of the Giles Blood-hand festival she and Monroe had breakfast in the dining room of the Radcliffe. He read his newspaper by the pool while she went off to the spa. Charges for a massage and facial appeared on their bill that morning. At noon they were spotted together near the mermaid fountain."

"That reminds me." She zipped through photos on her cell phone. "I captured spit from a mermaid's mouth at the exact second it landed in the center of a lily pad. This picture got seventy-one LIKES."

"Oh cool." He pointed to his computer again. "A valet went to get Ventresca's red Mercedes Benz coupe while they waited on the front steps. They're chatting and laughing about something. There doesn't appear to be any friction between the two of them."

"She's laughing because she's thinking 'You're dead meat, pal. Tonight my boy toy will be boning me in your bed'."

"We need to stay open-minded. Objectivity is the key. That's what Jay always tells us. The valet put her suitcase in her trunk. They disappeared for a few hours to the Giles festival."

"Will, switch to the security camera on the River Glen Bridge so we can follow their actions there."

"Okay." He typed across his keyboard and opened new footage. "Hey, look! There I am on the pier! See? I'm dancing with Alex and Carly."

"Partner, you have the moves!"

"Because Alex and I attend dance class. You should see us tango."

"Great costume. The green parrot on your shoulder really makes it." She tapped the computer screen. "Monroe and Ventresca are there. Boring. They're not wearing pyrate costumes."

"They went to the wine tasting booths, then got an outside table at the Dockside Café where they had a leisurely lunch."

"Despite a long line of customers waiting for a table. Inconsiderate hoity-toities."

He re-opened the CCTV footage from the Radcliffe. "At 4:38 pm the red Mercedes reappears at the front entrance of the Radcliffe. Monroe climbs out. He enters the hotel and Ventresca drives off. The cameras capture him as he passes through the lobby and enters the elevator. Next he's seen by the camera on the fifth floor. Room service delivers dinner to his room at 8:58 pm. At 11:38 pm he leaves his room, is captured both in the hallway of the fifth floor and in the lobby minutes later. He goes through the bar and the pool area, heading in the direction of the golf course. He's meeting someone by the shoreline. But who? That's the question. Who?"

"Ventresca!"

"But she entered her garage in Philadelphia at 6:56 pm. Her home security system verified her opening the garage door at that time. She entered her townhouse through the door between her garage and kitchen. She didn't leave the house until the next morning at 8:38 am to attend a yoga class."

"What if she climbed out her window and took a different car back to River Glen, then murdered Monroe at midnight? It's just a ninety-minute drive from Philly to River Glen. She would have had tons of time to kill him."

"There's no record of her returning to the Radcliffe."

"Maybe she was hiding in the trunk of her boy toy's car? Anything's possible. The security system at her house... does it have cameras?"

"No. Just a series of timestamps when someone enters or exits the doors."

"See! Told ya so! #guiltybitch. She definitely climbed out her window."

Will's laptop chimed. "Incoming."

"Who's it from?"

"The fingerprint database."

"What? What?" She spit her gum into the trash, unwrapped three more pieces and stuffed them in her mouth.

"In your words, Lisa. #theplotthickens. Professor Monroe Hadley's fingerprints belong to a Mr. Seymour Simon of Taunton, Massachusetts."

Ella was in no mood to socialize. The only morsel of good news that evening was the tip money from the twilight ghost tour, but most of it would go to dry-cleaning her gown. A potentially dangerous ex-convict like herself should be appreciative of steady work, but she was doing the same goddamn job she did when she was seventeen years old. Worse, she was now earning less—next to nothing—because Old Man Detrick's cheapskate daughter had taken over the business. Dana Detrick had always hated her, ever since she was a teenager and took the job in the first place. It was not her fault that Dana was a surly, ugly slob and that the old man had hired her, instead of his own daughter, to give ghost tours. It was a small miracle that Dana had re-hired her when she got out of prison, but she now earned minimum wage and Dana pocketed half the tip money. Worse still, the tip money was a fraction of what it had been.

Face it. At forty, her mysterious aura of ghostly sexuality had long vanished. She was no longer that saucy Darling of the Diabolic, that palpitating Princess of the Paranormal. Her black velvet gown now had bald spots and sagged off her. The torn hem collected dust balls as she moved with the tarnished candlestick through the grungy house. If she had to tell that ridiculous story of Robert, Elijah and Grace burning up in the fire one more time, she would scream. Why didn't any of the imbeciles on the tours ask her, just once, why the Ephram Whitson House was still standing if there'd been a catastrophic fire? Wooden houses burn, morons.

That evening the three families from Frederick, Maryland had snickered the whole way throughout the ghost walk. "What the hell is so funny?" she almost shouted. The source of their amusement was discovered when she peeled off her gown in the ladies room at closing time. She had led the tour with pink and yellow lollipops stuck to her butt! She might have felt the bratty little shitheads stick them there if she even had a butt to fill out her dress. Now the gown was going to need dry-cleaning unless she was willing to walk around with sticky sugar circles on her butt every evening.

Fuck everything! She threw her wrench into the dirt under her motorcycle. She was in no mood to socialize, but Keisha and Samantha had met some "nice guys" from a campsite by the bathhouse while she was at work. At any moment they were bringing over pizzas and beer. Maybe she could manage small talk for a few minutes if it meant free slices of za. Her two meals that day had been two PB&Js and a hand full of Keisha's Fritos.

"These alleged nice guys... they're not reenactors, are they?" she had warily asked her trailer-mates. "Remember our pact. No more reenactors."

"No, no, they're not reenactors," Sam had insisted. "One's a historian. The older one's hot. He looks just like Clint Eastwood."

Ella glanced at the dent in the Airstream trailer—Home Sweet Home—since her release from Cambridge Springs. The trailer wasn't even hers yet. She still had eleven more payments to Uncle Lyle. The dent was a daily reminder about messing around with reenactors.

Keisha and Sam had warned her off Tony, that Union soldier with the zany sense of humor. She blamed the fling on a nagging curiosity to see if her sex organs still worked after a dormancy in mothballs for nearly twelve years. They did work, in fact just fine. This prompted Tony to drive his truck and pop-up camper from Albany weekend after weekend. Then an unknown minivan with New York plates pulled into her campsite. The woman that jumped out grabbed the sledgehammer from the woodpile and smashed their lawn chairs, lantern and grill before whacking away at the trailer. The wife and four children had somehow slipped Tony's mind.

"Here they come," Keisha said. "Pizza and beer!"

Ella didn't bother to look. Her beloved BMW was the priority at the moment. After the near collision with the UHaul, the bike had miraculously started up and carried her home safely, but there was some minor damage. She pulled the wrench from the dirt and bent her head under the gas tank. Paws suddenly hopped onto her back, knocking her head into the carburetor. Long, eager tongues lapped at her cheeks. NASA must have a solo mission that could transport her off this twisted planet.

"Hey, Miranda. Hey, Clark," she sighed.

Chapter 4
Ghosts from the Past

Prison life had reset Ella's pineal gland that ran her diurnal clock. In another lifetime before Cambridge Springs, she had lived in the epicenter of Philadelphia's art scene, lounging in bed until noon with Ian Kent, afternoon seminars at the art college, evenings at exhibitions or galley openings, sampling wine and hors d'oeuvres prepared by the hottest new chefs, then carousing into the wee hours in pulsing night clubs. Now she, Keisha and Sam rose every morning with the sun. She remained in her sleeping bag while her trailer-mates headed off to work as housekeepers at the Lincoln Inn. Her work schedule was diametrically opposite to theirs. As they would be returning from the hotel, she would head off to the Ephram Whitson House for twilight and ten o'clock ghost tours.

Early morning in the campsite was the cherished time of the day. Even in the summer she would light a fire, put her bare feet on the stones of the fire circle and sip coffee. Tourists and reenactors wouldn't be up for hours. It was just her, birds and sunlight filtering through the tree canopy. She was filled with gratitude. Her debt to society had been paid.

She was free. High school and college friends had long disowned her, but she had found good companions in Keisha and Sam. The trio had made a pact to watch each other's back on that endless van ride from the holding facility to the arctic hinterlands of Cambridge Springs. That pact had proven fortuitous. They were hardened killers from the big bad city they had intimated to the other prisoners. The Terrible Trio was more or less left alone.

Nothing good would come of them returning to the temptations of Philly, they had decided upon their release. Gettysburg was not Ella's first choice of places to settle, but her uncle had an abandoned trailer where they could stay and figure out next steps. While she was in prison, her mother remarried and moved with her blended family to Florida where she painted sunsets and dolphins.

The thought of painting again sent a cold shudder through her. No painting for her, ever. With the ear-piercing crack of Judge Dickhead's gavel... four years for the forgeries, four years for fencing government documents... never, ever, she vowed, would she touch a paintbrush.

After her mother's departure for the tropics, her father had married a woman younger than Ella and had five-year-old twins. The little monsters were a perfect excuse to beg off on every holiday. Not that she, Half-sister Ex-Con was particularly popular among the relatives. Thanksgivings and Christmases were spent with Keisha and Sam, splitting a five-dollar rotisserie chicken and a bottle of cheap wine. Her father's twins had the same demonic tendencies as the monsters on last night's ghost walk. What the hell had the parents been doing while their cretins were sticking lollipops to her ass? Snickering with the other parents. Their little darlings were destined to become serial killers.

Who could afford dry-cleaning! She yanked the gown from a metal case on her motorcycle and entered the trailer.

At the sink she scrubbed the sticky circles from the backside of the gown. With any luck it would be a hot day and her gown would be dry by evening. A fly swatter caught her eye. That might be a useful weapon on future ghost walks. If any brats approached her—that would teach those little psychos. She left the trailer and spread the gown over a clothesline between the trees.

The only consolation from last night was the free pizza. Her impulse, after the shock of recognizing the black dogs, was to make a swift beeline to the trailer and crawl inside her sleeping bag. Her second impulse was to accuse that creepy Inspector Javert of stalking her to Gettysburg, but he seemed equally stunned to see her. Her strategy had been to silently monitor the situation. Sulky silence was her mood anyway.

Why had Jay Braden and James Collins from the River Glen Historical Society appeared at the campground in the first place? The whole thing was suspicious. Braden had not been wearing sunglass so she could see his whole face for the first time. Sam needed her eyes examined; he looked nothing like Clint Eastwood. Clint Eastwood was hot. Braden, well? True, with a nose that had been broken and a diagonal scar that divided his chin into unequal sections, he could have been from Hollywood's central casting for a hard-boiled cop. Braden could have played Clint Eastwood's partner, but he was no Clint Eastwood.

"Small world, Ella!" a cheerful James Collins had said from behind the pizza boxes.

"Nano small," she muttered.

Fortunately, she was altogether uninteresting to James. After distributing cold beers and pizza slices around the picnic table, he had asked Keisha and Sam about Civil War amusements in the area while she wandered back to her motorcycle. Still, her ears were poised.

"This is my first camping trip," he said with the enthusiasm of a schoolboy. "I'm meeting with the curator of the Battlefield Historical Society about my novel."

She had decided not to chime in on the nerdy curator Hazel Worth even though she had known her since childhood. Hazel had been a helpful supervisor on her high school Civil War art project and was a walking encyclopedia on the fighting at Gettysburg.

"Can you suggest fun things to do?" he asked her trail-mates. "I've never been to Gettysburg before."

Keisha and Sam reeled off a number of tourist attractions... bus tours around the battlefield, the diorama, Segway tours, wine tasting, when—Ella braced herself. Then came the dreaded words. Who to murder first? Keisha or Sam?

"You must go on Ella's ghost walk!"

"She's the best! The Darling of the Dead!"

"The Ghastly Ghoul Girl!"

"The Diva of Darkness!"

Nina tried to live in the moment and focus only on the exhibition hall filled with motorcycles and accessories yet a lecture at Tolchester College kept intruding its way into her thoughts. The topic of the campus lecture had been Visualization. The speaker's words... *intent to experience a beneficial effect... what you visualize will come to be...* seemed directed at her. That morning as she and Alex passed vendors selling bike luggage, leather gear and motorcycle tours to exotic lands, she was visualizing *a beneficial effect* with James Collins.

It was baffling how slow their romance—could one even call it that?—had progressed. She originally thought that James gay until she asked Alex about him. He definitely wasn't, she said. Alex and James had grown up in the same village but did not know each other particularly well until recently when she found out that he was her half-brother. An amazing revelation really. Alex and James had the same biological father, Colin Allaway. As the story goes, James' father Theodore Collins was infertile from a freak accident during the Dakar Rally yet he and wife Elizabeth desperately wanted a child. As a solution, the-then-teenager Colin had been recruited to inseminate Elizabeth while an impatient Theo paced the oriental carpet outside her bedroom. All went according to plan and young Colin delivered the goods; James was born nine months later and raised by the delighted couple while Colin departed for an architecture program at U Penn. It was obvious that James and Alex were related. They both had an endearing good-naturedness innate to all of the Allaways of River Glen.

It was time to give romance another go, Nina decided, and James was the one. It had been years since her then-fiancé Ricardo dumped her. Alas, there had been the misguided twenty-four-hour affair with Griffin Blake—or was it Blake Griffin? No matter. She had detoxed from men for long enough. It was time. Countless afternoons she and James had shared cups of tea, discussing Josiah and Abigail Wedgewood-Smyth and her fisheries research at the historical society. They seemed compatible intellectually, but how about sexually?

How convenient that James had a meeting with the curator at the historical society in Gettysburg during her bike convention! He had sent her a text inviting her to an early ghost walk at the Ephram Whitson House and a late dinner at the Dobbin's House. It all sounded wonderful to her. But what about *experiencing that beneficial effect* called dessert?

Visualize countless scenarios for dessert...

"But we haven't had lunch yet," said Alex looking up from rows of motorcycle boots.

"What?"

"You said something about dessert."

"Really? Did I?"

"Dessert sounds like a great idea for lunch," Alex said. "An ice cream sundae for me."

"Okay then, ice cream it is."

That settled, Alex made a beeline for a rack of leathers while her mind returned to James. What about a romantic moonlit walk in the battlefield? She and Alex had taken a spin through its picturesque forests and cornfields. The giant boulders at Devil's Den would be a perfect secluded place. Wait—what about snakes amidst the rocks? Were there venomous, nocturnal snakes in Pennsylvania? Maybe not there.

James' tent? It would be too hot and stuffy. Besides, Jay Braden might hear them. That's all she needed, for Miranda and Clark to bay as she bayed in ecstasy in James' arms. All that baying would wake the entire campground.

The sex was going to be extraordinary, she was sure of it. James reminded her of that dashing Josiah Wedgewood-Smyth. When she had stumbled upon the steamy letters between Josiah and Abigail in the archive that day, she found herself squirming in her seat. Abigail was so creative and Josiah so—open-minded.

How about the seduction in her air-conditioned hotel room while Alex partied with the Chrome Divas? With any luck Alex would be engaged in the poolside festivities again. Last night at the tiki bar, after crooning karaoke tunes, Alex and the beekeeper Janice Klein won the dance contest which meant free drinks for the rest of the night. Alex was flexible from climbing around boats so no one came close to her in the limbo contest. When the bar closed, Alex stumbled back to the room and collapsed into the pillows, plastic gold metals for the cha-cha, limbo and Name-That-Tune dangling from her neck.

"Chaps, Nina! Leopard spotted chaps!" Alex yanked a pair off a rack and held them to her waist.

"They're so you."

"So me!" Alex kicked off her sneakers and pulled the chaps over her shorts. "Perfect fit. They're mine." She dug through her backpack for her wallet and handed her credit card to the vendor. "I'm wearing these to the Hawaiian luau tonight!"

"What luau? When?"

"The luau by the pool after the ghost walk. I won't be back to the room for hours." Alex grinned. "And hours."

"Too bad Jay's not here," said Lisa Paco. "He'd be intrigued by this case." She studied the round, vacant face of Seymour Simon. "A case of a secret identity."

"I'm curious to know if the nephew, cousin or whatever Ian Kent says he is, knows who Monroe Hadley actually was," said Zera Lim.

"And what does Ventresca know about her darling Monroe? #shessofrickinguilty."

"What did you and Will find out about him?"

"I'll tell you if you let me have some gum."

"No. Absolutely no."

"Just one piece?"

"This is a sterile area," said Zera sternly. "No food or drink are allowed back here."

"I won't spit on anything!"

"Lisa—"

"#resignedsigh."

"#answermyquestionsorleave."

Lisa giggled. "When Seymour Simon was twenty-two, he stole documents from a library in Boston related to Paul Revere's midnight ride and tried to sell them to a rare book dealer. But the book dealer contacted the Arts Crime Unit of the F.B.I. Simon was prosecuted and spent three years in a Massachusetts prison for fencing stolen property. According to Immigration, two months after Simon's release from prison, he broke parole and fled to Spain. There was no record of him ever returning to the U.S., paying taxes, nothing. He literally vanished somewhere on the European continent."

"Interesting."

"Eight years after Simon disappeared, a British art professor named Monroe Hadley entered the United States on an H1B visa to work at a gallery in Philadelphia. He became a permanent resident when he married Ventresca. I burned the midnight oil reading his scholarly manuscripts. His dissertation was on a lesser American painter named Adam Eaton. Apparently in England, Hadley came across a collection of Eaton's paintings in the manor house of a reclusive lord."

"Reclusive lord?" Zera chuckled. "Sounds dubious at best."

"Allegedly the old lord permitted Hadley—Simon—multiple visits to his estate to view the rare Eatons. Since Hadley-Simon was the only scholar to have seen and studied the Eatons, he became the leading authority on the painter's unusual use of color and brushwork. Thereafter, whenever an Eaton painting was discovered, Hadley-Simon was brought in to authenticate it."

"Is that so?" Zera scoffed. She covered the face of Seymour Simon and slid him into the wall unit. "I want to see those paintings." She snapped off her latex gloves.

Lisa reached for her pocket. "Here. I have the Eaton link on my phone."

"My old eyes need to see them in a large format," Zera said tossing the gloves into a bin of medical waste. "Let's go to the computer in my office."

The second they left the morgue, Lisa whipped a pack of gum from her uniform pants. "Now?"

"Now."

They passed the offices and laboratories of the forensic scientists and reached Zera's office. Zera dropped behind her desk and logged on. "Here they are," she said after a moment. "Most of the Eatons are in Philadelphia."

Lisa bent over the polished desk. "That one there, *Whales* is owned by Hadley-Simon the Imposter and Ventresca the Guilty. Will saw it in their dining room. He says they're not really whales but Chessie the Sea Monster."

"Ah, Chessie," said Zera. "I've seen him myself after a few glasses of Clavados. Two more Eatons are at the Virginia Institute of Colonial Art. Two more are at the Old City Americana Gallery—"

"—that's owned by Hadley-Simon and Ian Kent."

"Really?"

"Really."

"According to this list," Zera stated, "five Eaton paintings in total are known to exist in the United States."

"And according to Hadley-Simon's dissertation, the others are in England."

"What others? How many? How did they get to England?" Zera said with a puzzled frown. "Why aren't they on this list?"

"Uh, I don't know. #pacounsettled."

"Please no." Jay pulled himself from his sleeping bag. His stomach quaked at the sound. Miranda was barfing. Julia had left him that bitch to torment him. Half his income was paid to the vet for Miranda's fragile gastrointestinal tract. He unzipped the tent and crawled through the opening. He groaned again. His back was too old to be sleeping on the corrugated ground. He lifted himself off his hands and knees in the outer screened room. It would be impossible to walk a single step until he stretched and flexed his back. His SUV was gone because James had taken it for an appointment with Dr. Worth at the historical society. Before leaving, James had whispered through the screened window that the dogs had been walked and fed and their leads were tied to a tree. He had moaned an "oh fine" and promptly dropped back to sleep.

He unzipped the flaps of the screened room and stepped outside. The guilty party was definitely Miranda. His Clark, who earned A's in obedience class, would never have perpetrated such a crime. Clark had smartly fled the crime scene and was hiding under the picnic table where he watched the culprit retch again. James had left the latch on the cooler unlocked so Miranda had nosed it open. Mushy pools of hot dog and plastic wrapper puke dotted the campsite. No way was he venturing forward without shoes so he lumbered back to the tent for his sneakers. The vomit was revolting. Goddamn Julia. This was all her fault. Miranda never had an ounce of discipline. All Julia had fed her was human food. He could still hear it.

"Eggs, sausage, bacon, mushrooms, tomato and toast," Julia lilted. "Let's not forget the brown sauce. Miranda loves the full English breakfast."

The vet admonished *him* about Miranda's weight—like he was to blame—and put her on a strict diet. The dog still pined for haggis. This explained her eating the plastic wrap; she thought it was stuffed intestines.

The warm puke had attracted flies. If he had a hose he could wash it away, but then the campsite would be a muddy mess all day. A shovel—that's what he needed. Keisha had been stirring the coals last night with a shovel. He craned his head down the dirt road.

There she was, the Philly Forger, drinking coffee by the fire. Last night she had been aloof while her companions Keisha and Sam were friendly and gregarious. They were ex-cons as well. He had encountered a thousand mouthy, street-smart women on the streets of Baltimore. The trio was eking out a living in Gettysburg, Pennsylvania, of all places. After a detour to the bathhouse to pee and brush his teeth, he wandered over to the women's campsite.

"Ella, can I borrow your shovel?"

She jumped slightly and spilled her coffee. "Um, yes."

She was not wearing sunglasses. In the broad light of morning he could see her face for the first time. He smiled wryly. Big baby-blues, long eyelashes, full lips. It was a face that swung open doors. He had seen that baby-face on the most treacherous of criminals.

"Miranda's gotten sick," he explained. "I'll wash it off before I return it."

"Do you want me to make her white rice? It's what my mother used to give our old dog."

"Would you? And could you spare a cup of coffee? We only have beer and water." No G & Ts for breakfast that morning. Not that James would have cared. He was a remarkably good traveling companion. Light-hearted and non-judgmental. That was an Allaway, not a Hale, trait.

"Yeah." She disappeared into the dented trailer.

So far, so good. She wasn't outright rude. She had not called him "Drunk. Noun." Nor had she told him to "hoof it to the camp store and buy your own goddamn coffee of cup." Instead he found her weakness—dogs. Last night Clark and Miranda had hovered around her and her motorcycle while ignoring the other two women.

Shovel in hand, he set off for his campsite. Thankfully he hadn't eaten breakfast because it was a nauseating chore to tiptoe around the picnic table and fire circle and shovel slimy-puke-paddies into the woods. He lifted the cooler on to the picnic table and locked the latch. Clark had remained under the table, shooting him a not-guilty look while a queasy Miranda slunk under a lawn chair and fell asleep.

Ella eyed the ground as if walking through a minefield. "Here." She handed him a mug. "It's black. We're out of milk and sugar."

"That's how I take it. Thank you."

"Also for you." She handed him a paper plate of toast slathered with jelly.

He didn't have the heart to tell her that he was cutting back on carbs because his metabolism had come to a screeching halt a decade ago. "You really didn't have to but thanks."

"The pizza last night... I forgot to thank you. Maybe Miranda will eat this." She placed a container of rice near the sleeping dog. "What are you doing today?"

"Hiking the battlefield if Miranda feels up to it."

"Do you want a tour guide? I know everything about the battle."

Toast paused in front of his mouth. There were a thousand reasons he should say no. But his ever hopeful, irrepressible libido tossed caution to the wind. "Wonderful."

James didn't know what to expect from the Battlefield Historical Society or its curator. The name Hazel Worth sound to him like an actress from the 1930s or a porn star; instead he found her to be a chatty frump with a super computer for a brain that had catalogued every minute fact about Adams County, Pennsylvania. She had obviously been anticipating his visit because the second he opened the front door and extended his hand in introduction, she tugged him inside.

"Don't let out the cold air, Mr. Collins," Dr. Worth barked. "We can barely afford air-conditioning."

"Yes, of course." He stepped quickly inside.

"We run this place on a shoe-string," another woman called from behind a laptop.

"My sister Phoebe," Dr. Worth explained. "Our book-keeper."

"Oh, hello," he said with a wave.

"I'll be baking soon," Phoebe replied.

"Oh. Lovely."

It was cleaning day at the historical society because the scent of lemon furniture polish mixed with his favorite smell, old books. Like the River Glen Historical Society, the collections had far exceeded the shelf space so stacks of books and file folders covered the tables. He scanned the one-room archive for a sliver of table space to place his briefcase, but all he saw were images of the same brawny military officer.

"Who is he?" he asked.

"My grandfather Tobias Worth. The hero of Gettysburg," Worth said. "Well, not really my grandfather because I'm not that old, but my many greats grandfather. I can't remember how many greats, but he was a great man." She giggled at her word play.

The number of Tobias sightings in the cluttered space was overwhelming. On every wall, in every painting Tobias was seen stabbing the air with swords and pistols, on a rearing horse amidst cannon fire or swirling a beauty around at a costume ball. Busts and statuettes of the captain lined the shelves. James had envisioned Josiah Wedgewood-Smyth in much the same way: dark and gallant, cloak furling on his dangerous midnight adventures. With a sweep of her dust rag, Dr. Worth directed him to a table near her desk, then set to the task of clearing a space for him. She took her time sliding books about as it was her opportunity to describe Tobias' countless achievements: his work at the orphanage, courageous cavalry charges at Bull's Run and Antietam, election for mayor of Gettysburg and his relentless pursuit of rebel spies that resulted in his untimely death.

"Hazel has an incurable case of hero worship," tittered Phoebe.

From what he could tell, Phoebe was streaming the movie *Troy*. That was definitely Brad Pitt speaking with Peter O'Toole.

"I'm just enumerating for Mr. Collins some notable accomplishments from Granddaddy's remarkable career," she huffed to Phoebe.

Dr. Worth suddenly recalled the reason for his visit and placed a stack of files labeled *Civil War Spies* in front of him. He sat down to work. Like the simple but effective record-keeping system at the River Glen Historical Society, there was a signature sheet taped to each file folder. For about an hour he sifted through the documents. There was an occasional brief mention of the Wedgewood-Smyths but no details that he hadn't discovered in prior researches. Abigail and Josiah were spies from Maryland. Their contacts with the spy network in Pennsylvania seemed limited at best. Admittedly he had become possessive—perhaps irrationally so—of anything related to the Wedgewood-Smyths. After all, his life's ambition was to write a blockbuster historical thriller about the daring couple.

He glanced around the musty room. While Dr. Worth was feather-dusting Tobias' bronze busts and Phoebe was baking cookies in the kitchen, he snuck a photograph of the list of individuals who had checked out the *Spies* folders. Maybe within the names was a competitor who was racing to write a Wedgewood-Smyth novel before him. What if this individual already had a book contract? With a giant New York publishing house? And had completed their novel? This was his greatest fear! He might compare this list against individuals who had been to the River Glen Historical Society. This way he might identify the potential competition. He scanned the names. None were familiar to him except Ella Winston's. He returned the *Spies* folders to Dr. Worth's desk.

"Maybe you have something on Adam Eaton who lived briefly with the Wedgewood-Smyths?" he asked. "Maybe by delving into his files, there might be a hidden gem on the Wedgewood-Smyths."

Dr. Worth turned from dusting marble statuettes of... who else. "Adam Eaton? Yes, of course." She climbed down a step-ladder and pulled two yellowing file folders from a cabinet.

A cookie tray clanked in the kitchen. "Mr. Collins, can I tempt you with peanut butter cookies?" Phoebe called. "Hot out of the oven."

"No thank you."

His mind was on a delicious meal with delicious Nina at the Dobbins House and with any luck after— He fought to focus his attention on the Eaton folders. Odd. No signature pages on them.

"Are you sure?" said Phoebe. "I used organic peanut butter. Omega oil is wonderful for the myelin on brain cells."

"I'm sure. But thank you."

"I hope Adam Eaton makes it into your novel," Dr. Worth said to him. "Adam was a fascinating character. He wandered into the village of Gettysburg two years before the battle. Where he came from was anyone's guess, but he had mentioned river towns along the Ohio River. His uncanny knowledge of machines resulted in his employment by the newspaper editor Clarence Stratford where he improved the performance of the printing press. I believe there are pictures in one of those folders."

"Yes. Here. I found it."

The first file folder labelled *Adam Eaton's Mechanical Drawings* contained sketches of gears and rotors that Eaton had used to modify the press that printed weekly news leaflets. It was really nothing that could go into *Subterfuge* though it was interesting background material nonetheless. And who knows how the plot might evolve? So far, the story had taken on a life of its own.

"Beautiful sketches," he said. "Do you mind if I photograph these?"

"As long as you credit our historical society if you use the images in your book. We're grateful for any publicity. We rely heavy on public donations."

"Of course. I'm happy to make a donation."

"Wonderful!"

"I hope I sell more than two copies of my novel," he said facetiously.

"The only person who bought copies of my book *The 1860s Guide to the Taverns of Gettysburg*," she laughed, "was my mother."

"Not true, Hazel," Phoebe shouted from the kitchen. "Remember that I got Reggie Westerly to buy ten copies that he sold at his pub."

"That was very kind of Reggie," said Worth who had moved on to polishing Tobias' pistol collection.

He snapped photos of Eaton's mechanical designs with his smartphone like Ella Winston had done with the files in the River Glen Historical Society months before. Ah, there it was—the signature page was stuck to a gear drawing. And there was Ella's name. It was no surprise that she would have studied these files. She lived in Gettysburg and was an expert on Eaton's paintings. Her name appeared on the list twice, almost twenty years ago when she would have been a teenager and a few months ago. He took a photo of the signature page in case his sly competitor lurked within the list of names. He opened the second file folder labeled *Adam Eaton's Art*.

"What do you think?" Dr. Worth asked over her shoulder.

"Of what? Tobias' pistols?"

"No silly. Adam's art."

"Let me see—" He studied the five brittle pages, each a colorful pastel sketch of Eaton's five known oil paintings. "Thought-provoking. Ahead of their time. Don't you think?"

"I agree on both points," she replied. "According to diaries from various villagers, he spent long hours wandering the countryside with his paints, canvas and easel. His favorite landscapes were the Round Tops and ridges. He often hoisted his materials and himself into trees which explains the near bird's eye perspectives of some paintings."

He re-examined them. "I see that now! Fascinating!"

The first sketch showed the hurried massing of the Union and Confederate forces around Gettysburg on the afternoon of July 1, 1863. It was painted as if from a great height, the clouds. The next three sketches depicted the violence of the battle: smoky air, roaring cannons, panicked men and horses—all in colorful swipes of pastels. He gingerly lifted the last one.

"*Whales,*" he said loudly to attract the archivist's attention. "Wasn't this one painted *after* Eaton left Gettysburg, when he had moved on to River Glen?"

"Oh, yes. The painting of *Whales* is the property of the art historian Professor Monroe Hadley. The other four are either in galleries or museums."

Best not to rebut, though he knew better. The original of *Whales* was in Grandma Julia's basement.

"But this *sketch* of *Whales*... how did it make its way back to Gettysburg?" he asked.

"Josiah brought it to Gettysburg a year before his death. He wanted the collection of sketches to be complete."

"Josiah resurfaced? He was a wanted man!"

"Just briefly. He gave this sketch to the newspaperman Clarence Stratford who had been collecting Eaton's documents. Stratford recognized his genius."

"That's it? Five Eaton paintings?"

"Only five have ever been seen. There are rumors, you know—completely unsubstantiated," said Worth in a secretive voice. "I was told by my grandfather that there's another series of Eaton paintings that chronicled Abigail's grisly—" She shuddered.

"—murder," he said quietly.

Will Wilkins tapped his foot on Julia Hale's porch step. What the hell was he doing here when he should be at headquarters, tracking down Hadley-Simon's killer? But no. He was fulfilling a filial obligation for the upteenth time. He was cursed! Cursed from birth! Why him? He never wanted to be a pyrate, but his last name inextricably bound him to the secret society in River Glen. Cursed immutable fate! All Wilkinses of River Glen were guardians of the treasure brought to the northern Chesapeake by Giles Hale and the crew of the *Raven* in the 1690s. Day and night he was at the beckon call of the two pyrate captains James Collins and Julia Hale. He was fine with helping James to install hidden cameras at the Wedgewood-Smyth mansion—except that he was late for Carly's swim meet. For Julia, he and his cousins Marty and Melvin had drilled tiny homing devices into the *Raven*'s treasure.

"Everything that's wood, lads," she had said while supervising the operation with a large glass of scotch. "Chests, barrels, figureheads, everything. In case a deranged Whitby locates the basement treasury."

The drilling took forever. He missed tango lessons which meant that Alex was without a partner and danced for the entire class with the charming instructor Braulio. Cursed immutable fate!

The never-ending chores weren't the worst of being a pyrate. Danger loomed around every corner. He had already taken a bullet in the shoulder while treasure hunting on Mutter Island with Alex, that terrible day that Clyde Whitby killed Jay's wife Laura. One consolation of the gunshot wound was that Alex massaged hot-cold cream into his shoulder on the nights it ached. Sometimes he whined about it just to feel her magical, kneading fingers.

If it wasn't bad enough contending with the Whitbys, there were the Dodds from Miami who were descended from the sadistic pyrate captain Bartholomew Dodd whom the *Raven*'s crew had cast into shark-infested waters. Only Bart Dodd was vicious enough to have survived an attack by tiger sharks, then lived to father a long line of equally vicious descendants. Three summers ago Pamela Dodd had kidnapped Alex, promising slow torture unless she divulged the whereabouts of the treasure.

Cursed immutable fate! Now he was bound by an exacting set of rules laid down by the pyrate-founders of

River Glen. Since greed was a heady motivator of dastardly acts, Giles had decided that there must be two crew members in charge of checking the treasury. As the legend goes, Giles cast his gaze around the tavern for two worthy candidates. The doe-eyed giant Barnaby Wilkins had a reputation for honesty. Aye, one treasurer would be the teenaged carpenter Barnaby. But the other? Twack twack... knives struck a smoke-greasy beam. Twack twack. The fire-haired pickpocket from Dublin had amazing aim with those throwing knives. No one was as ferocious yet loyal to the pyrate community as Shannon Allaway. Honesty and loyalty. A Wilkins and an Allaway would for perpetuity be the treasurers, Giles decided. So, it was his and Alex's blood destiny to check the treasury every Friday night.

Will's anxious foot tapping continued. He couldn't shake his unease. The murder of Seymour Simon, aka Monroe Hadley, was somehow tied to the paintings in Julia's hidden basement. But how? And why? Though it was not Friday, it was urgent that he get into the basement to check on those paintings. With Hadley-Simon's murderer skulking around River Glen, there was not a minute to wait. Alex was not available to assist and was thankfully safe and sound in Gettysburg, so in following strict Giles' dictum he had called Cousin Marty to fill in temporarily as a second treasurer. Will checked his watch again. He really should be at work!

But what to do with the information?

Jay knew of the treasury, but Lisa did not. No outsider could ever know of the treasure's existence. If word got out, they would be under constant siege.

"Finally."

Marty's pickup truck appeared on the river road. Two-by-fours and sheet rock jostled in the bed. The truck stopped next to his unmarked cruiser. Cousin Melvin waved from the passenger's seat, then held up his cell phone. "*Dexter* reruns," he called through the open window.

Marty slipped from the cab and ground his cigarette into the dirt. "The back deck at the Nauticus is riddled with termites. Amazing that none of those pretty boys crashed through it during a wild dance party."

"Thanks for coming," he said. "Alex is out-of-town."

"A miracle that no one busted something."

They entered Julia's empty house while Marty rambled on about planks, joists and wood screws. Julia's bedroom was on the first floor, right off the living room. They headed to her walk-in closet. There it was—the ornately carved wardrobe from Aberdeen, the portal to the unimaginable, the portal to an unspeakable treasure.

He typed the password into a hidden keypad and the outer doors of the wardrobe opened. He ducked into the cramped space and pressed another series of numbers; the back panel slid aside. He and his cousin descended the stairs and triggered a motion-sensor. Lights flicked on. The journey into the earthen chamber always filled him with awe and fear. So much blood had been spilt over the contents of the room.

He felt transported to a time of sail, wagon and plow. Figureheads, ship's wheels, spinning wheels, butter churns, sea chests and barrels filled the room. In the back corner were the paintings. A plume of dust rose as he pulled off the tarp. He had never given the paintings much attention, any attention for that matter, because his eyes were always drawn to the barrels and chests of coins and jewels.

"Marty, hold each one up while I photograph it."

"Can do."

The outermost painting was *Whales*. Marty positioned it under the light while he shot off pictures with his cell phone.

"Those two whales are swimming along the beach at the Wedgewood-Smyth place," Marty observed.

"Hey, you're right! It's definitely the beach by the mansion."

"Caught me the biggest eel there once."

"How big?"

"Must have been eight feet at least. It was a real monster. Took forever to reel it in."

A tarnished metal plate on the next painting read *Slaughter at the Berm*. He photographed that one as well. The one after that was *God Watches the Gathering*.

"It's as though the artist was painting from a bird flying over the battlefield," Marty said wondrously. "Look. You can see the position of all the regiments. Cool."

"Way cool."

The last two paintings *Ghost Riders* and *The Death of a Field Surgeon* were stylistically similar to *Slaughter at the Berm* and *God Watches the Gathering*. All were intensely colorful battle scenes. Will reviewed the images in his phone. In total there were four paintings of Gettysburg in Julia's basement: *Ghost Riders, The Death of a Field Surgeon, Slaughter at the Berm* and *God Watches the Gathering*. Only *Whales* depicted a scene in River Glen. Though he was no art expert by any stretch of the imagination, the style of the paintings foreshadowed the dramatic brushwork and hallucinogenic colors of the Impressionist movement that would appear a decade later in 1870s Paris. The swirling signature—A. Eaton—was in the bottom left corner of each one.

"Will, don't forget that one," Marty said.

"Oh. I never noticed it."

The painting was on the opposite side of the room, lodged between the wall and a battered sea chest. Marty lifted it toward the light and Will positioned his phone to snap the picture. It was another River Glen scene but definitely not painted by Adam Eaton. He recognized the setting immediately because he had fished there a thousand times with his father. It was that secluded marsh near the Wedgewood-Smyth estate and not too far from the beach in *Whales*. Like *Whales*, it was painted as though the artist had been out on a boat and looking back toward land. It depicted two men on the shoreline, both tiny in relation to the massive black object in the sand. Another whale? Had a dead whale washed up on the shores of River Glen? That seemed preposterous. Never had he seen whales swimming in the local waters, but maybe Alex had because she was a marine biologist and crabber. The nameplate on the warped frame read *Two Fishes*. Weird. All he could see was one black whale. The signature of this artist was in the lower right corner. The painter Abigail WS didn't know that whales were mammals, not fish.

Jay Braden was a cop but couldn't be entirely bad. Could he? Ella wondered. He was kind to his dogs. He had cajoled Miranda to eat the rice while stroking her head. The rice had perked up the dog and readied her for the walk. Nor did Braden seem the least bit drunk. If he was hungover, he disguised it well. Since she would be moving to River Glen and would inevitably run into him in the village, it couldn't hurt to become, not friendly, but at least neighborly with him. That was her rationale for offering a guided tour through the battlefield. In case Monroe Hadley and Ian Kent did send a hitman after her, it couldn't hurt to have a policeman aware of the situation, one who might understand that she was attempting life on the straight and narrow.

A trail at the back of the campground would lead them to the battlefield, she told Braden. The campground that morning was filled with women motorcyclists who were staying in assorted camp dwellings: tents, pop-up trailers, third wheels and vans.

UHaul trucks were also present. At each one she inconspicuously glanced at the front bumper for a black scuff from her back tire, but none had the telltale sign of nudging her bike off the road. There were thousands of UHauls in the U.S. and the guilty party was going to miraculously appear in her very campground? Ridiculous. Her paranoia was absurd. Her bike, though scratched and dented, ran fine. The driver was just a senile old woman who was not paying attention and never knew what she had done. Anyone with half a conscience would have stopped.

"What, Ella?" Braden said.

"What?"

"What about UHauls?"

"Nothing."

"It's something. What?"

He was perceptive when sober. He had been watching her. She was a criminal after all. His guard was up.

"Just yesterday—really it's nothing."

He pulled the dogs to a stop. "Just yesterday what? I'm not budging until I hear an explanation."

"A UHaul truck. It was a woman, probably texting. She almost ran me over."

He stared unnervingly into her face. "Where was this?"

"Near Taneytown. She grazed my back tire, but I swerved into the woods and crashed."

"So that's how your bike got damaged. I was wondering."

She exhaled. "I was lucky."

"Very."

"Today I can only show you sites from Day Two and Three of the battle," she said to change the subject. "The Day One fighting occurred mostly on the northwest side of town which is too long a walk from here. Days Two and Three are nearby, south of town."

The battlefield tour now held minimal interest for Braden because he had shifted into detective mode. At every UHaul in the campground he strode up to its front fender and studied it. The whole tenor of the walk changed instantly.

Now what to say? The tour was a boneheaded idea in the first place. After the fiasco with Tony's wife, she had promised that head-bashing bitch of a cop who responded to the call that she would stay clear of men. Other than male customers on the ghost walks, whom she only engaged in superficial chit chat, she had no idea how to talk to them. She had been surrounded by women for eleven years after all. Her strategy with Braden would be an informational historical lecture once at the battlefield. Nothing more, nothing personal.

"What got you sent inside?" he asked.

That was personal! She gazed forward and kept walking.

"C'mon, Ella. What happened?"

"I'm surprised you don't know that," she said hotly.

"I'm on vacation without my laptop so I don't have access to the database. Anyway, I want to hear your version."

"My version? When was my version ever important?"

No one except the useless public defender had wanted to hear her version. It had been an ironclad case against her. A staggering amount of preparation had gone into setting her up. She had been bedazzled by the whirlwind of the city and its crooks and walked blindly into their trap.

"Tell me," he insisted.

"It's an ages old story. The dim-witted country girl being set up by city slickers."

"Were you set up?"

"I was guilty and not guilty."

"How so?"

"Monroe Hadley, my thesis advisor in grad school, is the world's authority on a Civil War painter named Adam Eaton. Only a few Eaton paintings are known to exist. Three are in Philly and two are in Virginia though I knew Eaton's style very well because he lived in Gettysburg for a while. I produced paintings that looked like Eaton's other ones but with subtle differences so that it would be considered a new find."

"You grew up here?"

"Yes. This was the scam. My then fiancé Ian Kent, the dirtbag who owns the gallery with Monroe, would claim that a rare Eaton—my Eaton—had been discovered in a remote barn in West Virginia or Nebraska or some other bullshit location. The art world was abuzz with excitement. Then the painting would be taken to Monroe to authenticate."

"Monroe had you paint paintings that he'd later verify?"

"Yes."

He shook his head. "Audacious."

"Then it would be sold and I'd get a cut of the profits. I made a lot of money."

"You did this how many times?"

"Three times. Then one day the FBI's Art Crime Unit raided my Philly apartment. Someone tipped them off. I was caught red-handed. Paint brush in hand. In court Ian and Monroe denied any knowledge of the scam. I swear they had bought off the judge or were the judge's golf buddies, sex partners—who knows what?"

"But you said you weren't guilty."

"I was guilty of the forgeries but not the document theft."

"I'm not following."

"Here's the messed-up part. I was caught on a security camera, more accurately someone dressed as me was caught on camera, leaving the National Archives in Washington DC, with a satchel under their arm. I had allegedly checked out a historical document about Gettysburg and walked out with it. I've never been to the National Archives! I can't even tell you where the place is!"

"Was the document ever recovered?"

"I have no idea. But whoever it was, knew precisely how I dressed, even down to my blue hair, clothes and leopard sneakers. I admitted to the forgeries, thinking I'd get a reduced sentence but that, coupled to the security footage at the archives, nailed me."

"What about Ian and Monroe? Are you in contact with them?"

"You're kidding, right? I'm never going back to the city. I'm lying low in Gettysburg, then moving to River Glen to become a crabber."

"A crabber?"

"There's a Chrome Diva that I know who crabs. I'm going to ask her to teach me."

He smiled.

"You know her?"

"Quite well. It's a small place."

"Once I make enough money crabbing, I'm riding my motorcycle around the world so no one can ever find me and bother me again."

"Why River Glen of all places?"

"To crab."

"Who were you watching at the Giles Blood-hand festival?"

"Monroe."

"He was there?"

"Yes."

"Doing what?"

"Who knows? Probably doing what I was doing. Searching for Eaton's original paintings."

"But you said there are only five."

"I have a crazy theory—"

"Yeah?"

"That those five were produced by Monroe eons ago when he was a graduate student."

"Unbelievable. You were painting forgeries of forgeries."

Jay had half a mind to believe Ella Winston. Her story was so implausible that it might be plausible. Why couldn't a con man find an obscure painter, create a mystique about him and bring bogus works to the fore? Professors promoted oddball ideas all the time. That he had learned during the Cliff Top Murder investigation which led him to Tolchester College a few summers before. Entire academic careers were spent researching minutiae. Was it feasible that an art professor might devote a career to an alleged simpleton painter, then manipulate a trusting graduate student who needed cash? Absolutely.

It was a struggle to focus on Ella's description of the battles while roaming the Peach Orchard, Devil's Den and the Round Tops because his thoughts were mired in her crimes. It was the way his mind worked. He had no control over it whatsoever. His mind was attracted to crime like metal filings to a magnet. Laura had endlessly scolded him about his obsession with work.

"Jay, what did I just say?"

"What?"

"You're not listening to a thing I said."

"What?"

"What!"

"What?"

What? Did Ella just say that the Union forces retreated to the high ground on Day One of the battle, inhabiting

Cemetery Ridge, Cemetery Hill, Little Round Top and Culp's Hill? Was that what she said?

"On Day Two, July 2, 1863, the Union forces were aligned in the shape of an upside-down fishhook, with the hook end oriented to the north," she continued. He appreciated the fishing hook analogy as fishing was his other obsession. "That day the bulk of the Confederates attacked the Union lines or shaft of the fishhook from the westerly direction, with the exception of Ewell's men attacking Culp's Hill from the northeast."

After seeing the terrain, he could envision the attacks. But why was Ella sent inside for so long? Her sentence seemed excessive. The most murderous drug lords that he'd arrested in Baltimore were back on the streets after a couple of years, sometimes months, depending on the tenacity and political connections of their lawyers. She had been inside for an incomprehensible eleven years. What does that do to one's psyche?

Ella's physicality was another distraction. She was not drop-dead-gorgeous like Julia—and who knew it full well. Nor had she the delicate beauty of Laura. Her appeal was difficult to pinpoint. Ella was taller, leaner and meaner than the other two, a working-class woman in shoddy clothes yet with an upper-class education. Julia had smelled of whiskey and Chanel. Laura had smelled of paint and baby-powder, and Ella of campfire and gasoline.

Why was he comparing Ella's sensual elements to those of a wife and ex-girlfriend? And why was the prospect of her moving to River Glen titillating him? If what she said was true, she would learn to crab from Alex, the best crabber on the bay. Why should he even care?

Perhaps the battlefield tour felt vaguely like a date. Ella was not entirely unpleasant like their first encounter on the River Glen bridge. Nor did she insult him even once.

Twitches of a smile were evident and she had animated inflections in her voice, especially when describing Joshua Lawrence Chamberlin and the 20th Maine fixing bayonets and charging at the 15th Alabama down Little Round Top. Maybe his excitement was with Ella's age. Besides Alex and Lisa Paco, he was rarely around energetic young women. The hours of walking around the battlefield, that didn't wind Ella in the least, made him feel ancient.

"It's no use," he said collapsing under a tree. "My hip's on fire." Miranda was equally fatigued and flopped on his thigh.

"Sure. We can rest."

Ella's rest consisted of her throwing a stick to Clark in the meadow. End over end the stick flipped through the blue sky while the dog dashed after it. She had a remarkably good arm. Countless times she heaved the stick incredible distances.

He lifted binoculars to his eyes. Across the battlefield women bikers were on a guided motorcycle tour, though there was no sign of Alex and Nina amongst them. Over by a row of cannons was a solitary woman on a sport bike that looked like Ella's.

"Down, down!"

He pulled the binoculars from his eyes. "Off her, you pervert! She's not your species."

Clark was trying to hump Ella's long shapely leg. He could hardly fault the dog. Humping in the grass had crossed his mind as well.

Ella looked at her watch. "We should move on to Day Three and the site of Pickett's Charge."

He rose with a groan and leashed the dogs, but Clark only wanted to walk with his new beloved so he handed her the leash. At the Copse of Trees she told him of General Lee's plan to smash the Union line along Cemetery Ridge,

Longstreet's reservations and the massive artillery bombardment before the assault. On the afternoon of July 3rd the Southern army stepped from the forest into a deadly barrage of metal from the Union batteries on Cemetery Ridge.

The battlefield tour was done and they started back to the Round Tops and the campground beyond. Jay was tired yet impressed. Walking the undulating landscape gave him an appreciation of the distances and directions of the assaults. He understood the motivations and strategies of the generals and movements of the divisions as well as the challenges of terrain, inexperienced leadership, dehydration, heat and exhausting marches in the days and hours before fighting. All of it. But disturbing fragments of information... forgeries of forgeries... a stolen document from the National Archives... a heavy-handed sentence... had unsettled his history lesson. Ella was not a murderer, drug dealer or sex offender. Just a misguided painter.

As they passed through Devil's Den, he ducked behind a boulder and lifted the binoculars again.

Ella squinted into the distance. "What are you looking at?"

"The battlefield. It's a beautiful but eerie place. There's a definite vibe that something terrible happened here."

"Many people experience that—looming presence of death."

"Hm."

It was a stunning landscape; that much was true. But two things unnerved him. Maybe it was nothing. But probably not. The UHaul truck and now this—that solo biker watching them from afar.

"Always be sure before making an arrest, Paco," said Lisa said mimicking Jay Braden. "A wrongful arrest stigmatizes the person and casts a shadow of doubt on them. Yada. It impacts relationships with family, friends and colleagues at their place of employment. Yada yada. Be absolutely sure, Paco." She blew a bubble and popped it loudly for emphasis. "Yada yada yada."

She didn't want to be cocky and superior, but in ninety-nine percent of the cases she solved it light-years before Jay and Will. Criminal investigations were a team effort. That much was a no-brainer. The aggregated evidence from Jay and Will's thorough fieldwork and Zera's forensic examination of the body and crime scene were invaluable for her to link the critical bits of evidence. No way would she throw Jay, Will and Zera under the bus and take all the credit, but this time she would have to find Hadley-Simon's killer on her own because her partners were figuratively out-to-lunch.

Jay was vacationing.

Zera was moving her daughter and grandchildren into the spare room of her condo because the daughter's marriage had tanked.

Will was single-parenting Carly while Alex was in Gettysburg. This meant he was circling between Carly's swim camp, Hip Hop recitals and soccer games.

She, Maryland's Super Sleuth, was on her own with the Hadley-Simon murder investigation. Jay would return from his vacation with the case opened and closed. For the rest of the summer they would deal with banalities: DWIs, fireworks violations, domestic disputes and fender benders. Nothing serious would tax them. Jay's would be a placid summer of gin-drinking, fishing and dog-walking. Will could focus on his tango lessons with Alex. Zera could play with her grandchildren and she would stalk Pokémon.

FORGER'S REVENGE

Despite the paucity of evidence, something was nagging her about the wife Ventresca. She stuck her gum to the computer screen because mixing lunch with strawberry-flavored gum was plain gross. Jay always went ballistic when she stuck gum to her computer or desk. Same with Zera. What was it about fifty-somethings and germs? #whenthecatsaway.

She opened her lunch box and cracked open a Red Bull because she wasn't sufficiently wired from three cups of coffee. A balanced diet meant good nutrition. Good nutrition meant mental energy for crime-solving. Doritos were a source of carbs and sodium. The peanuts in the Snickers bar were a source of protein and the chocolate was good for the soul. And last but not least, an apple to keep the doctor away.

She gazed at the data on her computer while chewing her first course, the chocolate bar. Any second the clues would fall into place and the Hadley-Simon case would be solved. Ventresca would be arrested. Now to figure how the crafty bitch did it when she was allegedly at her posh townhome. Yeah yeah, likely story.

Detectives Haskell and Block from the Philly PD had said that IT found nothing unusual in Ventresca's computer: standard workplace emails between coworkers in her art therapy group and emails back and forth to her sisters who were planning a surprise party for their father's eightieth birthday. Ventresca had no role in the day-to-day operations of Hadley-Simon and Ian Kent's Old City Americana Gallery except for hiring caterers and choosing wines when a new exhibition or party was to be held.

Think, Lisa, think... clues clues... falling into place.

Hadley-Simon was a con artist who reappeared in the United State in the guise of a British art professor. Most academics were charlatans anyway. Why was he any different? She had learned all about academics during the investigation of poisonous spiders at Tolchester College summers before. Tolchester had their share of shady characters so why couldn't an art college in Philly? Hadley-Simon had spent an entire career writing about five Eaton paintings. The British lord, Sir Pompous Pompadoo or whoever the hell he was, whose paintings Hadley-Simon had studied for his dissertation, could not be located for questioning. #bigsurprisethere. The manor house where the alleged Eaton's paintings resided never freaking existed. #somethingisrotten. This wouldn't be first time that a dissertation had been written on falsified—in this case—non-existent material. The avuncular 'Brit' had bamboozled his colleagues with the fake goatee, cane, tweed suits, ascot and erudite accent. His marriage to the hoity-toity Ventresca secured his place in Philadelphia's high society. He bought the gallery with Ian Kent, taught art classes at the art institute and, according to his dean, had an impeccable record of scholarship. He paid his taxes and had not so much as a speeding ticket. Absolutely nothing came up on Monroe Hadley in the police database.

The wife had an equally spotless record. Ventresca Hadley, maiden name Wyndmor, had grown up on the Main Line in an affluent neighborhood outside of Philadelphia. She earned an art degree at the Massachusetts College of Art and Design in Boston. There, according to Lisa's phone interview with her father Benjamin, Ventresca had a brief marriage to a Spanish actor named Franco.

"Franco what?" she had asked Benjamin.

"There was no last name," he answered. "It was just Franco, I believe. Like Madonna."

"And Sting, Liberace and Beyonce."

"Quite right. A one-name stage name."

"And Prince and Adele."

"Before I could meet him, the marriage fizzled. After the thankfully speedy divorce, Ventresca returned to the books and graduated with honors. She then moved back to Philadelphia and earned a graduate degree in art therapy. She's been working for a hospital consortium ever since. Monroe was a good husband. Theirs was a happy marriage despite a difference in age."

Benjamin also corroborated what she and Will had learned about Monroe's business partner. Ian Kent had an undergraduate degree in Business from Gettysburg College and an MBA from Penn. He had grown up in King of Prussia, Pennsylvania. He had a brother and sister. Both parents were deceased. Kent was currently an investment banker in Philadelphia. When Lisa asked of Kent's relationship to Hadley—uncle or cousin?—Benjamin couldn't say for sure.

Lisa's back-checking found Benjamin's statements to be correct. Ian Kent had degrees from the two Pennsylvania schools, was a half partner in the gallery and had two siblings Lorena and Curtis. Lorena Kent was a nurse anesthetist living in Charlotte, North Carolina. She was married and had three children. When Lisa placed a call to Lorena, there was the chaotic sound of children in the background.

"Was Monroe Hadley your uncle or cousin?" she asked.

"Ian's partner who—?" said Lorena loudly over the din.

"What?"

"Died."

"Yes."

"Monroe was no relation to us, but Ian called him Uncle Monroe for some reason. They were chummy. Monroe took a fatherly interest in Ian after our parents died."

"How did they die?"

"My mother of a heart attack. My father a few months after, I guess of a broken heart. He missed her that badly."

"Where did Ian and Sey—Monroe meet?"

"I have no idea. Probably at an art gallery. Ian loves art."

Lisa rang off and checked Lorena's Facebook page. She was a stout, smiling woman surrounded by brood of children.

Lisa's next call was to Ian's brother Curtis who ran wilderness tours in the Canadian Rockies. Curtis could not be reached though she listened to the cheerful greeting on his phone. "Hey, it's Curtis of CanRock Outdoor Adventures. Please leave a message because I really want to hear from you, but right now I'm out with a group. No cell reception where we go and that's a good thing. Please visit my website CanRock.com for the next available tour. There's always room for one more. Join us! We have a blast. And be sure to check out our July discounts."

She logged onto the CanRock webpage. Curtis Kent ran a series of two-week tours from May to October, presumably until the weather was too cold to venture into the mountains. According to the online schedule, he was leading a white-water rafting tour down the Kicking Horse River. A website photograph showed Curtis to be a tanner, handsomer version of Ian.

It was time that she spoke with Ventresca directly. Though she had read Will's notes and heard his account of the interview in Old Town, sometimes another person asking a question in a different way or asking a new question entirely opened up new lines of inquiry. Ventresca answered her call immediately. She too was having lunch because the noise of a hospital cafeteria was heard in the background.

"I'm happy to answer any questions," said Ventresca eagerly. "Do you have any news yet?"

Don't be fooled by the woman's pleasant tone, Lisa cautioned herself. It was always the wife. Ventresca must have climbed out that townhouse window. "We're following several leads. You met Monroe where?"

"At an art auction to raise money for pediatric cancer."

Likely story. It was probably at a Philly sex club. "And you were aware that Monroe was wearing a fake beard and toupee."

"How would I not know that? He was my husband. Of course, I would know that."

That answer seemed reasonable enough, if not a bit curt.

"He was extremely self-conscious about his Alopecia universalis," Ventresca elaborated. "He spent a lot on high-quality hairpieces."

"Are you aware that Monroe Hadley was an alias? That he wasn't British at all. That he was an American named Seymour Simon from Taunton, Massachusetts."

Silence. Dead silence. "Ms. Hadley?" More silence. "Um, Ms. Hadley? Are you still there?"

"Th- there's some mistake," the widow quavered. "I don't know what you—"

"I'm afraid there's no mistake. You were married to Seymour Simon. A thief who fled to Europe, changed his identity and returned to the U.S. as an art professor named Monroe Hadley."

"I can't believe... this can't be!... he took me to England... we toured his university, prep school... his childhood village in Sussex!"

"Fingerprints don't lie. The man on the beach at the Radcliffe had the same fingerprints as Seymour Simon who served time in a Massachusetts correctional facility for stealing historical documents."

"Historical documents?"

"Do you remember him ever mentioning or having visitors from the past, from his days in Massachusetts?"

"No! Ridiculous. All of his friends were either British or fellow academics from the Philadelphia area. No mentions of Massachusetts ever!"

"He met Ian Kent where?"

"I have no idea. They've known each other forever. Long before I came on the scene."

"Did Seymour have any disputes at work, bad blood with neighbors, former girlfriends, relatives, anyone?"

"Seymour? Monroe? Now I don't know what to call him! The man I was married to was a kind, considerate person. An absolute gentleman!"

"With a dark past."

Ventresca sniffled. "Your mention of historical documents jarred something."

"What?"

"Monroe was called to testify at a trial many years ago. Over a decade ago. He had a very gifted student who was painting forgeries and fencing historical documents."

"What documents?"

"I don't remember the details, but it was a sad ordeal. She was a wild, impetuous girl but an artist of considerable promise."

"Her name? Do you remember her name?"

"Yes, of course. Such a tremendous waste of talent. Ella Winston. She's serving time somewhere in Pennsylvania, as far as I know."

Lisa whipped her cell phone from her ear and hit speaker mode. She pressed the screen and opened her text messages.

Sick sick ride! A BMW F 800 GS. Belongs to a forty-year old. Ella Winston.

Just released from Pa. prison. An art forger from Philly.

Camping with James Collins was excellent fun, Jay concluded. James had returned from town with the essentials: Cohiba cigars, a local IPA and a bag of ice. Better yet, he strode right over to the ladies' campsite to invited them for hotdogs. "Keisha and Sam are still at work," Ella told him. "But I can join you." What a perfect afternoon it was: chit-chatting about Gettysburg history with a lovely lady by a delightful fire.

"The ghost walk tonight?" James nonchalantly asked her. "Is it near the Dobbins House?"

Jay almost guffawed. The sly dog was in strategy mode, planning his seduction of Nina Vega.

"They're a block away from each other," Ella replied. "A short walk. The organizers of the women's motorcycle convention reserved both ghost tours for this evening. The twilight and ten o'clock tours should be packed with bikers, but anyone can tag along. The more, the merrier."

The more, the merrier. Jay liked the sound of that. He batted around the idea of inviting Ella for a nightcap after the ten o'clock walk, but much of the day had already been spent with her. He'd be pushing his luck. In truth, he chickened out.

After two hotdogs and a mound of potato chips, she pulled herself from a lawn chair. "I have to go to work. Thank you for dinner."

A vestige of gallantry remained in his aging body for despite a shriek by his arthritic hip he popped from the chair. "See you tonight!"

Ella smiled. "See you then." She returned to her campsite where she pulled a black gown off the clothesline, stuffed it into a metal case on her motorcycle and motored off.

Throughout the afternoon he had kept a close eye on the activities in the campground. The rider on the sport bike had vanished from sight when they climbed up the slopes of the Round Tops. Women on motorcycles had come and gone from their campsites. Nothing seemed amiss. The painter Adam Eaton, Monroe Hadley's presence at the Giles Bloodhand festival, the menacing UHaul and the mysterious rider who had followed them consumed his thoughts. They were somehow related. It was just a matter of connecting the dots. Every mystery was just that... finding logical connections between seemingly disparate bits of evidence, dots.

He settled back in a chair and stretched his feet toward the fire. "How did things go at the archive?"

"There was nothing new on Josiah and Abigail, but I now know that Dr. Worth's great grandfather Tobias was able to leap tall buildings in a single bound," James laughed. "What a yacker she is! She showed me two folders on Adam Eaton. Both files were the property of the nineteenth century newspaper editor Clarence Stratford who was interested in Eaton's inventions and artwork. Dr. Worth was kind enough to let me photograph the papers in two folders: Adam Eaton's Mechanical Drawings and Adam Eaton's Art. Have a look."

He swiped through the images in James' cell phone. Adam Eaton was clearly a jack-of-all-trades, equally adept as a machinist and painter. Eaton's modifications to Stratford's printing press meant little to him because he was a mechanical-ignoramus; it was Alex who tuned-up and winterized his outboard. But Eaton's sketches gripped him.

For a professional development activity last year, the River Glen police chief Herm Taylor had sent his team of detectives to a short course run by the FBI's Art Crimes Unit. It was three-hours of death-by-Powerpoint but a nice change of scene to spend the day in DC with Will and Lisa (though her gum smacking on the car ride drove him insane). He didn't want to sound the know-it-all, but he was familiar with art of the different periods from being dragged on Laura's museum tours of France and Italy.

The five Eaton sketches were mesmerizing. It appeared as though colors had been blown by a brisk wind. Brash swipes of pastels moved from right to left across each page. It was easy to visualize the paintings that resulted. Four were Gettysburg scenes and one was painted when Eaton had moved on to River Glen.

"Tell me about Eaton and your novel," he said, handing the phone back to James. "We have plenty of time before the twilight ghost walk."

"Marvelous!" James pulled a beer from the cooler and dropped into another lawn chair.

"What's the story called again?"

"*Subterfuge*. Let me give you the historical background on the main characters before we get into the plot. Josiah was born in River Glen and descended from Angus Smyth, a pyrate on the *Raven*. After Charles Allaway was decapitated by Neville Whitby, Angus fathered children with the widow Shannon Allaway. Shannon would later become the most fearsome pyrate queen who ever sailed the Chesapeake and Outer Banks."

He suppressed a groan. Every bizarre happening in River Glen was associated with those goddamn pyrates on the *Raven*. Now this.

"By the time of the American Civil War," James went on, "generations of Wedgewood-Smyths had occupied the coastal property north of the village and become wealthy farmers. One of Josiah's side businesses was the importation of rum from the islands. On a business trip to the Carolinas he met Abigail Leighton. He was smitten, she accepted his proposal and he bought her back to River Glen. I traced her genealogy. Here's the fascinating thing about her. Her great, great, great—three greats—grandmother was Anne Bonny!"

He grinned incredulously. "You're quite the story-teller."

"It's true! After Jack Rackham's pyrate ship *William* was captured, Rackham, Anne Bonny, Mary Read and the crew were taken to Jamaica and sentenced to be hanged."

"Yeah, I know the story. Bonny and Read got off by 'pleading their bellies' while all the men swung."

"Correct. Anne's father William Cormac, a rich plantation owner, bought her freedom and married her off to the Virginian Joseph Buerleigh. She had eight children with him and lived to be eighty-four. Abigail is descended from that union."

"Two pyrate families, the Smyths of River Glen and the Bonnies were united by the union of Josiah and Abigail."

"Exactly. Isn't it wonderful!" James said.

"If you want to populate the world with pyrates. That will keep me in work. Did Josiah and Abigail have children?"

"Yes, many. The Smyths of the Smyth Family Marina are their descendants. My novel's not about local genealogy but about Josiah and Abigail's dangerous double-life. On the surface they were simple farmers, but they also spied for the Union army. The couple had their servants watch over the children while they took midnight rides into the countryside to watch troop movements and assist in the Underground Railroad. Ella found the underground crypt where runaway slaves were hidden when she was wandering the house."

"What crypt?"

"The one under the cook's bedroom floor."

"She's a trouble magnet."

"With nerves of steel. I went down there with Judith Ann Smyth from the library. There's no way I'd go down there alone. Once was enough."

"What's down there?"

"Pitch darkness and spiders. I'm a wimp," said James with a self-deprecating chuckle. "It was terrifying. I took one quick look, then bolted."

"How did Eaton meet the Wedgewood-Smyths?"

"The spies were on high alert after mid-June of 1863 when the Confederates crossed the Potomac into Maryland

and headed north toward Pennsylvania. The Union army had moved in parallel, positioning itself between the Confederates and Washington and Philadelphia, anticipating an attack on one of those cities. Josiah and Abigail were on reconnaissance east of Gettysburg and west of Baltimore when they stumbled upon riders from Jeb Stuart's cavalry. Stuart's cavalry had strayed too far east to be effective as the eyes and ears of General Lee before the battle of Gettysburg. At the onset of the fighting a frustrated Lee lacked vital information about the size, number and positions of the Union divisions. Stuart would later be rebuked by Lee and blamed by contemporaries and historians, at least in part, for the rebel defeat there.

"But back to Adam Eaton. Riders from Stuart's unit spotted Josiah and Abigail and pursued on horseback. The couple rode off in a shower of bullets. Josiah was unscathed, but Abigail was struck in the hand and two fingers were blown off. The chase had been observed by Adam who had been riding around the countryside with his satchel of paints. He watched as a rebel rider slid off his horse and lifted Abigail's bloody fingers from the dirt.

"Those fingers would lead to Abigail's demise," said James ominously. "The Confederates knew to search for a spy that was a female with two missing fingers. Adam followed the cavalrymen back to their camp and watched the soldier toss the fingers into the fire. At daybreak, after the riders packed up and departed, Adam dug amongst the coals for the fingers. He then rode eastward. Near Havre De Grace Adam stumbled into a grove where Josiah was tending to Abigail's wounds. Josiah jumped to his feet, his pistol readied, when he noticed the child-like expression on Adam's face. Adam fumbled in his pocket and presented a knotted handkerchief to Abigail. In it laid her charred fingers. But missing from the ring finger was her gold wedding band with hers and Josiah's initials."

"Wow, what a story. I'll be first in line to buy your novel."

"If I can find a publisher—"

"Then what?"

"They shared a meal with Adam and he followed them home. There was plenty of room in the manor house. Adam painted with Abigail and... built stuff with Josiah."

He noted the hesitation. "What kind of stuff?"

James flicked cigar ashes into the fire and lowered voice. "Jay, you can't tell anyone this."

"What?"

"Promise?"

"Promise."

"It's the central part of my novel."

"I promise."

"You've heard of the legend of Chessie—"

"Of course. Julia and Alex love telling Carly about the Chesapeake Bay Sea Monster. A cousin of Nessie from Loch Ness, Julia used to say. According to her, the Scottish pyrates on the *Raven* brought a baby Nessie with them to America. When Nessie got too big for the jug, then the barrel, the pyrates released the monster into the Glen River where it fed on crabs and oysters and grew to a mammoth size. It's another crazy River Glen tall tale."

"I have news for you," James said. "Chessie was real. A destroyer of ships that had any affiliations to the rebs."

"And I've been abducted by aliens."

"Really! The monster was real! After Adam moved to River Glen there was a rash of unexplained shipwrecks, all with ties to the Confederacy. Witnesses on shore reported blazing ships sinking into the bay at night. The lives of many rebel sailors and sympathizers were lost."

"Adam trained a sea monster to attack southern ships?" he said absurdly. "So *Subterfuge* is going to be a fantasy?"

"Josiah realized that Adam was a mechanical wizard. He and Adam built a prototype submarine that had lethal capabilities."

He shook his head. "Preposterous."

"I can prove it!" James swiped through his phone. "You've seen Chessie. In fact, there was a pair of them. One operated by Adam, the other by Josiah. Two lethal killing machines as powerful and malevolent as Captain Nemo's *Nautilus*. Look!"

Goosebumps rose on Jay's skin. Mystified, he stared into James' phone—at a sketch seen minutes before—two bullet-shaped objects coursing through the green waters of the Chesapeake.

"Josiah cleverly named Adam's painting *Whales*," James whispered, "in subterfuge."

"We are working," Lisa told Norman from IT. "If anyone asks. Really. We're millennials and experts at multi-tasking. It just looks like we're walking aimlessly through the field behind the police barracks, staring into our cell phones. Searching for Pokémon Go characters *while* working on the Hadley-Simon murder investigation. #noproblem." She popped a bubble. "You know what Jay Braden always says to me?"

"What?" Norman replied.

"Paco, let the clues, the evidence, lead you to the suspect. Never make a prejudgment about a person, Paco. Invariably you'll arrest the wrong person, Paco. Paco, Paco, Paco. Like a myna bird."

"I'm getting close, Lisa," said Norman breathlessly. "I sense it. Oh, I hope it's Pikachu! My pokéball's ready to heave at that wily Pokémon."

"I'm trying to keep an open mind even though Ventresca's guilty as sin. Or maybe it's that BMW biker chick? Did you read the transcript from Hadley-Simon's phone?"

"What?"

"The transcript, Norman."

"Ur, no."

"What a blabbermouth Hadley-Simon is! It took me for-endless-ever to read the whole thing. First was his lengthy phone conversation with his next-door neighbor about the mysterious cat that had been leaving gifts of mutilated rats and squirrels on his doorstep. No one else in the neighbor had received dead animals. Only him. That's kinda weird."

"And really gross."

"Every cat owner on the block denied that their precious Felix was the vicious killer. Then he had texted Terry from the wine-tasting club about splitting season tickets to the symphony at the Kimmel Center because he and Ventresca could only attend half of the concerts."

"Lisa, do you know the millennial whoop?"

"You're kidding me, right? It's all over You Tube. Every song in the 2000s has it. Oh ah oh ah."

"Oh ah oh ah," giggled Norman.

"Then he was asked by his dean to serve on the scholarship committee. He agreed. #simonsabrownnoser. Next he had talked, whined mostly, to a colleague about their annual raises. The administrators got eight percent raises but the faculty only one percent. Who was he to complain? His salary was four times mine! Then there were gallery-related conversations with Ian Kent about city taxes and fixing the back window in the men's restroom. Other conversations went back and forth with Ventresca. Hadley-Simon was trying to avoid his father-in-law's birthday party because one of Ventresca's sisters was 'too obnoxious to endure.' Yada and more yada by the pontificating pompous Philly professor. Alliteration!"

"Pikachu picked a peck of Pokémon… oh ah oh ah."

She pondered the image in her cell phone. "I wonder if I should change my avatar."

"Keep it, Lisa. It looks just like you."

"Yeah, it does. Scrawny and mousy with Coke-bottle glasses. No one would ever guess from my inconspicuous, blend-into-the-crowd disguise that I'm the State of Maryland's Queen of Crime-solving."

Norman's avatar looked nothing like him. His avatar was not fifty pounds overweight.

"After all the yada in the transcript was the I-gotcha-moment. The smoking gun text!" she said.

"What was it?"

"Two weeks before the Giles Blood-hand festival an unidentified caller lures Hadley-Simon to River Glen."

"I'll try to track down that person when I get back to my computer, but it's difficult with those rental phones. Oh, Lisa, my heart's really set on Pikachu!"

"Rental phones, the cheater's phone. Ninety-nine percent of the time those phones are used to arrange affairs. But not this time. The unknown person said *I found the Eatons. All of them.*"

"Eatons?"

"Paintings, Norman."

"I'll even settle for Zubat or Rattata, if not Pikachu."

"The unknown person texted: *If you authenticate we split 60 40. No cut with K this time.* K must be Ian Kent. *This time* implies that they'd made a deal in the past. For some reason this person wanted Kent out of the picture. Then

Hadley-Simon responded cautiously with *I need to see them first.*"

"Oh ah oh ah."

"You're not paying attention to a thing I'm saying."

"I've been searching for Pikachu for days!"

"Okay, I'll shut up." She silently recalled the texts in the transcript.

Unknown: They're very fragile. Some will need restoration. I'm not moving them. But I've taken photos.

Simon: How many? Where did you find them?

Unknown: 4 River Glen scenes. Where is my business. 4 so we're talking a fortune. I don't blame you for before. I know it was K who set me up.

Simon: I'm so sorry it happened and am glad you're well. Where are you?

Unknown: In River Glen. Meet me next Saturday.

Simon: At the Radcliffe?

Unknown: OK. 11:45 pm

Simon: I'll leave your name at the front gate.

Unknown: We can't be seen together. I live on a boat in River Glen. I'll come by water. Meet me on shore by the golf course. 11:45

Simon: I'll be there.

Unknown: No K involvement. Just us. 60 40 split.

Simon: OK

The same day the message was received from Unknown, Hadley-Simon went online and booked a room at the Radcliffe. He then called Ventresca, telling her that he wanted to go to the Giles Blood-hand festival. They should take two cars, he suggested, so he could stay on. Perhaps he assumed that Unknown would show him the paintings. That seemed the logical reason for booking extra days.

Earlier that morning Norman had traced the phone of the unknown caller to a cell tower in the cornfields outside of

River Glen, confirming what the person had said to Simon—that the caller lived in River Glen. Ella Winston was at the Giles Blood-hand festival that day. Was it her phone?

Maybe Unknown had approached the shoreline of the Radcliffe by boat. That explained the lack of footprints, other than Hadley-Simon's traveling from the golf course to the beach. Unknown was not perceived as a physical threat or Hadley-Simon would never have agreed to meet him *or her* on the beach that night. Unknown must have crept up from behind, unheard in the sand, and slashed the professor's throat. Unknown's footprints were then erased by the tides.

"Easy peasy, Norman. We identify Unknown, we identify the killer. Oh ah oh ah."

"The sooner the move to River Glen, the better," Ella decided as she climbed off her motorcycle at the Four Score and Seven Hotel. She now knew a few people in the bayside village. James Collins was a nice guy who might help with her document search at the historical society during her days off. She might have the occasional neighborly chit-chat with Jay Braden if she passed him on the bridge during a dog-walk. He had seemed legitimately concerned about the UHaul incident, listened to her account of the Civil War battles and asked informed questions. He had an inquisitive mind that was requisite to being a good detective. Sam was right; he did bear a slight resemblance to Clint Eastwood.

She needed to learn to crab; she needed a job in River Glen. It couldn't hurt to ask Alex about it. Crab cakes instead of PB&Js! The worst Alex could say was "no... or get lost loser... or don't even think about encroaching on my business." Doors slamming in her face was the norm. But what if Alex said yes?

It was doubtful that Sam and Keisha would want to move with her. They liked Gettysburg and had a good boss at the Lincoln Motel. Gettysburg was exciting to them because they hadn't grown up there. And they had become lovers again. Last night they were whispering and messing around in the back of the trailer as she was falling asleep. They had had a long relationship in prison, then had a falling out over that meth dealer from Harrisburg. But the romance was rekindled. She was now underfoot, an awkward third in the trailer.

At the entrance to the Four Score and Seven Hotel women bikers climbed into a battlefield tour bus. Other bikers milled around the lobby, but there was no sign of Alex. Ella peered into the fitness center, then the restaurant and bar. Still no Alex. This whole thing was useless! The hotel had countless rooms. How was she ever going to find her? The pool? She followed a circuitous hallway to the back of the hotel.

The gods were smiling on her. The pool area was filled with Chrome Divas. Alex and Nina were on sun loungers by a plastic palm tree. Linda Radowski was having a coffee at the tiki bar and tapping furiously into her tablet. Other Divas were hanging off the edge of the pool, sipping from perspiring cocktails. Hawaiian music played from pineapple-shaped speakers.

"Hey, Ella," said Alex squinting into the late afternoon sun.

"Hi."

Nina held up a cocktail with a tiny umbrella. "Grab yourself a drink."

"I can't. I'm on my way to work."

Alex gestured to an empty lounger. "Then at least have a seat."

Ella exhaled. So far, so good. "I'm going to be moving to River Glen soon. That's why I was there a few days ago. On a scouting mission."

"Good," Alex said. "Maybe you'll ride with the Divas."

"Where will be you living?" Nina asked. "My apartment building's pretty affordable."

"I'll be in the campground until I find something more permanent. Um, Alex, I was wondering if you'd show me how to crab. Not to set up a business or try to compete with you in any way, but to get food."

The seconds of silence were excruciating. Then Alex held up her calloused palms. "Look at these hands. I can definitely use the help. Between work at the marine lab and hauling crab pots, my hands and back are getting destroyed. I set traps in the morning and pull up them in the afternoons after work. Then I deliver crabs to the dockside restaurants in the village. I can use another pair of hands, if you want a part-time job."

"Thank you!"

"No, thank you."

How wonderful will it be to give notice at the Ephram Whitson House! "Take this job and shove it!" she couldn't wait to tell Dana Detrick. "I'm leaving with no forwarding address." A new start! Her parole officer would need to be notified and a new one assigned in Maryland. Maybe Jay Braden could assist with that. Alex might have to write a letter to the parole board to verify employment. That would be embarrassing to explain to her, but she might be okay with it.

She checked the clock by the tiki bar and jumped to her feet. "That time can't be right!" If she arrived two seconds after five o'clock, Dana would dock her pay. That bitch used any excuse to short change her.

"Ignore that clock," Nina said humorously. "It threw me into a panic also. See the sign underneath it?"

"It's five o'clock somewhere," she sighed.

"It always reads that time," Nina said.

"I should be getting to work."

"Let's stay in touch about the crabbing," said Alex.

"Definitely."

"We'll see you very soon," Nina said. "We're coming to the twilight ghost walk. I can't wait."

"I can," Alex groaned. "I'll probably pee myself."

"It's July 5, 1863 when the beleaguered armies retreat south," said Ella in her mysterious ghoul voice. "The citizens of Gettysburg are confronted with a horrifying task... fields and fields of putrefying bodies..."

"I'm terrified already," Alex uttered.

Ella laughed. "I'll show you two an evening of terror that you'll never forget!" She was the Diva of Darkness, after all.

The search for Pokémon in the field behind the River Glen police barracks was a mixed success. It was not Pikachu he captured but a rare Dragonair. That was enough to mollify Norman. Lisa had captured one of her favorites—Gengar. Norman returned to his computer while she drove into the village. The unknown caller had mentioned living on a boat in River Glen. There was only one marina in the village, the Smyth Family Marina and the owner Gary Smyth was a poker buddy of Uncle Tommy. Gary could give her a list of the boaters renting slips. It was simply a matter of matching the name of a boater to the unknown caller and easypeasy... they had their killer.

Lisa climbed from the police cruiser. #frickininferno. It was too hot a day to be in a long-sleeved uniform, but Captain Taylor could not see her tattoos. He would go ballistic. Her tats depicted fascinating historical crimes, she might argue in self-defense, but Taylor would never buy it. He was that big of a prig. Luckily her immediate supervisor Jay was cool. He saw them when she was digging up a grave in the Sarova-spider investigation. "Impressive," he had said with a wry smile.

The marina was deathly still because a suffocating heat wave was keeping everyone in their air-conditioned cabins. Gary was nowhere to be seen on the docks. She headed into the garage where ceiling fans could barely move the oil-thick air. She knocked on the office door.

"Come in," grumbled Gary without looking up from a piece of equipment. "You need to be a goddamn rocket scientist to fix these new navigation systems. I hate touch screens."

"Hey, don't look at me," she shrugged. "I'm an ignoramus when it comes to science."

There was no time to chit-chat about boat instruments because she had to wrap up the case by the end of the day. That way she and Norman could search in earnest for Pokémon and edit the film footage from the Radcliffe without anything urgent hanging over their heads. Her film would lack a true star. No Ed Sheeran, Pitt Bull or a single Kardashian. That sucked.

"Gary, I need a list of the individuals renting slips this summer."

"No problem. It's been a good season. All the slips are full." He opened a folder on his laptop, found the list and hit PRINT.

"Any females who ride motorcycles?"

"Two, and both pains in my ass."

"Why?"

"They bicker all the time. Oil and water, those two. I assigned them slips at opposite ends of the marina this season to keep them apart. A lot of good that did me."

"Who are they?

He handed her the list from the printer and they walked to the entrance of the garage. "Blanche Hyde lives on that Gibson houseboat." He pointed toward floating Dock Four.

"What does she ride?"

"A Cam Am Spyder. She used to ride a Harley until her knee replacement surgery. She's a dog groomer. She burned out her knee standing all day." He pointed to a motor yacht at Dock One. "Linda Radowski and her husband Kenneth live on that DeFever 44."

"Does Linda drive a BMW?"

"No. A Kawasaki Vulcan."

"Neither woman drives a BMW sport bike? You're sure?"

"Positive."

She scanned the list. There was no female named Ella Winston amidst the boaters. Was Winston using an alias?

"Any other women bikers here?" she asked.

"Nope. Just Blanche and Linda."

In the texts to Hadley-Simon Unknown had mentioned living on a boat and traveling to the Radcliffe via water. She glanced upriver. The individual could have a mooring somewhere else, but where? Or were Unknown's words meant to mislead?

"Okay, Gary, thanks for your help." It was wasted trip to the village, an exasperating dead-end. No Ella Winston with a BMW was staying at the marina. She headed to her cruiser, then stopped. "Hey, BTW, what do Linda and Blanche fight about?"

"It's all Kenneth's fault, the way I see it. Every time Blanche puts on a bathing suit to tan, he wanders down the dock to flirt with her."

FORGER'S REVENGE

Lisa climbed into the car, turned the key and blasted the AC. Her cell phone vibrated. It was a text from Norman.

Unknown is a female named Jennie Wade. Phone charges are paid by Wade's bank account in Gettysburg, Pennsylvania.

Chapter 5
Ghost Walk

Alex's heart pounded. One would expect by the age of thirty that one would not succumb to peer pressure. She should be at the tiki bar, drinking Hurricanes and chatting about the Phillies or Orioles with the bartender Red. But no. Here she was in line with Nina and the Chrome Divas purchasing tickets to a ghost walk. The ghost walk through the River Glen cemetery when she was a teenager was terrifying enough. When the headless pyrate Charles Allaway jumped from behind a gravestone, she had shrieked and almost wet her pants. She never made it back to the town pier for cider and caramel apples. Instead she had lingered at the back of the group. When they turned to cross the bridge, she dashed madly down the river road, passing Papa Randy and Old Ben smoking weed on the porch, en route to the bathroom. The boys in her homeroom for weeks after had pulled their shirts over their heads, feigning headlessness. "Ooh ahh, Alex, I'm coming to get you!" How did she survive adolescence? Every second was agony.

She inched toward the ticket booth where the ticket vendor Dana was taking money and stamping hands. Dana's face was pierced with the same type of fishhook that she used to catch herring and menhaden for the crab traps. Dana had the demented, cockeyed look of someone who might jump out of the dark and strangle someone. Dana's Goth attire, she supposed, was a costume and her lugubrious demeanor intended to heighten the tension before the ghost walk, but it was no costume and no act. Dana was simply creepy by nature.

Alex willed her mind to safer places. At Ella's request to crab with her, she had almost blurted "Hell yeah!" but she didn't want to sound too desperate. She was burning out; that was the truth of it. With setting traps before work, then putting in an eight-hour-day at the marine lab, followed by pulling traps and dropping off the crabs at the dockside restaurants after work, there was no steam in her engine by the time she returned home to Will and Carly. She had dozed off on Will's shoulder at Carly's dance recital. When was the last time she and Will had sex on a week night? Last year? If Ella would be interested in forming a partnership, maybe pull the traps in the afternoons and make the deliveries in the *Vital Spark* to the dockside restaurants, she would be eternally grateful. Then she might be able to stay awake past eight o'clock. If Ella was game to expand their enterprise, she could show her other places to find big crabs. She knew all the best places because she had crabbed for years with the best of the best... Papa Randy and Old Ben.

A car door slammed in the parking lot and Jay and James stepped out. She had grown fond of Jay while he was dating Julia. He was good company at holiday dinners and summer barbecues on Julia's riverfront beach. Julia had handled the break-up all wrong—disastrously wrong.

"Some excellent grandmotherly advice for ye, lass," Julia had said while blowing smoke rings off the porch. "When it's time to end a fling, make sure it's cataclysmic so there's no turning back."

"Fling? You've been dating him for over two years!"

"Oh. Was it that long?"

James and Jay purchased their tickets and joined Nina and her. Jay must have noticed her anxiety because he gave her hand a reassuring squeeze. She squeezed back. She and Jay were inextricably bound by that tragic day on Mutter Island... when Clyde Whitby shot Will and killed Laura Braden. She—in self-defense—killed Whitby.

One last woman rushed to the ticket booth, paid her money and got her hand stamped.

"Line up by the front door!" Dana shouted. She slammed the window of ticket booth and disappeared into the Ephram Whitson House.

The Chrome Divas shuffled hesitantly toward the colonial house. Linda Radowksi and Blanche Hyde had had enough of each other and stood at opposite sides of the group. The woman who just joined the ghost tour was from the motorcycle convention because she wore scuffed up engineer boots, faded jeans and leather vest over a pink long-sleeved T-shirt. Her long blonde hair was covered by a black and pink skull-and-cross bones bandana. Papa Randy taught her never to be judgmental of people's appearances. "Honey, every woman's beautiful in her unique way." That sentiment caused him to marry six times, Julia being Wife Number One. Alex passed judgment just the same. The blonde biker was the homeliest woman ever. She searched the woman's vest for a club name or a home state, but there was none. The film *Deliverance* sprang to mind; the woman looked like an inbred hillbilly from a remote mountain village. Like she should talk about inbreeding and remote villages. As long as she was not related to Will Wilkins, she didn't care who was sleeping with who in River Glen.

The blonde smiled at her and she smiled back. She thought that she owned every piece of pyrate apparel... *Yo Ho Yo Ho The Pirate's Life for Me* shirts and pajamas and *Surrender the Booty* thongs but no.

"I love your bandana," she said. "Where did you get it?"

"Online, but I don't remember where," the woman replied pleasantly.

The front door of the colonial house creaked and Alex turned. In the doorway stood Ella Winston in a black velvet gown. Black eyeliner accentuated her blue eyes. Her lipstick was blood red. Jay gazed up the steps with a look she had seen on his face many times, when he was watching a sunset, mist on the river or Julia—when lighting on an image of incredible beauty.

"Welcome to my nightmare," said Ella mischievously. "If you would please silence your cell phones and put them away for the tour, the ghouls would appreciate it. Besides, where we're going, there's no cell coverage."

The Chrome Divas fumbled with their phones and stuffed them in pockets and bags. Ella stepped aside and, with a grand sweep of her wing-like sleeve, gestured the group inside.

Alex's heart heaved. She grasped Jay's hand with her sweaty one and proceeded up the steps—into the terrifying unknown.

"Damn that hotel manager Lionel Stevens!" Lisa said to Will. "What the hell is he hiding? Why didn't he give us all of the camera footage for the night of Hadley-Simon's murder? He probably whacked him and is banging Ventresca."

"Stevens is gay," Will said. "I've seen him at the gay bar at the Nauticus."

Lisa raised an eyebrow.

"I know because the bar has awesome hot wings. Alex, Carly and I eat there all the time. Alex and Carly love ukulele music."

"Because of Mr. Stevens, this whole investigation's been delayed. Norman and I should have found Pikachu by now. It was spite on Stevens' part. He gave us camera footage from the main building but not footage from the security booth at the entrance. Why's that? I wonder. What's really going on at the Radcliffe?"

"Stevens claimed that he was protecting client confidentially. I don't buy it. I wasted my entire afternoon going back there for the footage from the security booth." He looked despairingly at the wall clock. "I should be at Carly's swim meet right now. She holds the record in her age class for the butterfly. I shouldn't be reviewing footage that I could have looked at this afternoon!"

"And I haven't seen one frickin' celebrity there. Not even Janet Jackson or Gordon Ramsey! I bet the Radcliffe's PR people make that shit up to attract rich wanna-bes like the Hadleys."

He leaned toward Lisa's computer. "Slow down the scroll speed. It's going too fast. The only person I recognize so far is Chet Hathaway and his golf buddies checking in with the security guard. Hathaway will find Hadley-Simon's body the next morning. He has a nice set of wheels."

"An Escalade," she said. "Tony Soprano's car."

"Look who's following Hathaway's car! You recognize the driver, don't you?"

"Only one thing brings The Madam to town," she chuckled. "Horny men with deep pockets. One, two... five whores are packed into her car."

"That's why Stevens didn't want to release this footage to us. No doubt he took a sweet backhander to look the other way."

There was no activity on the footage for minutes until Lisa blurted "Ha! Too funny! Look who's partying with the hookers? The mayor!"

"Wait, stop scrolling. Who's beside him in the passenger's seat?" He leaned back in his chair. "I should have known! The banker Kenneth Radowksi. He was a few years ahead of me in high school. He was a senior when I was a freshman. We played football together. A complete a-hole."

"Who has a fancy boat at the marina."

"Yup. A DeFever. Alex hates that boat. He's run over her crab traps and doesn't know the boating rules of the road."

Lisa stretched her gum from her mouth and spun it around her finger. "I go to Radowski's bank. Piss me right off! I'm funding his lifestyle of hookers and yachts with the two-dollar-maintenance fee that I'm smacked with every month while my savings account generates three cents a year!"

"I don't remember these guys checking in at the front desk when we reviewed the footage from the lobby."

"Because the horny bastards and their lady friends never checked-in. They probably went directly to one of the time-share condos by the golf course."

"That was a busy night at the Radcliffe," he said. "While an orgy was happening with the River Glen fat cats and ladies-of-the-evening, Hadley-Simon wandered down to the beach to meet the elusive Jennie Wade."

"Jennie, incidentally, does not have a boat at the Smyth Family Marina and did not want to enter through the front gate for fear of being captured on film."

"But she, or he, still could have come by boat. That would explain the absence of footprints other than Hadley-Simon's leading down to the water."

They silently watched the footage scroll by. Nothing notable occurred other than a new security guard starting his shift at 10 pm. The night cleaning crew also arrived around 10. A Lexus of pyrates from the Giles festival entered at 10:24. Two teenaged girls in a Corvette were waved through at 10:43. Around 10:58 a sport bike slowed by the entrance but didn't turn toward the security booth. Instead it disappeared into the darkness.

Lisa rewound the footage and froze the frame where the motorcycle was poised at the entrance. "Weird!"

"What's weird?"

"I swear to God, I don't know how he does it."

"What?"

"Jay. He must have a crook sensor, sixth sense or something." Lisa's fingers pounded the keyboard. "Compare that image to this one."

She had split the screen on her computer. One image was of the motorcyclist at the entrance to the Radcliffe. The second image was captured by the security camera on the bridge during the Giles Blood-hand festival. In it, the biker and her motorcycle were under the shade of the oak tree.

"Jay solved the case in absentia," she said.

Will's eyes bounced back and forth between the two images. The BMW adventure sport bike was present in both. The rider was dressed in black boots and faded jeans and had a single dark braid and a high vis yellow helmet. The only difference was that the woman during the day wore a black leather vest whereas at night it was a leather jacket. That was no surprise; it was often chilly riding at night, even in the summer.

"Lisa, is this the woman Jay texted you about on the night of the Giles festival?"

"Ella Winston. It's gotta be. It's the same motorcycle."

"So Winston's story about the boat was a ploy to get Hadley-Simon alone on the beach. South of the Radcliffe is marshland. She could have parked her bike there, walked through the marsh and along the beach, then climbed over the wall at the Radcliffe's property. The wall's not that high."

Lisa opened new sticks of gum and chewed excitedly. "What a sick, sick puppy! She uses the alias Jennie Wade to buy the phone and send the texts that lure Hadley-Simon to the beach. Then she slashes his throat from behind—leaving a scarlet thread!"

"It's too late to pick her up for questioning today." He stood and pulled off his tie. "If I hurry, I might be able to catch one of Carly's races."

"Let's get Winston first thing tomorrow morning. I'll call the Gettysburg PD so they know we're coming. They'll have an address for her."

"Gettysburg?" he choked.

"I thought I told you. The phone payments were linked to a bank account in Gettysburg. All Norman could find was a Gettysburg P. O. box for Winston's address. An ex-con must be checking in with a parole officer. The police will know her whereabouts."

Will's heart lodged in his throat. His beloved Alex was in Gettysburg, Pennsylvania.

"Step back in time with me," began the tape in Ella's head. "It's July 5, 1863 when the beleaguered armies retreat south. Us citizens of Gettysburg are confronted with a horrific task... fields and fields of putrefying bodies...."

Rather than dead bodies on a battlefield, Ella was taking a head count of live ones stuffed into Ephram Whitson's living room. The twilight tour consisted of twelve customers: women bikers and husbands or boyfriends who had attended the convention as support members. Those she recognized were Alex, Nina, Janice Klein, Linda Radowski, Blanche Hyde, Jay and James. Thankfully there were no brats with lollipops. Because she had arrived to work on time, her stingy bitch of a boss would have no excuse to withhold pay and tips from twelve customers meant that it might be a decent night of wages. This plus her meager savings would be enough to move her stuff to River Glen. Sooner than later. Because future neighbors were present, she decided to give it her all.

"Those with an inquisitive mind might wonder how the Confederate and Union armies wound up in Pennsylvania in 1863 so let's start with a historical snapshot of the times. The South's surging confidence after victories at Chancellorsville and Fredericksburg spurred General Robert E. Lee to move his army into Maryland and Pennsylvania, with the goal to take Harrisburg and Philadelphia, then sweep southward to Baltimore and Washington. However, Lee's ambitious plan was foiled from the start when the two armies stumbled upon each other in the inconsequential village, mostly of buggy makers, called Gettysburg."

That much history caused the average ghost walker's eyes to glaze over so she shifted to the macabre. Since the story of Ephram Whitson and his house was a fabrication—there was not a historical grain of truth to any of it—fabricate she would.

"This house is not right," she said with a hush. "Ephram Whitson was a man of (she paused) unusual tastes." She stepped on a floorboard that Old Man Detrick had loosened decades ago. *Creeaak.* Gasps and nervous whispers filled the tight room. "A state archeologist climbed into the basement to investigate." Always smart to authenticate the creepiness with a bureaucrat. "He rushed out, pale-faced, shaken! He found evidence of disturbing practices. Rusty manacles, black candles, goat horns." Hm, what other objects to raise goosebumps? "Finger bones in a chalice, a baby's mandible. Evidence of devil worship."

"Jay, I'm outta here," whispered Alex from the back of the group.

"There's no turning back now." Ella felt a twinge of guilt at terrifying her future boss. "The good news is that the basement was sealed up, never ever, said the officials, to be opened again. Besides, we're going into the dining room, not into horrid dungeons. At least not tonight. This way please, to Dr. Caleb Morgan's surgery." She gestured the group through the doorway. "Please gather around the table."

Old Man Detrick had done a brilliant job with Dr. Morgan's surgical arena: a heavy wood table covered with a blood-spattered table cloth (who, in the gloom, could tell that it was faded red paint?), old surgical instruments and anesthesia (old whiskey bottles). It was time to graze the hidden switch. The dim lights flickered.

"That must be Robert. He's very shy, the shyest of the three ghosts. Visitors always upset him."

"Th-three?" Alex said to Jay.

"After Ephram Whitson's mysterious disappearance, the house was occupied by his cousin Dr. Morgan and his sixteen-year-old daughter Grace. In 1863 the fighting between the Union and Confederate armies raged for three days. The field hospitals were quickly overwhelmed so soldiers were brought to the village to be cared for. Dr. Morgan was a grim but reputable physician. This makeshift surgery was where he tended to both Union and rebel soldiers. Most procedures were amputations: feet, hands and legs. The body parts were tossed out that window." She pointed to a window covered with black paper. "Bloody, necrotic limbs piled up on the sidewalk outside the doctor's window. Stray dogs were well-fed."

"Sick!" Alex again.

"On July 5, as the two armies retreated, the villagers were left with the dreary task of burying the dead, in fact thousands of men, horses and mules rotting in the fields and forests south of the village. The stench of Gettysburg was smelled from fifty miles away. It was years before the village recovered, but in the short term the exhausted villagers scoured the blood-soaked fields and dragged bodies into shallow graves. But some of the soldiers were not yet dead. That's how Robert Harper from New Hampshire who was discovered in the Wheatfield and Elijah Jones from Pickett's Virginians made it onto this operating table." She lifted the hacksaw. "Dr. Morgan sawed off Robert's leg and Elijah's arm with this very tool."

Alex threw herself into Jay's chest. So that was it. That was the reason that Jay had come to Gettysburg. Not to follow her like Inspector Javert pursing Jean Valjean. This had nothing to do with her. Jay was visiting his young girlfriend Alex Allaway. That's why he had asked her on the River Glen bridge if she would be riding with the Chrome Divas. He was concerned that his sweetheart would be in the presence of an ex-con. His intentions had been cleverly disguised. Ella had mistakenly thought him a lecher hitting on her. Instead he was looking out for Alex. Of course. It now made sense.

Nina had a higher threshold for the ghastly than Alex. She and James had gravitated toward each other and grinned at her every ludicrous word. That's why James and Jay made no passes at Keisha and Sam last night while drinking beers and eating pizza. The men were here visiting girlfriends. This was a double date of sorts. It all made perfect sense.

Ella hit the hidden switch again; lights flickered. "Poor Robert... so shy. He can't tolerate visitors. Let's go upstairs to where the tragedy occurred and where the ghosts are sighted."

There was the usual hesitation until a brave soul ventured up the steps after her. In this case it was the Divas' president.

"I ain't afraid of no ghost," Linda Radowski quipped.

"We're in an episode of Scooby Doo," said Janice Klein.

"I love Shaggy," Blanche Hyde said.

"You would," Janice laughed. "He was a pothead. That's why he was eating all the time. He had the munchies."

There was muffled laughter.

"Shh!" Linda snapped. "I wanna hear about the ghosts."

Following Linda up the stairs was the ugliest woman that Ella had ever seen and there were some pretty rough looking women at Cambridge Springs. The blonde was tall and ungainly and wore a black and pink pyrate bandana. Next came Blanche and Janice, still giggling about Shaggy. The rest of the group dragged themselves up the narrow passage and assembled in the bedroom. Jay, tugging Alex, arrived last.

"This is where Robert and Elijah convalesced after their respective surgeries," she said. "Robert was painfully awkward and spoke to Grace in stammers while Elijah was a boisterous flirt. The soldiers discovered that they had fought each other at Antietam, a battle that resonated terribly with both of them. There Robert had lost his father and cousin and Elijah his twin brother. Now add a beautiful teenager to the mix. Grace brought them their meals, changed their bandages and read them passages from the Bible. Both men fell hopelessly in love with her and hatred brewed in this cauldron of a room that fateful July of 1863.

"Dr. Morgan was at a meeting of the Sanitation Commission the night the fight broke out. Who knows how it started, but Grace heard a commotion upstairs and rushed from the kitchen. Smoke poured from the bedroom where a lantern had presumably overturned. The two wounded men thrashed on the floor while fire climbed the curtains and ignited the straw mattresses. Screams were heard in the street as flames leapt from the windows. The next day three charred bodies were found amidst the debris.

"A grief-stricken Dr. Morgan left Gettysburg for his sister's lighthouse in Maine, never to return to Pennsylvania." She paused for dramatic effect. "Here's where the story gets bizarre. On hot summer nights like tonight residents of the house hear movements... pacing... scratching... knocking in this very room. Paranormal experts have combed the house, measuring unexplained temperature fluxes, sounds, energy fields and vibrations."

Alex squeezed her eyes closed; her fingers plugged her ears. Jay was poised at her side, preparing to catch her should she faint.

"Witnesses who have seen the ghosts report the same thing," she went on. "A stub-armed Elijah dragging an unconscious Grace from the room, a hobbling Robert in vicious pursuit, Dr. Morgan's surgical blade in his hand. This recurrent sight has led ghost chasers to conjecture that Elijah attempted to pull Grace from the fire, but Robert slaughtered them both, then died himself."

The bedroom went black—pitch black. Ella had no idea why.

"I'll never survive menopause," Detective Sharon Westerly told herself. "Besides, I'll kill myself first." Only one thing was going right that evening... the headquarters of the Gettysburg PD was nearly empty so her team didn't have to witness her yanking on and off her suit blazer. "I'm cold, I'm hot... hot cold hot cold. Fuck." Countless times she had walked to the thermostat, checking it for an electronics glitch and each time it read a constant sixty-eight degrees. Her imminent insanity would be caused by her thermoregulatory malfunction. Like that wasn't enough... hot zigs of pain shot across her pelvis every few minutes. Who has their period twice in one month? Her entire paycheck was spent on tampons and her son's data plan to play Pokémon Go. "Swear to God, that game is more addictive than crack cocaine," she muttered. Despite a body gone haywire, there were two positive developments in her otherwise abysmal life: a small profit made on the sale of her house and best of all, the finalization of her divorce from Ralph MacKenzie.

The whole neighborhood was privy to the fact that Ralph was father to the infant Jonathan born to Caroline, the twenty-something-next-door-neighbor. Sharon was a detective, supposedly astute and observant... how did she not see that coming? It was her catastrophically stupid decision to marry a younger man. Her father and brothers never failed to remind her that her marriage was a train wreck waiting to happen. And wreck it did, boulders tumbling down the shattered mountain, crashing onto twisted train cars, fuel igniting... the whole infernal mess burning long into the night.

When she first met Ralph, he was an undergraduate and a football star at the university. He was ecstatically loyal to a football program run by sexual deviants. That should have told her everything. But in a moment of temporary insanity she had agreed to date him. From an intoxicated, regretful night of sex at Devil's Den came her precious son Paul, who she dearly loved, but his computers, game systems (did he really need an Xbox *and* a PlayStation?), elaborate phone and monthly overages were bankrupting her. Retirement might be possible by age ninety-five if she wasn't shot by a cop hater first.

The phone rang. "Gettysburg PD, Detective Westerly here."

Westerly! That singular word a joyous declaration of freedom, escape from servitude, coercion, oppression and every other synonym for slavery. Never again Sharon MacKenzie!

It was the chirpy voice of—uck—a millennial. On and on went the young cop, chattering and gum-smacking into her ear. Ella Winston? Is that what the gum-smacker said? Ella Winston. Not again.

It was Sharon's rotten luck. Pennsylvania was a substantially large state of forty-six thousand square miles and yet three ex-cons had chosen to settle on her patch. It was just what Gettysburg *did not need*—on top of inebriated reenactors, a college of self-absorbed, selfie-snapping students and thousands of bikers during Bike Week—a drug dealer, cat burglar and an art forger. Now Detective Paco of River Glen, Maryland, wherever the hell that puny place was, was crossing state lines to take Ella Winston back to Maryland for questioning in a murder investigation.

"Yes, Winston lives here," she told Paco. "Who was killed? How was the murder committed?"

"Winston's former professor from her art college. He was killed by one well-placed swipe of a blade across the windpipe. Do you have an address for her?"

Sharon hesitated. Murder seemed out of character for Winston though anything could have happened in prison. Prison was a transforming experience. Some repented, but others were hardened. Still, to move from art forgery to murder? That seemed a bit extreme.

"Winston's in a trailer at the Blue and Grey Campground behind the Round Tops," she answered. "I don't know the exact site number, but I know the trailer very well. She lives with two other parolees from Cambridge Springs. When are you coming? I'll be there to assist."

"First thing tomorrow morning," Paco smacked again. "Can we meet at 7:30 am at the campground?"

"Roger that. I'll meet you at the entrance and take you to her trailer."

There was a reason that she knew the location of Ella Winston's campsite and that reason was named Charlette Fern. Charlette had decided to take a sledge hammer to Winston's grill, lawn chairs and picnic table before directing her displeasure at the Airstream. Seeing no end to the destruction, the three ex-cons had dashed to the safety of the camp store and called 911. She and a uniformed officer had responded to the call. Charlette had been impossible to calm; they finally had to cuff her.

"I'm suing you for Alienation of Affection, you bitch!" Charlette screamed at Ella.

"That dick never told me he was married!" Ella shouted back. "I'm suing you for destruction to my property!"

Tony Fern's pickup truck full of whimpering children arrived. "Maybe I forgot to tell Ella about my family" was his lame-ass excuse.

"Maybe, pal?" Sharon said with clenched fists.

Tony Fern was your average lying scumbag and Ella Winston was plain stupid for buying his crap.

She had informed Charlette that Alienation of Affection laws no longer existed in Pennsylvania and suggested the couple seek marriage counseling back in New York despite her personal conviction that the institution of marriage be outlawed. Charlette herded the children into her minivan and yelled through the window "Cheating asshole, get your shit from the house or you'll find it burning on the curb!"

"Mr. Fern," she had growled, "if I see your face in Gettysburg again, we're going to have another conversation. Next time I won't be so polite."

He nodded obsequiously and slunk off to his empty truck. As the Fern vehicles departed, she was sure that she'd be hearing about a homicide in New York that evening. Thankfully that would be in the jurisdiction of the Albany PD. Just another day in marital paradise.

"Oh, by the way, Detective Westerly," said Paco punctuating her remark with a popping bubble. Saliva probably covered Paco's desk in wherever-the-hell-River Glen was. "Winston's been operating under an alias."

"Why does that not surprise me?" she said with a tired sigh. "What is it?"

"Jennie Wade."

"What?"

"Jennie Wade," Paco repeated. "Does that mean something to you?"

"Yes, actually. Jennie Wade was the only civilian killed during the battle of Gettysburg. She died when she was twenty years old. She was making bread for Federal soldiers when a stray bullet pierced her door, then her heart. The Jennie Wade House is a museum and allegedly haunted by Jennie's ghost."

"I ain't afraid of no ghosts," Paco giggled.

"Nope, me either."

"See you at 7:30 tomorrow."

"7:30 it is."

They rung off.

Sharon pulled her suit jacket off the chair and slipped it back on because her body-on-the-fritz was now freezing. She glanced at the wall clock. In a half an hour her shift would be over. Within the hour she would be soaking in a bubble bath in her new condo, then to bed with warm tea and the clicker. Bliss, sheer bliss... reruns of *Downton Abbey* with no husband haranguing her about watching them again. Her killer cramps would not relent so she reached into her desk for two Midols and a tampon. No, it was a three Midol night so she knocked another into her hand. She lifted herself out of the chair and lumbered toward the ladies room. Again.

"You can do it, old girl. Just a half an hour to go."

Déjà vu. Ella had been here before, in this exact place, in this exact gown. Wait, wrong. It was no déjà vu. It was a flashback. In the black silence of the Ephram Whitson House the memory struck like lightning, quick and solitary. Then the frisson was gone, irretrievably gone.

Now any thought of Ian Kent was far from electric; it chilled her blood. Why had any time been spent with him? Ian's sole quest was to make money for: a Jaguar, penthouse overlooking the Delaware River, beach house in Cape May, ski chalet in Utah and private schools for their children. Incredibly they had even discussed a family. Frightening things, children. Her goals were simpler: to pay off student loans, teach art classes and paint. But three things bound her to Ian: a mutual love of art, her mentorship by his uncle Monroe Hadley—and the third.

"Leave the back door open for me, Ellie. The lights must be off," a garbled voice whispered into the phone.

She had waited in the blackness of Robert and Elijah's bedroom, her teenaged heart dancing. Old Man Detrick and Dana had closed up and left hours before. Then she heard it... footsteps climbing the stairs... ever so slow the footsteps. The grasp—hair ankle breast?—always surprised her, but the next gesture was always the same. A hand clamped over her mouth.

"Submit submit. Nod that you understand me. No sounds at all."

Nodding emphatically, she was pulled over to a straw mattress. It was never violent or restrained as submit submit implied. Rough yes, enthralling yes, deathly silent yes. After, the footsteps ever so slowly descended the stairs and disappeared into the night while she panted on the mattress, gown twisted around her waist.

Ella shook herself from the past. This blackness did not bewilder or arouse but was oppressive. She groped her way to the stone fireplace and flipped the light switch. Nothing. She tried again. Nothing still. Were the lights out in town? Maybe the heat wave had taxed the power grid. Was it a brown-out?

"This is super scary," someone whispered.

"We're getting our money's worth," whispered another. "I'm scared shitless."

There was apprehensive laughter and shuffling bodies.

"Ouch, careful! You stepped on my foot!" a voice cried.

"Please don't move," Ella insisted. "I'll get the lights on in a moment."

"It's part of the tour," a woman giggled. "It's Robert. Spooky Robert turned off the lights."

Swish gurgle aghh.

Warm droplets splashed Ella's neck and face. *Thud.* Movement... shifting bodies... "don't shove, jerk!"... patter of feet on stairs... a door squeak.

Silence. Black silence.

"Ella, can you turn the lights on?" Jay said. "Please?"

"I tried. Maybe there's a power outage in town."

"Then I'm turning on my cell phone."

A light from Jay's phone cast the uneasy faces a ghastly blue.

"Oh... my... god...."

Everyone backed away.

A Chrome Diva was sprawled on the floor. Blood oozed from a slice in her throat and crawled up the hem of Ella's black gown.

Alex pressed her face in Jay's chest and squeezed him so hard that air burst from his lungs.

"It's part of the act!" a Chrome Diva laughed perversely. "The woman was a plant in the audience. She's an actress! Brilliant!"

Jay scanned the room and found Ella by the fireplace. Her blue-tinted face was spattered with a glistening dark fluid. She shuddered and stared at the woman on the floor. Either she was a brilliant actress also, or scared out of her mind. The blood and woman's wound, even in the darkness, looked too real.

His own panic skyrocketed. "Ella?"

She shook her head. "No... it's... it's not...."

He struggled to calm his voice. "Not what?"

"N-not an act."

"L-Linda!" cried another Diva. "It's Linda Radowski!"

He whipped his wallet from his pocket and held up his ID. "Police! Please don't move. Turn to the wall, if you need to, but don't move."

Alex, Nina and James clasped each other in a bear hug while he circled the body from a distance to avoid the blood. Zera always castigated him for disturbing a crime scene. Yes, definitely. It was Linda Radowski who ran the insurance agency next to the Chinese restaurant at the strip mall. He'd seen Linda working at her desk when he went to pick up Laura's General Tso's chicken. Linda was married to that prick Kenneth who used to hit on Laura and Julia.

Jay stretched over the expanding puddle and lifted Linda's limp wrist. No pulse. No surprise there. He gazed hard at Ella Winston and called 911.

Sharon Westerly pressed her cell phone to her ear. A 911 had just come in from a dispatcher. "On it." Fuck all. Her evening with a heating pad pressed against her belly just went down the crapper. At the Tobias Worth statue on the corner she yanked the steering wheel to the right, instead of toward her condo. She stomped on the gas pedal. A homicide had been reported at the Ephram Whitson House where Ella Winston was employed.

She first heard the name Ella Winston years ago. Ella, Ella, Ella ad nauseam over every dinner over many years. Her brother Geoff was infatuated with his classmate, "the amazing artist" with pink, green, purple then blue hair, but mostly "her stunning blue eyes."

"Not a bland slate blue like yours, Shar, but a cobalt, maybe cerulean blue."

"Well, thank you very much, baby bro. Turd."

"Dad, she called me—"

"Turd," she said again.

"Sharon honey, your language—"

"Turd, turd, turd."

Stranger yet, right before the breaking news about Baby Jonathan next-door, Ralph had taken Paul for a ghost walk at the Ephram Whitson House, without inviting her. They returned home, buzzing with excitement. Ralph ran to his man cave, rummaged about and reappeared with his yearbook.

"Look, Paul!" he said stabbing his finger into the book. "I told you I went to high school with her. She was hot then too."

Curiosity piqued, Sharon had peered over Ralph and Paul's shoulders. The page appeared like a stamp collection of black and white headshots. It was impossible to discern Winston's hair color du jour or eye color that was so much more spectacular than own. She remembered being mildly unimpressed—BFD a smiling teenager—and never thought about Ella Winston until the incident at the campground with Charlette Fern. She had been taken aback when the woman dressed in a ragged T-shirt and faded jeans had said her name was Ella Winston. Winston was shaky and teary-eyed and anything but the stunner who had weakened the knees of her brother, husband and teenaged son.

Now this.

Police cruisers screamed toward the Ephram Whitson House and the CSI van lurched into the parking lot behind her unmarked sedan. Distraught women from the women's bike convention at the Four Score and Seven huddled by their motorcycles. She glanced at the ticket booth. Not her again. She had arrested Dana Detrick twice for shoplifting at the Walmart and Dana's old man for relic hunting in the battlefield, before his disappearance. Some of her detectives speculated that the shyster father had fled south-of-the-border to evade the IRS. Others guessed that a shady black-market-relic sale had gone terribly wrong. No one had seen hide nor hair of him for years. That was a good thing as far as she was concerned. It was one less scumbag on her patch.

Now what? A busybody tourist with snow-white hair was meddling with the uniformed officers. His was the most garish tropical shirt that she had ever seen. Not far from the busybody was Ella Winston in a slinky black gown. White and black make-up and blood streaked her face. Ghoulish indeed.

She climbed from her sedan into a Tim Burton movie. The scene was that surreal... biker chicks, tourists in horrible shirts and the Darling of the Dead herself. Upon graduating from the police academy, she had put in requests for PDs in Lancaster, Harrisburg and York but no—hers was the miserable luck of being assigned to her hometown where her father and uncle had been police officers. Hers was the thankless job of arresting friends, family and neighbors. Her whole career had been one big cluster fuck and three Midols had done nothing to diminish the bonfire raging in her uterus.

The pimply new recruit Trooper Hastings approached, saluted and awaited orders.

"Get statements, names and addresses of everyone here," she said. "I want to know exactly what happened."

"Yes, ma'am!" He scurried off.

At the CSI van she pulled a sterile jumpsuit over her slacks and blouse which meant that her body temperature would be three hundred degrees instead of her usual two hundred. She sensed a presence behind her.

"What?"

The tourist in the tacky shirt pulled a police ID from his pocket. "Detective Jay Braden from the River Glen PD."

Jesus Christ. Just what she needed... an interloper trying to pull rank. River Glen? Is that what he said? "River Glen, Maryland?"

"Yes."

"And you're doing *what* in Gettysburg, *Mr.* Braden?"

"I'm visiting the battlefield and hiking with my dogs."

"You're here in a civilian capacity? Vacationing?"

"Yes, but I was there... I can tell you exactly what...."

"Thank you," she said brusquely. "I need you to tell Trooper Hastings exactly what happened." She pointed to the young officer.

Braden's eyes narrowed. No doubt he was inwardly calling her bitch, cunt, dyke or other misogynist slur that she'd been called over the years. Sticks and stones, fucker. She bolted into the house.

Bloody footprints descended a warped staircase as she climbed up it to the crime scene. The bedroom was a literal and figurative bloody mess and Braden's mention of River

Glen made it impossible to concentrate fully on the situation at hand. Her first impulse had been to ask him about Lisa Paco and the murder investigation, but that would have led to irrelevant banter that at the moment there was no time for. It could wait. Was Braden really on vacation or undercover, checking out something in Gburg? He was suspicious, very suspicious.

The medical examiner Dr. Gordon Lombardo and his assistant Dr. Warren Goldstein were bent over the dead woman. The bedroom contained two straw mattresses and a wood table with a water pitcher and bed pan. The mattresses had acted like giant sponges drawing up the victim's blood. It was a tight space; she wasn't sure where to stand because a forensic scientist was clicking rapid-fire photographs of the walls and floor. Another man was dusting the doorframe for prints.

Lombardo handed her a plastic evidence bag with the decease's wallet, glasses and motorcycle keys. "Radowski, Linda. An insurance agent from River Glen, Maryland."

River Glen. Why of course.

"She died instantly," Lombardo said flatly. "Exsanguination from the carotids and jugulars and asphyxiation from a severed trachea."

"Weapon?"

He handed her a second bag and she held it to the light. Inside it was an old-fashioned barber straight razor, about four inches across.

"The last time I saw one of these was in *Sweeney Todd*," she said. "I hate musicals."

"Oh, but you should see *Hamilton*, Sharon," said Goldstein looking up from the body. "I took the kids to see it last weekend on Broadway. It was outstanding. Didn't you love it, Gordie?"

"Yes, but *Man of La Mancha* will always be my favorite. *To dream the impossible dream*," Lombardo crooned. "I'm terribly tone deaf, I know. In my next life I'm going to be Pavarotti."

"Anything else... about the victim?" she asked.

"Not yet. Not until we complete a post-mortem," Lombardo said. "I'll send you the report as soon as it's done."

"I'll be outside. I'll have a look around the place after the body's been removed."

"I'm serious, Sharon," said Goldstein. "*Hamilton.* Don't miss it."

"Okay," she said departing.

She dropped the evidence bags at the CSI van and peeled off the jumpsuit as her body plummeted to a subzero temperature. The parking lot was in chaos... weeping ghost walkers, tense policemen and the press gawking from behind the yellow crime scene tape. Where to even begin? The job rarely overwhelmed her, but she had lost too much blood that day.

Trooper Hastings, on the adrenaline high of his first murder investigation, flew across the parking lot. "Commander, here's the list of individuals in the room when the lights went off."

She scanned the names and addresses. Twelve people, including Ella Winston, had been on the ghost tour. Winston had listed her address as the Blue and Grey Campground so she had told the truth about that. The three males were associated with the eight women from the biker convention. The females were from the Chrome Divas motorcycle club from—well how interesting—River Glen.

"Detective Braden drew this for us," said Hastings handing her a second piece of paper. "This is where everyone was standing when the lights went off."

It was a map of sorts and helpful, if any of it was true. The names of the customers were grouped in front of Winston. That made sense since the ghostly tour guide was tantalizing them with a story of the supernatural. The whole story was a crock of bullshit. She had wikied Ephram Whitson after Ralph and Paul's evening there. No Ephram Whitson existed. Ever.

E. Winston, as designated on the map, was between the table and fireplace. Next to E. Winston was the victim L. Radowski and one B. Hyde. J. Braden and A. Allaway were farthest from E. Winston, across the room by the door. Next to J. Braden and A. Allaway were J. Collins and N. Vega.

Sharon searched the crowd for Braden. He was with three young adults by a retro motorcycle with a Union Jack sidecar and a blue sport bike. A nerdy thirty-something male was hugging a nerdy latina and a woman in leopard skin chaps. Braden was consoling Winston. He gazed over Winston's shoulder at her. She returned his gaze; their eyes jockeyed briefly.

Good cop or bad cop? Meddler or decent guy? It was time to find out. She strode over to the River Glen contingency. Introductions were made while she scrutinized their positions on the map. James Collins: polite lawyer. Nina Vega: equally polite academic. Alex Allaway: high strung, fashion-challenged marine biologist. Jay Braden: big fish in a little pond, ditto on fashion-challenged.

"Ella, how do you know these folks?"

Winston sniffed. "From doing research at the River Glen Historical Society and riding with the Chrome Divas."

Nina Vega, Alex Allaway and James Collins nodded in unison. How convenient.

"How do you know Mr. Braden?"

"Just from around River Glen."

"Pathetic answer, Ella. Really?"

"My dog Clark..." Braden butt in, "... is fixated with Ella. We met on the River Glen Bridge. Clark...."

"Yeah, yeah, okay. This is no time for a dog story. Ella, tell me what happened in the house tonight."

"Um, I led the group through Dr. Morgan's surgery in the dining room and upstairs to the bedroom where Robert, Elijah and Grace died. Then the lights went out."

"I know this house has all sorts of gizmos for special effects. You didn't cause the lights to go off?"

A guilty grimace appeared on Winston's face. "I can't divulge trade secrets or Dana will—"

"You goddamn better!"

Winston balked.

A wildfire of pain blazed across Sharon's pelvis at that second, her uterus strangling her vagina and bladder... a physiological phenomenon previously unknown to medical science. Her tampons were in her purse in the sedan—if only she could get to the ladies' room next to the ticket booth. Her patience was gone.

"Ella, we're continuing this chat at headquarters."

"Okay, okay! I can control the lights flickering on and off and I step on loose boards to make creaking sounds. In the hallway at the end of the tour, where holograms of the three ghosts appear, I turn on a cold draft of air, but we never got to that part because—"

"The lights went off in the bedroom."

Winston nodded. "People laughed and made jokes like it was part of the tour. Someone was moving about. I tried to turn the lights on, but there was no power. Someone was definitely moving. Someone's foot got stepped on. Then came a horrible gurgling sound dend a thump near my feet."

"Someone left through the door," Braden said. "I felt a breeze."

"I felt it too," said Alex Allaway.

Sharon studied the map again. Braden and Allaway were closest to the door. Or so they said.

"It sounded like someone crept down the stairs," Winston explained. "There was the squeak of a door downstairs. I thought it might be Dana in the downstairs hallway. She listens to the ghost story sometimes. To check if I'm doing my job."

Dana Detrick was smoking a cigarette by the ticket window. That interview, Sharon decided, would be postponed for as long as possible because Detrick did not own a toothbrush or a bar of soap.

"Ella, does this look like the position of the twelve people when the lights went out?" she asked handing her Braden's map.

"Twelve?" blurted a wide-eyed Allaway. "There were thirteen of us! That's how I knew the evening was going to be a disaster. Unlucky thirteen!" She searched the parking lot. "The blonde biker with the pyrate bandana wasn't there when the lights went back on!"

Sharon Westerly stirred. The clock on her bedside table glowed 12:35 pm and Paul was clattering about in the kitchen cooking pizza. On top of everything else, her stomach growled. He would be up all night, streaming movies and burning through the data plan. If she had had half a brain, she would have negotiated Paul's data usage into the child support payments. Plain stupid. The over-the-counter pain meds had done nothing to alleviate her cramps so she popped a codeine prescribed for Ralph's broken ankle. The only perk of having a jock for an ex-husband were the painkillers left in the medicine cabinet when he disembarked. The pill would provide the knockout blow, but until then her thoughts were stuck at the crime scene.

Dana Detrick had been next door at Wendy's having two double cheeseburgers, a milkshake and jumbo fries while Ella Winston was conducting the twilight ghost tour. Footage from Wendy's security camera showed Detrick stuffing herself at the corner table for the entirety of the ghost walk. When the police cruisers roared into the parking lot of Ephram Whitson House, she had rushed out, leaving food wrappers littering the table.

"This blows!" Detrick had ranted to her detectives. "I'm gonna lose revenue from the ten o'clock ghost walk! Do you know how fucking hard it's gonna to be to remove blood from a hardwood floor!" It was irrelevant to her that a woman had just lost her life. It was all about the bottom line.

After the removal of Linda Radowski's body, Sharon had walked through the house with a glazy-eyed Ella Winston. She had permitted Jay Braden to join them because he was the only one, besides her, thinking straight. He had mentioned a long stint on the Baltimore PD before moving to River Glen which meant that he had seen everything. Winston had rambled incoherently about squeaky boards and hidden switches while she and Braden entered the bedroom and sidestepped the blood and sticky footprints.

The bedroom glowed a sickly yellow from CSI's lamps and resembled a movie set—from a horror movie. Long ago the single window had been covered with black contact paper by Old Man Detrick so not a ray of outside light could penetrate. Braden pointed out the position of the customers. Winston had been standing between the fireplace and table. Sharon had flipped the switch under the table. It was dead. She tried the switch next to the fireplace. Also dead.

"When the lights went off, it was darker than pitch," Braden said.

"Then how did the killer see?"

He shook his head.

As the three of them left the house, Trooper Hastings rushed up to her. "Ma'am, ma'am!" A plastic evidence bag jittered in his gloved hands. In it was an unrecognizable electrical device.

"What the hell is it?"

"It was attached to the fuse box! That's what shut the lights off. The killer must have had a remote in her pocket which triggered the lights to turn off."

"Show me."

They hurried behind the house. The cellar doors were open so she followed Hastings inside.

"The device was attached right here!" he pointed to the fuse box. "The device shorted out the entire panel, flipping all the switches."

"Does Detrick keep the cellar doors locked?" she asked him.

"Closed but not locked."

"Get CSI in here to dust for prints."

"On it!" Hastings rushed out of the cellar, skipping steps at a time.

She slogged up after him. "I was never that young," she muttered to Braden waiting at the top step.

"Me neither." He lowered his voice. "These biker women usually wear their hair in braids. Both Linda Radowski and Ella Winston had their hair in one braid."

Winston had returned to the River Glen folks by the Royal Enfield and sidecar and the blue Suzuki. Braden was right. Her brown hair was bound in a long braid. Radowski's braid had appeared like a brown snake in a red pool. The killer might have been after Radowski and hit the mark—or was the killer after Winston?

"A UHaul nearly ran Ella off the road near Taneytown," Braden whispered again.

"When?"

"Yesterday. And today when we were touring the battlefield, a motorcyclist was following us in the distance. I only noticed because I had binoculars."

Interesting. But what if Braden was making this up to deflect scrutiny from Ella? Why trust him? Was he misleading her with the map and stories about UHauls and mystery riders?

Ralph's codeine kicked in and Sharon's mind drifted from the crime scene to that wispy place where essential clues... UHauls, braids and motorcycles... vanished in a narcotic fog. Tomorrow it will all make sense. What was she doing tomorrow... in all the confusion... what... what was it? Right. Detective Paco was arriving to interview Ella Winston. About what? She was so so tired. Float... drift... dream.

Bossy, bossy, Ella thought to herself. Jay Braden was just plain bossy. First he objected to her riding her motorcycle back to the campground for fear that a UHaul would emerge from the darkness and run her down. Perhaps he had a point so she agreed to drive back to the campground in his car. Second, he ordered James Collins stay at the hotel with Nina and Alex. "Just as a precaution. Safety in numbers." That meant following their motorcycles back to the Four Score and Seven Hotel.

The evening had unnerved everyone including James. "I have no stomach for this!" he admitted on the ride car to the hotel. "Law school never prepared me for murder. I'm a wills and estates lawyer, not a criminal lawyer." On and on he blabbed about this and that, about his half-sister Alex, her boyfriend Will and daughter Carly, and Nina who was a sociology professor at the local college. Jay Braden was the former boyfriend of his grandmother Julia who was in

Scotland caring for a dying aunt. Once at the hotel James climbed out and rushed over to Nina and Alex.

"Do not leave each other for one moment," Braden called out the car window. "Not one moment." He pulled away only when the trio had passed safely through the front entrance.

She and Braden drove back to the campground in a dismal silence.

"You and I will stay together since I'm your self-appointed bodyguard," he finally said.

Yeah, right. He was guarding her until Sharon Westerly and the prison van arrived.

"We'll stay in my tent," he added. "No one will come near us without the dogs going berserk. The UHaul incident, motorcyclist in the battlefield and Radowski's murder might be connected. I don't want to spook you, but it's better to face the facts. You might have been the killer's intended target, not Linda Radowski."

"That had crossed my mind."

"That's why I want you to be on guard and watchful at all times. Until the police catch this psycho."

"I need a shower," she said. "No way I'm washing off the blood of a dead person in my trailer. I'll curse the place. I'll use the bathhouse."

"I'll watch the door. Just in case."

"Just in case? In case what? Like I'm not spooked already!"

They swung by her Airstream where he flipped on the lights and peered inside. The trailer was empty because he had told Sam and Keisha to sleep in town at the Lincoln Hotel for the night. Bossy bossy.

"The coast is clear," he said.

"That's a relief."

She'd half expected the psycho to lunge at her from the dark. She picked up fresh clothes and toiletries and headed into the bathhouse. She stripped and stepped into a shower stall. One benefit of Sam and Keisha working at a hotel was 'free' soap, tiny as it was. Her vigorous scrubbing washed away the blood and make-up. Gone also was her black gown, now on its way to a crime lab. Gone and done with. Good riddance. Her days of ghost walks were finito. Unlucky thirteen, Alex had said. That was the truth.

What a messed-up reversal of luck! That day had a pleasant enough start—the walk through the battlefield in the morning and lighthearted conversation and hotdogs around the fire in the afternoon. Her plan for the evening had been to give the twilight- and ten o'clock ghost tours and with tip money head to the Four Score and Seven for a drink at the tiki bar with Alex, Nina and the Chrome Divas. Then Linda Radowski collapsed to the floor and she was splattered with blood! No doubt Sharon Westerly, Ralph's ex, thought her the murderer. The blade was found right by *her* feet. Blood was all over *her* face and *her* chest. No one else had a drop of blood on them yet she was covered with it!

Was the killer the woman in the pyrate bandana who had slipped out? Or was that woman terrified of the dark, too embarrassed to admit it, then fled in panic? Perhaps when the police located her, the woman would explain that the ghost story was too intense... her heart was seizing... she had to leave. It wouldn't be the first time that had happened. That meant that one of the eleven Chrome Divas or male support members in the parking lot was The Slasher. It couldn't have been Alex, Nina, James or Jay because they were across the room by the door. Who? Who? It had to be the homely blonde who left. Why kill Linda? Or was she the target?

What disastrous luck! She was going to take the fall for this—she could sense it. Just like the stolen document from the National Archives. She rubbed the soap over herself again. It was a miracle that the cops had let her go back to the campsite with Braden instead of hauling her off that moment. Westerly was probably at the police station, feverishly compiling the evidence and paperwork to make the arrest. At any second squad cars would scream into the campground, red and blue lights flashing, and she would be cuffed and dragged away. No minimum security prison like Cambridge Springs next time. It would be Muncy, the maximum security prison for all the capital cases. The rest of her life would be spent with murderers, psychopaths and sociopaths.

Should she make a break for it? Unfortunately, her motorcycle was at the Ephram Whitson House which meant an escape by foot over the Round Tops and out to Route 15. It was no use. Helicopters would be circling the night skies over Gettysburg, men with night vision goggles and dogs would stalk her through the forest. She would be captured within minutes and spend the night in a cinderblock holding cell. Those accommodations were all too familiar.

Yes, it would be Muncy. It's probably what Braden and Westerly had been whispering about behind the house. He had probably agreed to watch over her until Westerly had the documents in order to make the arrest. She was already on record as an art forger, document thief and home wrecker—why not add throat-cutting to her resume?

Ella peered around the shower curtain. With the mirrors fogged up, it was impossible to tell if the blood and make-up had been washed away. They had to be; she had washed her face ten times. Braden was smacking and cursing at mosquitoes in the doorway of the bathhouse.

Guard the door. Yeah, likely story. He was blocking her escape.

"You okay? You haven't gone down the drain yet?" he said through the steam.

"I'm done." She turned off the water and dried off. She slipped out of the shower in her towel and headed to her clothes on a bench. "Don't look."

"I'm a gentleman. I wouldn't dream of it. But hurry up. I'm getting eaten by mosquitoes."

"What time is it? I have no concept of time."

"Almost one."

She pulled on clean clothes and brushed her teeth. Braden walked her back to her trailer where she picked up her sleeping bag and pillow.

"Don't you think the trailer would be safer?" she said glancing about. "I can just imagine a giant blade tearing through the canvas of your tent, then—"

"You imagine too much. The person's been following you. She might know where you live."

"Maybe she's watching us right now?"

"She's running for the hills right now. The dogs will alert us if anyone comes near the tent."

They returned to his campsite.

"Now I need a shower." He grabbed a towel and his shaving kit. "Please stay in the doorway the whole time. Please Ella, will you do that for me? Please?"

"Alright."

He disappeared into the men's side of the bathhouse. The shower squeaked on. She peeked inside. His clothes were on a bench. If she was to make a run for it, now was the time. His car keys were in his shorts pocket; she had watched where he put them. If she tiptoed in and grabbed his keys, she could motor from the campground and floor it down Route 15. But by then he would have called Sharon Westerly. They would have set up roadblocks before she even hit the Maryland state-line. Flight would be an admission of guilt.

A guttural shriek burst from the woods. She jumped backwards into the men's room. *What the hell was that?!* A screech owl? Her mind playing tricks on her? She strained to listen. Nothing. It was nothing. Really. Nothing. It was only her imagination. She squinted into the forest, but all she saw were smoky orange campfires between black pillars of trees. Was someone watching her at that moment? No, impossible. The killer was running for the hills like Braden said.

It was best to give Braden the benefit of the doubt. Maybe he *did believe* that she was not the killer. Maybe he *did believe* that it was that blonde biker who killed Linda Radowski. Maybe he meant what he said... that she was in danger, he would be her bodyguard. Except that he was guy and therefore a liar and trying to get into her shorts. The next thing she would hear was that tired pickup line, "Oh Ella, your beautiful blue eyes," code for 'I want to fuck you senseless.' Maybe Sharon Westerly was making an arrest at this moment. Maybe tomorrow Braden would drop her off in town to get her motorcycle. Then she would pack it up and ride back to River Glen with Alex and Nina. In the best-case-scenario she would learn to crab from Alex by tomorrow afternoon.

The drizzle of water stopped and Braden rustled behind the shower curtain. He stepped out with a towel around his waist and paused at her presence in the men's room. For an older guy, he had a very nice body. Trim waist, muscular shoulders, arms and pecs. His short white hair stuck up in wet spikes.

"Don't look," he said imitating her. "Or look. What do I care?"

"I'm a lady. I wouldn't dream of it. But hurry up. I'm getting eaten by mosquitoes."

"If you want to get lucky on a date," the psychology professor had said, "take your date to a horror movie. Three

Fs work because of the same neuronal wiring. Fight. Flight. Fornication."

Ella remembered the professor's comments like it was yesterday. It was a lecture on the sympathetic nervous system and the fight-or-flight response. Now she was lying in a tent next to a man—worse a cop—that she hardly knew with F words preoccupying her, frustrating her, keeping her awake.

"These puny little fans do nothing to move the hot air," complained Braden.

"Puny and little are redundant." She had to agree with him; the battery-operated fan-lanterns hanging from bungee cords were less than useless.

"It's too goddamn hot." He ripped off his T-shirt and heaved it into the corner, leaving him clad in plaid boxers.

"This is a horrible idea. That demented slasher..."

"Demented slasher is also a redundancy."

"... is probably deciding at this second which of her many exotic blades she's going to use to slice through the tent."

"That's just what she's doing," he said sarcastically. He slapped at a mosquito. "Fucker."

Another F word. It was the darkness of the Ephram Whitson House that had roused her salacious thoughts. *Submit submit.* Ian had been such a turn-on in that dark room. Then the strange thing. When they had later cohabitated in Philly, the sex was... well, different. Not edgy and passionate. In truth, Ian was pathetic in bed. When she had suggested that they play the *submit submit* game, to spice things up a bit, he became surly and uncommunicative. He would put on his jacket and walk around Center City for hours.

Then, while fantasizing about *submit submit*, Linda Radowski dropped dead at her feet! Worse still, Sharon Westerly aka Sharon MacKenzie, of all of the cops on the

Gettysburg police force, appeared at the crime scene which replayed her night with Ralph at Devil's Den when they were high school students. She was never much of a party animal. She had had the occasional beer with her girlfriends or a glass of champagne at a family celebration. Plain and simple, she was a lightweight. It was a beautiful moonlit evening when Ralph pulled a bottle of wine from his backpack. That loosened her right up. Then came the final blow... literally. He pulled a vial of white powder from his pocket.

She had jerked up from the blanket. "No, no way."

"One little sniff. Just one," Ralph coaxed. "C'mon, Ellie, you'll feel so good."

She caved and took a snort. Whoa! Wonderful! She was suddenly in the mood. What was the word for horny magnified to the nth degree, then doubled?

Now she was in a dark tent with a man who looked just like Clint Eastwood—and she was too wired and anxious to sleep. She flipped and flopped on her sleeping bag.

"Can't sleep?" he said.

"No. You?"

"It's too damn hot."

"It's hot."

"We could take off more clothes," he said jokingly.

"We could do that."

"You first then."

"You take them off me. I dare you."

"No, I'll watch."

What to do? Really? Should she do it? It had been ages since... but the stuffy tent was not the setting for a tantalizing striptease. The low ceiling and useless fans made it impossible to stand up and her clothes were an unglamorous tank top and gym shorts. How could she think finesse at a time like this? Her vagina—or was it her uterus?—some organ between her legs was pulsing. Just do it! She whipped off her shirt and shorts and heaved them into the corner with his rejected shirt. He tore off his boxers and yanked his sleeping bag next to hers. She expected him to jump on her at that very second, but instead he lay on his side with his head propped on his hand.

"Okay, be that way." She propped herself in the same position, mirroring him. Her eyes roamed down his body. It was not too dark to notice that he was very glad to see her.

"You make the first move," he said.

"You."

"No."

"Then tell me something sexy."

"Okay. It's about you."

"But if you say anything about my eyes, all bets are off."

"What blue eyes? I never noticed."

"Go on."

"The single sexiest thing I ever saw you do is..." he whispered.

"What?"

He said nothing.

Her heart pounded. "What!"

"When you're by your motorcycle." His hand stroked her thigh. "And you take this beautiful leg and swing it over the seat of your bike, straddling—"

"You just made the first move."

"I'm helplessly weak."

"I'm making the second move."

She slid on to his sleeping bag. At daybreak cop cars might wail into the campground and drag her off to an endless eternity at Muncy. This might be her last night with a man. Forever. Better make it a good one.

Chapter 6
Broken

The jangle of dog tags roused Jay just after sun up. Despite the lack of sleep, he felt absolutely refreshed. In fact, invigorated. During the night, when he had escorted Ella to the bathhouse—she had to pee and he was her bodyguard after all—they had ended up cooling off in the shower. She was still asleep on her rumpled sleeping bag. He couldn't resist. He twisted her hair off her shoulders, kissed the nape of her neck and down her spine, culminating with a kiss on each perfect ass cheek. She murmured from a dream place.

A car door slammed. It had to be James who had taken a cab from the hotel. It explained the opening and closing of a single door. James was familiar to the dogs. Otherwise they would be howling and clawing at the screen of the outer room. Of all the ironies, it was James who had come to Gettysburg to get laid, but instead it was his lucky night and hopefully not the last. She was perfect. They were perfect together. Everything perfect. Beyond perfect.

The screen door unzipped. It was definitely James taking the dogs for a walk. Only this morning he prayed that James would not leave the cooler open so that Miranda could raid it. The last thing he wanted to do on this perfect morning was clean up puke paddies. He was sure that he had placed the cooler on the picnic table and out of Miranda's reach.

Ella gave him a sleepy smile. "Good morning." She outstretched her arms and pulled his head into her breasts. His ear rested on her heart. The *thumpa thumpa* pacified him. If he could stay like this, unmoving. Here.

More car doors slammed. Clark and Miranda barked. Ella tightened.

"The people next door have dogs," he whispered. "It's nothing. It's just James walking about."

"Are you sure?"

"The slasher's not going to attack in broad daylight."

"Sir?"

That was not James' voice outside the canvas. Nor did James ever call him Sir.

Jay's head sprang up. "Will?"

So that's it. Alex must have called Will last night. Will would have rushed to see if Alex was okay, after having dropped Carly off at the grandparents' house for the day. But why was Will in the campsite? Maybe killing time while Alex and Nina packed their bikes? Yes, Alex had probably told Will that he was at the campground.

"Yes, sir," Will whispered. "We're here to pick up the suspect in the murder investigation of Seymour Simon."

He shook away the cobwebs. "Who?"

"The thief Seymour Simon who went by the alias Monroe Hadley."

Ella shoved him off.

"Her trailer is on this loop," Will said.

Hadley? That name was so familiar. Why? Who the hell was Hadley?

Ella scrambled on all fours in a mad search for her clothes. Her alarm was contagious. He jumped to his feet, slamming his head into the lantern-fan. "Ouch!" She whipped on her shorts and shirt at lightning speed. He tripped on the sleeping bags. Where were his goddamn boxers?

Monroe Hadley was Ella's thesis advisor! That was the name she mentioned on the battlefield walk! He's dead?

"The police have surrounded her trailer," Will whispered again. "She must be asleep. It's very quiet down there. Her name's Ella Winston."

Ella's incredulous stare turned molten. Her lips moved silently, then words were audible. "You set me up... here to spy on me... you shit!"

"I don't know... what... I don't know!" he sputtered.

A furious sweep of her arm unzipped the tent flaps and she rushed into the screened room. She searched the nylon floor for her flip-flops, but the dogs had chewed up them up during the night. He pulled up his boxers and lunged through the tent flaps after her. She ducked through the outer tent flaps and froze. So did he. An impenetrable wall of bodies—the giant Will Wilkins, Lisa Paco smacking gum, a dour Detective Westerly and the gangly trooper Denny—blocked the way. Ella looked desperately toward her campsite as if to seek refuge there, but police cruisers were parked at her trailer.

"Braden, you user... you shit!" Ella pushed through the barrier of police officers and headed toward the bathhouse. "I'm washing that slime off of me. If I'm lucky, one of you will put a bullet in my brain and put me out of my misery."

A bullet in the brain. Jay's knees wobbled. *Clyde Whitby had slaughtered Laura with a bullet to the brain. He had raced his boat to Mutter Island, staggered over the gunwale, dashed across the beach but...*

"Let her shower," said Westerly.

"I'll watch the bathhouse," Paco volunteered.

Ella lifted a lawn chair and folded it, then disappeared from view behind the officers.

Westerly leapt aside. "Duck!"

... around Laura's head was a halo of sandy blood...

Jay saw it—hurling at him—a spinning disc of silver. But too late. Crack blackness. "What the—!" He found himself in the dirt. Pain surged across his face and a hot fluid streamed across his eyelids and cheeks. He reached gingerly for his nose. There was a crack between his nasal bones and cartilage. He wiped away blood that was pooling in his eyes. Two silhouettes peered down at him and blocked the sunlight through the tree canopy.

Lisa Paco could barely contain a grin. "#busted."

The second person leaning over him was Sharon Westerly. He half-expected her to offer him a hand-up, but instead she said "You so deserved that." She walked away with a frown of disgust.

What the hell just hit him? What knocked him off his feet? He wiped more blood from his nose and eyes. A lawn chair lay next to him. His sweetheart flung a chair at him. It was a direct hit. She had a great arm after all.

At least Detectives Westerly and Paco had the decency to let her shower and change into clean clothes in her trailer. Ella's initial thought was to pack a duffel bag of clothes, but why bother? Where she was going her attire would be an orange jumpsuit. All she needed was a cell phone for her One Call.

Ella scribbled a note to Sam and Keisha saying that the Airstream was theirs, if they wanted the piece of junk. Last payments for it could be sent to Uncle Lyle. She flung the pen on to the table. Done. That was the end of all financial worries. Where she was going she would be fed, housed and given healthcare until the day she died, if that was any consolation.

Westerly and Paco stood apprehensively against her kitchen counter as though she might throw something at them or pull out a gun and start shooting, except that she had never held a gun in her life and the only approximation of a weapon was the fly swatter over the sink. Anyway, the trailer was too stifling hot for physical exertion. Westerly obviously thought the same and pulled off her blazer. She was wearing a shoulder holster and revolver underneath. Paco had a gun on her belt. Guns were no match for a fly swatter; it was a pathetic idea in the first place.

How could she think straight? Guns? Fly swatters? She had lost her mind and her will for anything—like life. With any luck, a serial killer at Muncy would take an instant dislike to her and kill her within days of her arrival. She could only hope.

The heat also got to Paco because she rolled up the sleeves of her uniform. Like Sam and Keisha, Paco had tattoos down to her wrists. As an artist, one would think that the ink artwork might hold some fascination, but she would soon be surrounded by tattooed women. So many lifetimes to look at flash, tribal, native American and military tats... how many lifetimes would she be given for killing both Linda Radowski and Monroe Hadley? Hadley was a thief called Seymour Simon? Isn't that what Detective Wilkins had said?

Paco blew another obnoxious bubble and held out her cell phone to Westerly. "I found Dragonite and Mewtwo last night."

"My son Paul found Blastoise and Charizard," said Westerly with an exasperated sigh.

"Sweet. Do you play?" Paco asked Westerly.

"No. It sucks up too much data."

Paco stared back at her phone. "I have the unlimited plan."

What the hell was a Blastoise? Ella wondered. Clearly the cops were talking in code. She circled the cramped space one last time. "I'm ready."

Westerly and Paco escorted her back to the men's campsite where a Maryland State Police cruiser awaited. A trooper called Denny cuffed her. "Cuz you assaulted a police officer, but he's not pressin' charges."

Ella laughed derisively. "Like an assault charge on top of two life sentences is going to make a damn bit of difference!"

The Royal Enfield and blue Suzuki were parked by the tents. It was mortifying to be paraded in handcuffs in front of Alex, Nina and James. In the less than remote chance that she did get off, Alex would never teach her to crab. James would never allow her access to the historical records. Nor would she be welcome to ride with the Chrome Divas. James and Nina sat awkwardly at the picnic table while Alex was in a hot conversation out of earshot with Detective Wilkins. The Shithead and his two dogs were thankfully absent. He was off gloating about the big score between her legs, perhaps anticipating a promotion, citation, maybe even a plaque.

Ella climbed into the back seat of the cruiser and the door slammed behind her. Denny and Paco clipped themselves into the front seat while Wilkins squeezed himself into the back next to her. She turned suddenly to a tapping sound by her ear. Alex's splayed hand pressed against the window and she gestured with her eyes that Ella reciprocate.

"Ella, we crab by the end of the week!"

Alex's unrealistic optimism and kindness hit like an avalanche. She placed her cuffed hand over Alex's on the glass. Alex had admired her motorcycle and she had no more use for it. "My bike, Alex! Take it. It's yours."

Alex adamantly shook her head. "Where is it? The keys?"

"It's behind the Ephram Whitson House. The keys are on my kitchen windowsill. Take it, please. It's a gift."

"I'm bringing it to you!"

The cruiser backed out of the campsite and Ella looked out the back window. An inscrutable Sharon Westerly, arms folded across her chest, watched her. She was wrong about Muncy. This would be the last time she would see Pennsylvania. The rest of her days would be lived out in a women's prison in Maryland.

Never shed a tear, Ella reminded herself. Tears are blood. You bleed and sharks tear you limb to limb.

Sharon was all too happy to open up the Airstream and give Ella's motorcycle keys to Alex Allaway. It would be one less chore that the Gburg PD would have to oversee... the removal of the BMW from the parking lot of the Ephram Whitson House. The bizarre motorcade: a Maryland State cruiser, a blue Suzuki and Union Jack Enfield-sidecar combo disappeared from the campground. Good riddance.

If Casanova and James Collins would pack up and go, she would be rid of the whole freak show. They would be gone from her patch and back to that kooksville called River Glen where waterfalls and hot springs must spew love-inducing pheromones into the atmosphere. Alex Allaway was the girlfriend of the crew-cutted giant Detective Wilkins; there was an unsettling sexual tension between those two. James and Nina, unnerved as they were, seemed ready to jump into the nearest tent and have each other for breakfast. And last but not least. Mr. Braden, who had gallantly volunteered to watch over Winston last night, had succeeded quite intimately in that.

Sharon had a newfound respect for Ella Winston. Her choice of words, "you user... you shit," was brief yet on point. But what was most impressive was Winston's athleticism. She recalled little brother Geoff remarking on Winston's eyes and artistic talents but never her extraordinary aim. She was never the intended target because Winston's eyes were blue lasers of rage fixed on Braden. Winston had picked the lawn chair, folded it snugly and flung it backhand as if hurling a discus. It was a brilliant throw and direct hit to the bridge of his nose, throwing him off his feet. Sharon had mustered all self-control to mute a "You go girl!"

The presence of the River Glen oddballs made Sharon want to take a cold shower except there was too much goddamn work to do. She climbed into her sedan, glancing once more at the campsite. James was milling around his tent, trying to figure out how to pack it up. His ineptitude was too painful to watch. Anything to get those two moving and on their way. She rolled down her window.

"Pal, it's not rocket science. Pull up the stakes, roll it up, wrap a bungee cord around it and toss it in the car. Done!"

"Oh yes, wonderful!" James said with a wave.

Braden was nowhere to be seen. He had leashed the dogs, pressed a roll of paper towels against his face and staggered up the forest trail, still in his scotch plaid boxers.

Good riddance River Glen.

With any luck those two would be gone by day's end. Her phone vibrated. "No way. Impossible." It was only mid-cycle and Paul had used up the monthly allotment of data. She tossed back two Midols with her black coffee and turned her car in the direction of the morgue. Hers would be death by data overage charges.

Nina jerked down the throttle of the Royal Enfield in attempts to keep up with Alex's sport bike zig-zagging along the forest road. The Enfield-sidecar was a lumbering elephant compared to Alex's bike, a fast and agile cheetah. Passing them in the opposite direction were motorcycles rumbling their way to Gettysburg. The women's motorcycle convention overlapped with Bike Week.

The road trip to Gettysburg was nothing like what Nina had imagined. It resembled a sine wave of peaks and troughs, ups and down. Up, the euphoric ride along scenic country roads. Down, Linda Radowski and Blanche Hyde's bickering. Up, partying at the poolside tiki bar with the Chrome Divas. Then the trip flat-lined in a trough. There was no date with James and tragically Linda, a friend and fellow Diva, was dead. That was the terrible reality of it.

Last night Jay Braden had ordered them back to the hotel where they sequestered themselves in the room and had a dinner of lukewarm room service. Their unanimous decision was to get the-hell-out-of-Dodge since a slasher was on the loose. They had been too agitated to watch pay-for-view movies or drink at the bar and instead spent the evening discussing Linda's murder. They would be lowest on Detective Westerly's list of suspects since they were across the room from the killing. Blanche Hyde would be high on the list since she and Linda had been arguing.

"And there was the blonde with the pyrate bandana who mysteriously disappeared," Alex had reminded them.

"Ella will be top on the list since she was right next to Linda and covered with blood," she said.

"Especially since Ella's an ex-con," James mentioned.

Alex looked up from her jalapeno poppers. "What?"

It was then that James told them of Ella's research at the historical society, her secret trips through the Wedgewood-

Smyth house and his pizza dinner with the ex-cons in the campground. All of this fascinated Alex who barraged him with questions for the rest of the night. Alex's logic was a bit off-kilter and by the time they crawled into bed she was convinced that art forgery was a requisite skill for her new crabbing partner.

Nina flexed her numbing fingers while holding down the throttle... not an easy feat. It was going to be an endless day of riding. The plan was to ride to River Glen and empty the sidecar of luggage. Then Alex would hop into the sidecar and Nina would drive them to Gettysburg where Alex would pick up Ella's motorcycle and ride it back to River Glen. Back and forth, back and forth. It would be a minimum of ten hours on the road. At day's end their butts, backs and hands would ache, but it seemed the only way to get Ella's motorcycle to River Glen.

Alex, despite Will and Lisa Paco's evidence, was convinced of Ella's innocence. "Will's been distracted lately. He's picked up the wrong suspect. He's off his game. Something's on his mind. Once the BMW is in River Glen, all will be well." Alex had a simple life philosophy: as long as boats and motorcycles were operating, crabs climbed into her traps and treasure-hunters stayed out of River Glen, then the gods were smiling on the insignificant mortals of the Chesapeake Bay.

The Suzuki's turn-signal flashed. Odd. It was too early for a gas stop or bathroom break. Ah, good call, Alex! It was a gas station and adjacent UHaul rental company. Please, please have a van or truck available! Nina checked her odometer. They were only twenty-three miles outside of Gettysburg. All they would need to do was load the bikes into the truck, return to the Ephram Whitson House to pick up the BMW and drive back to River Glen in air-conditioned comfort. No sore butt, back and frozen fingers. No ten-hour drive in the summer heat.

An attendant at the service station hurried outside when Alex climbed off her motorcycle and removed her helmet. His eyes traveled up and down her leopard chaps.

"Do you have a truck available?" Alex asked him. "To rent this morning?"

"You're kidding me, right? It's Bike Week. Trucks have been rented out weeks in advance."

"Okay. Thanks anyway." Alex headed back to the Suzuki.

A second man stepped from the garage. "Wait. One came in late last night. Just as I was closing up. It's out back. I haven't had a chance to tank it up or clean it. It's been trashed."

"Can I have a look?" Alex said.

"It's this way," he said.

Nina removed her helmet and followed Alex and the mechanic around the building. He opened the back doors of the truck.

"It's definitely big enough to hold two motorcycles and a motorcycle-sidecar combo," Alex said to her.

"See?" the man said. "Trashed."

Wadded bags from fast food restaurants and empty water bottles were scattered across the floor.

Nina scrunched up her nose. "Strange smell."

"Rancid." Alex turned to the mechanic. "But we'll still take it."

Ella fidgeted in the handcuffs. Alex's kindness still moved her. Not even a half-witted jury would believe that she didn't kill the man who had sent her away for over a decade. She appreciated Alex's concern, but she was never being released. Nor would she ride her motorcycle again.

Besides, if Alex did go back for the bike, it would be long gone. Once Dana heard of her arrest, she would remove the plates and sell it on the black market or for parts at a chop shop. The thought of the beautiful BMW dismembered and sold for scrap was too painful a thought. Everything hurt: the cuffs, her growling stomach since she had missed breakfast, being screwed by that shithead cop—her surreal existence in totality.

How could this be happening again? She was lying low in Gettysburg minding her own business, harming no one. Now was she stuck in a police cruiser with nitwits. For the entire two-hour drive back to River Glen Denny talked about his wife's orthodontia and Detective Paco was on and off the phone with someone named Norman discussing the capture of cyber-creatures. Detective Wilkins was lost in thought when out-of-the-blue he asked "Do you follow the Eagles or the Steelers?"

"Neither. I hate professional sports," she said as a conversation stopper.

"I played tight end for the Maryland Terrapins until I blew out my knee," he said undeterred. "Twice."

Perhaps a bit of tedious small talk might show her in a more sympathetic light. "Did you know Ralph MacKenzie who played tight end for the Nittany Lions?"

"No."

"I guess not. He's older than you."

"Did he go to the pros?"

"No, he partied too much."

"You have a great arm. How'd you learn to throw like that?"

"Prison."

She turned to the window to signal that her quota of mindless chit-chat had been exceeded, although she did want to ask him questions about Alex. Best to avoid personal stuff.

FORGER'S REVENGE

Who knows where that might lead? The BMW would have a good home with Alex.

Never in her wildest dreams did she imagine that she would own such a splendid motorcycle. It was acquired on her release day from Cambridge Springs. A prison guard had called for a cab to drive her to the bus station, but it never showed. By this time her mother had moved to Florida and her father was too busy with the twin monsters to pick her up. It wasn't too far a walk to the town center so she had started to hoof it. Keisha had already been released and was staying with an old friend near Allentown. Sam had another two months to go. The plan was to reunite at Uncle Lyle's trailer in Gettysburg and figure things out from there.

A dinged-up Buick pulled up next to her. The driver was the oldest guard at the prison. Joe Cameron was one of the good ones—not a goon or lecher. It was Joe who had organized the softball games, East versus West Pennsylvania. She either pitched or played shortstop. The Easterners were much better athletes than that group from Pittsburgh, Erie and Altoona.

It was Joe's day off. He drove her to his home where his wife cooked them a lunch of fish sticks and crab cakes. A home-cooked meal! Never had she tasted better food.

"I need you to do me a favor," said Joe taking a last bite of apple pie. "Take something off my hands."

She followed him to the back of the house where he pulled at a leaf-covered tarp. There it was. A dusty F 800 GS adventure sport bike.

"Gorgeous. Whose is it?"

"Yours. I have no use for it. I know you can ride. I saw the motorcycle pictures in your cell."

"I can't take this. This is a very expensive bike."

"It was my boy Tim's." Joe's mouth twitched. "He was going to ride it around the world but—"

She was afraid to ask.

"He didn't come home from Afghanistan."

"I'm so sorry."

"Sit on it," he said to change the subject. "See how it feels."

They dragged the motorcycle from seasons of debris and she slung her leg over the seat. He handed her the key. The battery was not dead. The engine purred. No wonder. There were only nine hundred miles on it.

"Please hon, take it off my hands. It needs a good home."

It was love at first sight, sound and feel. "Yes. Okay. Once I get on my feet, I'll send you monthly payments. Promise."

"No rush. When you can."

She never made it to the bus station that day. Instead she had put on the leather jacket and helmet from a fallen soldier, stuffed her backpack in a metal saddlebag and headed in a diagonal trajectory across Pennsylvania.

Suddenly she remembered it. At the time it meant little, nothing really.

But now.

She turned warily out the back window of the police cruiser. Will Wilkins looked at her and turned as well. All she saw were cars inching along Interstate 95. On the day of her release from Cambridge Springs, as she rode her new BMW F 800, barely visible in the rearview mirrors was another motorcycle. It was no more than a speck in her mirrors. But that speck had followed her all the way to Gettysburg.

Jay handed the SUV keys to James. "I'm drinking. You're driving." He wedged the cooler between the seats within easy reach. Boodles gin was not an option so the plan was to get drunk on beer. He cracked open a cold one. James had the discretion not to talk or ask questions about the previous evening; nor did he choose one of Laura's cheery Broadway musicals. He would kill himself if he had to listen to a perky tune from *42th Street* or *Hello Dolly*. Instead James found a jazz station on the radio. Perfect. The blues suited his mood.

He checked his face in the side mirror. This was the third time his nose had been broken. The first time was by a dockworker in Baltimore, then by a drug dealer. Already his eyes had taken on a peculiar hue... when blue and purple watercolors run together. By tomorrow there would be traces of yellow. Why, he wondered, had he never matured beyond adolescence? He was that stupid when it came to women. He had never had a one-night-stand until last night. He loved courting Laura and wining and dining her on his tiny paycheck from his work-study job at the cafeteria when he was an undergraduate at the University of Vermont. The same was true when courting Julia. He loved their seafood dinners, dog walks, weekend get-aways and picnics along the Glen River. A woman's friendship and the love-making were inextricably linked, one as satisfying as the other. Many men were, but he was not, a one-night-stand-type-of-guy. The evening with Ella Winston, he had assumed was a prelude to something longer.

Jay's phone vibrated. Oh fuck. He knew this call was coming. He was not drunk enough to say something regretful; shame about that. Captain Herm Taylor blatted on and on about the Seymour Simon-Monroe Hadley case. "Braden, do not compromise the investigation any further!" No doubt the big-mouthed Denny had tipped off the equally big-mouthed secretary Cloris about The Lawn Chair Incident. Had someone photographed him sprawled in the dirt in his boxers? Likely. The image was probably on the River Glen PD's Facebook page by now. The story must have spread like wildfire across headquarters and prompted his constipated captain "to remind him about policies about messing with suspects."

"How was I to know that she was a suspect in a murder investigation?"

"You're on vacation so stay out of this!" said Taylor ringing off.

"Yes indeed, James. I'm on vacation. Another compelling reason to get drunk."

After guzzling who-knows-how-many beers and who-knows-how-many roadside pee stops, he reclined his seat and fell asleep. On the coastal road leading into River Glen, James nudged him awake. They passed the vine-covered estate of Josiah and Abigail Wedgewood-Smyth, traveled through a valley of summer corn, through the pine forest near Alex's marine station and down the hill into the village.

"Let's stop at the hospital and get your nose set," James suggested.

"I can fix it myself. I've done it before."

James winced. "Are you sure?"

"Yeah."

"Suit yourself."

In his driveway he climbed out of the car and opened the hatch of the SUV. Clark and Miranda took off in pursuit of Canada geese at the river's edge while he and James offloaded camping gear into the garage.

"Please don't drive today," said James handing him a flash-drive. "Here."

"What is it?"

"A folder with photographs I took at the Battlefield Historical Society archive. There's nothing in there about Josiah and Abigail to assist with my novel. Who knows. Maybe there's something to help Ella."

"Okay, thanks."

James ducked into his sports car and drove off while he dragged himself back to the garage for the dreaded task. He pulled a bottle of Boodles from a case and took a long swig. He fumbled through his toolbox for the right sized hammer. Laura hated when he did this to himself, but it beat the shit out of sitting in an ER all day. Then would be endless calls to insurance arguing about what percent they were going to cover, or mostly not. It wasn't worth the hassle. He propped a hubcap on the workbench to use as a mirror and firmly pressed one finger along the side of his nose so he wouldn't knock it off in the opposite direction. Right there... he needed to hit it right... there. He paused. Shit, did he hate realigning his own nose!

"Just do it, you wimp."

He snatched up the hammer. *Smack snap.* "Yow!" Blood spurt from his nostrils on to his favorite tropical shirt. He leaned toward the hubcap and studied his handiwork.

"Good as new."

Sharon Westerly read the autopsy report on Linda Radowski. The perp had grabbed Radowski by her single braid to expose her neck and killed her with one rapid, deep swipe. The medical examiner Gordon Lombardo had located tiny bits of leather in her hair, presumably from a black riding glove. There were no prints on the blade. Not one Chrome Diva interviewed the night before could recall the blonde in a skull-and-cross bones bandana at any event at the Four Score and Seven Hotel. Nor did they know which State chapter she belonged to. All of them had corroborated the same points. The blonde had joined the ghost tour at the last second and she did not ride into the parking lot. The Divas would have noticed if she rode. After all, that's all they did—check out each other's motorcycles. The blonde had walked to the Ephram Whitson House, but from where?

If her team of detectives could gain access to footage from security cameras in the vicinity of the Whitson House, the killer might be caught on film. It would be a cumbersome job acquiring footage from the local businesses and scrolling through it all. It was a perfect job for the go-getter Trooper Hastings. Yup, Hastings could review footage while she interviewed Kenneth Radowski who would be arriving at any time. She left her office and weaved through the maze of cubicles.

"Where does Hastings sit?" she asked a trooper.

The man looked up from his computer. "There, ma'am."

Hastings' desk was in the corner with a view of a gray wall. He was so new to the job that his work space hadn't yet accumulated photos of family and vacations or stickers and magnets of sports teams.

"What's his first name?" she asked.

"Connor."

"From where?"

"Somewhere in the Poconos, I think."

"Where is he?"

"I haven't seen him yet today."

She tilted her head toward the trooper's computer. "Anything coming in?"

"Two car break-ins."

"If people wouldn't leave CDs and valuables on front seats or dashboards as thief bait—"

"These thefts are different. A park ranger had his dry-cleaning taken from his car. Only his uniform was stolen. The other man, a construction worker was really pissed off. He had his hardhat and yellow high vis vest taken from his truck."

"Where?"

"Up at the battlefield."

"Only clothes? Strange." She crossed the office to the duty sergeant. "Connor Hastings. Did he call in sick?"

"No, Commander," the woman answered.

"Can you call his home?"

"Yes, of course."

"I'll wait." Sharon pulled her phone from her blazer pocket to appear as though she wasn't hovering. Miraculous... additional gigs hadn't been added to her data plan.

The sergeant hung up. "His wife said that Connor never came home last night. He had texted her that he'd be late. He was working late on a murder investigation, he told her."

"But all of us cleared out of the Whitson House around ten."

Linda Radowski in the morgue. Clothes stolen from cars. Now this. Sharon's heart skipped a beat. A missing greenhorn.

JW unfolded the foil and sniffed the fillets. For hours the meat had been marinating in a special blend of her own creation. After months of experimentation the precise spices had been identified. A touch of Cajun flavors to enliven the palate but not overwhelm the flavors of the meat. Today the fillets would be cooked in foil, simmering in juices, Polynesian style amongst the coals. She stirred the fire with a green stick from the forest. The coals had that grey sooty coating and glowing orange core. With tongs, she laid the foil packet in the fire and placed a few coals on top. The cardinal rule of cooking on fire, stove or any heat source was to never overcook the meat. This dish must have a blackened exterior yet be tender to the touch. Moist but not runny. She set the timer on her cell phone. Fortunately, there were no texts from her boss. *Do this, do that, day and night.*

"Don't think about work," JW told herself. "Savor this quiet moment to cook." She pulled herself off her knees and searched a metal case on her sport bike for eating utensils. The Ella Winston job necessitated her riding the BMW instead of her preferred Harley Fat Boy. The upside to all that waiting in Gettysburg was an interesting tour of the Harley Davidson plant in York. She missed the throaty grumble of her Harley and its low-slung comfortable seat. The sport bike sounded like a pesky gnat though it had superior handling around corners and over rough terrain that allowed her to find secluded patches of forest to camp in.

Another downside of the sport bike was that it was European. It was her patriotic duty to purchase American products to stimulate the economy. Harley Davidson, LLBean, Heinz 57, Campbell's Soup. Always American food products, especially meats. Who knows what prions or other contaminants might have infected a foreign meat source? That's all she needed... mad cow disease. And always American spices (preferably from Louisiana) for her recipes. Once she got paid for this job, she could get her life back on track. Finish school. Start her career. Maybe write a cooking blog on the side. What about a cookbook? A publisher would jump at her unique approaches to seasonings and marinades.

The foil packet sizzled and smoked. JW rushed back to the fire, pulled the packet from the coals, placed it on a stone and peeked inside. Perfectly done. The exterior was lightly blackened and the interior a white-pink. Moist but not runny. She blew at the meat on the tip of her fork, then held the slice on her tongue, concentrating on the contrasting flavors. Perhaps a little more cayenne next time. It was delicious nonetheless.

What *nom de plume* to blog under? Mack the Knife had a zany ring to it. Or would that be too off-putting to readers? What pen name would appeal to a female readership?

A crunch of leaves caused her to jump to her feet. Two deer hunters stepped into the clearing.

"My, my," said the scrawny, unshaven one.

"You alone, honey?" the second one asked tugging a flask from his camouflaged vest. His smile looked like a dried corncob.

Scrawny One's eyes raked over her. "A biker chick and a big 'un."

"You know what they say about chicks and bikes. It's like riding a vibrator."

"She ain't too pretty but hell... she has a pussy."

Yellow Teeth stepped toward her and held out his flask. "How 'bout you party with us, sweet thang?"

Incredible but true, Kenneth Radowski's repugnance eclipsed Ralph's, Sharon concluded. Linda had been murdered and Kenneth was swaggering around her office, stinking of cheap aftershave and new money. She had arrested countless good-old-boys just like him, a redneck who had lied and cheated his way up the ladder of the Old Boy Network. The fact he was an ex-football player also turned her stomach, but his most nauseating feature was the dull, lifeless eyes looping in figure eights across her breasts. Her strategy for the interview was to button her blazer and shield her lower torso by remaining behind her desk. Radowski could have been Ralph's long-lost brother separated at birth.

The mourning husband act was pathetic. Good thing he chose banking as a career because he would have failed miserably as an actor. An encouraging piece of news was that there were no children from his union with Linda which was a small coup for human evolution. His DNA was not polluting the *Homo sapiens* gene pool. According to his testimony, he had been at a banquet of the River Glen Rotary Club last night while Linda was at the women's bike convention in Gettysburg. He was a speaker at the dinner, lecturing on his bank's mutual fund advisement services. He was seated next to the mayor who would vouch for his activities. Radowski's movements would be easy enough to corroborate, but what if the slasher was an accomplice? Was Radowski wanting Linda out of the way? Or was the intended victim Ella Winston as Jay Braden had insinuated? It was pitch black after all. It would have been impossible to tell who was who.

Radowski confirmed that the River Glen PD had come by his motor yacht to impound his and Linda's laptops. "Anything to help," he said with a disingenuous smile.

"Any disputes, arguments, anyone who might want to harm Linda?"

"No, no."

That, Sharon knew, was an outright lie. A few Chrome Divas had mentioned the tension between Linda and Blanche Hyde over Kenneth and Blanche's "Facebook friendship." Hot words between Linda and Blanche had been exchanged on at least three occasions: at last month's breakfast meeting, a gas station on the ride to Gettysburg and at the hotel's poolside tiki bar.

"Linda was a pillar of the community," he boasted. "Her insurance agency sponsored the town's breast cancer 5K. Her agency sold Girl Scout cookies. She was the secretary for the Friends of the Wedgewood-Smyth House."

"Which is?"

"A village committee to raise funds for converting a colonial estate into a museum. I'm the treasurer."

On and on he praised "his wonderful Linda, his paragon of virtue" while his rodent eyes tried to squeeze between the buttons of her blazer. Instead of note-taking, she found her fists unconsciously clenching and unclenching in her lap. She searched her desk for a projectile. No lawn chairs were available but that paper weight might rearrange Radowski's nose. There was a good chance that her aim might be as accurate as Winston's. After all, she only had to hurl the object over the distance of her desktop. She sighed. If only. She had heard enough and ushered Radowski from her office.

Note to self: contact the River Glen PD about the contents of the Radowski laptops and any background on the prurient husband. Possible mistresses, business operations and the like. Like it wasn't bad enough dealing with the assorted personalities and head-cases in her own PD. Now was the complication of a new cast of characters: The Big Fish in the Little Pond, the Earnest Giant and the Tattooed Gum Smacker. The first second she could retire... she could hardly wait! But what to do? She had no idea, no plan. Where to go? It would be some place with a water view because she was so goddamn tired of cornfields, cannons and split rail fences. A cabin on a lake... thatched hut on a tropical island... beach house on the Outer Banks?

A tap at her office door interrupted her reverie. "What?"

"Um, ur, Connor Hastings has been located," said the trooper hoarsely.

Will Wilkins' day was going from bad to worst. Now a text from Jay's cell phone—not asking—demanding that he stop by on his way home from work. It was against regulations to talk to Jay who "was compromised," according to an irate Captain Taylor. Yet there he was, obediently turning into Jay's driveway. First and foremost, his loyalties were to family, the River Glen pyrates, then Jay and Lisa. If nothing else, the detour to Jay's house postponed another heated conversation with Alex about *his* bringing in Ella Winston for questioning. His ears already burned in anticipation of that discussion. Now Alex would certainly say "No."

For months he had the engagement ring hidden in the back of his sock drawer. He and Alex had lived happily together for over two years. Carly adored Alex. Why shouldn't they marry? He had been in love with her since he was a timid five-year-old setting off for his first day of kindergarten. At the bus stop was that skinny second grader who was always out on the crab boat *High Times* with her grandfather Randy and Old Ben Hancock. He could finally see the black-haired girl up close. She was off by herself, arranging mermaid figurines along the curb.

It was going to take some convincing for Alex to marry him. Randy who raised her had had six ill-fated marriages that repelled her from the idea, and their high school friend Gillian White was stuck in a bitter divorce and custody battle over the Siamese cats. That didn't help his cause. But the Ella Winston case was the final nail in the coffin. He had just brought in one of Alex's riding buddies. Could he ever catch a break?

Now this. How drunk was Jay going to be? He had been the talk of headquarters that day. The lovesick spinster Cloris had barraged Lisa with questions about Jay in boxers which prompted Captain Taylor to stomp from his office.

"Get back to your desks! All of you!"

He and Lisa had skirted the captain's wrath by questioning Ella Winston in the interview room for much of the afternoon. Winston's mood vacillated between despondency, sarcasm, condescension and resignation. "I'm being framed *again*," she repeated.

"What did you do on the evening of the Giles Blood-hand festival?" Lisa had asked.

"I went back to my campsite, cooked dinner, went into my tent and went to sleep. That was it."

"Were you with anyone?" he said. "Can anyone corroborate that?"

"I was camping alone, but maybe you can track down the people from Virginia in the next campsite. They saw me. One guy was really annoying and kept asking me to come over for beers."

"But then you took a ride down the coastal road around eleven," Lisa stated.

"No, I didn't!" said Winston jerking up from the chair.

"But you and your motorcycle were seen at the Radcliffe."

"What the hell's the Radcliffe?"

"The posh golf resort," Lisa said. "You should see the cool mermaid fount—"

"Do I look like I frequent posh resorts?" Winston cut in.

"But you were caught on their security camera at the guardhouse," he added.

"What!" Winston went pale. "I want to see your evidence!"

He slid a folder across the table.

Winston leafed through the photos. "This... this can't be happening again."

"What?"

"That's not me!"

"But it's your motorcycle and Pennsylvania license plate," he informed her.

"It's not me or my bike! The license plate is a fake, a duplicate, a forgery. I don't even know where the Radcliffe is! I can't believe this! Just like I've never been to the National Archives. Don't you dolts see a pattern here? I'm being set up, just like before. Can't anyone see that? Someone wants me sent away again!"

"Why?" he and Lisa blurted at the same time.

"I have no clue! I haven't done anything!"

"Who knew you were going to the River Glen pyrate festival?" Lisa asked.

Winston paused to think. "A few people. My trailer-mates. My boss at the ghost walk. The lady at the camp store where I bought provisions for the trip."

He and Lisa had terminated the interview at 5:48 pm. Lisa rushed off to tell Norman from IT to check the phone records of Dana Detrick, Samantha Ramirez, Keisha Long and the cashier from the camp store to see if there were any communications with the Hadleys or Ian Kent.

If what Winston said was true, the murderer knew she was coming to River Glen. If true, a tremendous amount of forethought had gone into planning the crime—all the way to identical motorcycles with identical license plates. The person behind this had deep pockets.

Will climbed out of his sedan in Jay's driveway. Clark and Miranda charged around the corner of the house which meant that Jay was out back. The dogs escorted him to the deck. Jay was in the hot tub, his head resting on the edge. A plastic bag of ice covered his face. There was a bottle of Gatorade nearby instead of the usual beer stein of G & Ts. That was a good sign.

Jay didn't move. "Tell me everything that Ella Winston said today and everything about the Monroe Hadley investigation. *Everything!*"

Her son was safe. That was the only thing that mattered to Sharon Westerly. Paul could have stayed at Ralph's house while she traveled, but she nixed that idea. With her shitty luck, the new wife Caroline in a tiny bikini top and tinier shorts would be watering plants in the front yard when she dropped off Paul. In her current mood, she would throttle Caroline by the hostas, an action witnessed by Paul and toddler Jonathan, and the Gettysburg PD would have another homicide on their hands. Caroline could die another day. The PD was too stressed at the moment to deal with her rampage against the MacKenzies. Instead she brought Paul to her father and Uncle Reggie's place. After retiring from the police force, the two brothers had pooled resources and bought a small apartment building with a pub at street level.

She gave Paul a hug by the bar. "The data plan," she implored. "I really don't want to be eating cat food in retirement."

"Yeah, yeah Mom," he said rolling his eyes. Juggling his backpack, laptop and game system, he disappeared up the stairs to her father's apartment.

A pub of retirees would be a safe place for her teenager. She pulled her hand from the pocket of her jeans; it still jittered. Reggie gave her a sad smile from behind the taps.

No tea or glass of wine that evening. "Scotch, Reg."

"But you're driving."

"A double."

Sharon's knees still felt fluid. Her gaze would be permanently fixed over her shoulder until they caught this monster. So far, so good. Just regulars at their regular places.

The old lush Mrs. Hildenbrand sat on her stool by the juke box. The Turner cousins, the chatty sisters Phoebe and Hazel Worth and the sullen widower Teddy Ferraci had appropriated their usual table for the weekly Scrabble tournament.

Reggie reached to the top shelf and poured her a drink. "Bad, uh?"

She climbed onto a bar stool. "What's worse than your worst nightmare?" she whispered. "After the perp cut the biker on the ghost walk, she must have hid somewhere and watched us. She was waiting for a cop. It could have been Lombardo, Goldstein or—"

Reggie's calloused hand covered hers. "But it wasn't you, honey. It wasn't. Thank the Lord."

"Who would stay and watch us? How brazen was that! That sicko was already looking for her next victim."

"I heard through the PD grapevine that Hastings—"

Sharon downed her drink. "With surgical precision. At the origins and insertions of the muscles. Gone were the gastrocnemius, biceps, triceps, masseters and tongue. That bitch filleted him."

Chapter 7
A Village on the Bay

"A charming bayside village of Crabbers, Artisans and Pyrates" proclaimed the glossy tourist brochure in Sharon Westerly's room at the Tides Inn on the highway. There she was in the center of River Glen on the bridge over the Glen River, sipping watery hotel coffee from a Styrofoam cup. FBI agents and profilers had descended like a swarm of hornets upon Gettysburg, Pennsylvania while she had been sent to a backwater in Maryland. At any other time being elbowed from the eye of the hurricane would have infuriated her, but her captain's rationale made sense. "If the killer watched your team at the crime scene, who knows who else is on her hit-list?" At that chilling remark she hadn't complained or put up a fight which shocked them both. The fire-in-her-belly was extinguishing itself ever so slightly with each passing year. That was the sad truth of it. Retirement was not too far on the horizon. If her banishment to partner with the River Glen PD meant living to see Paul grow to adulthood, then so be it.

Countless times she had witnessed the violence of semi-rural America: deaths by gun-shot wounds and stabbings, suicides and overdoses. Most assaults were perpetrated by drug dealers, disaffected loners or mentally unstable husbands (she was an expert on those) who had circumvented Pennsylvania's gun laws. In most cases the perps were white males. But never had she seen anything close to what was left of Connor Hastings and the handiwork of a woman. He had been tied to a tree in the woods near the Round Tops. His remains had been found by Eagle Scouts on a hike, all of whom would need psychological counseling for years to come.

All said, being sent to River Glen wasn't so bad an assignment. The narrow bridge was an excellent vantage point to watch the village. The place was no more than piers on opposite riverbanks, dockside shops and restaurants, a boat yard and marina. Up the hill was a village green with a post office, historical society, law office and township administration building. In the distance, at the intersection of the river and Chesapeake Bay was the Point with a bathhouse, picnic tables and beach. The houses that lined Main Street were brightly painted Victorians whose front porches were draped with flags of blue crabs, the Maryland state flag and skull-and-cross bones. A brochure in her hotel room described the local history, but who had time to read about silly pyrate legends at a time like this—when a ripper was on the loose? The last thing she wanted on her nightstand were images of lunatics wielding daggers and cutlasses.

The now infamous Gburg Ripper had struck twice in one night. Could the same perp have struck last week in River Glen? The slashed necks of Linda Radowkski and Connor Hastings were identical to the MO of Hadley-Simon's murderer. But Hastings had further treatment. Gordon

Lombardo told her that the excision of Hasting's muscles was exacting in technique. Only skeletal muscles were removed. The major organs: the brain, heart, liver and lungs were left intact. Why remove only skeletal muscle? There was no frenzied hacking suggestive of rage or panic. Just precise surgical cuts at the origins and insertions. Why? Stranger yet, none of the muscles were found on site. Why take them with her? The FBI was scouring the databases for similar murders, perhaps by female surgeons, in particular orthopedic surgeons. And to complicate matters, the perp might be disguising herself as a construction worker or park ranger.

Sharon couldn't help herself—couldn't repress the maternal urge. She pulled her cell phone from her pocket and sent Paul a text. *Good morning, sweetheart. Hope you have a nice day. XO Mom.* She just needed to hear a response, any response—annoyed, surly—it didn't matter. To know that he was okay. His last text read: *im fine mom go away*. But that was last night. How was he today?

Through the morning haze she watched the village come to life. Alex Allaway and a black Labrador retriever climbed onto an old tugboat and motored out to the bay. James Collins left a majestic mansion on the bluff and wound down the hill to the law office. An old hippie from the Psychic Readings shack sang incantations and sprinkled herbs along the dock, presumably to bless the fishing boats. Outdoor tables at the Dockside Café were filling with customers, including Nina Vega setting up her laptop. Faint ukulele music played from the tiki bar behind the Nauticus restaurant where well-groomed waiters were setting tables.

And last but not least. The Big Fish had been watching the village awake also. He hurried toward the bridge, the two black dogs at his side. She was his intended target.

JW read the text and heaved her cell phone onto the sofa bed. She had organized her entire day and now this! Yesterday, when she had arrived back in South Philly, she had stopped at the grocers for extra cayenne before unpacking her motorcycle in the alley. She was supposed to be cooking today! The text from Jennie Wade—a stupid alias—upended her day.

Jennie: *E's been taken to River Glen. Go back and watch what's happening. Pronto!*

No "please go back" or "would you kindly go back?" Another imperious command. "Go back... Pronto!" What ever happened to civility?

JW circled her studio apartment. Now what? The road trips had become so tiresome. She had not slept in her own bed for a week, instead tossed and turned on the hard floor of a UHaul. She ripped off her apron and flung it on the kitchen chair. "So much for making stew." She snapped off the Crock Pot, returned the cutting board to its drawer and shoved the block of knives against the backsplash. "Dicing meat and vegetables—that clearly isn't happening." A drive to River Glen was another in a long list of frustrating postponements. By the time she finished school she would be as ancient as the Cryptkeeper. She bent under the kitchen sink for the VacMaster. Another road trip meant vacuuming sealing and freezing the fillets.

"Ugh. They're never as tender after freezing them."

Deal with it. Just finish the job, then focus one hundred percent on career objectives and composing a letter to cook book publishers.

Her previous boss was so organized, his instructions clear and simple. The new boss Jennie was so capricious. All over the map... like her. Go to Cambridge Springs... River Glen... Gettysburg... now River Glen again.

FORGER'S REVENGE

JW pulled the fillets from the fridge, slipped one into a vacuum bag and placed it in the VacMaster, then another and another. Who could remember whose were whose? Why did it matter as long as the meat was tender and tasty? She had almost passed on the skinny guy because there was not much meat on him. If he was too tough and gristly, the worst she could do was put him through the food processor and make burgers.

The phone chimed from the bed. She crossed the apartment and read the text. Not her again.

Jennie: *All over the news! A murder at the Ephram Whitson House. Did you?*

JW: *NO!*

Jennie: *FBI are swarming the place!*

JW: *i know nothing about it!*

"There are a lot of things Jennie doesn't need to know," she said turning off the ringer. She had been hired for a twofold task: to take out Seymour and implicate Ella. Both had been flawlessly accomplished. Seymour's murder had been conducted with clockwork precision. Every detail of Ella's motorcycle and riding gear had been precisely replicated, even down to her boots, jacket and helmet. She had even stolen a motorcycle license plate in Center City and painted over it with Ella's plate numbers and letters. She had followed Ella for months—when she should have been in school! She should be starting a clinical internship by now but no. Submit submit to Jennie's every whim.

Jennie didn't need to know about the word carved into Seymour's chest or the Confederate kepi. Those dramatic touches were fitting for a traitor in their midst. Ella had been picked up and fingered for the murder of Seymour. Job done. Once payment was received, she was done with Jennie. The tenuous partnership would be dissolved for good.

The next phase of the plan required a new disguise so JW dropped on to her throw rug. Seated Indian-style, she placed her hands' palms-up on her knees. Middle fingers touched thumbs. Meditate breathe meditate breathe *erase. Erase* JW from your psyche. *Erase* her personal history, physical appearance, quirks and internal monologue. *Erase* her aspirations and thought patterns... all of it gone. Breathe meditate. JW was gone, but the personality transformation was only half complete. JW was gone. *It* was present. *It,* without identity and gender, sat on the throw rug, breathing meditating breathing. Who to become next? Whose history to create, appearance to assume, mind to occupy? Whose thoughts to think? Who?

Ah, yes! Breathe mediate *create.* Create *his* past, *his* dreams, *his* thoughts and personality. *He* rose off the rug and opened the closet door. Rows of wigs and costumes lined the shelves. Which to choose from? No blonde wig this time. The itchy long hair had driven him crazy. The nape of his neck was covered with blisters of prickly heat. This time a character with short hair. How about the grey toupee covered with a skull cap motorcycle helmet? A black Harley Davidson T-shirt covered by a black leather vest. A long grey beard and thick sideburns. What name for a grizzled biker? Clayton, Bobby Joe, Roy?

Roy sprinkled baby powder onto his bald scalp and pulled on the toupee. With actor's glue he adhered the sideburns and beard. He smiled at himself in the mirror. The upside to the road trip to River Glen was riding the all-American Harley Fat Boy instead of that whiny German sport bike. The personality transformation was one hundred percent complete. In the next command performance, a *She* would become a *He.*

None of this felt right. Jay Braden, for fraternizing with a suspect, had been ordered from the Hadley-Simon case, but there Sharon was, watching the millennial detectives Paco and Wilkins create a time-line on poster boards on Braden's kitchen island while he attempted scrambled eggs. The kitchen strategy session was a bit too cozy for her. The only plus was that Braden's coffee was marginally better than the watery swill from the hotel's free breakfast buffet.

Most murder investigations have convoluted histories and this one was no different. Paco and Wilkins recounted the essential points from yesterday's interview with Ella Winston for Braden and her. Winston had met Ian Kent and Hadley-Simon went she was a high school senior. While an undergraduate art major at Swarthmore College, she had been invited to receptions, seminars and exhibitions organized by the professor. Hadley-Simon had exhibited her works at his newly purchased gallery in Old City. Upon her graduation he had encouraged her to apply to the MFA program at an elite Philadelphia art college where he taught. She was accepted and he became a hands-on mentor, closely supervising her master's thesis (painters of the Civil War era) and career in general. He had introduced her to "everybody who was everybody" on the Philadelphia art scene.

Winston's companion at the art events was the doting boyfriend Ian Kent. Holidays were spent at Kent's family home in King of Prussia, a suburb of Philadelphia. She was a bridesmaid at Lorena Kent's wedding where she had danced up a storm with the handsome brother Curtis who made a surprise appearance at the reception hall in Valley Forge. Only in the summers did she return home to Gettysburg to work the ghost tours. It was easy money.

According to her testimony, Ian Kent had a brilliant plan to make more easy money. "You pay off your student loans, Ellie. Monroe and I will pay down our mortgage on the gallery faster. Big deal if a rich geezer or heiress purchases a bogus Eaton? They'll never know. As soon as we pay our bills, we can buy a house together."

Greed got the better of her. As instructed, she painted the Eaton and sent a text to an unknown deliveryman. She wrapped the painting in bubble wrap and heavy brown paper and placed it at the back door of her apartment. Three times she followed these exact instructions and three nights she heard the same thing—a motorcycle cruise slowly through the alley. She had peered from the window. The rider in black leathers strapped the package to his motorcycle and vanished into the cobblestoned labyrinth of Center City.

"Did Kent or Hadley ride? Or Ventresca?" Wilkins had asked.

"No," she had answered. "No one I knew rode."

"Can you remember the make of the motorcycle?"

"It was too dark to see."

"Gender of the rider?"

"Don't know. There were no lights in the alley."

Then a rare Eaton—her Eaton—would surface.

"Yes indeed! It's an Eaton!" Hadley had proclaimed. "How extraordinary!"

The auction was quiet and quick. An envelope of cash... untraceable cash... was delivered to her mailbox when she was on campus. The delivery person clearly knew her schedule of classes. The money was always delivered when she was out.

Cagey Ian had put none of their conversations in email. Nor had she discussed the scam with Hadley-Simon in emails, texts or in person. Never. Later at the trial nothing could be traced to either Kent or her professor. It was her word against theirs. They had hired the best lawyers money could buy. She had a public defender who had just graduated from a third-rate law school.

"They used me plain and simple," Winston had told the detectives. "I was too blinded by ego to see through the seduction."

Sharon pulled her vibrating cell phone from her pocket. Damn it. The text wasn't from Paul. Why wasn't he responding? He was certainly awake by now. Her father would insist that everyone have breakfast together at the crack of dawn. He had raised her and her brothers like police academy recruits rather than children.

The text with attached images was from a detective on her team in Gettysburg. He had written two words—*Two hunters.*

She opened the attachments. Braden's scrambled eggs and coffee rolled in her stomach. She jumped to her feet, raced to the powder room and splashed cold water in her face.

The detective's subject line was completely wrong. It should have read: *What had been two hunters.*

A world in cinderblock. How many hours had Ella's eyes traveled the roughened cement next to her pillow at Cambridge Springs? For countless hours—days, weeks, over a decade in totality—she looked into the undulating cement world, willing herself into the tiny valleys and ridges where she was not a Gulliver-like giant in an orange jump suit but an inhabitant of an enchanted world... one of Degas dancers... a gypsy among Rousseau's lions... a cubist bull or horse of Guernica... a soldier amidst Rembrandt's dark captains... a dog playing poker... one of Eakins' surgeons bent over a patient... her character in the landscape changing at whim. The cinderblock was her canvas of distraction and escape.

Other times, to chip away at the monotony, she had mentally matched the colors of the cellblock to the paint tubes in her Center City apartment, though none matched exactly. No greys in her palette were that dismal. If she was a paint manufacturer and had to name the hue of the cell, she might have called it desperation grey, perhaps suicide grey. Here she was again, head on a snot-yellow pillow, facing another future of cinderblock. The grey of this cell was a shade whiter than at Cambridge Springs and with a hint of green. The paint had more gloss and less grime, but it was a depressing grey nonetheless. This hue might be called hopelessness grey.

Would she be called in for more questioning or were Wilkins and Paco done with her? Birds chirped outside the barracks and they had fed her something called breakfast so it must be morning. They were probably deciding what exactly to book her with. Something that would stick and ensure a conviction and a life sentence without parole. That was the reason for the delay. Her eyes roamed the cinderblock, but no images could be conjured. Nor could she shrink herself into a pleasant imaginary world. She was no nude descending a staircase, nor a jolly flatboatman frolicking on a Midwest river. Not a pale human inhabiting a garden of earthly delights, nor Venus emerging from a scallop shell. Her mind was devoid of color, light and imagination.

Stern, clacking shoes approached. A key rattled in the lock. She swung her socked feet off the cot. One of the men was the trooper Denny. The other man was about sixty, highly decorated and taciturn. His nameplate read Herman Taylor. The bars of the cell slid aside. More questioning, she figured, though this time by the captain of the barracks.

"You can go," said Taylor through taut lips. "To sign for your belongings."

She sprang to her feet. "I can go?"

"Yes, but you must stay in River Glen. We'll need to talk later."

"Did you catch who—?"

"That way," he said gruffly. "Trooper, show her to Processing." He spun on the waxy floor and departed.

"What's happened?" she asked Denny.

"Ms. Winston, we can't say."

She rushed down the hallway beside him. She was free? My god! She was free! Where to go? Who cares? Think about it outside. Just sign for her belongings and get the hell out. She was free to go! Free... free... free! Maybe they had made an arrest. Maybe she had been cleared. That's why she needed to stick around. To be a witness at the trial. She would get the details later. She just needed fresh air and sunlight.

The secretary Cloris, whose desk was covered with cat figurines, assisted with the discharge. Ella was given her sneakers, belt, wallet and cell phone. Then Cloris handed her an unfamiliar envelope. She shook the contents into her lap —her motorcycle keys and a note. She read and re-read the childlike handwriting.

An address. A place to go. A promise of work!

She tugged on her shoes and flew out the front entrance while slipping her belt through the loops of her jeans. There it was, parked in the back of the police barracks. Her motorcycle glistened in the morning sun! Her helmet hung off the handlebars. She sprinted across the parking lot. Just as the note said, her boots, gloves and leather vest were in the saddlebags. She pulled on her riding gear and helmet and climbed on the seat.

The best melody in the world... a motorcycle engine!

All of it—too good to be true—her bike and a full tank of gas. She kicked the bike into first gear. Her heart leapt. She released the clutch and pulled down the throttle. Her destination was the coastal road and the marine lab beyond the pine forest.

Hell yeah! She was going to be a crabber.

Jay moved next to Sharon Westerly at the make-shift crime board—poster boards propped along his sofa.

"Too many incongruities," he said. "Let's assume Ella is telling the truth. She admitted to painting the Eaton forgeries but denied the theft of the historical document from the National Archives. Her thesis advisor Monroe Hadley aka Seymour Simon had a previous conviction for selling historical documents. Decades later he sets up his graduate student for a crime he had committed years earlier in Massachusetts. But why frame her if the forgery scam was so profitable? According to her, she, Hadley-Simon and Kent made tens of thousands of dollars."

"I bet someone was on to them," said Westerly standing with hands on her hips. "Three rare Eaton paintings surfacing from nowhere in the span of a few years must have raised eyebrows in the art community."

"True. Ella said that Hadley-Simon and Kent wanted her to take the fall and disappear for a long time. And there was the mysterious motorcyclist-courier who picked up the forged Eatons from the alleyway in Philly. So at least three people were in on the operation." He sidestepped to the poster board with the time-line. "Ella disappears for almost twelve years and all is quiet on the Eaton art front."

"Then she's released. According to her statement, a motorcyclist followed her back to Gettysburg. The courier from Philly? At that point the motorcyclist definitely, and possibly Hadley-Simon and Kent, knew where she was. Then she started looking for the real Eatons in River Glen. Maybe she found something. Or was getting warm?"

He headed to the coffee pot in the kitchen. "Another cup?"

"I'll take a pass. My stomach's still in knots. I have to leave soon and meet up with Paco and Wilkins at headquarters." She pondered the time-line a moment longer. "Someone got rattled by Winston coming to River Glen. They needed her to go away but this time permanently. They decide that Hadley-Simon must also go."

"It's a twofer," he said over the kitchen island.

"Yup. They kill Hadley-Simon and frame Winston. Viola, both are gone. But here's the biggest incongruity of all—"

"What?"

"Why go to such intricate lengths to frame her, then try to run her over with a UHaul? Then having failed at that, try to slit her throat on a ghost walk?"

"Who the hell knows? How does one rationalize the actions of a psychopath?"

"A sociopath," she corrected. "This killer's impulsive and erratic. A psychopath is methodical and cautious."

"But renting a pay-as-you-go phone under the alias Jennie Wade and luring Hadley-Simon to the beach as Ella takes forethought. So does getting a motorcycle that looks like hers and dressing like her, all for the purpose of riding by the security cameras at the Radcliffe. All of that takes a lot of planning and a lot of money. BMWs are expensive motorcycles. Multiple wealthy people were involved in the art forging scam. It has to be some of the same individuals. Don't you think?"

She nodded. "Maybe the psychopath is in charge of the planning and the sociopath is doing the dirty work?"

"Dirty work's an understatement," he said grimly. "How did one person... I hate to sound sexist... one female... take on those two hunters?"

"That is sexist." She frowned at him. "But in answer to your question, one who knows martial arts or is ex-military. According to a preliminary toxicology report, the hunters were drunk which made her job easier."

"I've never seen such butchery," Jay said. "At least Ella's out of harm's way. There's no safer place in the world than a holding cell at a police barracks."

The motorcycle unburdened, Ella leaned low into the turn. She had passed the sign for the River Glen Marine Station many times en route to the Wedgewood-Smyth estate but never ventured down the dirt road. Her strategy was to swerve around the rivulets and potholes, chin over handle bars, as if maneuvering a complicated obstacle course, but they were too numerous. She gave in to childlike impulses, deciding instead to bounce in and out of them, her seat and shock-absorbers squeaking. Her senses were alive for the first time in... who could remember back that far? Sunlight filtered through the pine trees. Hot air grazed her bare arms. An occasional pebble plinked against her face shield. The scent of warm sap gave way to acrid marsh grass and brackish water. The forest parted. Amidst the *Spartina* was a clapboard building. So that was it, Alex's place of work. A one-room laboratory from what she could tell. No car or motorcycle was out front; Alex must have motored there on her tugboat.

Ella climbed off her motorcycle as a black Labrador Retriever leapt on her and knocked the helmet from her hands. Ropes of dog spit were flung onto her jeans. "Down, wild thing, down!" She pushed him off and peeked through the screen door. No one was inside. She walked behind the lab, passing an outdoor shower, sink, collecting buckets, rakes and nets.

Alex was dumping bags of ice into coolers on the *Vital Spark*. She waved tentatively. "Hey."

"Hey!"

"I'm heading out in a minute if you want to come. The traps will be bursting."

"Yes, definitely!"

She stepped on to the warped dock and Alex tensed. She had witnessed this response a thousand times. 'What have I gotten myself into? Is this ex-con potentially dangerous... the murderer? Going to attack me?' Would Alex renege on the job offer? Alex had brought her motorcycle to River Glen, but was she having second thoughts?

"Alex, I swear to God, I didn't—"

"Oh, I know," said Alex. "Or Will or Lisa wouldn't have released you."

"I was released by Captain—" Her thoughts locked up. What the hell was his name?

"Herm Taylor."

Alex would obviously know him. Captain Taylor was Will's boss. Everyone mentions their boss to their significant other at some point.

"Let's head out," Alex said untying the lines. "There's a lot I need to show you. First how to drive the tug." She whistled and the black dog bounded onto the boat. "My first mate, Water Boy."

Ella stepped onto the sturdy vessel and followed Alex and the dog into the cabin. She knew absolutely zero about boats but from what she could tell the little tug was a well-loved, well-tended-to rust bucket; though ancient, the electronics at the helm seemed modern. Alex pushed the starter and the boat vibrated below their feet. The propellers eased them off the dock and churned the water from olive green to a muddy ochre. She tried to concentrate on how Alex was operating the wheel and two throttles, but the cabin's décor was captivating. The boat was decorated like a pyrate ship. Tattered black flags from notorious pyrate captains hung off wooden bulkheads. Dangling from a ship's wheel lamp were plastic shrunken heads and tropical birds. Over the hatchway a blue-gowned figurehead was wearing Hawaiian leis. Pictures of iconic pyrates were taped around the cabin: Captain Hook battling Peter Pan, Johnny Depp's Jack Sparrow and N. C. Wyeth's images from *Treasure Island*. Alex had even drawn magic-marker eye patches on the dogs in *Dogs Playing Poker*.

"Crabbing is dirty, hot work, Ella, so be sure to hydrate. Water bottles are in there."

She pulled a bottle from a small fridge. "I'm parched from the motorcycle ride. Thank you."

"Let me find us some tunes," Alex said adjusting a satellite radio. "What do you like?"

"Anything." She had expected Alex to select country music, maybe southern rock, Zach Brown, Jimmy Buffett or Bob Marley, but instead she would be learning to crab to tango music.

The hours on the water passed quickly and though Alex had countless eccentricities, she was an expert on boats and the Chesapeake wildlife. She had pointed out to her bald eagles, sea hawks, skates, eels and fish. Best of all Alex had shown her everything about crabbing. Dirty, hot work yes, but exhilarating nonetheless. No more pushing soap suds over prison floors. No more walking creaky hallways while brats stuck candy to her ass. No more escaping into an alternate reality in cinderblock. This reality, hard and hot as it was, was a damn good one.

FORGER'S REVENGE

By afternoon's end she knew how to: drive a tug, operate the navigational equipment, bait traps, use the pot hauler to raise and lower the traps, avoid the menacing claws of crabs and pack the crabs in ice. Alex had shown her the marshes and inlets where the biggest Jimmies hid. She knew how to determine the sex of the crabs, measure them and toss back the juveniles and females.

"I know of other places packed with crabs," Alex said, "but I don't have time to get them and still do my day job at the marine lab. I can show you if you're interested in expanding the business. What do you think?"

Unbelievable! Never was she asked for her input by an employer. Never.

"I'm definitely interested. I have no other plans, nothing else going on. I'm not supposed to leave River Glen until things get straightened out. I'm really grateful for the work."

"Okay then. Let me show you this great place."

They motored northward. The Wedgewood-Smyth manor house appeared around the bend. After tiptoeing from room to room searching for Eatons, it was intriguing to see the house from a different perspective, the water. The coastline was beautiful... stunningly beautiful... inspirational and worthy of painting. Except not by her. She was not touching another paintbrush in this or subsequent lifetimes. Still, the scene was easy to envision as a painting. Impressionistic or surreal possibly, because the house appeared like a mirage, hazy and floating on glistening water and steamy marsh. The expansive lawn was overgrown with weeds and scrubs trees; vines coiled through the hurricane fence. The property was book-ended by a dark green forest and an orange cliff crowned with trees.

"One of the best crabbing places is there," said Alex looking out a porthole. "There's a deep hole near the mouth of that creek. No one ever sets traps back there so there's a ton of monster crabs hiding in it."

"Why is that?"

"There's all sorts of junk on the bottom. Generations of Wedgewoods and Smyths must have used it as their garbage dump. But there's also cool historical stuff. My grandfather Randy and I pulled a Penny-farthing high-wheel bicycle from the hole. I rode it around for an entire summer until the spokes rusted out. I'll show you the place, but we have to be careful that we don't get the prop or rudder snagged on the bottom." Alex reached to an instrument above the windshield and flipped a switch. "This is a side-scan sonar. You'll see stuff on the bottom in a sec."

She gazed up at the screen. Scattered bits of debris soon appeared on the smooth bottom. "Did you ever dive on this stuff?"

"Not here, but I dove in other places. The bay has bad visibility. The water's so rich with nutrients, algae and microbes that you can barely see your hand in front of your face."

"More and more junk," she observed.

"If we do decide to set traps here, we'll have to position them away from this stuff and closer to the marsh grass. That's where crabs hide anyway."

Shadowy objects continued to appear on a grey silty background. "Wait, Alex."

"What?"

"Can you stop here?"

"As much as a boat can stop." Alex threw the throttles into neutral. "What is it?"

"Look at that."

Alex studied the screen. "What do think it is?"

"It's big whatever it is."

"Really big."

"A propane tank?"

"Or a septic tank?"

"A World War II torpedo?"

"Maybe."

Alex pushed a button on the helm and a heavy chain unspooled at the bow. The anchor splashed into the water. "I hope that didn't stir up too much muck or we'll never find it."

"Find it?"

"Crabbing is dirty, hot work, Ella. We're taking a swim."

Querida Mama was reeling in her grave for the umpteenth time. Were Mama still alive, she would have insisted that Nina move from River Glen after the incident at Tolchester College that severed her fingers. Mama would be equally shocked by her motorcycle riding, getting tipsy on Hurricanes with Alex and Julia, eating marijuana brownies and wild dancing at the Giles Blood-hand festival... dancing that was recorded by a student in her Social Problems seminar, posted on You Tube and resulted in requests for dates from two seniors, the chairman of the Political Science Department and the women's basketball coach. When did she even get on the picnic table with Alex? That afternoon, when she was about to give James a passionate kiss, every sphincter in her urinary tract let loose. Her bladder could never endure the endless lines at the porta-potties. Then she remembered the ladies room in the historical society. Her dash across the village green while yanking up the petticoats of her wench gown also made it on to You Tube as *The Effect of Luna's Magic Brownies on Tolchester College Professor Babe Part 2.*

Mama was reeling once again because Nina was in the stacks of the historical society reading (re-reading more accurately) what was the equivalent of pornography. Her four-year review in the promotion and tenure process was fast approaching and she was supposed to be working on her manuscript "A Post-modern Interpretation of the Deconstructional Matrix of the Socioeconomics of blah and more blah," but instead she was surreptitiously reading through Box 4: The Letters of Abigail Wedgewood-Smyth.

Box 4 contained Abigail's love letters to Josiah. Abigail had many intertwined interests: sex, history, art, cosplay and bondage. Her favorite past-time was to dress Josiah as a historical character—Julius Caesar, Henry the 8th, or Genghis Khan—then he would let Abigail do anything her heart desired. Her heart desired a lot. Some letters even included sketches of elaborate contraptions and sex toys. 'Submit Josiah submit' Abigail had written in letter after letter. In the current one Abigail was coaxing Josiah—Eric the Red—to... she was very imaginative.

A sound. Nina froze and stopped reading. Footsteps in the hallway. A key slipped imperceptibly into the lock. Oh my god... who? Only a few people had keys to the rare documents room. It wasn't the librarian Judith Ann Smyth; she was on vacation. And the assistant librarian Burt Sweeney had taken Burt Jr. to an Orioles game at Camden Yards. James also had a key, but he was at the county courthouse.

Was it the killer from the Radcliffe, searching for something in the stacks?

Do not move... not even twitch! She held her breath. The footsteps stopped. Had the intruder moved onto the carpet? Now she had no idea which direction he was heading! No idea whatsoever! Do not move, not even to slide Box 4 into place. What if he heard her frantic heart? It must sound like a gong! Who? Where was he? Could she tiptoe to the door, bolt down the hallway and out the front door to the village green without being caught and killed? Absolute silence. Where was he?

A swift tentacle of an arm encircled her waist and a hand clamped against her mouth!

"Mmm!" She twisted.

Silence.

"Mmm!"

"Abigail, you're reading Box 4," said a hot whisper to the nape of her neck.

The aftershave and voice were immediately familiar and she exhaled into his hand. He removed it from her mouth. "Yes, Josiah."

"Your letters so delight me," he whispered again.

She grinned. "That's why I write them."

"We have the archive to ourselves for the afternoon."

"And four tables to... work on."

"Only four?"

"Submit, Josiah, submit."

"Anything you desire, my beauty," he replied in Josiah's exact words.

She turned and pressed a kiss onto James' mouth. It was long overdue.

"You know how to swim, don't you?" Alex asked Ella.

"Do you think I'd be working on a boat if I couldn't?" she replied.

"Just checking." Alex dug through a sea bag. "I don't know where they all went. My bathing suits must be at the cottage. Here. Change into these. We're about the same size." She handed her a wad of clothes and disappeared from the berth.

Ella shook out the clothes. That morning she had been in a holding cell at the River Glen police barracks, expecting to be given an orange jumpsuit to wear. The ironies of fate. Instead this. Corona beer shorts and a Sponge Bob T-shirt. She sniffed the clothes. Clean but rumpled. She slipped out of her shirt and jeans and pulled them on.

She stepped outside and looked into the motionless green water. When was the last time she had been swimming? Not in prison, grad school or college. It had to be during high school gym class. That's where she had met Ralph MacKenzie. It was the semester after volleyball. At the shallow end of the pool he had sidled up to her in his smarmy way and said that he liked her bathing suit. There was nothing remarkable about it; every other girl at the pool's edge was wearing the identical one. "No bikinis, ladies," the swim coach had told them. That meant using ghost walk money to purchase a hideous one-piece black Speedo—that she wore for only one goddamn semester. The reason she spoke to Ralph at all was to get a closer look at his cut body. The following year in college art classes she would be sketching nude models. She was just getting a jump-start on her study of muscle anatomy. Ralph's body was pretty perfect though in all other respects he was a dullard. Because libido triumphs over reason every time, she agreed to a date where she ended up ankles on his shoulders at Devil's Den. Afterwards that user never called her back. She obviously lacked the right skills in the romance department. What did he expect? It was her first time. Maybe he was already boning Sharon Westerly. Being older, Westerly would have been very experienced—probably expert. She got a call back because he married her. No more thoughts about one-night-stands with bastards like Ralph and Jay Braden. She would distract herself by watching Alex attach long orange tubes onto a scuba tank. Yikes, two tubes.

"Alex, um... we're not..."

"Yeah, we are."

"But I don't know how to scuba dive."

"But you know how to breathe."

"Well, duh, but—"

"This isn't exactly scuba diving. You don't need to be dive certified." Alex strapped a Velcro belt around Ella's waist and fastened an orange tube to the belt. Then she gave her a scuba mask. "I taught Carly, Will's daughter, to use the hookah hose and she's only eight so you can do it. You simply breathe in and out of the regulator. According to the side scan data, the propane-septic-torpedo is only in eighteen feet of water so there are no decompression issues."

Ella's heart pounded. Crabbing was one thing but diving on a junk heap was another.

"Adjust the mask to your face and make sure it's snug," Alex said. "Climb overboard and try breathing and swimming with the regulator."

What choice did she have? She would have swum with piranhas to please her new boss and keep the job. Besides, how dangerous could a quiet inlet be? She climbed over the gunwale and down a rusty ladder. The water was lukewarm, hardly refreshing at all after a sweaty afternoon of hauling crab traps. Alex spooled the orange tube and regulator over the side.

"Just breathe relaxed and normal," Alex called down to her.

She put the regulator in her mouth and submerged her face in the water. The world beyond her mask shimmered green and yellow, so dense were the shiny particles. Pressurized air shot into her lungs and bubbles burst around her head. She found herself hyperventilating. Relaxed and normal, Alex had said. She willfully slowed her breathing. In out in out. Nice and slow. In out. If an eight-year-old could do this, then so could she.

She was doing it... breathing underwater! She jerked her face from the water and ripped the regulator from her mouth.

"I did it, Alex! How long was I breathing underwater? Two minutes, three?"

"Maybe twenty seconds," Alex laughed. "I'm coming in." She flung another orange tube over the side and climbed down the ladder. Hanging off the ladder, she tied a rope between their Velcro belts, tethering them together. "We're sticking together all the way down and all the way up."

"Works for me."

"The sunken object is right over there," Alex gestured. "Let's go down to the bottom and swim over to it. Remember, just breathe slow and relaxed and kick gently so we don't stir up the muck."

"Got it."

"Ready?" Alex put a regulator in her mouth.

She did the same and nodded. Down they went, tugging on each other in descent. The visibility was terrible in these waters. Six inches at the most. They kicked forward in green blindness, distance impossible to gauge. Then thump. Her hand bumped into a smooth object. Alex shot her a mystified look. She felt it too. Their hands slid along its side. Whatever it was, it was metal and slippery with algae. On they moved. A seam of corroded rivets appeared. Alex's suggestion of a septic tank seemed most likely.

Until.

They turned to each other in mutual dismay. In front of them was a mechanical arm shrouded in seaweed. Alex reached cautiously for the appendage as if it might grab back. The joints of the arm were stiff but mobile. Rags of seaweed swayed languidly as she moved the arm back and forth. At its end was a claw like those of the blue crabs in ice.

FORGER'S REVENGE

Alex checked the air gauge hanging off her Velcro belt and motioned that they move on. More algae-slick surface, seams and rivets. It was a man-made object but what? It narrowed to a point and at its tapered nose cone was a sturdy metal eye to attach to a hefty tow-hook. There were no windows or a hatch. Was it hollow or solid? What was it? Despite ample air in the tank, Alex gave a thumbs-up that signaled ascent. They had only just begun to explore the wreck. Why ascend now? But who was she to question the dive master? She followed Alex up to the surface.

"What the hell was that?" she gasped.

"Captain Nemo's *Nautilus*?" Alex said. "Who freaking knows?"

"Why'd we come up so soon?"

"I need the remaining air for one more dive. This old tug used to pull barges up rivers so it should be able to lift this thing off the bottom."

"We're bringing it up?"

"Why not? The visibility sucks. It's the only way we'll know exactly what it is. I think I can attach a cable from the winch to the wreck's nose cone."

First crabbing, then diving with a hookah hose dive apparatus, now nautical salvage. They returned to the deck where Alex tinkered with the winch's motor and cable for a few minutes. "I think this will work." She reattached her Velcro belt and hookah hose and climbed down the ladder. "I'm ready. Send it down."

Hand over hand Ella lowered the winch's hook down the side of the *Vital Spark*. Alex grabbed it and disappeared in green glitter and bubbles.

Sharon rung off with a detective in Gettysburg and swiveled her chair toward Lisa Paco and Will Wilkins. "Why does this not surprise me. A number in the contact list from Dana Detrick's iPhone belongs to the phantom Jennie Wade."

Paco glanced up from her laptop. "Who's Dana Detrick?"

"Ella Winston's boss at the Ephram Whitson House."

"Jennie's was the number that texted Hadley-Simon and lured him to the beach at the Radcliffe," Wilkins said.

"If some nefarious business is going on in Gburg, one of the Detricks is invariably involved," she said. "Their combined IQs are in negative numbers so they always get caught."

Paco chewed excitedly. "Did your officers bring Detrick in? Did she reveal who Jennie Wade is?"

"Yes and no. Yes, Detrick was brought in for questioning. No, she couldn't identify Jennie Wade."

"How come?"

"According to Detrick's statement, a female parole officer approached her upon Winston's reemployment at the ghost walk. The officer told Detrick to inform her of Winston's comings and goings and gave Detrick a number—the Jennie Wade number—to call when Winston was traveling. And Detrick was given a backhander every time she notified the parole officer of Winston's activities. How nice to incentivize Detrick with cash... untraceable cash."

"What's the name of the parole officer?" Paco said.

"JW Booth. Detrick described her as a large female in a business suit. Big hair. Thick glasses. Briefcase."

"Let me guess," Wilkins said. "There's no parole officer in your jurisdiction by that name."

"You got it. The person of interest in Linda Radowski's murder, the biker who split early from the ghost walk, is also a big stocky woman."

Paco popped a bubble. "That's how the perp knew that Winston was going to be in River Glen."

"Messed up," Sharon uttered. "Jennie Wade. Now JW Booth."

"Why?" Wilkins asked.

"John Wilkes Booth was Lincoln's assassin."

The algae-slick object spun like a hooked fish. Muddy water drizzled off it creating a silty puddle on the deck of the *Vital Spark*.

"What a catch!" said Alex looking aloft. "A primitive submersible and definitely a home-made job. No wonder we couldn't tell what the thing was. It was upside down in the muck. We were swimming along its underbelly."

"What if we found Nemo's *Nautilus*?" Ella wondered aloud. "What if it wasn't fictional? How cool would that be?"

"Very cool. But that *Nautilus* was a giant sub that held an entire crew. This is only big enough for a few people at the most." Alex's amazement turned to worry. "This might be a priceless historical artifact. Until we know what it is, we say nothing to no one."

"Agreed," she said emphatically.

"Help me clear a space for it."

They slid aside crab traps, nylon lines and coolers.

"Stand back, Ella. Water Boy, move or you'll get crushed," said Alex at the winch controls.

The cable squealed and the sub thudded onto the deck. Water Boy cautiously sniffed it as clumps of black anaerobic mud slipped down its sides. It was definitely a sub... cylindrical in shape, tapering to a nose cone and eye, and at the opposite end a rudder and propellers. A circular hatch door was its only entry point. Alex stood on a crap trap, climbed up its side and pressed her face to the glass windshield.

"What do you see?"

"Nothing. The glass is encrusted with eons of green slime. Let me try the hatch."

"Do you think we should?"

"Why not?"

"I don't know. Just a feeling."

"It's probably filled with putrid water. Nothing more."

"I'll get ready to plug my nose."

Alex reached for a lever on the hatch and pulled. "Nothing." Ella climbed up to assist and grabbed the lever also. "On the count of three," Alex said. "One, two, three." They threw their weight into it. Nothing again. "It's completely corroded." Alex slid down its side, disappeared into the cabin and returned with a sledge hammer.

"What if we damage the thing? Maybe historians should have a look before we hammer away at it."

Alex flashed her a devilish smile. "There's pyrate treasure stashed all over these parts. Who knows what we might find? What if Nemo of the Chesapeake found the treasure of Giles Blood-hand or Juan Carlos del Castillo and loaded his sub with pieces of eight?"

"Treasure? Okay then. I'm in."

Alex tapped at the lever as gentle as was possible with a sledge hammer. Miraculously it didn't break off because it was made from a heavy iron alloy. She tapped again. She hammered more forcefully and the lever squeaked to the side. She struggled to lift the hatch, but it wouldn't budge. "Also corroded." She disappeared into the cabin once again then reappeared with a crowbar. She jammed it under the lip of the hatch. "Ella, again on three. One, two, three." They thrust their weight down on the crowbar and the seal broke with a crackle.

"Well?" she said to Alex.

"I guess we should open it. Shouldn't we?"

"We've come this far."

"Yes."

"Okay then."

"Let's do it."

"Yes."

"Okay."

They lifted the hatch and bent over the opening. Barely visible through the gloom was the sub's floor.

"Strange, Alex. No water. It's bone-dry. The person who built this knew what they were doing. Weird smell."

"Way funky. I never smelled anything like it." Alex pushed her head farther inside.

"What do you see?"

"Nothing. It's too dark. There's a short ladder. Let's me check it out."

"You sure?"

"Um, yeah." Alex disappeared into the grey circle.

"Anything?"

"I'm outta here!"

"What?"

Alex launched herself up the ladder and collided with Ella's chin, knocking her off the sub. Alex spilled next to her onto the deck.

"Alex, what!?"

"This isn't a sub! We opened a goddamn tomb!"

Jay Braden's blood was boiling. He was that stunned and that furious. His ignoramus boss Herm Taylor had released Ella Winston while a slasher was terrorizing River Glen and Gettysburg! What staggering stupidity! According to Will, their captain's rationale was that Trooper Hastings and the two hunters Eddie Malloy and Clayton Underwood had been killed while Ella was in the custody of the River Glen PD, therefore it would have been impossible for her to have committed the crimes. Hastings had been dispatched like Hadley-Simon and Radowski, by one exacting slice to the throat, but then the killer methodically dissected his skeletal muscles. The Malloy-Underwood crime scene was radically different. From the extensive defensive wounds on the hunters, it was clear that they had stumbled into the wrong campsite at the wrong time. They had enraged the killer. After the frenzied hacking was done, she removed what was left of their skeletal muscles. There was evidence of a recent fire and fresh motorcycle tracks amidst the butchery.

Ella should be in protective custody, not walking free! When the Whitby cousins were stalking Alex three summers ago, he had assigned Will to act as her bodyguard. Thank god he did. Alex was unharmed but his beloved Laura—

How to reach Ella? He never thought to ask for her phone number. Should he reach her, he might offer up a room in his house until the whole mess was over, but she certainly wouldn't speak to him, much less answer if she knew it was him.

Herm Taylor had closed him out of the case. While Westerly, Paco and Wilkins were at headquarters piecing together the evidence, he was stuck at home like a prisoner under house arrest. It was not his fault that Herm's wife Janine hung all over him at Laura's funeral. Or that Janine insisted on being his partner in the three-legged race at the annual picnic, or drank too much egg nog at the Christmas party... that incident with the mistletoe was outright mortifying. If Herm could rein in his needy wife... shit, no wonder the man abhorred him.

Ella, Ella, focus on Ella. Where would she have gone? To find Alex. Yes. Ella had mentioned crabbing with Alex. He pulled his phone from his shorts pocket and sent a text: *Hey Alex, is Ella with you? If no, do you know where she is? J*

He gingerly pressed his swollen eye to Laura's telescope. In the last days of her madness she had searched the Glen River for the ghost ship *Raven* cruising the mists. He swiveled the telescope toward the village. There was no sign of Ella at the dockside shops and restaurants. He inched the telescope along the riverbank. The windows in Julia's house were a lifeless black. The *Vital Spark* was gone from the dock. No surprise there. Alex and Water Boy motored the tugboat to the marine lab every day. The telescope swept across the tacky lawn ornaments. Wait. What was that in the driveway between Julia and Alex's houses?

A UHaul.

He whistled for Miranda and Clark. He locked them in the house while he hurried to the river's edge. He jumped into his Boston Whaler, ripped the cord on the outboard and sped across the river. He tied up at the cleats for the *Vital Spark* and rushed down the dock to the driveway and truck.

"Son of a bitch." A black smudge, definitely rubber, was on the front bumper of the UHaul.

He checked his cell phone. No response from Alex. She had lost two cell phones into the bay that summer. Had she bought a third or given up on owning one? He walked to the back of the truck. In the pocket of his dress pants for work he always kept a spare pair of nylon gloves so as not to contaminate a crime scene but at the moment, the only thing in his shorts pocket was a roll of poop bags for the dogs. He fitted one over his hand, opened the latch on the back door and climbed into the bed.

Vile smell. The odor was not from the fast food garbage in the corner but of gasoline and something else, something stale and organic. The floor was covered with droplets of motor oil, gasoline and—he sent Zera Lim an urgent text—blood.

Ella paced the deck of the *Vital Spark*. "I'm screwed! Cursed! How can one person have such horrendous luck? First *my* professor gets killed, then Linda Radowski on *my* ghost walk. Now two bodies in the sub! This is going to seal the deal with the cops. They'll think I'm behind this. Does Maryland have the death penalty?"

Alex bit her nail. "I need to think."

"I'm definitely going to take the rap for this! Four bodies, Alex! Four!"

"Four? But the two in the sub are ancient."

"What?"

"Yeah. Ancient."

"How ancient?"

"I don't know but very ancient." Alex disappeared into the cabin and returned with a flashlight. "See for yourself. No one can blame you for those. It's a male and a female. I didn't stay around to see much more, but the woman was in an old-fashioned gown. A wooden crucifix was by them."

"I need to see for myself."

Ella grabbed the flashlight, climbed up the sub and dipped her leg into the cool opening. She stepped onto the first rung, the second and third. Her sneakers hit the metal floor. *Scrape scrape.* In a panic, she leapt up the rungs. It was only Alex with a filleting knife, scraping away the algal film from the window. The light of late afternoon poured through the green streaks. She exhaled and lowered herself to the floor. Her head nearly grazed the ceiling; the sub was that shallow. She knew two corpses would be there, still she gasped.

The sub was a tomb as Alex had said. Lifting it off the bottom had jumbled the two skeletons into one another. There was a crucifix amidst a heap of bones and fabric. Despite the disturbance, the woman's bony arms were frozen in an X across her concave chest. The male, locked in a fetal position near the woman's feet, was clothed in wool knickers, suspenders and a cotton shirt. Both individuals wore nineteenth century garb.

Ella knelt beside the male to examine the spatters and smudges on his shirt. Motor oil? Engine grease? Paint? She wasn't about to press her nose into a skeleton's shirt to find out. The flashlight beam moved back to the female whose leathery face nested amidst thick red hair. The light beam traveled down the skeleton's collapsed gown and hovered over her crossed wrists.

"Oh my god." Ella grasped the flashlight with both hands to stop the shakes.

Two fingers on woman's left hand were missing.

She illuminated the male's shirt again. The colorful spatters in the spotlight were paint—most definitely dried oil paint.

"Hello Abigail. Hello Adam," she whispered.

Fishing hat low over his face, Jay climbed onto a stool at the outdoor bar of Harlow's Pub. One benefit of the busted nose and black eyes was that he looked like such a low-life that no one would bother him. House-bound during an investigation of this magnitude made him antsy. In the end he had ignored Herm Taylor's orders to stay put. Harlow's Pub in the village center was the ideal vantage point to look for Ella Winston.

"I'm allowed to go out for a beer," he might argue should he be caught. "I'm on vacation after all."

Nor did Herm need to know that Sharon Westerly had agreed to meet him after work. The pub was a strategically-located sentry post and place to wait for Westerly that conveniently sold alcohol. He looked between the neon beer signs to the pub's interior. Miles Harlow was at his usual place behind the taps. Locales, mostly fishermen and boaters who rented slips at the Smyth marina, were watching the Orioles game and other sporting events from a row of TV screens above the bar.

And there were bikers.

He had had enough of them for one lifetime, but River Glen had become a popular ride destination. At a corner table was a group of women bikers who, according to the rockers on their leather vests, belonged to a club in Plumsteadville, Pennsylvania. None bore any resemblance to the tall woman who was part of the ghost walk then mysteriously disappeared. Two couples from Indiana rode in on big touring bikes, Honda Gold Wings. A grey-bearded biker with a Bikers for Jesus vest sat at the bar, eating a steak and chatting with Miles. The Christian biker must own the Harley Fat Boy with the Massachusetts plate. But there was no sign of Ella Winston and her BMW.

He checked his phone. Still no word from Alex though a text from Westerly said that she was on her way. *I'm at the bar outside*, he texted back. Nor was there feedback from Zera whose forensic team was lifting prints and analyzing the blood samples in the UHaul.

How did the UHaul that tried to kill Ella end up in River Glen and in Alex's yard? Was Alex driving? Why kill Ella? No, impossible. Nothing made sense. Will had no knowledge of the truck at the cottage that he shared with Alex because he hadn't slept there last night. After their conversation last night at the hot tub, Will had stopped by his parents to pick up Carly. Will and Carly got delayed watching Ravens' highlights with Will's father and in the end decided to sleep at his parents' house. It was Will's ploy to postpone a hot conversation with Alex about Ella Winston's arrest.

Jay tossed down the rest of his beer and headed to the men's room. He unzipped his fly at the urinal. The prostate meds allowed for an unobstructed flow. The bathroom door opened. The Christian biker stopped at the urinal next to his. The man had obviously drunk a lot because he pissed for a while. Jay glanced down, then took a second look. Whoa, lucky guy. This dude would have no problem getting a date on a Saturday night. Jay washed his hands and left. Westerly was buying herself a drink at the outside bar.

"Let's not talk here," she said. "It's too crowded."

"There?" he said pointing to the solitary bench at the end of the pier.

"Fine."

He and Laura had sat on that bench countless times to watch an orange sun drop into the bay but before he could wallow in sadness, his phone vibrated. "It's Zera Lim."

"Who's that?"

"Our medical examiner."

He and Westerly walked down the pier while he spoke with Zera. Westerly dropped tiredly onto the bench and slipped off her shoes.

"Alright," he said to Zera. "Let me know when you know." He rang off.

"What's up?" asked Westerly kneading her ankle.

"There are prints from many individuals on the UHaul. Not surprising for a rental vehicle though most are from Alex and Nina. Will couldn't reach Alex, but he got in touch with Nina. Nina said that they drove it from Gettysburg to River Glen with the three motorcycles."

"Alex and Nina have prints on file and police records?" she said suspiciously.

"No records, but they were printed for other reasons."

Westerly's face remained doubtful.

"In two previous murder investigations," he clarified.

"Two?"

"It's a tiny town. Our suspect pool is limited."

"The other prints?"

"Nothing yet. CSI found cut marks in the floor of the truck made with a sharp implement like a razor. The human blood and muscle tissue belonged to Hastings."

She gulped fast from her drink.

"A possible breakthrough," he said.

She looked unabashedly at him. "What?"

"The fast food trash in truck. Saliva on a water bottle."

"Whose DNA?"

"CSI is on it as we speak."

"Good for us. Bad for her," she said with a hint of optimism. "A careless killer. A sociopath."

"With a psychopath pulling her strings?"

"Jennie Wade has to be Ventresca, Will," said Lisa Paco twisting her gum around a pencil. "She just has to be."

"But Ventresca has no direct association with Gettysburg. Only indirectly through her husband. Immigration does have a record of her visiting England with Hadley-Simon. She mentioned visiting his birthplace and art school in London. The two of them visited the UK ten years ago. Her passport confirms that trip. So far all of her statements have checked out."

"What about her first husband What's-his-name?"

Will sat up in his chair. "What What's-his-name?"

"The Spaniard that she married. Ferdinando? Frederico? Franco! That's what the father said. An actor. What if her long-lost-love Franco returned from Spain and they schemed to knock off the geezer husband, collect his life insurance and inherit half the gallery? I bet that's what happened. #pacoisbrilliant."

"When was this?"

"When Ventresca was a college student in Boston." She turned to her laptop. "Let me find her resume online. Then we'll know the time-frame."

"Remember that Boston is where Hadley-Simon was convicted of stealing historical documents."

"Spain is where he fled to when he broke parole!" she said.

"And what about Hadley-Simon's make-up case with the toupees, beards and actor's glue? Our killer's pseudonym is JW Booth. John Wilkes Booth was an actor."

Ella sat on a crab trap amidst coolers of blue crabs while Water Boy gnawed on her shoe laces and Alex drove the tugboat to sultry tango music. Tied to the *Vital Spark*'s transom was a primitive submersible. Who knows what other crazy stuff she and Alex might pull from the bay on future cruises? In one day she had become a crabber, diver and marine salvor. Extraordinary boat adventures were her new normal.

In hindsight, she wished that she had paid more attention to Adam Eaton's mechanical drawings. She had only considered his engineering innovations to contextualize his art. His drawings were first seen when she worked as a student intern at the historical society in Gettysburg during her senior year in high school. She was researching Civil War artists for her honors history class. Dr. Worth couldn't pay her student wages, but she had been happy to file, photocopy and transcribe documents in exchange for unlimited access to the stacks and Phoebe's gooey peanut butter cookies. Besides, she had no need for a second paycheck. She was at the pinnacle of ghostly fame.

It was then that she discovered in a dusty box what appeared to be submarine designs. Adam Eaton and Josiah Wedgewood-Smyth's names were on the plans which put the Wedgewood-Smyths of River Glen, Maryland on her radar screen in the first place. She had walked over to Dr. Worth's desk with the submarine sketches but hesitated. Worth was engaged in a heated conversation with Old Man Detrick. He had been relic-hunting in the battlefield again, and again she was barking "No!"

"I will not buy your illegally obtained belt buckles, caps, shoes and bullets. No, no and no!"

Detrick persisted.

"And no! I will not set up a display of your stolen artifacts next to the Tobias Worth exhibits! They do not belong in the same room!" The exasperated curator shooed him away with his box of ill-gained booty.

Worth turned to Ella. "An absolute crook."

Ella grinned. "My boss."

Worth looked curiously at the papers in Ella's hands. "Well, my dear, what do you have?"

"Pretty cool. Adam Eaton and Josiah Wedgewood-Smyth were building submarines."

The curator gently leafed through the brittle papers. "Where did you get these?"

"From the Wedgewood-Smyth files."

Nonplussed, Worth had handed them back to her. "Submarines were around long before the Civil War, Ellie. Historians believe that they date back to Alexander the Great who used diving bells. Several inventors, starting in the Middle Ages and Renaissance, were experimenting with different submarine configurations. During the Civil War there were of course the *USS Alligator* and the Confederates' *H. L. Hunley*."

FORGER'S REVENGE

What obscure minutiae didn't this bitty know? Ella had wondered at the time. If it didn't apply to art and artists, she had listened with half an ear. She never gave the submarines a second thought until James Collins mentioned his novel *Subterfuge*.

That day she and Alex found Adam and Josiah's sub! Their designs on paper had been brought to life. The men had built one! She was overcome with a strange compulsion to call Dr. Worth and tell her of the astonishing discovery, but she and Alex had vowed secrecy until they could find out more about the men's activities. And why were Abigail and Adam entombed in it? Were they there by choice or had someone put them there?

According to Alex, no one visited her at the marine lab so the quiet marsh would be a good place to hide the sub. They lowered it onto a narrow beach surrounded by *Spartina* grass and covered it with tarps. But their day was not done. Fresh crabs had to be delivered to the Dockside Café and Nauticus, then their final destination was James Collins' house to learn of a dastardly killing machine called Chessie.

Starring in the role of Roy the Bible-thumping Biker is actor extraordinaire...

Setting of the play: A sports bar in a Chesapeake fishing village.

He could barely stay in character. One minute he had been contentedly watching the Orioles game and eating a T-bone when Jennie's latest text ruined his mood. *What a total cock-up!* Fuck her. Fuck her anal-retentive perfectionism. This job had been anything but a *total cock-up*.

When the fat Goth Dana had informed them that Ella was heading to River Glen for the pyrate festival, Jennie decided to act. "Seymour goes." Prepaid cell phones were purchased and "Ella" texted Seymour to arrange a meeting at the Radcliffe. Greed got the better of Seymour and he agreed to a meeting—behind the back of his partners. That was a costly mistake.

"Ella kills Seymour and gets sent back to the slammer," said Jennie thinking aloud. "The second conviction for murder. This time life."

He had pondered Jennie's scheme and became irked by the finer details. He had been watching Ella for some time ... years in fact. So delicious she was and would be again. What a waste for her to waste away in prison. What if instead of being sent back to prison as Jennie planned, Ella were to disappear? It would implicate her further in the eyes of the law. The inevitable conclusion would be that she had murdered her thesis advisor and successfully escaped, perhaps fled the country.

What if there was a deviation in Jennie's game plan? What if JW ran Ella off the road? Knocked her off the motorcycle, stashed her in the UHaul, then had a bit of fun with her? Submit, Ella, submit. Those had been wonderful romps on the straw mattress in the Ephram Whitson House. Ella's fate would never be known. She had cleverly evaded law enforcement, he might tell Jennie.

But then...

Ella's riding abilities had been vastly underestimated. She was amazingly quick in veering off the road and navigating the forest's rough terrain. Within seconds she was lost in the underbrush. JW thought to pursue her into the woods, but it would have been impossible to stop the speeding UHaul and offload the motorcycle in time to catch up with her. She would have been long gone.

Ella's escape enraged JW. How she hated revising well-conceived plans. Fuck Ella slipping from her realm of control! Improvisation was in order. JW strategized while watching Ella and the white-haired man tour the battlefield. How dare Ella defy her! Improv, improv... she was an expert at improvisation from acting school. But how?

Exert the ultimate control.

The lights went off according to plan. JW grabbed the braid and sliced. She skirted the crowd and fled down the stairs. She ducked into an alley, whipped off the blonde wig and bandana and changed into the stolen hardhat and high vis construction vest. Hiding in plain sight, inspecting power lines between the buildings while watching events unfold at the crime scene.

What? Ella staggered out of the Ephram Whitson House on the arm of the white-haired man! How?

JW seethed. Why didn't the voluptuous detective-in-charge drag Ella away on-the-spot? That made no sense. She had to know that Ella was an ex-con. Ella would return to the Ephram Whitson House parking lot that night to pick up her motorcycle, JW figured, but instead the young trooper showed up. That was an opportunity not to be missed.

Miles the Bartender: Would you like anything else?

What was the next line? How to answer? As JW or Roy? At times the lines were completely jumbled. Which character was he? Roy. He was absolutely sure. The personality transformation had been complete. JW, the manipulative murderess, was gone. He was Roy. JW was gone, long gone. The Roy character was a good-natured lover-boy, as docile as a kitten.

Roy (smiles pleasantly): Another Bud please.

Miles departs for the taps.

Roy turns to a noise offstage and cranes his head toward the plate glass window. Between neon beer signs he spots a tugboat chugging to the pier by the Dockside Café. On it are a skinny black-haired woman and—how very interesting—Ella Winston.

Roy pulls bills from the wallet chained to his belt loop and tosses them on the bar.

Miles (approaches with a frothy mug of beer): But your—

Roy: Keep the change.

He departs stage left toward a Harley Fat Boy in the parking lot.

Alex pounded on the skull door knocker. Nothing. "His car's here," she said to Ella. She pounded again.

"One minute" sounded James' voice through the intercom.

"Ella, wait 'til you see this place," she whispered. "It's super cool. The whole place is decorated with nautical stuff."

The massive door swung open and Alex's eyes widened. "Bro, Halloween's in October."

A ruddy-cheeked James bowed and waved them in with a gallant sweep of his arm. His attire was from the eighteen hundreds: knickers, a billowing blouse with laces across his chest and a velvet coat. His usual meticulous hair was in unusual disarray. "Nina and I were in the basement, checking out my mother's costume closet."

"Were you?" she said comically.

"Yes. C'mon in. Let me get you ladies drinks."

She glanced over his shoulder. A lust-flushed Nina was leaning against the marble counter, sipping wine. Her likewise messy hair fell over an ornate gown.

"Having fun, Roomie?" she smirked.

"A fine time," Nina smiled.

"Tipsy are we?"

"On my way."

"Beer, wine, cocktails?" said James cheerfully.

"Just water," she said. "I'm dehydrated from a day on the water."

"Water's fine for me also," Ella said.

He ducked into the fridge and pulled out water bottles. "Alex, wouldn't it be marvelous to resurrect the Collins tradition of annual costume balls? I was just telling Nina about them."

"Papa Randy told me that they were drunken orgies," she said. "He lived for them."

"How wonderful! Nina and I thought that we might go as Josiah and Abigail Wedgewood-Smyth." He glanced down at his belly. "This costume is a perfect fit, but I can't put on another pound."

She looked ironically Ella. "On that topic. That's why we're here."

He cocked his head. "Oh? Why?"

"We were crabbing near the ruined estate today and got on the subject of them. We wondered what really happened to Abigail. I heard stories about the hanging tree. Is any of it true?"

James' face darkened. "Let's sit. But let me give you fair warning, it's a horrible story."

The four of them crossed the spacious room of seafaring curios. Paintings of ships and storms and stuffed marlins and sharks covered mahogany walls and stone pillars. There was a Steinway piano, suits of armor and weapons: small cannons, blunderbusses and rifles at every turn. It was the preponderance of spears, swords and throwing blades that always unnerved Alex. They settled into leather sofas by a wall of glass. Beyond it was a groomed lawn, the cliff's edge and a dusky bay.

"The only account of Abigail's death that I know of is from Josiah's diary," James said snuggling next to Nina. "Josiah wasn't there when it happened. Everything was told to him by his foreman Moses so it's a second-hand account.

Had he been there that evening, there might have been a different outcome or it might not have happened at all."

"Which diary?" Ella said anxiously. "I never saw it at the historical society."

"It's the private property of a local family," he replied. "It has other family information. Very personal family information so they won't release it to the public."

Alex nodded imperceptibly. It probably verified the existence of the *Raven*'s treasure and revealed that the treasure was moved every few years for security reasons. The treasure presently resided under Julia's house along with other nautical trinkets and worthless paintings that her grandmother had picked up at flea markets.

"Maryland was a hub of spy activity," James began. "Being the Old Line State, it had sympathizers from both sides of the Cause. In the summer of 1863 someone in River Glen, certainly one of the deranged Whitbys, alerted the rebel spies to Abigail's lost fingers. They waited for Josiah to leave on business."

She leaned forward. "Then what?"

He put down his wine glass and held Nina's hand. "A group of horsemen stormed the estate. They rounded up the farmhands and imprisoned them in the servants' quarters. Abigail scooped up her children and ordered Moses and another worker, Seth, to hurry them into the underground passage."

"Under the kitchen?" Ella asked.

He nodded. "It was part of the Underground Railroad. Abigail told them to get the children into a Chessie and flee out to the bay."

"Where was Adam Eaton?" Ella said.

"Who knows?" he said. "Maybe on one of his painting walkabouts?"

"And Abigail?" Alex asked. "Why didn't she go?"

"She stayed behind to cover the trap door with dirt and drag the bed over it."

Nina had sobered up. "She sacrificed herself for her children."

He nodded again. "The workers trapped in the servants' quarters heard gunshots from the manor house. They watched through a crack in the shutters. Rebel bodies fell off their horses and dropped in the fields. It was Abigail racing from window to window with rifles and pistols, but there were too many raiders. They swarmed the house and chased her from room to room until—"

A terrible punctuation mark, until. There was no need for elaboration. Each of them sat silently, imagining the horror.

"The rebels drank up Josiah's rum, ransacked the house, desecrated the family graveyard and set the crops ablaze while the servants remained captive at gunpoint. Abigail was finally dragged outside to the maple tree. The dirty work done, the men disappeared into the forest as her broken body swayed under moonlit branches."

"But her children must have survived," Alex said. "There are many Smyths in the village today."

"Yes, Moses and Seth motored a Chessie down the bay and up the Glen River."

"How many Chessies were there?" she asked.

"I'm not sure, but Josiah always referred to them in plural. Chessies. The children were delivered to relatives in the village. The villagers tore up to the estate, passing toppled headstones and fires raging in the fields. Screams rang out from the servants' quarters. They rushed to release the imprisoned workers and beat down the blaze before it spread to the dwellings and barn. It was then that Adam charged from the forest on horseback and clambered up the tree to cut Abigail's noose. He carried her limp body into the forest, presumably to mourn his dear friend. Moses' account ends here. Neither Adam or Abigail's body were seen again."

Alex's pulse quickened. "Ever?" She glanced surreptitiously at Ella who gazed remotely outward.

"The servants waited and waited, assuming that Adam would bring her body back for burial. Perhaps the smoldering graveyard and fields frightened him. Who knows why he did anything?

"Days later Josiah returned from his trip. He and the servants scoured the forest for weeks, but they were unable to find Adam or Abigail's body. He feared that Adam had stumbled upon a rebel hide-out in the forest, that Adam had been killed, that he and Abigail had been dumped in a shallow grave.

"Josiah returned to the manor house, boarded it up, took his children to cousins in the village and freed the servants. Then he and Seth vanished. The Chessie attacks in the bay increased. Ships burned in the night; dead sailors washed up onshore. Over the next months there was a string of unexplained murders. Savage murders, all with the same MO. The mutilated corpses were found without their heads."

"Beheading was the MO of the River Glen pyrates in the seventeen hundreds," Alex interjected. "Who were the victims?"

"Men reputed to be from a network of rebel spies scattered throughout Maryland, Delaware and Pennsylvania. Northerners, traitors. The perpetrator was never caught but the main suspect was Josiah gone mad, ferociously mad."

Chapter 8
Dark Places

At 6:03 am Jay Braden awoke and tiptoed downstairs. Coffee would have to wait. Beyond the kitchen island someone else besides him was passed out on his sofa. Sharon Westerly had been in no state to drive back to her hotel. God help the MacKenzies when she returned to Gettysburg. The wall-to-wall carpet allowed him to silently make his way to the bar where he kept his laptop. He unplugged it and crept past her.

The empty glass of water and bottle of aspirin on the coffee table were telltale signs of a seasoned drinker who has the forethought to dull the impending hangover—at least enough for a minimal job performance the next day. He glanced at Westerly one more time. Her long hair had escaped its bun and spread across Laura's needlepoint pillow. Pink shirttails were splayed across gray suit pants. Bare feet, maroon toenails. A prizefighter named McClellans had given her an upper cut to the jaw and laid her out flat. He found himself smiling. Handsome woman. Curvy body that would be fun to get lost in.

Success. He made it to the dining room without waking her or without her hurling an object into his head. There would be no knot protruding from the back of his head to match the purple swollen mess that was once a nose. He quietly set up his laptop on the dining room table.

He couldn't imagine Westerly's sense of loss. He and Laura had had no children despite years of trying. Perhaps it was for the best. How would he ever have cared for a child *and* Laura during her descent into madness? *And* do his job. The incident that precipitated Westerly's drunk was a text from her teenager received yesterday while sitting on the pier near Harlow's.

"I've been waiting to hear from Paul all day," she had said pulling the buzzing phone from her pocket.

She read and re-read her son's text, then shoved the phone back in her pocket. He had tried not to pry, but he couldn't help but notice. A film of tears coated her eyes. Then, like water on a blue hot stove, the tears beaded away and she stared ferociously into space. A windless silence fell over the pier. A flip of her wrist downed her drink.

His hand had reached consolingly toward her, but her sizzling eyes halted it. "Is everything—"

She stood abruptly. "I'm getting another drink."

He scrambled to defuse a potential disaster in Harlow's. If a man at the bar crossed her, hit on her... that's all River Glen needed... another homicide. "I haven't had dinner yet. I bet you haven't either. Let's go to my place."

The contents of the text had bewildered and infuriated her, rendered her speechless. Her eyes bounced from him to the bay to the pub.

"I can grill us something," he added urgently. "My bar has a better selection of scotch than Miles Harlow."

That got her attention and she slipped on her shoes. They walked in swift silence to her unmarked police sedan parked at the pub. Gone were the Gold Wings from Indiana and the Harley Fat Boy from Massachusetts though the motorcycles belonging to the women bikers from Pennsylvania remained.

"How about I drive?" he suggested.

"You're not insured for this vehicle."

He climbed reluctantly into the passenger's seat, tightened his seat belt and clamped the door handle in a death grip. "If you want to talk—"

"I don't!"

She pulled onto the road and stared murderously at the pedestrians on the sidewalk. He feared for the lives of Luna and her dogs, and Mrs. Kandle pushing her walker across the bridge. His heart lurched as they passed Leo and Nancy Smyth and the twins in a baby carriage at the crosswalk. Miraculously they made it down Main Street and his dead-end road without an accident or incident of road rage. In his driveway he jumped out and unlocked his front door. She made a beeline for the bar in his den while he fired up the grill out back. She obviously knew what she wanted because in no time she appeared on the deck with a bottle and— thoughtful of her—two glasses.

"Good choice," he said. "McClellans."

She filled the glasses to the brim and looked at the edge of his property. "What's there? Any neighbors?"

"A forest. No one can build there because it's a very swampy forest. That's why I live amidst a hoard of mosquitoes." He tore the plastic wrap off a package of ground beef. "I hope you're not a vegan."

"Nope. I'm a carnivore."

Something about the forest interested her because she hefted his green recycling bin of Boodles bottles and beer cans to the weedy border by the trees. What the hell? She lined up the bottles and beer cans, crossed the yard, then disappeared around the front of the house. He flipped burgers until she reappeared. No, no way! She had retrieved her gun from the car and strode toward the center of his lawn.

"Um, Commander—!"

"If we're going to get drunk together, then at least call me Westerly," she shouted.

"I don't know if that's a good idea," he shouted back. "What if you hit a fox, squirrel, gnats?"

"I won't miss."

How courteous of Not-Sharon-but-arms-distance-Westerly; she'd put a silencer on the pistol so as not to piss off his neighbors. She positioned herself as if at a shooting range, feet slightly spread, one eye closed. *Plink plink shatter shatter plink shatter plink shatter.* Cans hopped and glass shards exploded into the weeds. Impressive. Not one miss.

She returned to the deck, the gun pointed to the ground and the safety on.

"Feel better?" he said.

"No." She rolled up the cuffs of her suit pants and stuck her feet in the hot tub. She fixed her hand like a gun, pointed it toward the forest and moved it horizontally. "Ralph, Ralph, Ralph."

"Bad end to that fling, I guess."

She chose not to comment.

He handed her a burger on a paper plate and they ate wordlessly while crickets chirped under the deck.

"Paul's text," she finally said. "I'm boring, he says—"

He shrugged. "I wouldn't know."

"I'm not boring! I have an amazing career, fascinating, dangerous at times, full of adventure. I head up a whole division of detectives. Paul no longer wants to live with me. He wants to move in with his father."

"Sometimes a boy needs to be with a man."

She shot him a lethal glare. "Where he'll be exposed to Ralph's cocaine, porn and wife-swapping parties. Paul is closer in age to the new wife Caroline than Ralph is. I have a very bad feeling about this. I don't care what adults do on their own time. If Ralph wants to watch Caroline get fucked at sex parties, then that's their business. But I just don't want Paul, any child, near it!"

He recoiled. "You're more open-minded than I am. As far as I'm concerned, Ralph's prostituting his own wife. If anyone came near my Laura—"

"Because you're a sane man."

He pointed at his nose. "Is this the face of a sane man?"

She half-smiled. "You're a cop. It's par for the course."

He glanced down at his vibrating phone. "It's Lisa Paco."

"The gum smacker."

"Bugs the shit of me."

"It's a millennial thing."

He answered. "Hey, Lisa, I'm putting you on speaker. Commander Westerly is here." He held up his glass and silently mouthed 'Cheers'. "We're discussing the case."

"Hey, Commander," Lisa yelled through the phone, "tell your son that I found the Pokémons Squirtle and Venusaur!"

"Will do," Westerly said flatly.

"Lisa, the case—"

"#onit. Ventresca Hadley and Ian Kent lied to us. Both of them! They said that they met Hadley-Simon at some art function in Philly. Wro-ong! I knew that Ventresca was a lying bitch and that Ian was a slimy eel! I just knew it! They all met in Boston decades ago when Hadley-Simon worked as an actor at a little theater called the Back Bay Murder House where they produced mysteries like *The Mousetrap* and musicals. Ian's family lived in the Boston suburbs before moving to Pennsylvania. Ian worked there part-time in the summers as a stagehand and props manager. Ventresca was an art student at a nearby art college. This was around the same time that Hadley-Simon got caught by the feds for stealing documents about Paul Revere. They all lived and worked within blocks of each other and at the same time!"

Sharon Westerly's bare feet shuffled into the dining room and drew Jay back to the present.

"Anything new?" she asked.

"I don't know yet. The laptop's still booting. Coffee?"

"Please. It's my life's blood."

He stood. "I'll make us some."

She gestured upstairs. "Do you mind?"

"Second door on the left. Clean towels are in the hall closet."

He plodded about the kitchen while the shower turned on upstairs. Bacon, scrambled eggs and toast were within his culinary abilities. He set two places on the kitchen island like the housekeeper Mrs. Pulacki had done for him and Laura once upon a time. His mind wandered outside. Mist floated on the green water. Clark and Miranda were performing their morning ritual of harassing the Canada geese. Gnats hovered in clouds over the damp lawn. Another steamy Chesapeake morning. A stunning steamy Chesapeake morning.

Westerly reappeared. Despite sleeping in her clothes, she had managed to pull herself together. Her hair was atop her head in a loose bun. She had applied a tasteful amount of makeup. His asking her how she felt wasn't going to make a hangover disappear so he didn't bother. Besides, he already knew her answer: a dismissive "I'm fine. Now let's get to work." She was a type AAA who would give two hundred percent even if she had cholera or the bubonic plague. A hangover, small beans.

He handed her a cup of coffee. No doubt she drank it black.

"My shoes are somewhere," she said mildly amused.

"By the hot tub."

She stepped outside and paused, obviously entranced by the river. She stepped back inside. "Lovely view out there."

"Yes, lovely."

"Shall I get the laptop?"

"Sure."

It was going to be a working breakfast. Her cursing about father-son threesomes and the mental defectives and perverts that constituted the MacKenzies of Gettysburg was done with. They filled their plates and bent over his laptop.

A new email held their attention.

Last evening Paco and Wilkins had been busy working with Interpol's division in Spain because they had young brains that could function beyond six o'clock. According to their email, Ventresca Hadley's ex-husband had been located. The lengthy interview with Interpol was attached.

Franco Montero had provided a detailed account of the actors at the Bay Back Murder House. The Spaniard had met Ventresca Wyndmor when she attended a cast party for *Dracula*. She had been the guest of the actor Seymour Simon. Ventresca had a thing for men with exotic accents and all but threw herself at Montero. That introduction was followed by a whirlwind courtship and impulsive marriage until Montero discovered men. He and Ventresca had an amicable separation and divorce. After much soul-searching, Montero had a second discovery: his theatrical talents were minimal so he returned to Spain to attend dental school. For over a decade he had been living with his partner Rodrigo while raising two adopted sons and running a successful dental practice. Years before, Seymour Simon had appeared on Montero's doorstep in Barcelona. Montero never liked the man—Simon and Ian Kent had been accused of stealing props and costumes from the theater. Montero politely turned Simon away and never heard from him again. The rest of the dentist's interview included gossipy critiques of the actors in the troupe and the plays performed during his brief time in Boston.

Westerly checked her watch. "The saliva in the UHaul. Do you think Zera has that information yet?"

"Very likely. She's always the first to arrive at the crime lab." He called Zera's number. As expected she answered. He put the phone on speaker mode.

"We completed the analysis late night, but I didn't know if I should call since you're on vacation," Zera said kiddingly. "Great photo, by the way."

"Photo?"

"The famous campsite photo."

"Who took it? Lisa or Denny? They're dead!"

"I'll never tell because I don't want them on my slab," Zera chuckled. "I've always liked scotch plaid."

Westerly scowled.

He smiled back at her. "Next time I'll wear the ones with the red hot chili peppers. Any matches with the database?"

"No, but here's the interesting thing. The DNA's a partial match to that from a paper cup at the morgue."

"Someone in CSI?" The implications were appalling. The killer was an insider to their team?

"No," Zera replied. "From a visitor to the morgue to ID Simon's body. Ian Kent."

"You said partial," Westerly cut in. "Not the same?"

"That's right."

"Lisa told us that Kent's parents are deceased," he said. "A sister lives somewhere in the south."

"Lorena lives in Charlotte, North Carolina," Westerly said. Hungover or not, she had instant recall with the specifics.

"Is there another sister, one who's a biker, that we don't know about?" he wondered. "I'm going to get Lisa and Will to check again. Maybe there's a psychotic aunt?"

"Sisters? Aunts?" said Zera. "The DNA is male."

The girders of the investigation shifted—swayed—underfoot. They, the FBI, everyone had been looking for a large female but instead ... he and Westerly shot each other a mystified look.

"Are you two still there?" Zera asked.

"There's a brother," he suddenly recalled.

"The adventure guide Curtis," Westerly said. "Who lives in Canada."

"Maybe not," Zera said.

Jay's fingers flew across the keyboard. He re-opened Franco Montero's statement and found the section where the actor-turned-dentist had remarked on his fellow actors at the Back Bay Murder House.

"Simon Seymour..." he read aloud, "... dreadfully bombastic but a master at British and French accents. So-so tenor singing voice. Leona Jolt. Ridiculous stage name, but she played a convincing Mrs. Lovett in *Sweeney Todd* though she couldn't hit the high notes. Ian Kent. A pathetic no talent. Good only for non-speaking bit parts, otherwise he should be nowhere near a theater. Curtis Kent. Gorgeous baritone with an amazing range. Was brilliant as Sweeney Todd and Mackie Messer aka Mack the Knife in the *Threepenny Opera*."

"In both those plays murders are committed by a knife or blade," Westerly said. "I hate musicals."

He shoved his plate across the kitchen island, his appetite gone.

"What, Jay?"

"I was pissing right next to him at Harlow's. He's now a Biker for Jesus who's riding a Harley Fat Boy with a Massachusetts plate."

Ian Kent looked in the mirror and liked what he saw—a clean shaven face for a breakfast date with a lovely Asian doctor. Zera Lim had changed her mind after all.

My schedule just opened up so I have a little time this morning, read her text. *I was wondering if you were free for an early breakfast? Short notice, I realize.*

The Kent charm never failed, Ian thought as he slapped on cologne. He texted his secretary to have his eleven o'clock meeting in Philly postponed. It was summer so half of his investment group was on vacation anyway.

Yes. I can change my plans, he texted Zera.

Good, she replied. *There's a little park with a boat ramp. Take the southern trail and you'll spot a quiet strip of beach where we can breakfast-picnic. I've included a link with the address.*

The picnic sounds idyllic. See you soon.

He opened Google Earth on his cell phone. The park was shady and secluded. It was considerate of Zera to choose a location not too far from the Radcliffe. He slapped on more cologne for good luck and hurried from his room. He climbed into his Jaguar and sped down the coastal road. What might they discuss? He had absolutely no interest in Zera's career as a medical examiner. Blood, body fluids and tissues revolted him. If talk of messy crime scenes, mutilations, guns and knives could be avoided, breakfast might be semi-enjoyable. He wasn't particularly fond of the outdoors and that included picnics. Ants, flies and mosquitoes were abhorrent beasts yet he would endure the meal long enough to convince Zera to call in sick. Then they might have a swim back at the Radcliffe because under no circumstances was he putting even a big toe into the silty muck of the bay. Maybe she'd be game for a couples' massage, culminating with champagne, strawberries and sex in his waterfront room. Why not, if he played his cards right? The massage, champagne and strawberries could be written off as business expenses so he wouldn't have to pay out-of-pocket.

Ian turned his car into the waterfront park. This was definitely the right place; there was a mossy boat ramp and a trail leading south. His was the only car in the parking lot. Zera must be running a few minutes late. Or did she live nearby? She was athletic in build. It was entirely possible that she had walked there with her picnic basket and was already on the beach. Perhaps her blanket was spread out and delicious food awaited him. He wound along the trail, stopping every few feet to knock sand from his Docksiders. Dreadful substance, sand.

Bushes rustled. Pain surged across Ian's temple. Before he could turn, his knees buckled. Duct tape was smacked on his mouth and a blindfold yanked around his head. It was not one mugger but two! One tied his feet while the other bound his hands behind his back. Why not take his wallet and leave? Where was Zera? Also tied up? Abducted? Did the kidnappers expect a ransom? The pair of assailants lugged his writhing body onto a scratchy blanket, rolled him it, tied its ends and dragged him over roots and rocks. Then came the nauseating sensation of being swung like a sack of potatoes. "One, two, three."

He thudded into a boat. The boat rocked as his captors climbed in. An outboard engine sputtered. Time and distance were impossible to gauge in the suffocating wool blanket. The boat rose and fell over swells until the motor cut off.

Shadows of light and dark sifted through the blindfold as his captors unrolled him. There was a muted lap of water and smell of musty wood and gasoline. The place was cool, damp and shady. Was he in a boathouse?

"Time to talk, Ian," a male voice echoed in the enclosed space.

"Mmm!" he screamed.

The man ripped off the duct tape, taking the skin of his face with it.

"Ow! Fuck! What the fuck did I do to Zera?"

"She has no idea that you're boating with River Glen pyrates," the man said drolly. "But hell, if she invited me to an intimate bayside picnic, I'd jump at the chance too."

Ian struggled to identify the voice, but he was sure that he'd never heard it before. It was not a Philly accent, nor the accent of an educated person. The voice belonged to a dumb hick.

"Ian buddy, you're gonna to tell about me about how you and Seymour set up Ella at the National Archives. Then you're gonna to tell me about your brother Curtis."

"I don't know what you're talking about! I'm telling you nothing!"

"Shannon," the redneck said to his companion, "do you wanna hear how the pyrates got Old Ned MacDuff to talk?"

Ah, so one of the assailants was named Shannon. The only Shannon he knew was Dan Shannon from the Accounting Department. But why would Dan kidnap him and want to know about Ella Winston? It couldn't be the same Shannon.

"Why sure, honey," replied a female.

"Well now, it must have been around seventeen hundred and ten when the pyrates discovered that some of the *Raven*'s gold was missin'," the male captor explained in a slow country drawl. "All clues led to Old Ned, but he was a closed-lipped sort of fella. Kinda like our Ian here. So they decided to feed his foot to blue crabs."

"Did they cut it off?" she asked with a perverse giggle.

"Why no, doll. They tied chicken gizzards to Old Ned's foot and tied him up to a pilin' at the town dock so everyone could watch. After the gizzards were eaten away, the crabs gnawed away at Ned's toes. That stubborn old bastard had three toes chewed off before he de-vulged the whereabouts of the gold."

"Giles, you're pullin' my leg!" Shannon laughed.

"I swear on the Holy Bible it's true," Giles chuckled. "Let's see if this truth serum works today. There was no time to go to the hen house to slaughter a chicken and yank out its gizzards so I'll have to use leftovers from KFC."

"Finger lickin' good!" she hooted.

"You wouldn't dare!" Ian hissed. Plastic bags rustled and he was hit by the disgusting odor of greasy chicken. His Docksiders were tugged off. "No! You maniacs! No!"

"A little chat about the National Archives and Curtis saves your toes," Giles said.

These yokels had to be bluffing. They had to be! But then he felt it—his toes were parted. There was childish giggling, then hysterical laughter as his captors lashed drumsticks between his toes. He was manhandled onto the edge of the boat so that his bound feet dangled in the water. The boat tilted and water splashed as one of them jumped overboard.

"You'll never get away with this!"

"Doll, can you hand me that anchor please?" said Giles politely.

"Why sure, hon."

The weight of the anchor pulled Ian's feet under the water. "I'll never talk to you assholes!"

The boat rocked and shifted as Giles climbed back in. "Shannon, do you play Crazy Eights?"

"I haven't played that in coon's age. You'll have to re-teach me."

"Tunes?" Giles said to her.

"What do ya have?"

"Have look."

Ian heard the shuffling of plastic as though she was flipping through CDs.

"Well, I declare," she said. "Glenn Campbell. I love this one."

"So sad about his decline."

"*Wichita Lineman* is my favorite Glenn song."

"Mine is *Gentle on My Mind*."

"True classics."

'Nothing motherfuckers! I'll tell you nothing,' Ian urged himself. 'Despite my prone, humiliating position on the edge of your fucking boat. Nothing motherfuckers through your games of Crazy Eights, Gin Rummy and Go Fish. Nothing motherfuckers through half of *Glenn Campbell's Greatest Hits*. Nothing fuckers, absolutely nothing!' Then pointed appendages, like pin pricks, scurried over his foot. "Get them off!"

"Shannon, looky there," said Giles rocking the boat. "The crabs have arrived."

"Really? Let me see. My, my, there's a few of 'em."

"There's nothin' better than steamed crabs in Old Bay spices on a summer day," Giles said.

"Washed down with an ice-cold Pabst," she added.

"I'm a Bud man, myself."

"Get them off!" He twisted and strained against the anchor line.

"Tickle do they?" she said.

"Get them off!"

"Patience, buddy," Giles replied. "They're feastin' on the chicken. Not you yet."

"It was Curtis dressed as Ella!" Ian panted. "Now get me out of the water! Their spiky legs are stabbing me! I'm bleeding... I'm sure I'm bleeding!"

"Blood? Blood will attract bull sharks," Giles said. "You better talk in a hurry."

"Sharks in the Chesapeake?" he choked.

"Bull sharks make great whites look like gentle little lambs," Shannon said.

"Okay, okay!" he said. "I stole Ella's clothes from our apartment in Philly! Curtis cut a wig like Ella's hair style, dyed it blue and went to DC disguised as her. It was Seymour's idea. All his idea. He had Ella take the fall. Now pull me out!"

"Tell us about Curtis," Giles said.

Ian's lungs heaved. His head throbbed from the strangulating blindfold. The pinpricks on his feet were making him insane! He, his parents and Lorena had promised each other never to say anything about—

"Two more crabs just arrived," Giles chuckled. "That chicken's goin' fast. You're next, Ian buddy."

"C-Curtis is different..."

The swaying nooses, blazing cornfields and stampeding horses in Ella's dreams that night were prompted by James' tale of Abigail's terrible end. Now she and Alex held an incalculable piece to the puzzle. Still they had said nothing to James and Nina. For years the ghost walk job had necessitated her telling a fabricated ghost story about three fire-ravaged spirits haunting the Ephram Whitson House but as fate would have it, she found herself in an actual ghost story. Within twenty-four hours her life had taken surprising turns—piloting a tugboat, crabbing, hookah hose diving and marine salvage, after which she had slept on a tugboat tied up by two riverside houses tacky with lawn ornaments. The sleeping hammock onboard was not entirely comfortable but infinitesimally better than a lumpy mattress enclosed by iron bars and cinderblock. The strangest turn of all was the discovery of a primitive submarine that entombed two real-life ghosts… the long missing Adam and Abigail.

While listening to James' account of the raid, the same question had nagged Alex and her. If the estate had been surrounded by rebel marauders, how then had Moses and Seth snuck the children from an underground hideaway to a Chessie on the shoreline without detection and capture? That question prompted their return to the estate that morning. It was Alex's suggestion to take her grandmother Julia's Royal Enfield and sidecar. "Let's keep our bikes off the road. Especially yours, Ella. Just in case."

Just in case. Again. The phrase gave her the willies.

Ella climbed into the sidecar, tucked her backpack deep in the cockpit and strapped on a Union Jack helmet. Alex pushed the starter and the Royal Enfield awoke. They bumped and rumbled along the coastal road and headed into the pine forest near Alex's marine lab. Between the arrow straight pines a brief light flashed in her peripheral vision. A reflection from a mirror? Alex's helmeted head turned reflexively toward it. In an instant the shimmer was gone. It was nothing, really nothing. Sun glinting on a beer can. They emerged from the forest into fields of summer corn and turned at the dirt road leading to the abandoned mansion.

If she could just find Adam Eaton's original paintings! It would solve so many problems. It would solve everything. *Whales* in the Hadley's dining room in Old City was an obvious fake, flashing BOGUS BOGUS like a neon sign. It was probably painted by Monroe during his dissertation studies or by Ventresca who was also a decent painter. *Whales'* fraudulence was certain; every Eaton sketch in Dr.

Worth's archival collection appeared as though the colors had been blown across the paper by a brisk wind. Eaton saw the world in turbulent motion. The objects in each sketch—plumes of smoke, cannon fire, charging horses and rushing water—whisked horizontally across the page in an unwavering right to left direction. But *Whales* in the Hadley's dining room, the two alleged Eatons at the Old City Americana Gallery and two more at the Virginia Institute of Colonial Art were painted in multi-directional brush strokes interspersed with pointillism. Wouldn't she know better than anyone! She had meticulously studied the style of those five pieces before painting the forgeries for Monroe and Ian.

What if Eaton's original paintings had been burned during the fire ignited by the rebel attackers or tossed in the marsh dump eons ago? This caused her incessant worry. What if his images never made it beyond the form of a sketch? What if the paintings never existed at all but were figments of her unsettled imagination? Then what?

Alex slowed the Enfield in the circular driveway and flipped up her face shield. "Where to?"

"Hide us behind that hedge."

Alex turned the handlebars and they squeaked and rattled over tufts of grass. Behind the hedge at the hurricane fence they pulled off their helmets and grabbed flashlights from the cockpit.

"Did you see that strange light in the forest?" Alex said. "It was like someone was signaling us."

"No."

"It was a quick flash of light."

"Sun glinting on a beer can?"

"Maybe."

"Here's where I enter." Ella pointed to a depression in the soil under the fence. She squeezed under first and scanned the grounds. All was silent except for bugs chirping in the weeds. "The coast is clear." Alex was a slender woman and slipped easily under the chain links.

They crossed the lawn and climbed in a broken window. They tiptoed across the creaky floor to the cook's bedroom off the kitchen, slid aside the rickety bed and pulled back the trap door. After dropping her flashlight into the hidden cellar months before, she had swished the light around before scampering out, but with Alex as a companion the whole room could be explored.

They followed their flashlight beams down the dark stairway. Like the submarine yesterday, their heads just grazed the low ceiling of the cellar. They beat away cobwebs as they moved forward. Wooden cots covered with mold-flecked sheets and pillows lined one wall. There was a shelf of dusty water pitchers, chamber pots and unburned candles.

"Ahh-choo!" Alex sneezed.

"God bless you."

Alex sniffled and pulled a doll from a chest. "Abigail and Josiah had attempted to make a frightening hiding place along a frightening journey as habitable as possible. Toys for the children."

"Hey, check out this mirror," she called from across the room. "A work of art in its own right. Look at the carved frame and feet."

Alex joined her and moved her flashlight in an oval path around the massive mirror. "Mesmerizing. I would have expected carvings of crabs or fish, not whales. There are no whales in the Chesapeake. It's too brackish."

"Maybe Eaton carved it? To match *Whales*."

"Eaton painted *Whales*?"

Blood surged in Ella's head. Alex was a biologist and a crabber, but her question reflected a familiarity with *the painting*. Alex had used the verb *to paint*. How would Alex have known of it? Eaton, after all, was a lesser painter known only to a handful of artists and art historians. She had never discussed any of Eaton's individual paintings with Alex. She was sure of it. "How do you know that painting?"

Perhaps the tone of her question sounded hostile and accusatory because Alex stalled. "Um, I'm not sure. Maybe I saw it at an art gallery?"

"Impossible. A bogus version of it is in the private collection of Monroe and Ventresca Hadley in Philadelphia. Can you remember where you saw the painting? It's really important! *Whales* and Eaton's other paintings are what I'm looking for!"

Alex shook her head confusedly.

"Alex, where?"

"Sorry," said Alex looking at her feet. "I don't know."

Ella sighed despondently and stuck her flashlight between the intricate mirror and wall. "No Eaton paintings there. Just a tiny door. Probably a supply closet for bedding."

"Who knows?" said Alex with some optimism. "Maybe your paintings are amidst the sheets."

"Doubtful."

"It's worth a look."

They dragged aside the heavy mirror and Ella tugged on a knob. She bent down and shone her beam into a pitch-black space.

"This is no closet, Alex! It looks like a mine shaft. This is it! I knew it! There had to be a way for Abigail's children to get outside during the rebel raid. Maybe it exits into the forest?" She ducked into the opening. "Maybe the paintings are hidden in here!"

"I'm not loving this," said Alex backing away. "What if there are bats or snakes? What if the bats are vampires?"

Adrenaline surged through Ella's veins. "Let's take a look!"

"No way."

"C'mon."

"I hate dark places like the ghost walk house. This tunnel gives me the creeps."

"Please? Just a quick look, then we get the hell out."

Alex gnawed her thumb nail.

"Please! The paintings will exonerate me. Clear my name."

"Shit. Okay. In and out."

"Promise. No dawdling. Just in and out. I'll go first."

They crouched forward, their flashlight beams jittering over the dirt walls and floor. The tunnel was exactly like a mine shaft, the walls and ceiling supported by logs and unhewn boards.

"What if we run into a creeper like Injun Joe?" Alex worried aloud. "He gave me nightmares as a child. Or the floor oozes with venomous snakes like in the Indiana Jones movies? There are copperheads and water moccasins in these parts, you know. What if they've mutated in the darkness and grown to gigantic proportions like in the movie *Anaconda*?"

"You're a biologist. Do snakes really breed in caves?"

"How do I know? I'm not a herpetologist. If our flashlight batteries die, we're screwed."

"We can use the lights on our cell phones."

"Except that I don't have one because I keep losing mine," Alex said. "I don't know which slow death would be worse, being swallowed whole by a gargantuan snake or having blood sucked from my neck by a vampire."

"It's too dark for anything to live. Nothing is in here. Believe me. Nothing."

Alex slowed. "Don't you think we've gone far enough?"

"There are no such things as vampires, Injun Joes, man-eating snakes or ghosts," said she over her shoulder. "Just a little farther. It can't be too much farther."

"We've been walking forever."

"Weird. The air's getting warmer and more humid."

"Ahh-choo!"

"God bless again."

"I'm going to be blowing dust out of my nose for weeks."

"Hey, Alex, the tunnel's widening." She lurched and gasped.

"What?"

"There!"

The flashlight beams lighted on them at once.

"I'm outta here!" Alex cried.

"Wait!" she said, grabbing Alex's hand.

"No, Ella!"

"One quick look!"

"My heart's in my throat! I can't breathe!"

They inched forward, hand in hand.

They were in a row. Skulls on pikes. Five of them.

"Pyrates," said Alex with a hush. "Beheading is the ultimate form of revenge. The victim wanders the netherworld sightless and soundless forever and ever."

"James said that Josiah murdered and mutilated the rebel spies who—"

"Shh!"

"What, Alex?"

"Did you hear that?"

"No. What?"

"Shh!"

Alex flicked off her flashlight and she did the same. They waited in the blackness.

"I don't hear anything," she whispered. "What was it?"

"Something. I'm not sure what," Alex whispered back.

"Maybe it was a mouse or vole."

"Or a vampire bat!"

"I'm putting my light back on. It's nothing."

Alex snapped her flashlight on also.

She wandered over to the skulls. "I wonder who—"

"Ella, look!"

In the quivering bull's eye of light was a crucifix of fabric, a shredded gown nailed to the dirt wall.

She leaned toward the dress. "Those stains are blood."

"It must be Abigail's," Alex said. "This is Josiah's shrine of retribution."

"Let's go on a bit farther."

"Like we haven't seen enough."

Ella stepped into the widening passage. "Well, well."

"What?"

"Sea Monster Number Two."

"No way? Incredible!"

Their beams zipped wondrously around the cavernous room. Against one wall were tables with tools and a forge for metallurgy. But their attention was irresistibly drawn to the center of the room—to a mobile platform on railroad tracks. On it sat another Chessie. The Chessie that had saved the Wedgewood-Smyth children. The Chessie that sent fiery rebel ships sizzling to the bottom of the Chesapeake.

"Nemo's secret workshop," said Alex awed.

"Except that it was Josiah and Adam's."

Alex followed the tracks to a pair of wooden doors. She opened the latch and shoved. Nothing. She threw her shoulder into it. The door gave an inch. Green light slipped through the crack and illuminated the dim room. She pressed her eye to the opening.

"What do you see?"

"Vines," replied Alex. "That's why no one knew this was here. Vines have overgrown the door. I can smell the marsh. Help me open this."

Together they leaned and pushed. The door gave another few inches.

"Maybe I can dig the dirt away," said Alex dropping to her knees. She pushed her head through the crack and shoveled with her hands.

Ella crossed the room. Amidst old-fashioned tools on a worktable sat two incongruous objects—hot pink bike helmets.

"We're at the base of the cliff," sounded Alex's voice from outside.

"Someone else found this place before us."

Alex pulled her head back inside. "Who?"

"The owners of these." She lifted the bike helmets. "Their names are inside. Sandra and Megan Larson."

Alex sprang to her feet. "Those twins disappeared years ago! They were here? Way creepy! Will and Jay need to know about this."

"And that's not all. Look at this."

Alex brushed dirt off her hands and approached the table. "What is it?"

"Sketches. Extraordinary. Adam documented the attack on the estate. He must have been watching from a hiding place."

Alex stared wide-eyed at the flipping papers in Ella's hands. "They're like frames from a movie. Rounding up the servants by gunpoint. Abigail in a window shooting at the rebels. The siege of the house. The desecration of the family plots." She swallowed. "This gets bad."

"Really bad. Adam showed Josiah exactly what happened to Abigail at the tree."

"With names of the attackers so Josiah knew who to— I recognize those two names. Their descendants still live around here and they're still pricks."

Ella pointed to the other names. "And I know those three. They're folks from Gettysburg. Adam would have known them from his time there."

"Two plus three. Five skulls."

Click.

They turned... into the barrel of a gun.

"I'll take that, thank you," said a man stepping from the tunnel.

"K-Kenneth?" Alex said.

"Both of you against the wall!"

"H-here, take it." Alex lifted the yellowed sketches. "We didn't see anything! Promise!"

"Pricks was it, Alex? Turn to the wall."

"If-if this is your secret place, we'll never—"

"Who, Alex?" she asked under her breath.

"Linda's husb—"

"Shut-up, you cunts! Turn to the wall!" Kenneth Radowski's gaze lighted on the bike helmets.

Oh god... the missing twins...

"We'll never say a word," said Alex futilely. "Never. Really. Promise."

Did something move? Something behind Kenneth? A black fluttering *something* in the tunnel?

Alex must have noticed it also; her panicked eyes were fixed over his shoulder. "O-kay. W-we'll go to the wall."

They stepped backward to the crack of green sunlight. Something... yes... definitely... black... fluttered in the tunnel.

"Ah!" Kenneth gargled. His eyes bulged. He staggered. He thudded face-first into the dirt.

A black-cloaked ghost spun and vanished into the blackness.

At 11:13 am a hollow-eyed man appeared at Lisa Paco's desk at the River Glen police barracks. He was barely recognizable from his former self. Lisa had meet Ian Kent once before, when he had identified Monroe Hadley at the morgue and then dropped by for questioning. At that time the man with slick black hair had been polite yet glib. Why not be smugly confident? Kent had an iron-clad alibi; he had been dining with friends at Cuba Libre in Philadelphia on th e night of his partner's murder. Security cameras in OldCity verified his presence there that night, but now his Ralph Lauren shirt was streaked with mud and oil and his cargo shorts were equally rumpled and dirty. One of his eyes twitched uncontrollably.

"They said they were going to kill me if I didn't come here—if I didn't confess!"

Lisa stood abruptly. "Who? Confess to what?"

"Whacked-out private eyes or bounty-hunters. Who the fuck knows! They fed me to crabs! Look! Look at my ankle!" He pointed frantically downward. "Complete sickos!"

She leaned over her desk. There was nothing unusual about Kent's leg, ankle or foot. They were tan and hairy; on his foot was a sandy Sperry Docksider. There was no evidence of his foot being eaten by crabs.

She pulled Denny away from his morning gossip session with the secretary Cloris and they shuttled Kent to an interview room. She flipped on the recording equipment and entered the date and time. "Confess to what? Tell me everything."

Kent slumped into a chair. "To framing Ella Winston. It was Monroe's idea... all *his* idea."

"Seymour Simon," she interrupted. "Call him by his real name. You knew him from your days at the Back Bay Murder House."

He picked at his cuticle.

"Did you and Simon have Ella Winston paint the forgeries?"

"She wasn't forced," he said in sulky defense. "She got off on it. It was an adrenaline thing. She's an adrenaline junkie."

"Who was the courier on the motorcycle?"

"My brother Curtis."

"Whose DNA was in the UHaul."

"What UHaul? Curtis? He's around here?" His voice pitched octaves higher. "He's supposed to be in Canada."

Lisa popped a giant bubble. "Winston admitted to her involvement in the forgeries but denies the theft at the National Archives."

"What UHaul!"

"I'm asking the questions."

"I need to know where Curtis is!"

"Answer my questions, Ian. Tell me about the National Archives." She popped another bubble. "Then we can talk about UHauls."

"That was Seymour's idea also. He was always back and forth between Philadelphia and Washington DC tracking down historical documents related to Gettysburg. He found something important in DC that he wanted. Curtis dressed as Ella and stole the document for him. She was going down for the forgeries. Why not take the fall for the theft as well? That was Seymour's rationale."

"That added four years to her sentence! She was your girlfriend, you cold-hearted di—" The door opened so she paused the recording equipment and stood deferentially. "Ian, this is Commander Westerly from the Gettysburg PD."

Westerly's "Good morning all" was vaguely sarcastic like Jay's greeting when he was hungover. Kent responded with a lecherous gander down her body. Westerly's eyes boiled. #howcoolwasthat? She looked like she was going to reach across the table and rip out his trachea.

Lisa turned the recorder back on, noting again the time and date as well as the presence of the detective from Pennsylvania. "What specifically was the document stolen by Curtis?"

"How the hell would I know?" he replied.

"I'll contact the Art Fraud unit ASAP," she said to Westerly. "They'll know what it was." She turned back to Kent. "Did Curtis kill Seymour?"

"I have no idea. I didn't even know he was around. He had set up an outdoor adventure business in Canada or so he said."

"When?"

"I don't know. Years ago. He comes and goes."

"You never visited him there?"

"No. He's a loser who can't hold down a job. First it was acting and singing. Then he learned judo to become a Hollywood stunt man, but he never made it to California as far as I know."

"But he was an actor for a time in Boston."

"And failed miserably at that. Then he worked as a mechanic."

"Where?"

"Also in the Boston area. At a motorcycle dealership. Then he was going to culinary school to be a chef. Then acting again, but this time he thought he might have more luck as a female so he went to the auditions in drag. He completely gets into character, becomes the character, assumes their personality and gender, thinks their thoughts. He's absolutely cracked. After no success as an actor, actress, transgender or otherwise, out-of-the-blue he decides to get a degree in kinesiology. He showed me apps on his phone that he was using to study muscle anatomy. With the kinesiology degree, he was going to grad school, he told me, to become a physical therapist or personal trainer. He has a thousand kooky ideas and does none of them. He's all over the place. He's delusional, I think."

"What would be his motivation to kill Seymour Simon?"

"I have no idea. Seymour paid him well as a courier and to dress as Ella to steal the document."

"Why would Curtis want to kill Ella?" Westerly jumped in.

Kent sat up. "What?"

"By running her down with a UHaul," Westerly said. "Having failed at that, he tried to kill her on a ghost walk in Gettysburg. Why? What does he have against her?"

He stared defiantly across the table.

"Answer the Commander," she said.

More defiant silence.

"Let's return him to the bounty hunters so they can feed him to the crabs," she said to Westerly. "He's wasting our time."

"What bounty hunters?"

"He was *allegedly* attacked by bounty hunters." Lisa rolled her eyes. "Who *allegedly* fed him to the crabs, but as far as I can tell he's still in one piece."

"They did!" he shouted.

"Who's the delusional one?" she smirked.

"I swear they were real!"

"What does Curtis have against Ella?" she asked, repeating Westerly's question.

"Who fucking knows." He slumped deeper in the chair. "I thought he was hot for her."

"Elaborate, Mr. Kent," Westerly ordered.

He folded his arms across his chest. An obstinate silence engulfed the room again.

The fuse of Westerly's patience sparked to its end. Her fist clenched—opened—clenched. "What's that static, Sergeant?" She stared at the recorder. "The equipment?"

"Ur, yes, ma'am. I believe so."

"Equipment malfunction." Westerly flipped off the recorder and stepped behind Kent. He jerked up in his seat, his head whipping to the glowering Westerly, then imploringly to her.

"Kick his ass, Commander," she giggled. "I'll never tell."

"You'll be wishing that you were crab bait, Mr. Kent," said Westerly quietly, "when the perverts in the county jail get their hands on you."

"Jail? But I've been cooperating!"

"Do you see cooperation, Sergeant Paco?"

She grinned. "I see obstruction."

"This interview's over," said Westerly walking to the door. "Sergeant, call for a van to take Mr. Kent to the county jail. He's dim-witted. He needs more time to think about his answers."

He jumped from his chair. "Wait! Wait!"

Westerly turned slowly.

"I don't know how many times they met! Curtis came to visit me when I was a student at Gettysburg. I took him on Ella's ghost walk. He was infatuated. He had me call her to arrange a date at the Ephram Whitson House. Keep the lights entirely off, he said. But I didn't go. Instead—"

"You're kidding!" Lisa laughed. "You lured Ella into a tryst with your own brother?"

"I didn't have a choice. Curtis is...."

"What?"

"... very persuasive."

"Because he has a propensity toward violence," Westerly filled in. "He'd hurt you."

"Yes."

"The dates. They happened how many times?"

"I don't remember. He started calling her on his own. But I do remember that he'd gave me a play by play of how she liked it when ... the sadistic bastard got off humiliating me!"

Westerly sat down. "Now I want to hear about those *alleged* bounty hunters."

"They—were—real!" he said blood vessels popping at his temples. "They entrapped me by telling me they were Zera Lim."

"Zera?" Lisa burst in laughter. "She'd never go out with a scumbag like you. #itstoofunny!"

Kent dropped listlessly into a chair. His eye started to twitch again. "They told me they were River Glen pyrates, that their fellow pyrates worked at the Radcliffe and throughout the village, that all of them were watching my every move. That's why I was forced to come here. They knew a lot about the case so I figured that they must be private eyes or bounty hunters. They were two sick rednecks who strapped chicken to my foot!"

"No way," said Lisa giggling.

"KFC," he huffed indignantly.

"Original or extra crispy?"

"It's not funny!"

"Hey, it sounds like the torture of Old Ned MacDuff," she suddenly realized.

"Who?" asked Westerly.

"A local pyrate who—"

"MacDuff's real?" he interrupted.

"Of course," she said. "There were pyrates all over these parts."

"My kidnappers were a male and a female," he grumbled. "I heard their names. Giles and Shannon."

Lisa guffawed and grabbed her sides for dramatic effect.

"Why's that so funny?" he yelled.

"Giles and Shannon?" she said comically. "Really?"

"Educate me, Sergeant," Westerly said. "Who are they?"

"You've never heard of Giles Blood-hand, the avenger of Charles Allaway who had his head stuck on a pike by Neville

Whitby in 1692? Giles was really pissed off at that. Charles was his best friend. They grew up on the same estate in Aberdeen, Scotland. Giles responded by slaughtering Neville Whitby and his entire family. Hence the name, the Bloodhand."

"News of his wonderful deeds has not yet spread to Gettysburg, Pennsylvania," Westerly said. "And Shannon?"

"She was a pickpocket from the slums of Dublin. Instead of being hung, she was sent to Virginia as an indentured slave. When the pyrate ship *Raven* sailed up the coast, some of the women including her, escaped from the plantation and joined the ranks of Giles, Charles and the other pyrates. River Glen was settled by the crew of the *Raven* and women criminals. Shannon was meaner than all of them combined. #uberbadass. She was the wife, then widow of Charles Allaway."

"So these pyrates were real?"

"Of course, Commander! Shannon had many lovers after Charles was killed. She's the great—many greats grandmother of the Allaways, Collinses and Smyths, probably the whole village."

"This explains everything," Westerly muttered.

Jay fumed. Another text from Herm Taylor ordered him to stay home during the biggest manhunt in River Glen history. He was under house arrest, thinly veiled as a vacation. His attention bounced between the coffee pot and gin bottle. He checked the time. It was almost noon. Gin definitely. A late morning G & T could be justified as an analgesic to suppress the lingering throb in his face and blot out the Taylor's maddening text.

Wait. Not yet.

He refilled his coffee mug and walked to the den where Will and Lisa's poster boards of suspects and victims lined the sofa. Photos of the suspects: the haughty Ian Kent, haggard Ventresca Hadley, baby-faced Ella Winston—all with alibis of some sort—and the victims: the sly goat Seymour Simon, ambitious insurance agent Linda Radowski, two homely hunters and eager-to-please Connor Hastings stared back at him. His cell phone vibrated in his pocket. It was a text from Sharon Westerly at headquarters.

Just emailed you 2 files on C Kent.

Westerly was the only one keeping him in the loop. God only knows what Will and Lisa were up to. Herm Taylor had probably confiscated their phones to prevent them from contacting him. He went to his laptop and printed out the two files. The first was a photo of Curtis Kent: motorcycle courier, hitman and chameleon. He was a robust, muscular version of his fraternal twin Ian. Thick black beard and wavy head of hair, glistening-light eyes, engaging smile. A charming mountain man from the looks of it and nothing like his current disguise, a paunchy Bible-loving biker.

Jay dropped into his recliner and read the second file, a police report. Curtis Kent's education at community colleges in Boston and Philadelphia was sporadic. There were likewise brief stints of employment as a singing waiter, actor, female impersonator and motorcycle mechanic. Nothing was out of the ordinary. On the surface Kent seemed to be a restless free spirit with a love of the outdoors.

Then came the red flags, more like detonations.

At the same time Curtis was working as a river guide in the Canadian Rockies a backpacker was found tied to a tree and dismembered, skeletal muscles excised like that of Trooper Hastings. Years before that, mutilated animals had been left on doorsteps, then dogs and cats went missing in the Kents' suburban Boston neighborhood. The then-teenaged Curtis was captured by local authorities at a forest encampment that showed evidence of butchery. This led to two-years of incarceration at a Massachusetts state hospital and prompted the Kent family to up and move to Pennsylvania. While in the mental hospital Curtis became involved in theater- and art therapy, was a cooperative patient and ultimately released for good behavior when he turned eighteen.

"I'm a carnivore." That's what Westerly had said to him last evening as he patted ground beef—skeletal muscle—into patties. The two of them then slathered the burgers with Heinz 57 and washed them down with McClellans.

Curtis Kent also was a carnivore but with a taste for human flesh!

Coffee upwelled in Jay's stomach. He sprang from the recliner and whipped his phone from his pocket. Westerly picked up immediately.

"The bastard's eating them! Their skeletal muscles! He's hiding in these woods, waiting to trap Ella. I know these woods like the back of my hand from chasing my dogs. Fuck Taylor's orders. I'm going to find him!"

"Odd." Lisa Paco leafed through an attachment from the FBI. "Very odd."

"What?" said Norman looking up from his computer screen.

"The document from the National Archives stolen by Curtis Kent dressed as Ella Winston for Professor Monroe Hadley aka Seymour Simon was not about art but Civil War spies."

"The name is Bond, James Bond," Norman said in an atrocious British accent.

"This theft would make for an awesome limerick," she said. "Many words rhyme with Kent like tent and vent."

"Lament."

"Convent."

"Prevent."

"And Simon... pie-men, thigh-men, hymen. It stinks that nothing rhymes with Winston, but stuff rhymes with Ella. Don't tella fella!"

Norman snort-laughed. "That's a bad smella."

"Ha ha. You made a funny. How about this? There once was an actor named Kent, Who stole spy documents to pay the rent. What do you think? Is biker a better word than actor?"

"More words rhyme with biker like piker liker hitchhiker."

"Norman, you're almost out the door, man," said a glowering Herm Taylor.

"Good one, Captain!" She burst in laughter.

"Paco, we're cops, not poets," Taylor groused. "Norman, where are we with Jennie Wade's bank statements?"

"Ur, uh, Jennie's account was opened thirteen years ago and with a social security number stolen from a deceased woman in Gettysburg."

"Sir, it occurred around the same time that Ella Winston started to paint the Eaton forgeries for Seymour Simon," she said. "After the sale of the third forgery ten thousand dollars was deposited into Jennie's account. #morethancoincidence!"

"You're sure this bank account doesn't belong to Ella Winston?" Taylor said.

"Positive, Captain," she said resolutely. "Her accounts were with a bank in Philly. With the forgery money, she paid off student loan debt and pissed away the rest living high in the city." She paused. "I have a hypothesis. That Jennie was blackmailing Simon. She was on to his Eaton forgery scam. He paid her 10K for her silence. That's when he decided to end it and finger Winston."

"Interesting, Paco," Taylor said. "Very interesting."

"Oooh, but it doesn't end there," she said mysteriously. "Then I think Simon turned the tables on Jennie because two thousand dollars every six months started to be withdrawn from her account."

"When?"

"The withdrawals started two weeks after the theft from the National Archives. They continued for the past thirteen years to this year. That's 52K total!"

"In what form?"

"Cash withdrawals from random ATMs around the Gettysburg area," Norman said.

"Could you see who it was from the security cameras?"

"Some guy," Norman answered. "Big hat, beard, sunglasses."

"Someone in disguise," she added. "Withdrawals from Jennie's account coincided almost exactly with deposits to Simon's personal bank account, one that he didn't share with Ventresca. Only his name was on this particular account."

"So Jennie the blackmailer becomes the blackmailee," Taylor stated. "What did Simon suddenly have on her, do you think?"

Lisa tapped the paper on her desk. "I think your answer is in the document that Curtis Kent stole for Simon. The FBI just sent it to me. If my hypothesis is correct, the document's important for two reasons. First, Simon found incriminating info in it that Jennie paid sorely to keep hidden. Second, by linking Ella to its theft, it sealed her fate with the jury. This one document silenced Jennie and Ella at once."

Taylor pulled up a chair. "Show me."

LEAH DEVLIN

"Here, sir. Curtis Kent tore pages from a Civil War-era diary written by a woman named Mary MacKenzie from Gettysburg. The pages pertain to the activities of villagers—specifically spies—in late August 1863. I'll read you the salient passage."

My suspicions arose the night I heard noises in the cellar. My husband Hiram was absent so I grabbed a pistol and tiptoed downstairs. Hiram's nocturnal absences were not uncommon for he was amongst the clandestine vigilantes that scoured the countryside for enemy spies and troops. I pointed the pistol outward with a shaky hand, fearing a rebel intruder or a deserter foraging for food. The clink of bottles and quiet laughter drifted up the earthen stairs. I recognized the voices as belonging to Hiram, Jed Detrick and the Captain. They were stacking boxes embossed with Carib's Finest Black Rum, Wedgewood-Smyth Import Co. Hiram was a farmer. What was he doing with a cargo of liquor in our cellar? The three of them were filthy, their clothes encrusted with mud—and blood.

I backed away and crouched in the darkness, listening.

They were drunk, quite drunk. The subject of their low, diabolic laughter was a woman named Abigail. A bottle sloshed between them and a contest to outboast the other in lewdness and savagery began. A sick horror subsumed me. My ears were deceiving me, I first believed. It could not be possible. It could not be possible that Hiram had—no, no it wasn't possible! I was walking in my sleep. I was in a nightmare, a sleep-walking nightmare. Yet I knew I was not. I was very much awake, my every nerve and fiber of being crackling awake. The men toasted their atrocities with celebratory gulps of liquor and vulgar belches. Abigail fought and thrashed like a wild cat but they finally subdued her then... after they hoisted her bloodied body up a maple tree. At this Hiram and the men laughed. They laughed! My sobbing heart I feared was rattling the beams and rafters of the farmhouse. God help me! Lord, what to do with the child I was carrying... the child of Hiram MacKenzie... Devil incarnate?

The arrogant captain snarled an order. "Ride south tomorrow, Jed. Catch up with Longstreet's army."

Longstreet? How could that be? Longstreet? I must have misheard. But thrice the Confederate general's name was mentioned.

"General Longstreet must know of our victory. Abigail Wedgewood-Smyth of the missing fingers has been dispatched! Josiah will be next!" laughed Captain Tobias Worth.

"You're not going alone," Sharon Westerly whispered hotly into Jay's phone. "Remember Hast—wait for me. I'll be right there. This is an order, Civilian-on-Vacation! Wait!"

Last evening his empty gin bottles had exploded by the swamp's edge. Westerly was a crack-shot and a very smart cop. It couldn't hurt to have a second pair of eyes searching the forest. "I'll wait but hurry." He rang off, rushed to the safe in his office, punched in the password—his and Laura's anniversary date—and pulled out his Glock. Now what? How to kill the endless time while waiting for Westerly? Do something constructive. Work. Look at the images from James' flash-drive taken at the historical society in Gettysburg. That would pass the time until she arrived.

He popped the flash-drive into his laptop and hit print. Sheets of paper slid from his printer. "Shit. Really?" Just drawings of gears and rotors from a printing press belonging to a nineteenth century newspaperman named Clarence Stratford. Basically useless. He checked his watch. One last page pushed from the printer. A faded list of names and dates from what looked to be lined notebook paper—individuals who had checked out the Eaton folder.

This was interesting. Ella Winston's name. Twice.

The first time was nearly two decades ago when she would have been a teenager; the second time was a few months ago. Jay felt momentarily light-headed as though a storm cloud was blowing out to sea, allowing a clear view of the horizon. Nearly two decades ago, a few weeks after a teenaged Ella had visited the historical society, was a visit by two brothers: Ian and Curtis Kent. Three days later was another visitor, one Professor Monroe Hadley.

Jay walked out to the deck and rotated the telescope down river to the town center, but there was no sign of a grey-bearded biker on a Harley. His dogs barked and shot off around the side of the house. He unsnapped the Glock from his holster.

"Thanks for answering the front door," said a testy Westerly as she rounded the corner. "Down, you monsters, down!" She shoved off the dogs.

He pushed his gun back in its holster. "Who runs the Gettysburg Historical Society?"

"It's the Battlefield Historical Society," she corrected. "Phoebe and Hazel Worth. The sisters are two Scrabble-crazed bitties. Phoebe used to date my uncle Reggie while he was still married to Aunt Marjorie, Wife Number Three. I should hate Phoebe for breaking up the marriage, but she's quite sweet. Far nicer than Marjorie ever was. Phoebe still brings Reg a tin of peanut butter cookies every week. Has something happened?"

He handed her the list of names.

She shook her head. "What is it?"

"Visitors to the historical society. Look who was there twenty years ago, looking at the Eaton files. The entire Philadelphia art mafia."

"Why do you ask about Phoebe and Hazel? Are they okay?"

"That's what I want to know. Are they *okay*?"

His meaning sunk in immediately. Beads of sweat broke out on Westerly's nose.

"Sharon, last night you mentioned that your father and uncle were cops."

"Retired. Dad and Reggie now own a bar frequented by burnt-out cops and firefighters, widows and spinsters." She paused to think. "I thought the Worth sisters hung out there because they felt safe. Two single women surrounded by a bunch of kindly old men—"

"Or were they listening for police information, insider gossip?" His phone vibrated. He frowned. "An unfamiliar number. Another goddamn courtesy call. I put my name on the no-call-list and I still get bullshit calls all day long."

It vibrated again. This time it was a text.

its me alex on ellas phone! pick up pick up!

Lisa Paco looked slyly around the office. Would anyone at the other desks notice if she read Mary MacKenzie's diary for a third time that afternoon? Perhaps if she made a don't-fuck-with-me expression, like on Commander Westerly's face all the time, then no one in the office would hassle her for reading it—again.

Shit! This was worse than her crush on Justin Timberlake when she was at the police academy. Far worse. She couldn't help herself. She looked around and slipped the Xeroxed pages from the folder.

Double shit! It was just her luck to fall hopelessly in love with a person who lived over a hundred years ago! Josiah Wedgewood-Smyth was way hot. If she tweeted about a steamy dead guy, would her followers unfollow her? Like that wasn't bad enough, Josiah was a psychopathic serial killer. But the brutal murders then decapitations of Abigail's killers were so justified. Sheez, now she was defending him!

She wasn't the only one excited by JWS. He obviously palpitated every palpitatable organ in Mary MacKenzie, even if he did murder her husband. According to Mary's diary, Josiah was a genius at psychological torment. In monthly intervals after Abigail's death the rapist-murderers disappeared from beds, brothels and bathtubs. Then a headless body would appear in the apple orchard, livery, or town square. "Which one of us is next? Who? Who?" the rebel spies whispered in panic. Despite Tobias Worth's formidable sentries and defenses, Josiah and Seth, as elusive as vapor, slipped into the village, struck and vanished. Tobias' paranoia and madness festered.

Lisa opened three new sticks of gum and began to read. 'Chew slowly and nonchalantly. Act like you're reading something uber mundane like the new HMO options.'

It was the night that the grey foal was born when Josiah appeared on the farm. Hiram and I were in the barn. Lisa's heart always skipped at this part. *An arm snaked around my waist and a black gloved-hand clamped over my mouth. "Mmm!" I twisted.*

"Shh, Mary. It's only me. You knew I'd be coming. I mean you no harm."

The words, spoken in a low gentlemanly drawl, seemed sincere so I pulled my nails from his wrist.

"But Hiram is going with me," he said. "His place is in Hell with Jeb Detrick and the others."

I nodded.

"Please do not scream," he coaxed and commanded at once.

I nodded again. Josiah released his hand from my mouth and I turned into his shadowed face. Over the shoulder of his black cape I spotted his manservant tying Hiram behind a horse. Hiram was sniveling into a gag. Where ever they were taking him, before an eternity in Hell, he would be dragged there.

Josiah's bright green eyes drew me under the ledge of his hood. I felt no fear instead a strange warmth and disequilibrium.

"Captain Worth drinks and whores at the Plow and Scythe every Tuesday night," I said loudly so Hiram knew of my disgust for him and his companions.

"I know, but thank you. Tobias will wait a little longer. We will make him wait the longest." Josiah turned to his black-caped companion who was finishing with Hiram's ropes. "Ready?"

"Aye, sir."

Josiah placed a gentle hand on my belly. "This will be a good child for he has a good mother."

"Godspeed, sir."

"God bless you, kind woman."

Jay's thoughts were a tornado of confusion. There was too much information swirling in his head in too short a time. "Kenneth Radowski... a tunnel... pink bike helmets... the missing Larson twins... Chessie..." Alex rambled to him as they rushed along the forest trail toward the abandoned estate. Ella's words were equally baffling. "We can't get to the workshop by the tunnel. That's where the black-cloaked ghost is! In the tunnel!"

What he gleaned from them was that they had fled through doors of a secret underground workshop and pushed through vines and brambles after Radowski's killer— a black ghost—had vanished into a tunnel. Absurd all of it, but that was their story. That was why they were covered in dirt and burrs. If they would just hush for one moment, he might be able to think straight. Compounding all of it was the bossy-take-control Sharon Westerly.

"Braden, you should stay behind. You're not supposed to be here. We should call for back-up."

"I'll be dismissed for disobeying orders," he retorted. "Herm Taylor is looking for any excuse to can me."

"With more man-power we can enter the tunnel at both ends and trap the perp in the middle," she said stomping through the underbrush.

"He's long gone by now but I *am* calling for back-up," he said. "I'm calling Will."

"Good. Call him."

He slowed enough to call Will, but there was no answer. He then sent him a text, beat away swarms of gnats and checked his phone again. Still nothing.

"Goddamn it! Alex, where's Will?" he shouted ahead.

"He mentioned a doctor's appointment," she called back. "Carly has an ear infection from all the swimming."

He smacked a mosquito on his neck. "Shit!"

"Shh!" said a glaring Westerly.

He glared back. "There's no one to hear us. The perp is gone. Alex said that Radowski's dead. I just want to have a look at his body and the workshop. Do you know how long we've been looking for the Larson girls? Eons! I should have known it was that pervert. One quick look at his body, then I'll leave. You call it in, Sharon. Taylor will never know I was here."

"Alex said she thinks he's dead," Westerly said. "She wasn't certain."

"He didn't move after the black-cloaked ghost whacked him. He had blood on his head," Alex said. "I'm sure of it."

"Alex is right about the ghost," Ella said. "And the blood."

"Ladies, there are no such things as black-cloaked ghosts," said Westerly sternly.

They halted at the forest's edge and looked both ways down the narrow beach as if crossing a dangerous road.

"There." Alex pointed. "The entry is at the cliff."

"Where?" asked Westerly.

"Behind those vines."

"Fuck. It's a wall of poison ivy," Westerly said.

They traipsed down the beach in the opposite direction to Alex and Ella's earlier footprints, widely spaced furrows dashing away from some indeterminate terror.

"Here!" said Alex parting the curtain of vines.

Westerly unsnapped the service revolver from her shoulder holster. "Move aside, Alex. I'm going first. Civilian-on-Vacation, take up the rear."

"Yes, ma'am," he said caustically.

Westerly didn't deign to reply because she had already ducked, then disappeared into tendrils of leaves and branches. Next went Alex, then Ella. It was his turn. He felt vaguely like Tarzan climbing through green and brown vines. There it was, just as Alex said. A crack between two doors. He turned sideways, sucked in his gut and pushed himself through.

Incredible! Westerly, gun lowered, seemed equally awestruck. Their flashlight beams zigzagged around the cave-like room but ultimately rested on one singular object. Chessie did exist! Just as James had said. It was on a sturdy wooden platform affixed to railroad tracks. That's how Josiah and Adam had moved such a behemoth to the water, then back to its secret cliff-side lair.

Alex's flashlight spotlighted a patch of dirt. "No way! He was there! I swear it! Kenneth Radowski was right there!"

Westerly swept her pistol around the room. "If this is a practical joke, I'm hauling your ass in."

"He was!"

"I swear it too!" Ella called from a worktable. "He was there! Right where Alex is standing."

Guns readied, he and Westerly followed a gesticulating Alex into the mouth of the tunnel.

"The ghost was right here!" Alex explained. "Fluttering about here. He was all black and fluttery and faceless." She dashed back to the workshop. "And Radowski was here. Exactly here. Ordering us to the wall with a gun! Then the ghost hit him with something." She pantomimed Radowski falling face first into the dirt.

The room near the worktables suddenly went dark.

"Ella?" he said quickly. "What's wrong with your light?"

"It just flickered off. Maybe there's a bad connection with the batteries." The light went back on. "Oh good. It's working again. Here are the bike helmets. Megan and Sandra's bike helmets. See?"

"I wish you hadn't touch them," he said. "Now your prints are all over them."

Westerly walked to a bench by the forge. "Paintings."

Ella spun. "What?"

"I don't remember seeing these before," Alex said.

"Me either!" Ella sped across the room and circled her beam over the canvasses. "These weren't here before! Oh my god! This is Eaton's *Ghost Riders*." She slid it away. "And *Slaughter at the Berm*." Her flashlight illuminated the last one. "*Whales*," she whispered reverently. "These are all originals. Even in the dim light I would know his style anywhere. These will—" She turned toward the tunnel with an expression of bewildered gratitude. "Thank you, Black Ghost. You've saved me. These paintings will clear my name."

"The Black Ghost must know of Josiah's death shrine," Alex said.

"What death shrine?" he and Westerly said.

Alex pointed to the tunnel. "It's horrible. Josiah beheaded the rebel spies who raped and murdered Abigail. Their heads are on pikes in there."

"How far in there?" he asked.

"Not very," Ella said. "We'll show you."

"I'm going first," said Westerly.

They snaked along the musty passage in Westerly's footsteps until she halted. "Gruesome." Jay's stomach knotted. Alex's description was accurate. It was a shrine to serial murder. Five nameless skulls. At the base of each pike were the victims' mangled weapons: bent knives, smashed pistols and twisted sabers. Candles and a tattered Bible were propped against the wall under the crucifix of a gown.

"Who were they? Do you know?" he asked.

"Two locals," Alex replied. "Ezekiel Whitby and Andreas Radowski."

"And three rebel spies from Pennsylvania," Ella said. "Hiram MacKenzie—"

"Why of course," Westerly cut in.

"And Jeb Detrick and Tobias Worth."

Westerly shook her head. "You're mistaken. Tobias Worth was the hero of Gettysburg and a staunch Unionist."

"No mistake," Ella said. "He was a spy for the Confederates."

"All of the men were," Alex agreed. "Eaton drew a series of sketches documenting what happened on the night that Abigail died. He labeled the men responsible. That's how Josiah knew who to murder."

"What's down here?" Westerly said stepping from view.

"Sharon, let's get the hell out of here," he called after her. "We can explore another time. Your team needs to question those Worth sisters and we need to put out an APB for Radowski."

BANG! Metal thudded into flesh. Only one thing made that sound.

"Bastard!" Westerly cried. Her gun flashed like lightning.

He pushed Alex into the wall, shielding her body with his. "Get out of here! Get the paintings and get out! Take them to Herm Taylor. You and Ella go! Call Will. Send back-up!"

"B-but?"

"Go!"

Alex and Ella scrambled away.

BANG-thud again. Westerly sprayed the tunnel with bullets. He tore past her and unloaded a clip into the blackness. Fleeing feet echoed on dirt and stone. He found her clinging to a root from the dirt wall.

"Where are you hit?"

"Leg and chest," she gasped.

"Can you move?"

"Nothing's keeping me in this hellhole."

He slung her arm around his shoulder and they limp-ran to the workshop.

She slowed, her lungs heaving. "I can't go any farther. I can't breathe. Place me there by the doors so I can see sunlight. Then get the hell out of here."

"I'm not leaving you." He whipped his phone from his pocket. "Shit! No cell reception!" He squeezed himself through the crack and called 911 and Will and Lisa from amongst the vines. He returned to Westerly who was in sweat-drenched pain. He knelt next to her.

"Sharon, talk to me. Keeping talking."

"My only hope was to make it to retirement. Will you tell my boy Paul that I—"

"You'll make it to retirement. Definitely. You will. Tell me what you want to do."

Her eyes closed, her breathing gurgled.

He grabbed her hand, shook it, squeezed it and pressed it to his lips. "Hey, Sharon, tell me what you want to do. When you retire. Please. What do you want to do?"

"Do you hear that?" she rasped.

"What?" he said despairingly. Was it a sound one hears when passing to the other side?

"Don't you hear it?"

"What, Sharon? What?"

She opened her eyes and tried to move her head, but it was impossible. Instead she averted her eyes toward the center of the room.

"There's something alive in that Chessie."

Alex and Ella sprinted along the beach and forest trail for a second time that day but now juggling three paintings. At the forest's edge they peered through the low scrub.

"Ella, call Will and call 911!" she said. "I think we're in the clear. No one followed us."

Ella urgently patted her pockets. "The phone must be in the sidecar! I think I left it there after you called Jay."

"As soon as we get there, call!" She scanned the fallow field and overgrown lawns around the mansion, but there was no sign of the ghost anywhere. The only evidence of a ghostly or human presence was Westerly's cruiser parked in the circular driveway. "Ready?"

"So ready."

They dashed through the tall grass and ducked behind the hedge. Ella pushed the paintings deep into the cockpit of the sidecar.

"Call 911, Ella!"

"Yes, okay!" Ella dug through her backpack. "My phone! It's not here!"

"But we called Jay from the sidecar."

"I can't remember if I put it in my pocket. Or? Maybe it fell out when we were running? I can't remember!"

"You're as bad as me with phones. We have to hurry and get to a phone!"

She tugged on her helmet and climbed on the Enfield while Ella put on the Union Jack helmet and hopped into the sidecar. "Hold on, Ella. We're outta here." She pushed the starter and kicked the Enfield into first gear. They veered around the hedge. In second gear they bumped over tufts of dried grass. At the circular driveway she kicked the bike into third gear and accelerated.

Ella grabbed the throttle.

"Hey, it's better if I drive!" she shouted over the engine. "You watch that the paintings don't jump out."

No response. Weird. Instead Ella stared at the forest from behind her face shield, her white-knuckled hand on the throttle beside her own.

"Let go, Ella! Hold onto the hand-grip in the sidecar! It's safer."

Still no response.

"Please let go! We're going to have an accident! Let me drive!"

Ella's eyes remained laser-focused on the forest.

"This is no joke! Let go!"

She fought to twist the throttle upward and slow the bike, but Ella's wrist tugged downward increasing their speed. The Enfield-sidecar hit the dirt road and picked up speed. What the hell was going on with Ella? 'Steer into the clumpy field,' she told herself. 'The clumpy field will slow us down.' She jerked the handlebars to the left, but Ella wrestled them in the opposite direction which kept them on the compacted road. What the hell!

"Ella, not funny! Stop it!"

Ella's strange gaze at the forest was unwavering. What was she looking at? Why no response?

Tug pull tug pull on the handlebars, they battled for control... snaking across the shoulder, swerving and bumping from grass to road, road to grass. The erratic motions made the sidecar rise and fall, at times nearly flip. Alex turned to a blip in her peripheral vision. A black object emerged from the forest. Its timing was no coincidence. Her heart clicked into high gear. Like a shark cutting through yellow water, the black motorcycle motored across the hazy field. She blinked sweat from her eyes. It was a low-slung cruiser. A Harley? A Fat Boy? It was moving directly into their path... on a collision course.

Alex's eyes ricocheted between the cruiser and the maniac next to her who crouched in the sidecar like a cat poised to pounce. Metal flashed at the side of her helmet. What? A pistol? Hard metal jabbed into her neck. Where did that come from? Ella's backpack?

"Jump, fucker!" Ella shouted, shoving the gun deeper. "Get off!"

Alex jerked the handlebars. The sidecar surged off the ground, throwing Ella back into the cockpit.

"You stupid fuck! I'm blowing your brains out! Jump now! Or!"

The pistol cracked against Alex's helmet, stunning her. It cracked again.

"Get off or you're dead!"

The gun barrel stabbed her neck again. Ella had gone mad... had been feigning sanity... feigning the victim... feigning the pursued. And she had been blindly reeled in.

There was no choice. Alex whipped her leg over the Union Jack gas tank and leapt outward. She hit unrelenting dirt and rolled to a stop. She scrambled into the field and flattened herself between clumps of weeds to duck a possible bullet. Her face shield was covered in dirt; she couldn't see a goddamn thing. She inched it up to watch. In a cloud of dust and exhaust Ella reached out for the handlebars, stretched out her leg and pulled herself onto the seat of the Enfield. Bent over the gas tank she raced up the dirt road. The Fat Boy waited by the coastal road. Ella accelerated as she approached. He revved his engine in greeting. They rode off in tandem. With the *original* Eatons in the sidecar.

"Sir? Sir!"

"Here, Will!" Jay released Sharon Westerly's hand and jumped to his feet. "Right here!" He pushed his head between the doors and shook the vines to attract attention.

Will Wilkins and paramedics followed the footprints in the sand to their vanishing point at the curtain of vines. The paramedics rushed to Westerly who had lost consciousness and was breathing in whistles and gasps. They jerked IV lines and oxygen tanks from their bags.

"How is she?" Will asked him.

"She's going to be fine," he said hoping that at a subconscious level his words might register with her. "And she's going to have a wonderful retirement."

"That's great news," said Will with a doubtful smile. He turned toward the submarine. "What is *that*?"

"Chessie is apparently real. Alex and Ella? Are they okay?"

Will's eyes flashed in rare anger. "Alex is banged up but fine. She's with James. We found her on the coastal road."

"Banged up? What happened? Ella?"

"Is not what she appears. We were duped. Really duped. She pulled a gun on Alex. Forced her off the motorcycle, took off with the bike and sidecar full of paintings."

"That double-crossing—when I catch her!"

"It gets worse. She's in cahoots with the Harley rider. Our serial. They rode off together. We've set up roadblocks between here and the Pennsylvania state line."

It took Jay a moment to cool down and compose himself. "She was using us to acquire the Eatons," he stated in realization. "That was her end game all along. To gain our trust, get us to assist her."

"Looks that way."

"And assist we did. All of us. A treacherous charmer. The worst kind. Those paintings will never see the light of day."

"Who knows?" Will shrugged. "What is this place?"

"The secret laboratory of Josiah Wedgewood-Smyth and Adam Eaton. According to Alex, a Black Ghost lives here. One who killed Kenneth Radowski, then carried his body away. A cop-hating ghost who shot Sharon. But oddly, put out the Eatons to be found. A ghost who's sympathetic to Ella."

"We'll find her, sir."

"Sharon thought she heard a sound in there," he said glancing at the Chessie. "Can you climb up there and have a look? My arthritic leg could never—"

"A sound?" said Will quizzically. "Yeah, sure." He effortlessly swung himself onto the platform. "Someone wedged a wrench behind the lever. Someone doesn't want this opened."

"Well, I do. Open it."

"Okay." With a groan Will lifted the hatch.

"Air! I need air!" shouted a desperate voice.

The paramedics looked up in terror; their hands with tubing, tape and syringes halted over Westerly.

Will poked his head into the opening. "Sir, you might want to see this."

"Get me out!" the voice shrieked. "Get me out!"

Jay rolled himself onto the platform and pulled his bad leg onboard with both hands. He groped upward along the rivets until he was on his feet. Will's face caused him pause. In all his years of supervising the young man, he had never seen this expression... sorrow, fury and revulsion at once.

"What is it, Will?"

Will seemed to be murmuring a somber prayer. He did not have Will's tremendous height so on tiptoes he shone his flashlight into the submarine. He was overcome by nausea. Even in the gloom he could see them—two small skeletons clothed in pink shirts and plaid shorts. One's T-shirt was embossed with an image of a Disney Princess, the other Snoopy. Carly Wilkins was roughly the same age as the Larson twins. This was a parent's worst nightmare. Fecal material had long dried in one corner. There were empty potato chip bags and water bottles. He closed his eyes as though it would erase the scene and reverse time so that it had never happened. Chessie had been a chamber of horrors until the killer had bored of the girls and decided to entomb them alive. The ladder to the interior had been long removed.

Hands upstretched and flailing, Kenneth Radowski jumped up and down, rattling the platform like a dog anxious to be freed from a pen. "Will, it's me, Kenny! From the football team! Remember? Kenny Radowski. Pull me out! Please? Pull me out!"

Radowski's hair was spiked with dried blood, confirming what Alex had described... the Black Ghost whacking him from behind, permitting time for the women to run. Did the ghost place Radowski in Chessie? It seemed a herculean—no impossible—feat. Radowski was a large man. Only a ghost of remarkable strength could have heaved him onto Chessie's platform, then lifted him up to dump him inside. Incredible really. The ghost had attacked Radowski, saving the women... deposited the paintings in the workshop to clear Ella's name... but then blasted away at Sharon Westerly. Completely illogical, contradictory actions. The ghost was benevolent then crazed in turns. What if there were two ghosts? A sane ghost and a mad one? A sane one who saved the women and delivered the paintings... and a mad one, Ella's accomplice the Harley biker? Had Curtis Kent found the tunnel and shot Westerly? After all, the gunshots were the diversion that allowed Ella to escape with the paintings.

The paramedics slid Westerly onto a gurney so Jay climbed off the platform. "How is she?"

"Um—" said a paramedic uneasily.

"Sharon, let's do something together when we're both retired," he said squeezing her limp hand. "Do you like to fish? I have a little boat. I could teach you to fish."

"Will! You've got to remember me!" Radowski screamed. "From River Glen High School. Football, buddy, don't you remember? We won the state championship in... please get me out! It's terrible in here! Please!"

"Sir?" said Will from the platform.

"Looks like Chessie's captured a pedophile who's going to stay there until forensics shows up to take swabs. Until they arrive, that hatch is staying closed."

"Yes, sir." CLANK.

Chapter 9
Bait and Switch

"You're a prick," said Ella smacking Curtis Kent's shaved head. "You could have killed me with that UHaul!"

Curtis grinned across the front seat of the truck. "It was only a nudge to give you a thrill, a rush of adrenaline between your legs."

"That did not turn me on," she grimaced. "You're so fucking disturbed."

"Submit, Ellie, submit," he chuckled.

"Shut-up. You're never touching me again. Like I didn't know it was you from the start. Your body is nothing like Ian's. Like I'm that stupid?"

"Give me a kiss, honey. We're together now."

"That mess on the ghost walk, Curt! That was way over the top. You could have cut me!"

"That wasn't me."

"Don't bullshit me. I'd know one of your costumes anywhere. And you wore that same biker chick costume when you visited me at Cambridge Springs."

"Oh. Did I?"

She whacked his head again and he laughed.

"Which costume did you like the best?"

"Hm. Let me think. I loved you in the three-piece suit. You looked so debonair. The guards were completely convinced that you were my new lawyer. The beach bum surfer boy was also a turn-on because I like you with long hair."

"I had fun with that character. Declan, your college friend from California."

"I hated you in polyester with the oily comb-over. Yuck. Absolutely repulsive."

He grinned again. "That was your second cousin Emmit from Bayonne, New Jersey. He was a used-car-salesman." His stomach grumbled. "Are we almost there? I'm hungry."

She checked the GPS on one of the Jennie phones. "We're very close. A hot dinner's waiting, she said."

"Good. I'm starved."

She turned out the window. "Pretty forest. I love the Poconos, especially in the summertime. I hated that tugboat. Yeah, right. Like I was really going to be a crabber."

"I'm not loving that you fucked that cop."

"It was just part of the script."

"Yeah, but—"

"Curt?"

"What?"

She gave his hand a squeeze. "Thank you."

"For what?"

"Teaching me how to get into character, assume their personality, inhabit their thoughts to become... to totally embody that character. I never would have survived Cambridge Springs without your visits and what you taught me about character assumption."

"Not character assumption, El. It's called personality transformation."

"I did exactly as you said. I meditated and breathed, erased my true personality and became an *It* without thoughts or identity. Then I transformed myself into all sorts of different things to kill time in prison."

"Like what?"

"Crazy stuff. One of Degas dancers, Rembrandt's soldiers and Rousseau's Gypsy. For a time I even imagined myself as a dog from Dogs Playing Poker."

"That painting cracks me up. Which one were you?"

"The gray collie. In creating the new Ella, the victimized woe-is-me biker for this job, I'd have these pathetic internal monologues about being a NASA astronaut or a crabber in River Glen. Can you imagine me living in a dull backwater shithole! Once we sell these paintings, it's the high-life for us. Paris. Rome. Stockholm. Baby, the sky's the limit."

"Personality transformation really works. That's how I became JW Booth the parole officer and the biker chick when I knocked off Linda Radowski. The cops thought the killer was going after you. You gained their trust and sympathy as you predicted."

"Everything worked like clockwork. I can thank the dick Seymour for that. He insured that I had years to plan my revenge down to the micro detail."

"I can't wait for our trans-global motorcycle trek when the dust clears. We'll have a ball."

She squeezed his hand again. "We will."

A log cabin appeared down a leaf-matted road. She checked the GPS. "That must be it."

"If those walls could speak. I bet it was a writer's retreat." He patted her knee. "And a romantic hide-away for lovers."

The cabin seemed a natural outgrowth of the landscape rather than a manmade construct. Moss and ivy were reclaiming the walls. Weeds and wildflowers parted the planks of a sagging porch. Seasons of leaves were plastered to plastic lawn chairs. A fishing rod leaned on a tangle of deer antlers. Languid smoke from a chimney hovered over the bowed roof. A rusty axe and chopping block were next to a wood shed.

"Our home for a while," she said with disappointment. "A dive, but anything beats a stinky crab boat or crowded Airstream."

Curtis rolled down the window and inhaled. "I like it. It has a rustic charm. There's nothing better than the smell of a wood fire."

"The Jennies are here. There's the minivan."

"I hope dinner's ready. Let's unload the bikes later and eat first."

"They'll want to see the Eatons before anything."

"And his sketches documenting Abigail's murder. How did you lift those without anyone noticing?"

"When Alex was acting out Radowski's attack by the Black Ghost, I was by the tables and bike helmets and stashed them in my shorts."

He looked blatantly her crotch. "I wanna stash something in your shorts."

"I almost didn't succeed. While I rushed to hide the sketches, my flashlight flicked off. I was in panic mode! Then Braden accused me of getting my prints all over the helmets."

"The Black Ghost? Who do you think that was?"

"It could be any weird local who's squatting there, maybe living in the tunnels." She became pensive. "You know that you hit the detective Westerly, don't you?"

"Not my problem. She headed down the passage. She was going to see me. I had to improvise fast. It became the perfect opportunity for you to grab the paintings."

"If she dies—a cop."

"Oh well. We're going to be here for a while anyway. This is a good place to lay low. You paint. I'll cook..."

"I'm not eating your road-kill."

"... and give you lots of great sex." He stopped the truck next to the minivan and they slid from the cab. "I'll get the paintings." He departed for the back.

The cabin door opened and Hazel stepped onto the porch, her hands jittering with anticipation. "You had no trouble getting here?"

"Nope," said Ella. "The truck was hiding at the Whitbys' farm. Right where you said it would be."

"My girl, what you've been through!" Hazel gave her a kiss on the cheek. "I'm so proud of you. What focus and concentration! What a stellar performance!"

She sighed with bombast, then laughed at herself. "I'm so glad to be here."

"Seymour is out of our hair," Hazel said with finality. "Blackmailer, thief, framer—"

"All-round shit. Ian and Ventresca?"

"Must know they're next. But later. They're squirming right now."

Curtis approached with the paintings.

"Get them inside," Hazel snapped.

"Yes, Jennie," he grumbled.

Hazel shushed him in with a flapping hand. "Put them right there." She pointed to a cracked wicker sofa.

Spatula in hand, Phoebe rushed across the cabin and gave Ella a hug. "Congratulations, sweetheart. I'm so glad you're okay! Curtis, I made your favorite... my world-famous peanut butter cookies. All organic, all natural. They're hot out of the oven."

"I'm starved. Can I have one now?"

"Before dinner?"

"Don't be so rigid, Phoebe," said Hazel. "In light of our victory, let's celebrate. Cookies before dinner, it is."

Phoebe pulled him toward the kitchen counter. "A glass of milk or a Yuengling?"

"Milk with cookies always," he said. "I could smell them all the way from the truck. What's for dinner?"

"Shepherd's pie," Phoebe answered.

"Did you use cayenne?"

"No, but you'll love it. It's one of my best recipes."

"Oh my, Ellie," Hazel said wondrously. "*Ghost Riders*. Incredible. It exceeds the beautiful sketch."

Ella moved next to Hazel at the sofa. "Eaton's use of black and white... the starkness is haunting. How about this one? *Slaughter at the Berm*. Look at the transition from reds to maroons. Impressionistic but with hints of abstract expressionism. He was so far ahead of his time."

"*Whales*," Hazel said breathlessly.

"By far my favorite Eaton," she told Hazel.

"My goodness, slow down, Curtis," said Phoebe. "Save some room for dinner."

"You're not eating the whole plate yourself, are you?" Ella admonished. "You better save me some."

"I missed breakfast and lunch because I was following your butt around a sweltering River Glen," he replied.

"No bickering, you two," Hazel said.

"A Yuengling, El?" Phoebe asked. "We're celebrating."

"Yes, we are!" She strutted to the kitchen area, grabbed a beer and flipped off the cap. She held it up. "To our brilliant success."

Phoebe held up a glass of wine. "Cheers. To well-laid plans."

"I ate too fast." Curtis collapsed into a chair at the kitchen table. "Way too much sugar on an empty stomach."

"Ellie, the other two?" Hazel said. "*God Watches the Gathering* and *The Death of a Field Surgeon*."

She returned to Hazel by the wicker sofa. "I have no clue. I don't even know where these came from. But one of the villagers knew of my plight and the paintings miraculously appeared in the tunnel."

"I'd put my money on the wanna-be-novelist Mr. Collins," Hazel said. "He knows a lot about the Wedgewood-Smyths. A disconcerting amount. He certainly knows about Tobias and Abigail. Seymour can no longer hang that over our heads."

"That's fake news, Hazel," Phoebe said adamantly. "Nothing from Mary MacKenzie's diary was true. All a pack of lies. Tobias would never have... fake news, fake news."

"It's doubtful that it was James," Ella said. "He's a ditz."

"Is he?" Hazel said warily. "Let's watch his movements."

"Please not me," Curtis groaned. "I'm so tired of traveling to River Glen. Phoebe, do you any antacids?"

"No traveling for a while," Hazel reassured him. "You and Ellie need to stay put and keep out-of-sight until we plan our next steps."

Ella took a thoughtful sip of beer and cocked her head at the row of Eatons.

Hazel looked at her and then the paintings. "What, dear? What is it?"

"Something. I'm not sure what. Something about this one. This. *Whales*."

Ping ping

The pyrates of River Glen were far from their native waters, on unfamiliar ground, inland and mountainous. Fish out of water. Between the black tree trunks the log cabin was just visible. The moon's glow had casted the dwelling an eerie shade of grey. If James had to describe its color for a scene in *Subterfuge*, he might call it necrotic grey, even better silent grey. The only movement in the clearing was a wisp of smoke from the crumbling stone chimney.

The tracker app on James' phone *pinged* again. "The three paintings are together," he whispered to his mates. "That's a relief. I was worried that they were going to be separated, divided up amongst the thieves. Alas, we'd have to chase them all over kingdom come. Then I'd never get my novel finished."

"Whose idea was it to put micro transponders into the picture frames in the first place?" Alex asked. "No one tells me anything."

"Julia's. 'Drill them into anything that's wood, lads'," James said mimicking his grandmother's Scottish lilt. "'Treasure chests and barrels, everything, in case the deranged Whitbys locate our hoard.' While we put trackers on the treasure, we decided to do the paintings and figureheads as well."

"We filled in the bore holes with a special glue-sawdust mixture," Cousin Marty said. "It exactly matched the type of wood... oak, mahogany, pine...."

"You'd never know there was a drill hole at all," said Cousin Melvin.

"I miss all the interesting activities," Alex said. "When was this discussed?

"At the April meeting," he answered.

"Honey, I think we missed that one because of tango lessons," Will said.

"Okay, gang. Let's focus. We all know the plan?"

"Aye, Captain," whispered his comrades.

"No one gets hurt," he repeated. "We grab the paintings and sketches and go. The police can pick them up later. Will has the best aim. He'll have the tranquilizer gun for Curtis

Kent. Kent's the one we really have to watch. Everyone be really careful of him. Really, really careful. Alex, you're outside with the boat stuff. Right?"

"I'm ready."

"No conversations with any of them. I'll do the talking. No one else. Remember. We're the *silent* guardians of the River Glen treasure."

"Aye aye, Captain."

"But do I have words for that skank!" Alex whispered hotly. "She used me, then almost killed me on the motorcycle. I told her my best crabbing secrets! Did she mess with the wrong pyrate!"

"Shh."

"Skank!"

"Shh! Let's get ready."

They slid on their pyrate surveillance attire, black cloaks and night vision goggles over black face masks, and tiptoed from behind the trees to the clearing. Two yellow windows glowed under the collapsing awning. There was a murmur of women's voices and bursts of raucous laughter. Why no male voice? Where was Kent? Did he know they were coming? Was his deadly blade sharpened? Was he hiding, readied to spring and slash? Where was he! They fanned out in pairs around the house and regrouped a moment later behind the truck.

"There's no back door," the Wilkins cousins reported.

"Good. That means the front door, or a window, is their only means of escape."

"No sign of Kent anywhere!" Will worried aloud. "Did he leave on his motorcycle?"

James shrugged uneasily. "Back to our positions. Be ready for anything."

They slipped silently across the clearing. Weeds and wildflowers muted their steps on the porch planks. The female voices got louder. Through a grimy window he spotted Hazel and Phoebe Worth and Ella Winston at a table, helping themselves to a casserole. They seemed supremely pleased with themselves. The log room was filled with smug laughter.

But where was Curtis Kent? James looked nervously around. Alex was tying seaweed encrusted ropes to a sturdy tree near the wood shed. He could only hope that Kent was long departed! Perhaps he had received payment and was on a backroad heading to the Canadian border. The giant silhouette of Will was in the center of the yard, providing cover for Alex and aiming the tranquilizer gun at the black unknown. She was done with the boat lines and gave him a thumbs-up.

It was time.

The black-cloaked pyrates smashed open the door. The three women jumped to their feet. Beer bottles and wine glasses toppled to the floor. He motioned with his pistol for hands-up. Their shocked hands sprung into the air. Marty and Melvin dashed from room to room, black cloaks furling and unfurling, but Kent was nowhere to be found! The Eatons were propped along a wicker sofa. There were two tins of cookies on the counter and a half-eaten casserole on the table.

They nudged the women outside by gun point. Ella Winston started cursing like a sailor. "Shut-up lass," he said in a Scottish brogue to disguise his voice. "Or I blow ye brains out." He pushed his pistol into the base of her skull which quieted her. The Worth sisters locked fingers and marched solemnly forward. A circle of pistols directed the women to a place under a thick branch.

"Back to back. One move, we shoot ye."

The pyrates stepped away and grabbed the ropes. The women looked down in confusion. Something, they were instantly aware, was odd about the black leaves under foot.

"Heave ho!"

"No!" Ella yelled.

Up went the corners of the net around the women.

"You shits!" she screamed.

"Heave ho!" The ropes squeaked. Off the ground the net lifted.

"When I get loose, you're all dead!"

"Heave ho!"

Up into the leaves the stinky fishing net was hoisted until three furious Jennies swayed under a moaning branch.

Will cautiously opened the back of the truck, poised for Kent to lunge at him. But no attack came. He shone his flashlight into the bed. It was empty except for a Harley Fat Boy and Julia's Enfield-sidecar combo. The Harley!

"The slasher's still about!"

Will and the Wilkins cousins stormed the darkness in pursuit of him, while he and Alex dashed into the cabin. He slid the Eatons into a lawn bag as she disappeared into the bedrooms, searching for the sketches depicting Abigail's death.

"Found them!" she said.

"Let's get out of here!"

She veered over to the kitchen counter.

"What are you doing?" he called from the porch. "Come on!"

"Captain!" called Will.

Marty and Melvin ran over to Will at the wood shed.

"Captain, please let us down!" said one of the Jennies. "I'm sure we can work out some arrangement. Mutually beneficial to all of us."

Ella writhed, shaking the branches. "I'm gonna kill you fuckers!"

"Shut-up, you moron!" shouted another one.

"Don't moron me!"

"Captain, how about a generous percentage when we sell the paintings? We have a very interested buyer. He'll pay handsomely—"

"It's really quite tight up here. Horribly constricting actually and difficult to breathe."

Ella spit through the mesh. "Fuckers, you're all dead!"

"Please, please, let us down! I'm sure we can work something out!"

He and Alex joined the Wilkinses at the shed. The women's implorations from the tree branches were suddenly background noise, incessant yet inconsequential like a departing rainstorm. He put his arm around his sister's shoulders. It was difficult for him to discern the age of men with shaved heads. Perhaps the man was in his early forties. Whatever his age, he was tremendously fit. His jeans were faded, engineer boots worn and the once black Harley Davidson T-shirt was a sun-bleached gray. Will illuminated shelves of Civil War relics: caps and kepis, belts and buckles, cannonballs and bullets, boots and banners... a treasure trove of black market memorabilia. The flashlight beam returned to the man. Nowhere were there signs of physical trauma yet Curtis Kent was very dead.

"Poisoned," Will said.

James felt a frenetic rustling against him. It was Alex fumbling for something under her cape. Peanut butter cookies dropped into the dirt.

"Not hungry," she whispered.

Julia took a thoughtful sip of Royal Lochnager and cocked her head at the Eaton on the stone mantle. She knocked a Dunhill from the pack, twisted it into her cigarette holder and flicked a silver lighter. She inhaled deeply and exhaled slowly.

"Done, Randy my love," she said to the photo in her locket. "My obligation to you is done. Our grandchildren in the Americas are fine."

A metallic slide and clang sounded as Aunt Beatrice pushed her walker into the library. "You're still indulging that vile habit."

"They haven't killed me yet."

"We're all mortal, darling. Even you." Beatrice gazed up at the mantle. "This painting. Of all the baubles you could have brought home as a souvenir, why this? It's quite atrocious. It looks like it was painted by a child, one with no hope for the University of the Arts in London."

"*Whales* by Adam Eaton. It's a worthless Allaway family heirloom. I found it and some other paintings in Randy's attic, amidst his vinyl albums of the British Invasion bands. Randy had ghastly taste in art but excellent taste in music and women." She grinned a cagey grin. "First wives anyway."

"But why this painting?"

"Adam Eaton was an insignificant painter as American artists go. But this painting is the essential link between the civilized world of Aberdeen and a land of rustics on the Chesapeake Bay." She pointed. "Those two black objects in the waters..."

"The whales."

"... are not whales but two sea monsters called Chessie."

Beatrice guffawed. "You're full of it!"

Julia smiled back. "Nessie of Loch Ness, you see, had two sprogs that Giles Hale and Charlie Allaway brought to the Americas as pets. The slimy little creatures had voracious appetites and grew too big for jars and beer mugs, then the rain barrels on the *Raven*. In the end Giles and Charlie had no choice but to release them. The Chessies slithered overboard as the *Raven* entered the Chesapeake, but the lads had grown fond of them so as the ship sailed north, they tossed them goat entrails, pig hooves and other discards from the galley. The Chessies followed the *Raven* all the way to River Glen."

"How many glasses of scotch have you had today?"

"Only three. I'm quite sober." With a cigarette-in-the-lips squint, Julia stretched and lifted the painting off the mantle. "*Whales* holds the key to the *Raven*'s lost treasure."

"My dear, the treasure's location has always been known. That was my understanding anyway."

"Yes, yes. It's under my house in River Glen but only a small portion."

Beatrice's eyes sparkled. "You mean that the bulk of the treasure has never—"

Julia shook her head mysteriously.

"How do you know this?"

"Luna the Psychic told me when we went to Burning Man in the Nevada desert. One night she was hallucinating on ayahuasca tea when she began to ramble on about a painting with two whales. We were with this handsome, young cowboy from Wyoming—"

"Oh, lass," Beatrice sighed. "Thank goodness your mother is not alive. Cowboys... Americans... psychics... oh my."

"I was wankered also, but not enough to forget that *Whales* was tucked between Randy's *Rolling Stones* and *Guess Who* LPs. 'On the shoreline half way between the two whales,' Luna mumbled, 'is the location of the mother lode.' You can imagine my excitement. The second I got home I scrambled up to the attic and found the painting and recognized the shoreline as the one by the Wedgewood-Smyth plantation. I took photographs of the painting and sent them to that cowboy, who was not really a cowboy but an artist from New York City who had exiled himself to a dude ranch in Wyoming. He painted me a copy of *Whales*."

Beatrice sighed again. "He painted you a forgery."

"Yes. Sadly, it was far from perfect. The cowboy, I suspect, was dyslexic or stoned because he had the Chessies swimming in the opposite direction than in the original. But that's neither here nor there. Alex and James will never notice. They're darlings but numpties. How exhaustingly competitive Alex is! She could never admit that I was better at everything."

"The forgery, Julia—"

"I put the cowboy's *copy* in the old picture frame and placed it and the other Eaton paintings in the basement, then sent *the original* here to Aberdeen. Clever me!"

Beatrice was unimpressed. "You're a scoundrel like your father."

"Don't you see? This painting's our insurance policy! Couldn't we send one of the gillies, Nigel or Cedric, to recover the treasure? Bring it back here by boat to bypass scrutiny and taxation? The leaky roof in the south wing could be fixed and the stained glass windows in the chapel. We'd never have another money worry! Ever, Aunt Bea!"

"There's not an altruistic bone in your body. This is not about leaky roofs and chapel windows. Your money for roulette and whiskey has been frittered away. Months ago, I received an overdue bill for a Royal Enfield and sidecar. Did you really need the deluxe Union Jack paint job? Your inheritance ran out. That's why you're here."

"Not true! I came back to take care of you!"

"I do just fine with the hounds and gillies. Giles' intent was that the treasure be used for communal purposes, always for the good of the community. Never for personal motive or gain."

"The villagers in River Glen are frugal with their allotment of the treasure. There's still plenty left. Besides, they'll never know about it."

"No, lass. I'm not sending Nigel and Cedric to treasure hunt along the banks of the Chesapeake."

Julia irritably tossed her cigarette butt into the fire. "You lack the pyrating Hale spirit."

"Possibly because I'm ninety-three." Beatrice pulled spectacles from her bathrobe pocket and slipped them on her long elegant nose. She leaned over the painting. "It is a lovely coastline, but that's a formidable expanse of beach between the two Chessies. Finding that treasure would be like finding a needle in a haystack."

"Ah, ah," said Julia teasingly. "There's a treasure map."

"Of course, there is," Beatrice said with a facetious laugh. "And pray tell. Where is this map?"

"So I've piqued your interest?"

"Not so much that I can't leave right now for a wee nap."

"Bea, indulge me!"

"You're about to ask me for money."

"I'm not! Okay, I'll show you the map."

"You haven't seen it?"

"No. During Luna's cosmic trip, she mentioned a secret map. Adam Eaton stood on the cliff's edge and drew the exact location of the treasure from a bird's eye view. The map, she said, was hidden within the painting by Josiah Wedgewood-Smyth. It's from the 1860s and therefore old. I dared not remove it until I arrived in Scotland for fear it might crumble to bits."

"My interest is piqued. Let's see it."

Julia flipped over the painting. She pried back the tacks and hesitated to heighten the suspense.

"Well, go on!" Beatrice said.

Julia pressed her fingernails behind the cardboard backing and lifted. A yellow envelope was visible through diaphanous contact paper. She gently peeled aside the paper. The envelope was stuck to the back of the canvas.

Aunt Beatrice's eyebrows rose in anticipation. "Open it, lass! Open it!"

Julia belted down the last of her whiskey. "Aye, Pyrate Queen." She opened the envelope. The texture of the paper inside was not at all rough and ancient but glossy and modern. She unfolded it. "Bugger all!"

"Brilliant!" said Aunt Beatrice laughing. "Dogs with Eye Patches Playing Poker. Numpties, are they?"

Chapter 10
The Wedgewood-Smyth Museum

Ten months later

Women in shimmery gowns and tuxedoed men swirled across the floor to the music of a five-piece band while children clambered on *Chessie 1*. All of them are in a state of happy ignorance, Will realized. If they only knew the full of it.

Chessie 1 was the name assigned by the forensic scientists to this submarine, the one winched from the marsh by Alex and Ella Winston last summer. DNA analysis had confirmed that the female skeleton was Abigail Wedgewood-Smyth. Since Adam Eaton's origins were unknown, the male could not be identified conclusively by molecular techniques, though most agreed that it was the missing painter. The Smyth family had requested that the two friends be laid to rest in the family plot, at long last uniting Abigail with Josiah and their children. Why Adam entombed himself in the sub with Abigail's body would forever be speculation. The presence of the wood crucifix suggested premeditation to his actions. Perhaps he was preventing her corpse from further abuse at the hands of her killers. An environmental historian suggested that a hurricane around that time had caused the Chessie to roll, making it impossible for Adam to release the hatch and escape. A more romantic interpretation was that Adam was guarding his beloved friend and patron through eternity.

Carly waved to Will from *Chessie*'s platform. He mouthed "Be careful." She mouthed a sassy "Daaad." His heart leapt at that singular word. If anyone dare lay a finger — His mood darkened.

Chessie 2 had a different fate. Out of respect for the Larson family it would forever be relegated to the space metal building behind Zera Lim's crime lab. Out of sight but not out of mind. Its final fate was to be a tomb, like its counterpart *Chessie 1*. When the police pulled a froth-mouthed Kenneth Radowski from the sub, he had ranted that it was all Linda's idea. They had been unable to have children of their own... had tried to get pregnant for years... with no success.

Then they came upon Sandra and Megan riding their bikes one summer evening. That was their chance to be parents. Most locals had heard rumors of a hidden labyrinth under the Wedgewood-Smyth estate. Years before, on a lark, he and Linda had gone searching for it. The underground workshop would be the perfect home for Sandra and Megan, they had decided. He and Linda joined the Friends of the Wedgewood-Smyth House to be privy to activities on the grounds. The girls were kept there for months until Linda's insurance business began to flourish and she lost interest in parenting. It would have been impossible to return the girls at that point, Kenneth said. This left them in his sole care.

Will felt his heart pound. Where was Carly? A second ago she was playing with the little boy in the red shirt. Now she was gone! He pushed through the dancers and circled the submarine. Oh, thank God! There she was on the portside, pressing her nose against the window. He sensed eyes on him. From the bar a tuxedoed James gave him a tacit look. He gave his captain a subtle salute. James smiled and saluted back. He, James and the other River Glen pyrates had no luck in identifying the pyrate imposters Giles and Shannon who kidnapped Ian Kent and tied chicken to his feet to force disclosure of the slasher Curtis Kent. The texts to Ian were not from Zera's phone. The number was untraceable, from a pay-as-you-go phone. But whoever the imposters were, they were accelerants to solving the case.

What a day that had been!

He and Carly had been driving to her doctor's appointment when he got the call. James' app to the security system in the Wedgewood-Smyth house was pinging. Someone had entered the tunnel. He rushed Carly to his parents' house so his father could get her to the appointment and he floored it to the mansion. The Enfield-sidecar combo was hidden behind a hedge. Alex was somewhere on the premises! In the tunnel? He hid his car in the barn where James was waiting. They donned the black capes, masks and night-vision goggles worn when haunting the house—the strategy of the River Glen pyrates to frighten away trespassers until the remainder of the *Raven*'s treasure had been located—and entered the tunnel through the egress passage in the barn. The timing was bizarre to say the least.

Just a week before he and James had discovered the workshop but had no time to explore it that day because of Carly's swim meet. They had only poked their heads into the space.

"Chessie exists!" James had declared. "This will be the centerpiece of our museum. It will attract busloads of school groups and tourists!"

What they did not see across the dark room were the pink bike helmets. Had they known! James' plan was to discuss the tunnels at the next meeting of the River Glen pyrates and schedule a time for the group to search the tunnels.

James' app had pinged again. Another intruder! He and James crept along the black passage. Voices were heard in the workshop, one menacing and male, and the other all too familiar... Alex's. Kenneth Radowski was forcing Alex and Ella to the wall for an execution style murder! In a black furl and swoop James struck Radowski with a rock. He and James stepped back into tunnel and watched the women flee through a green crack in the doors. Alex and Ella were safe! They had a little time but not much before the women would contact him or Jay.

"Feed Radowski to Chessie, Will! I'll be right back!" James disappeared into the tunnel.

Radowksi had a pulse. He was knocked out but not dead. Will dragged the horrid man across the floor, lifted him onto the platform, then lugged his body up the side of the sub. Radowski dropped through the opening with an echoing thud. Will clanked down the lid and jammed a wrench behind the lever to prevent an escape. In his haste he had never looked inside, never knew that the remains of the Larson twins were within!

A winded James reappeared with a stack of paintings and dropped them in a puff of dust. "For the police to find. To help Ella. Let's get out of here!"

He and James drove back to the village and sat at an outdoor table at Harlow's Pub, chatting with the owner Miles and Aunt Luna, creating for themselves a most conspicuous alibi. He waited for Alex and Ella to rumble into town on the Enfield. He waited for a call. Alex had no phone but Ella did. Why weren't they calling? His fingers drummed the table. Where were they?

James' app pinged again. Another person had entered the tunnel, but who? Had Alex and Ella gone back in? For what reason? What if they inadvertently released Radowski? What if the intruder was the biker-slasher? Oh god, what if?

Will's phone rang a second later. It was Jay. *Westerly down... need medics... perp in tunnel... send backup... quickest way on beach... cliff... curtain of vines.* He and James flew to their cars. They tore up the coastal road, through the pine forest and valley of summer corn and turned off on the dirt road. An ambulance and police cruiser converged on the estate at the same time as them. A dazed and dusty Alex was on the coastal road, a scratched pyrate helmet in her hand.

"Ella's gone! That psycho stole our Enfield and paintings!"

"Not for long," he said.

"I'll assemble our group," James said.

That afternoon from a laptop on James' kitchen island, the River Glen pyrates had watched three red dots, micro transponders embedded in the picture frames, move across the Maryland-Pennsylvania border, along the Pennsylvania Turnpike, up the Northeast Extension and eventually stop in the Pocono Mountains.

Twenty-four hours later an anonymous tip from one of the Jennie phones was placed to the Gettysburg PD. The police and FBI agents who swarmed the cabin found, in addition to three irate women who had been suspended in an old fishing net overnight, pay-as-you-go phones labeled Jennie 1, 2 and 3, two tins of peanut butter cookies—one normal and the other deadly with arsenic—a day-old Shepherd's pie casserole and a wood shed containing illegally-gained Civil War relics and a poisoned cannibal named Curtis Kent. In a shallow grave behind the shed was one decomposing Daniel 'Old Man' Detrick.

"It was their idea!" "No, it was her idea!" Accusations hurled from Jennie to Jennie told a story of treachery and murder long in the planning. Over an eleven-year period there were repeated visits to Cambridge Springs by the hapless messenger-guardian-assassin Curtis Kent and the devious Worth sisters. The blackmailer Seymour Simon would be murdered so Tobias Worth's crimes would never see the light of day. Winston would be framed once again. She would seduce a police officer to gain his trust and assistance. A lonely widower with a drinking problem seemed the ideal candidate. She would befriend the locals—the Chrome Divas, Alex, Nina and James—who might know something of the Wedgewood-Smyths and the whereabouts of Adam Eaton's paintings.

Will and Lisa had sat in on the interviews with Ella Winston and the FBI agents. She answered their questions with a chilling dispassion.

"Why was Linda Radowski killed?" an agent asked. "Why her?"

"In the end Curtis went off script," she said. "He ran into Linda while surveilling the Wedgewood-Smyth place months before. She told him to get off the property. It was her land, she said. He was trespassing. Then she committed a mortal sin. She told him that his Harley was an oil-spewing piece of junk. That was the final straw. When he saw her again at the motorcycle conference he decided to act. He knew that she was attending the ghost walk. Another murder, he figured, heightened the level of threat to me. More police protection, more sympathy. He wasn't as dumb as he seemed," she scoffed. "Just dumbly loyal."

"And Trooper Hastings and the two hunters? Why them?"

Winston shrugged indifferently. "I don't know. Who are they? I don't know anything about them."

"You're sure?"

"I have no clue."

"Did you ever dine with Curtis Kent at his apartment in South Philly?"

"Occasionally."

"He cooked?"

"Yeah. He was an excellent cook."

"Ms. Winston, his last laugh was on you," the FBI agent said.

Will felt a warm hand slip into his which drew him to the present.

"You're thinking about work," Alex said. "I can see it in your eyes. Whatever it is, leave it be. Dance with me, baby."

Alex's hand was firmly in his and Carly was just yards away, playing happily on the Chessie. He was a blessed man. "Yes."

"Yes, what?"

"Yes, beautiful wife! Let's show these folks how to dance!"

Jay took a thoughtful sip of champagne and cocked his head at the Eaton painting.

"What?" Sharon Westerly asked him. "What is it?"

"Something. I'm not sure what. Something about this one. This. *Whales*." Then it dawned on him. "Ah."

"Ah what?"

"Look carefully. Do you see how *Whales* is different from the others?"

She shook her head uncomprehendingly.

"In Adam's world view, colors and objects were in constant motion and moving from right to left. Consequently, dashes of painting sweep in that same direction as though the paint was blown across the canvas by a swift breeze."

She sidestepped along the first four paintings—*Ghost Riders, The Death of a Field Surgeon, Slaughter at the Berm* and *God Watches the Gathering*—intentionally keeping the weight off her bad leg. "I see what you mean." She paused at the last one. "It should be called *Chessies*, not *Whales*."

"The title was a subterfuge, one of Josiah's many. Speaking of which." He lowered his voice. "The man of mystery approaches."

James Collins waved and dodged guests and waiters balancing trays of hors d'oeuvres and glasses of champagne. "I'm thrilled that you two could make it!"

"I wouldn't miss this. Congratulations." Jay extended his hand but James clamped him in a bear hug and then gallantly kissed Sharon's hand.

"Can you believe it!" James' cheeks flashed with excitement. "The Wedgewood-Smyth Museum is finally a reality. Did you walk through all of the exhibits?"

"Not yet, but what I've seen has been impressive."

"The Friends of the Wedgewood-Smyth Museum are a terrific bunch of volunteers," James said. "If it wasn't for their tireless efforts—"

"How was this put together in such a short time?" Sharon asked.

"An anonymous donor came forward. He brought in an army of architects, historians and conservationists. He wanted the job done expediently. My head's still spinning! Oh, Nina just arrived. I must run! Submit, submit to her every need. Drink more champagne!" He dashed away.

"The host with the most," said Sharon wryly.

"An anonymous donor appears out of nowhere? How convenient. Why don't I believe that man?" Jay turned back to the paintings. "That *Whales* is an obvious forgery. All of the brush strokes are going from left to right, instead of right to left. I wonder if James sold the original to fund this museum."

"That wouldn't be enough for a renovation of this scope." She limped to the works of Abigail Wedgewood-Smyth, whose style was vastly different from Adam's and painted in the Romantic tradition of the early eighteen hundreds. "Another subterfuge, Jay. Abigail speaking in code. One Chessie and two black figures on the beach, yet it's entitled *Two Fishes*. The fishes of course being the men who were able to swim and breathe underwater in the Chessies."

"And use a mechanical arm to stick explosives onto the hulls of ships and blow them sky-high. Talk about mass murder."

"Spies are often assassins, justifying their murderous activities under the veil of nationalism or patriotism." She studied the museum's floorplan in a glossy brochure. "Where to next?"

"Can you handle seeing the Chessie?"

"Don't baby me. Of course, I can handle it."

"But the last time we were by it—?"

"I was shot, but I survived. Don't baby me. I'm an adult."

The music got louder as they walked through exhibits on the Underground Railroad, Civil War Spies, Civil War Submersibles and the Old Line State during the Civil War. They rounded the corner. Was this a party! What had once been Josiah and Abigail's ballroom now was an exhibition hall filled with drinking, dancing people and children climbing on a polished Chessie. The entire village was present. There were generations of Smyths, Colllinses and Wilkinses. Will and Alex were tangoing. The carpenters Marty and Melvin frowned up at the ceiling, obviously bothered by some aspect of the crown molding. Luna was dancing with the twenty-something gay waiters from the Nauticus. Herm Taylor and his wife were... oh god, his wife!

"Shit, Sharon!"

"What?"

"Janine Taylor! She's making a beeline for me. Can I pretend you're my girlfriend?"

"Okay. But—"

He grabbed Sharon and pressed his mouth to hers. Better make this kiss passionate and convincing. That would dissuade Janine. Sharon's mouth tasted heavenly... champagne and chocolate covered strawberries. She was a good sport and kissed him back, expertly in fact. From the corner of his eye, he saw Janine stop, then swerve to the bar. Hell, he had Sharon in his arms and she hadn't punched him or broken his nose so he might as well prolong—

"Someone's enjoying the party," laughed Lisa Paco.

"Mom!"

Sharon pushed Jay off. "Paul, it's not what you think."

Lisa stuck her cell phone into Jay's face. "We found the Pokémon Snorlax by the back patio and Muk in the flower garden. See?"

"We haven't checked the field by the parking lot yet," said Norman.

"Let's go, team!" Lisa commanded.

Paul Westerly lingered.

"Hey, aren't you coming, Paul?" Norman asked.

"Um, I'm not sure. Jay, are we fishing today?"

"Sure."

"When?"

He looked to Sharon for an answer.

"We can come back another day and see the exhibits when it's not so crowded," she said. "I wouldn't mind a swim while you guys fish. The swimming's improving my lung volumes."

"Now, Jay?" said Paul expectantly.

"Now."

"Paul, we'll text you if we find anything cool," Lisa said. She and Norman disappeared into the crowd.

The second he and the Westerlies left the mansion, he yanked off his tie. He couldn't wait to change into his comfy boating clothes. They passed by the maple tree with the new statue of Abigail. Its creation had generated a lively debate amongst the villagers. Some had hoped for a ferocious pistol-wielding Abigail shooting at the rebel invaders. Others wanted to portray her gentler, artistic side, Abigail behind her easel. The romantics had suggested an Abigail tangled in the arms of Josiah in a passionate kiss. But the majority had voted for the statue design of Abigail in an evocative moment of sacrifice and salvation. The statue made Jay shudder. Abigail is kneeling over the trap door, kissing her small children goodbye as they descend into the hidden cellar.

The dirt driveway encircling the maple tree and Abigail memorial was long gone. The anonymous donor had paved it and created a parking lot nearby. Jay located his SUV amidst a sea of cars. Paul climbed into the backseat and pulled on headphones while he followed Sharon to the passenger's side door. He leaned to assist.

"Don't!" she said.

"I'm just trying to help!"

"I'm not an invalid!" She lifted her leg with her hands and dragged it into the car.

Testy testy 24-7. How the hell did he get himself into this colossal mess? Maybe his *yes* had something to do with it.

He was distraught and not thinking straight on the day of Sharon's shooting. Curtis Kent had shot her not twice as she thought but twice in the right lung and once in the right leg, shattering her femur. He had been sitting in the hospital when two unshaven old men and a gangly teenager dropped into the seats next to his. It was clear that they were Westerlies; the resemblance to her was uncanny. They paced to dead-end hallways, sprang up and down for no reason and bought cafeteria food that they didn't eat. His black eyes and broken nose didn't exactly invite conversation, but he introduced himself anyway and described the events in the tunnel. Her father Murphy and Uncle Reginald seemed relieved to hear some account of the incident and bombarded him with questions for the rest of the day. An exhausted surgeon appeared. "The procedure is taking longer than expected. Go home, get some sleep. We'll have news by tomorrow morning." He ducked back into the surgical suite.

The next thing Jay remembered was Paul eating Big Macs at his kitchen island while Murph, Reg and him swapped police stories at his bar. During the following days his house looked and smelled like a frat with half-drunken men and a teary boy sleeping fitfully on spare beds and sofas and fast food containers accumulating on his counters. When it seemed certain that Sharon was going to pull through and the old men prepared to leave, a sniffling Paul had tugged on his sleeve. "Jay, can I stay here? To help my mom convalesce."

What could one say to that?

No would have been his inconvertible answer had he been working, but Herm Taylor had placed him on administrative leave pending an investigation for: 1) fraternization with a murder suspect and 2) disobeying orders. If Murph and Reg were okay with it, then why not? He and Paul could visit Sharon in the mornings and fish in the afternoons during her rehab sessions with the physical-, occupational- and pulmonary therapists. Murph and Reg were okay with it, in fact emphatically so. River Glen, they told him, would be the best place for Paul. A pestilence of news crews had descended upon Gettysburg, titillated by three murderesses in their midst and the brouhaha over the removal of the Tobias Worth statue. Paul could stay only until Sharon was done at the rehabilitation hospital, Murph said.

Then came the setbacks, an aggressive respiratory tract infection that sent Sharon back to the ICU followed by a bad reaction to the antibiotics. By September Paul had enrolled at River Glen Junior High School while she recuperated on a portable hospital bed in his living room until she could do stairs.

For months now, Sharon rented out the spare bedrooms in his house. She swam a mile down the river every morning, blasted away at Boodles bottles by the swamp and lifted weights on his deck. She stomped around his kitchen in hot-headed battle with her insurance company and placed unreturned calls to her captain, insisting that she was too young for early retirement. "I'm getting better. You'll see," she tried to convince his voicemail. Not that he was complaining but Sharon seemed to have an aversion for clothes and conducted all activities—the stomping, blasting and weight-lifting—in a very attractive bathing suit. And there was Paul who made pizza in the microwave at three in the morning, commandeered the TV for video games and had taken over his hot tub with a little minx from the marching band. Yes, the domestic disaster was entirely of his making.

The SUV passed through a valley of summer corn and the pine forest near Alex's marine lab. Down the coastal road was the village of River Glen. They rattled over the bridge and drove along Main Street where pyrate flags flapped on lamp posts. He turned down his dead-end road.

Whose car was in his driveway? It was an old clunker from the last century and covered with dings and dents. The front fender was held on by duct tape and wire. The antenna was a pink coat hanger. A skinny African-American woman was sitting on the hood, smoking a cigarette and gazing into a smartphone.

"One of your friends, Sharon?"

"No, but she looks familiar."

"I have a bad feeling about this. It's Ella's trailer-mate. Keisha."

"Keisha Long."

"Hello Keisha," he said climbing from his car.

"You remembered."

"I have a memory like a trap," he lied.

"I've been waiting forever. I was just about to leave."

"Are you okay?" Sharon said. "Is everything okay?"

"Still on the straight and narrow, Detective Westerly. And you? I heard about—"

"Almost back to fighting form," said Sharon dismissively. "And Samantha's okay?"

"Good also. It's more than I can say for some individuals," she said ironically. "Sam and I had no idea what Ella was up to. You gotta believe me!"

"No one's been accusing you, I hope," he said.

"Nope."

"Why are you here?"

His question prompted Keisha to jump in her car and start the ignition. "I'm making a delivery," she said through the open window. "Ella's returning a gift that you gave her. I've gotta get back to P A. Early shift tomorrow morning. No give backs, she says. She never wants to hear from you about it. Ever. Ever. No give backs!"

"Give backs? I never gave her a gift!"

"Yeah, you did old man!" Keisha laughed uproariously, rolled up her window and drove off.

"Where is it?" he called into her exhaust.

"There," Paul said. "On the door step."

"What do you think it is?" Sharon asked.

From what he could tell, it was a battered cardboard box. "If they're peanut butter cookies, I'm going to take a pass."

Paul walked over to it.

"Careful sweetheart," Sharon said. "It could be dangerous."

Paul pulled back the flap and leapt backward, his arms flailing overhead. "Yikes! So scary! So dangerous!" He doubled over in laughter.

She tentatively peered inside. Whatever it was, it rendered her speechless. "It's a gift, alright. And beautiful. Well done, old man."

"What beautiful gift? I have no clue."

He looked inside. It was alive and awake and staring straight at him with dazzling blue eyes. He grabbed his mailbox for support; he was that light-headed and unsteady.

"Ur, um, this can't be, Sharon. There's been a mistake. Laura and I could never—"

"How do you know? Were you both tested?"

"Uh, we never, neither of us wanted to know who—"

"There's nothing wrong with your sperm count."

"Mom, not PC!" Paul said.

"What if it's Curtis Kent's?" he wondered.

"Ella would know, wouldn't she?" she said. "Zera can check for sure. Well, don't just stand there, Papa. Pick up your child."

He lifted the squirming baby from the box. "It's bald. Is it a girl or boy?"

"There's one way to find out. Does it need a change?" She sifted through the box. "There's diapers, powered formula, a bottle and a paper." She unfolded it. "It's a birth certificate from the State Correctional Institution Muncy in Clinton, Pennsylvania. It was dated last month. Mother: Winston,

Ella Emily. Father: Braden, Jay. Name of child: Baby Boy Braden."

"What are you going to call him?" Paul asked.

"How about Ned MacDuff?" he replied. "After the wickest pyrate to sail the Chesapeake."

Paul moped. "I guess this means we're not fishing."

"Why not? Throw your tackle and rod in the boat. We need to teach this little tike to fish."

"Yes!" The teenager fist-pumped the air and disappeared around the side of the house.

"Shannon, doll, what do you think of the name Ned MacDuff Braden?" he jested in a redneck accent.

"I'm preferential to Glenn Campbell MacDuff Braden, myself," she said in her country accent.

"Glenn MacDuff Braden has a certain ring to it," he said grinning.

The silliness ebbed and the gravity of his situation rushed in. He exhaled and stared at the tiny child in his arms. His child. His son. He had a son.

"Sharon, I can't do this on my—"

"Giles, hon, I wouldn't miss this cruise for the world. Now let's take the boys fishing."

The End

About the Author

Leah Devlin

Leah Devlin is a mystery writer and marine biologist whose novels of the Chesapeake Tugboat Murders—*Vital Spark*, *Spider* and *Forger's Revenge*—are inspired by adventures on her mini-tugboat and motorcycle. Intrigued by many periods of history, Leah weaves historical mysteries into stories of present-day murder. *Vital Spark* and *Spider* delve into the history of piracy on the Chesapeake Bay while *Forger's Revenge* recreates a world of Civil War spies, art forgers and women bikers. Leah's first book series, the Woods Hole Mysteries, is set in the real-life village of Woods Hole on Cape Cod and chronicles the misadventures of a woman inventor and Nobel Laureate.

Leah enjoys travel on her boat *Vital Spark*, her Yamaha motorcycle and retro teardrop camper... in pursuit of thrilling stories and adventures. Please drop by Leah's website: www.leahdevlin.com and Facebook: Leah Devlin's Mystery-Thrillers for blogs, short stories and photographs from her travels and adventures. She's on Twitter as @SeaThriller.

If You Enjoyed This Book
Visit

PENMORE PRESS
www.penmorepress.com

All Penmore Press books are available directly through our website, amazon.com, Barnes and Noble and Nook, Sony Reader, Apple iTunes, Kobo books and via leading bookshops across the United States, Canada, the UK, Australia and Europe.

THE BOTTOM DWELLERS

BY

LEAH DEVLIN

Bioengineer and Party Girl...

Lindsey Nolan has it all: inventions paying large dividends, a dream job in the scientific village of Woods Hole, Massachusetts, and a stable of eager playmates. But when Lindsey wakes up in rehab with no memory of how she got there, her world is turned upside down. Her roommate, an HIV-positive teenage prostitute named Maggie, is the most volatile patient on the ward. The facility is plagued by disturbing thefts. And another theft unfolds when her competitor, an engineer named Karen Battersby, discovers and steals Lindsey's astonishing new invention from her Woods Hole lab. Lindsey and Maggie must face the consequences of past transgressions if they hope to deal with present perils and ascend from the desolate world of the Bottom Dwellers.

PENMORE PRESS
www.penmorepress.com

ÆGIR'S CURSE

BY
LEAH DEVLIN

A thousand years ago, the Viking colony of Vinland was ravaged by a swift-moving plague ... a curse inflicted by the sea god Ægir. The last surviving Norseman set the encampment and his longboat ablaze to ensure that the disease would die with him and his brethren.

In present-day Norway, a distinguished professor is found murdered, his priceless map of Vinland missing. The ensuing investigation leads to the reclusive world of Lindsey Nolan, a scientist and recovering alcoholic who has been sober for five years. Lindsey reluctantly agrees to help the detective who's hunting the murderer, but she has a bigger problem on her hands: a mysterious disease that's spreading like wildfire through the population of Woods Hole. As she races against a rising body count to discover the source of the plague, disturbing events threaten her hard-won sobriety—and her life. Will Lindsey be the next victim of Ægir's curse?

Leah Devlin is rapidly establishing herself as a writer of modern day mystery-thrillers. This story is as tight as a piano wire. Life at a seaside town in New England is full of treacherous undercurrents and peril, as residents are threatened by a menace from a thousand years ago. Murder, romance and deceit are a potent mix in this gripping novel, which I didn't want to put down.—James Boschert, author of the Talon Series and *Force 12 in German Bight*

PENMORE PRESS
www.penmorepress.com

THE BENDS
BY
LEAH DEVLIN

Maggie May has only weeks until graduation when Edward Gripp, a wealthy benefactor and the architect of Maggie's art college, goes missing from a campus Halloween party. Bill Bleach, the gawkish young detective assigned to the case, discovers a mysterious labyrinth within the walls of the art college where it appears Gripp spied on the activities of the faculty and students. When Gripp's mutilated body is found and a gorgeous art professor is also slain, panic spreads through art college. No one escapes Bleach's scrutiny, from the party's most distinguished guests to the terrified art students. But his investigation is complicated when he finds himself attracted to Maggie, whose dark and troubled past makes her a prime suspect. Bleach fights to stay focused, determined to untangle the web of lies and stop a devious serial killer from striking again.

Leah Devlin is rapidly establishing herself as a writer of modern day mystery-thrillers. This story is as tight as a piano wire. Life at a seaside town in New England is full of treacherous undercurrents and peril, as residents are threatened by a menace from a thousand years ago. Murder, romance and deceit are a potent mix in this gripping novel, which I didn't want to put down.—James Boschert, author of the Talon Series and *Force 12 in German Bight*

PENMORE PRESS
www.penmorepress.com

Vital Spark

by

Leah Devlin

After eking out a living as an adjunct professor in Washington DC, fisheries ecologist Alex Allaway lands a job running a small marine station back in her hometown. Arriving in River Glen to surprise her grandfather with her the good news, Alex is horrified to discover him dead, a bloody dagger in his heart. His clenched fist grasps a piece of pirate gold and a cryptic map with her name on it.

While the police investigate the murder, Alex begins her own search for answers. Aboard the tugboat Vital Spark she sails the Chesapeake in pursuit of treasure that belonged to a distant relative, the pirate Giles Blood-hand. But descendants of a rival pirate family are also looking for the bounty that's been hidden for over three centuries, and they'll think nothing of dispatching Alex once they discover she's in the way.

The first book in the Chesapeake Tugboat Murders series, Vital Spark draws us into a world where ancient feuds lurk beneath hidden waterways.

Leah Devlin is rapidly establishing herself as a writer of modern day mystery-thrillers. This story is as tight as a piano wire. Life at a seaside town in New England is full of treacherous undercurrents and peril, as residents are threatened by a menace from a thousand years ago. Murder, romance and deceit are a potent mix in this gripping novel, which I didn't want to put down.—James Boschert, author of the Talon Series and *Force 12 in German Bight*

PENMORE PRESS
www.penmorepress.com